The BRADENS
of KANSAS CITY

G.P. SCHULTZ

The Bradens of Kansas City

Copyright © 2019 by G.P. Schultz

http://www.gpschultz.com/

Published by Shadow Mountain Press LLC

Library of Congress Control Number: 2019904097
ISBN: 978-0-9626324-8-8 (paperback)
ISBN: 978-0-9626324-5-7 (e-book)

Cover and interior design by Deborah Perdue,
Illumination Graphics

Printed in the United States of America

Dedication

To the men and women of the greatest generation,
whose courage and sacrifices
during the Great Depression and World War II
made all things possible.

Also by G.P. Schultz

Gully Town

The Ghost Dancers

Incident at Simms Center

The Girl Who Loved to Run

The Kennedy Club

Please visit the following website for more information
about the author and these books.
http://www.gpschultz.com/

Acknowledgments

A special thanks to—
my editors, Joni Wilson and Susan Barnes.

Andrea Warren for her contributions to the novel.

Line editing and proofreading by Lori Sieber.

Cover and book design by Deborah Perdue—Illumination Graphics.

The staff at the Kansas City Public Library.

Cover postcard image courtesy of Missouri Valley Special Collections.

The apron and the store-within-a-store concept described in the novel
were created by legendary Kansas City fashion designer Nell Donnelly.

AUTHOR'S NOTE

The use of the N-word in this book is used as part of the culture of the era and not meant to offend readers.

The makeup of the various Kansas City political wards is my own creation and not part of the historical record.

G.P. Schultz

PROLOGUE

Kansas City
Christmas Eve 1971

LIZABETH BRADEN SAT IN HER TOP-FLOOR OFFICE looking out over the Garment District. To the north she could see the Missouri River flowing past the city, and to the northeast, old town and the City Market. The December snows had swollen the river, the water lapping halfway up the pillars of the Broadway Bridge. She was 56 years old and lamented the passage of time. She remembered when Broadway Boulevard had been bustling with activity, the Garment District servicing the Midwest and the fashionable stores on Petticoat Lane. The lane was so named because at the turn of the century the winds whipping between the buildings would, on occasion, raise the skirts of women shopping the lane and reveal their petticoats.

The most difficult time of her life had been the 1930s, when she and her family were struggling through the Depression and then in the 1940s with World War II. Life was hard, to be sure, but the fight for survival had brought out the best in everyone, as they met one challenge after another. Somehow, their troubles had brought them closer together, as they struggled against the Dust Bowl and then Germany and Japan's goal to rule the world. Living life on the edge had somehow seemed more exciting and dangerous. Her only regret was not spending more time enjoying her family. She had been so self-focused that she hadn't realized that one day time would run out. Life with her siblings had been interesting, because they were adventurous and not afraid to fail.

They had their faults, of course. Her brother, Walter, had his battles with the bottle, and her brother, Cam, was dour and self-absorbed. Like her father, her two brothers were handsome men and attracted more than their share of women. Her older sister, Eileen, had such style and grace that Lizabeth had spent a good deal of her life trying to emulate her. Lizabeth had known that she was not as physically attractive as her siblings, but she knew how to present herself to make the most of her attributes. Looking back on it now, she realized that she had tried to keep up with them through drive and ambition. She thought back to that April day in 1934, when it had all begun. She was 19 years old and emerging into womanhood. Her siblings were in their twenties and trying to make their way in the middle of the Depression. Her father had lost his job selling advertising for the *Kansas City Journal* and her family was facing an uncertain future.

CHAPTER ONE

April 1934

LIZABETH SAT IN THE LIVING ROOM, cautiously watching her parents and her brothers huddled in conversation in the kitchen. She tried to ignore them as they occasionally glanced her way, but they were making her very uncomfortable. The huddle broke up and her father approached her. He had olive skin, inherited from a Spanish grandmother, that he had passed on to Lizabeth's two brothers and her sister. The Spanish gene apparently expired at Lizabeth's birth, leaving her the quintessential Irish girl, with fair skin, auburn hair, green eyes, and a life among the perpetually tanned. Her father's hair was light brown, as were his eyes and well-trimmed moustache.

His name was John Morris Braden, but the family had long ago dubbed him J.M. From bits of whispered conversation Lizabeth had overheard, her father was not unsuccessful with women. There had been talk of a scandal years ago, involving a waitress who was a Harvey Girl at Union Station. The romance had been nipped in the bud when Mother confronted the girl and told her she could have Father but she would also have to take his four kids. That had evidently put a damper on the budding romance, left Father without a girlfriend, and confirmed for Mother that J.M. was not a man to be trusted. Despite that, Lizabeth loved him dearly and had decided not to hold his indiscretions against him.

"All right, Lizabeth," J.M. said, leaning over her. "Your sister has been gone all day and not a word about where she might be. Is there anything you want to tell us? You must know something."

"What makes you think that I know anything?" she asked defensively.

"Because you seem to know everything that goes on with this family."

If you only knew what I know, she thought. Her brothers, Walter and Cam, came over to join the conversation

"This is serious business," Walter continued. "Something could have happened to your sister."

Eileen had not sworn her to secrecy, so she felt free to speak. "All I know is that she has been seeing that stockbroker she met at Harzfeld's department store."

"When was that?"

"A month ago."

"Then they have been going out for a while."

"I guess so."

"Why haven't I heard about this?" J.M. asked.

"Because she knew you would blow your stack."

"And why would I do that, young lady?"

Lizabeth hesitated for a moment. "Because he's an older man."

J.M. looked at her with a curious expression. "How much older?"

"He's in his forties."

"In his forties!" J.M. turned red and looked like he would explode.

"Eileen's suspicions confirmed," Lizabeth said.

"Now don't raise your high hat to me, young lady."

"Sorry, Father."

"This is the first we've heard about it," Cam said.

J.M. took a deep breath. "Is there anything else we should know, Lizabeth?"

Lizabeth paused and wondered if she should give up her incendiary piece of information but decided to go ahead.

"I did overhear her whispering something to one of her friends about marriage."

Mira Braden took a deep breath. "We have to think this through calmly," she said. "And we have to stop her before she does something foolish and ruins her life."

4

Lizabeth's mother was of medium height, with hazel eyes, and a touch of gray starting to streak her hair. She was a devout disciple of Mary Baker Eddy and the Christian Science movement. As a Christian Science practitioner, she had a strong moral conviction and felt that she could handle any situation or illness that came her way. And they came her way often, because her husband was a hypochondriac and embraced any illness, real or imagined.

Mind over matter might work for Mira, but J.M. needed his pills. Mira never tried to instill her beliefs on her family, or insist that they attend church, but sometimes she required that Lizabeth accompany her on her rounds. Lizabeth carried the Bible and Mary Baker Eddy's book, *Science and Health with Key to the Scriptures*, that Mira read from. She was proud that her mother wanted to help the sick, but from an early age was dubious that prayer and mind over matter could heal the afflicted. She and the rest of the family were more than happy to let Mira be their sole representative in all things religious.

"You must have an idea of where she might be," Walter said.

"I have no idea," Lizabeth replied. She too was beginning to worry about her sister. Eileen was innocent in many ways, and Lizabeth loved her for it. She had raven hair, brown eyes, and a figure that made men melt. Unlike her brothers, Eileen had no ego and could not understand why she had this effect on men. The floor manager at Harzfeld's had wanted to fire her, because she attracted too many would-be suitors to her station in the perfume department. But he soon realized that these men made a purchase just to have a conversation with her, and, as a result, store sales had tripled.

Eileen had no clue and thought her success was due to her sales expertise. Her passion in life was being an actress with a local theatre group called the Red Barn Players. It was so named because the plays were performed in a converted barn south of the city. Actor types swarmed around Eileen but were kept at bay by her father and her brothers. J.M. felt that play actors were shiftless vagabonds and not fit for polite society, much less suitable for his daughter.

"Cam, you and Walter have to find her," Mira ordered.

"We'll go pick up Jimmy," Walter said. "He knows some downtown cops who can help us track her down."

Lizabeth slipped quietly out the door with her two brothers. She was not about to miss the search for her sister.

They piled into Walter's 1924 black and tan Chrysler sedan, then picked Jimmy up on the way downtown. Walter parked the car and they all got out and hurried down 12th Street. At the suggestion of the police, they had checked about a marriage license at the Jackson County Courthouse and discovered that Eileen and her boyfriend had taken out a marriage license an hour ago. The group headed to the closest justice of the peace, hoping that Eileen would be there and that they were not too late.

"This sure doesn't seem like something Eileen would do," Jimmy said. "That guy must have done some fancy talking to get her to fall for him."

Jimmy Dolan was Walter's best friend. They had met when they were six years old and had been inseparable ever since. In contrast to Walter, Jimmy had light blond hair and blue eyes. He was thin, but muscular, and had a scar above his lip where he had been hit with a brick when he was a kid. Walter had chased down and beaten up the boy who had thrown the brick and sealed a lifetime of loyalty from Jimmy. Jimmy was a middleweight Golden Gloves boxing champion and could more than take care of himself, but he accepted his subservient role to Walter and would follow him anywhere. His mother was dead and he had been abandoned by his father so his grandmother had raised him. They lived in a run-down Queen Anne house on the west side of Kansas City. He had no siblings, so he had adopted Walter's family as his own. His most identifiable mark was a gray fedora hat, with a black ribbon headband, that he hardly ever took off.

"It's probably some older man who told her a good story to get what he wanted. And I don't mean love and devotion," Jimmy said.

Walter gave Jimmy a hard look and nodded his head toward Lizabeth.

"Sorry, Lizabeth," Jimmy said.

They ran up the steps and into the office of the justice of the peace. Eileen and her future husband were sitting in chairs in the waiting room. Eileen jumped up from her chair in shock when she saw her two brothers, her sister, and Jimmy.

"What are you doing here?" she asked in panic and embarrassment. She took a deep breath and tried to regain her composure. "I want you to meet—"

"We don't want to meet anyone," Walter said coldly. "We are here to save you from a big mistake. Cam, you and Jimmy take Eileen to the car."

Lizabeth stepped back into the shadows and watched Cam and Jimmy escort Eileen from the building. She stayed put because she wanted to see what happened next.

"Now wait just a minute," the man said, getting up from his chair. Walter shoved him back down. He looked to be in his mid-forties and was much too old to be courting Eileen.

"Shut up and listen," Walter said menacingly. "You thought you could have your way with my sister, you sleaze bag."

"We love each other," the man protested.

"You're confusing lust with love."

"That's not true."

"How old are you?"

"I'm forty-five."

"My sister is twenty-one years old. You would have ruined her and then moved on to someone else."

"That's not true."

"Let me tell you how it's going to be, lover boy. You come anywhere near my sister and you will regret it."

"You can't keep us apart."

"Try me and you will wish you hadn't," Walter threatened.

Lizabeth slipped out the door so Walter wouldn't be embarrassed by her presence. She loved Walter dearly. He was of medium height, with black hair and a moustache. He had soft brown eyes that held a touch of mischief, and he had a great sense of humor. Walter could tease anyone out of a bad mood and was a joy to be around.

Walter gave the man one more menacing look before turning and heading out of the building.

Out on the sidewalk, the three men surrounded Eileen.

"What in the world were you thinking?" Cam admonished her.

Lizabeth put her arms around her sister to show her support.

"I'm very fond of him," Eileen said meekly.

"You don't marry a man because you are fond of him," Walter said.

"He's very well off," Eileen replied.

"So that's it," Cam said. "This was about money."

"Mother and Father are struggling. Father's prospects of getting a job are not good. My salary at Harzfeld's is not enough to pay the bills, and I'm afraid they will lose the house."

"That's not your responsibility," Walter said. "That's up to Cam and me."

"You haven't been able to find work."

"We are close to finding something," Walter said. "Cam might get a job selling cars, and Uncle Ray made me an appointment with Tom Hannon. Boss Tom controls everything in this city and Uncle Ray is tight with him. There is a good chance he will find me a job."

"Times are hard, and few people can afford a car, so a car salesman isn't a great idea," Eileen said. "And Hannon might not have any work for you."

"You let us worry about that," Walter said.

Eileen had to admit that her two brothers were resourceful, so she hoped for the best, as they all walked to Walter's car, got in, and drove away.

Lizabeth wondered how much trouble Eileen would be in, as Walter stopped the car in front of the family bungalow. J.M. had purchased the home in the Brookside area several years ago when the stock market was booming and times were good. Brookside was near the streetcar line and comfortably upper middle class. The homes were not as large and ornate as the homes along Ward Parkway or the mansions of Mission Hills to the west. The Braden home was built in the Idaville bungalow style, with seven rooms and a bath. Lizabeth shared an upstairs bedroom with Eileen. Her parent's bedroom was across the hall, near the bathroom. Walter and Cam slept downstairs in a bedroom in the back of the house, next to the kitchen.

The house had a spacious living room, a dining room, and a small den for J.M. But for Lizabeth the best feature was the sunporch, where the family could rest in the shade and be out of the elements. Her mother had surrounded the house with all types of flowers, from daffodils and daisies, to roses, alyssum, and bluebells. But Mira's pride and joy were the big blossomed hydrangeas. In another month, the sweet-smelling flowers would waft through the house, a daily reminder that spring had finally arrived.

"I had better go in and clear the way," Cam said. "I'll tell our parents that Eileen was getting married for the good of the family, that she was only trying to bring in some money to help us through these hard times." He paused and looked at his sister. "I'll tell Father you were led astray by an older, more experienced man."

"That's not exactly true," Eileen said.

"We're not looking for truth here; we are trying to smooth your way back into the family."

Lizabeth knew that Cam, as the oldest child, was the golden boy and could do no wrong in the eyes of his parents. Cam was the taller of the two brothers and his personality was the opposite of Walter. He was clean-shaven with dark brown hair and brown eyes. His only defect was a bit of separation between his front teeth. He had a bevy of women hounding him, who found his dour moods and sarcasm somehow exciting and dangerous. He could turn on the charm when it was to his advantage but preferred to be critical and suspicious of all who passed his way. There was not a lot of brotherly love between Walter and Cam. The only thing they had in common was golf, and they had teamed up to win the city championship.

Cam's elite status with their parents did not bother her or Eileen, but Lizabeth suspected that it irritated Walter. However, he never challenged Cam's standing with their parents. Lizabeth knew that her parents saw Walter as shiftless and a drinker, while Cam was grounded and the son who could be counted on in a crisis.

After a few minutes, Cam came out and ushered Eileen into the house. Lizabeth followed closely behind. Her mother took Eileen upstairs for a talk, as Lizabeth waited anxiously in the living room for them to reappear. After about an hour, her mother came down the stairs and Lizabeth hurried up to be with Eileen. She was sitting on the bed, wiping her eyes with a handkerchief. Lizabeth sat down next to her and gave her a hug.

"I'm so sorry this happened," she said. "Was Mother very upset?"

"Yes. I guess I didn't realize how much my actions would affect the family."

"It's your life," Lizabeth said.

"Not entirely, if it upsets Mother and Father so much. I don't want to cause them any more pain. With Father losing his job, they have enough to deal with."

"Are you in love?"

"I'm not sure I know what love is. I enjoy his company."

"How are you feeling?"

"Shocked. I've gone from being a bride to sitting in my room wondering what happened."

"You will always have me," Lizabeth said. "I don't know how I would ever be able to get along without you, so I can't say that I'm sorry this happened. We've been sharing a room and each other's secrets for so long that I would be lost if you went away." Eileen squeezed her hand. "Now you need to get some rest after all this excitement," Lizabeth said. "We will talk some more after you take a nap."

Lizabeth went to the little sewing room down the hall from her bedroom that was her sanctuary. Her Aunt Erma had taught her how to sew when she was 10 years old and she had loved it since her first stitch. She found it fascinating that she could create beautiful fashions from a plain piece of cloth, and for her, it became more of an art form than a chore. She was the family seamstress and she made all of her clothes and some for Eileen and her mother. She had been using an old Singer, rotary needle, sewing machine. But this past Christmas, the family had shown their appreciation for her work by scraping enough money together to purchase one of the new Singer treadle machines that she could operate with her feet. She could now double her output.

Eileen's selflessness for the good of the family had impressed Lizabeth greatly and now she felt it was her turn to help. She would start by taking in sewing for the people in her neighborhood and by creating her own dress designs that she would try to sell to the department stores and dress shops around town. She had a hunch that even in hard times, women would want to look fashionable. It was an ambitious goal, but it was what she wanted to do with her life, and she was not intimidated or afraid of hard work and she could hardly wait to get started.

Walter stood in a line that snaked out of Tom Hannon's Main Street office. The line ran down the stairs and around the corner. He wondered if there would be any jobs left by the time it was his turn to see the boss. An hour later, he was standing in front of the big Irishman's desk. Boss

Tom stood up and shook his hand. The political boss had a huge head set on a large frame. His eyes were penetrating and set under bushy, black eyebrows. He looked like the brawler of his youth.

Walter had heard from Uncle Ray that Tom was quick to anger and not a man to be crossed. Tom's older brother, Jack, had carved a political empire out of the first ward. He had arrived in Kansas City during the Industrial Revolution and quickly realized that by befriending and controlling newly arriving immigrants, he could form a political base and eventually control city government. His philosophy was "If you do for the boss, the boss will do for you." Jack's influence reached to the governor's office in Jefferson City and to politicians in Washington, DC. Before Jack Hannon passed away, he handed the empire over to his younger brother, Tom. Tom took firm control of the Hannon political machine and his rule was absolute.

"What can I do for you, son?" Tom asked.

"I'm Walter Braden, Ray Braden's nephew, and I'm looking for work."

Boss Tom sized him up as he shuffled through some papers. "Tell me about yourself, Walter."

"What would you like to know?"

"What do you want out of life?"

"I never thought much about it. I guess I'm like most men in wanting a good job and time to enjoy my friends and family."

"No driving ambition to make your mark on the world?"

"None. I'm your average guy and glad of it."

"I doubt that. Once you've had a taste of success, you might feel differently."

Walter had no comment on that.

"Have you ever tended bar?"

"No, sir. But I'm good with alcohol and I'm a quick learner."

Walter noticed the flicker of amusement in Tom's eyes. Tom grabbed a piece of paper and a red pen and signed his name. "Take this to the Hi Hat club on Twelfth Street and the manager will get you started."

"Thank you, sir." Walter was ecstatic about getting a job in these tough times. And he would be working in an atmosphere where there was a lot of action. A drink after a hard day's work was a working man's right, not a luxury, so even in the Depression it would be steady work.

There was no hesitation from the manager of the Hi Hat club when Walter handed over the paper. After a couple of days of watching and learning, the manager put him to work as an assistant bartender on the evening shift. He was successful from the start because he liked people, had a good sense of humor, and could talk with anyone. And it gave him a window into the workings of the city. He made friends with construction workers, white-collar workers from City Hall, drovers from the stockyards, and farmers from the City Market.

He knew the contacts he was making would hold him in good stead in the days and years ahead. And best of all, women were everywhere and readily available in the red-light district. The only concession he made to his lifestyle was to never drink while he was working. For him, one drink led to another until he was out of control, and he could not afford to be out of work. After a month on the job, he was so well-thought-of that he talked management into giving Jimmy a job as a waiter. The two of them fed off each other's jokes and made the work fun for themselves and for the customers.

Walter stepped outside the Hi Hat club to take a smoke break. He took a long drag on his cigarette and listened to the music pouring out of the clubs. The sound mixed with laughter and honking horns, as revelers made their way up and down the street. If ever a man was born to a city, it was Walter Braden. He loved the fast-paced energy of his hometown. It was a melting pot of Irish, Italian, German, and Polish immigrants, all struggling to make their mark in the city. And he loved the wildness of it all, because he never knew what would happen next. If it wasn't a fire, it was a fight.

From his perch behind the bar, he followed his customers down a trail of broken romances and failed careers. He was sympathetic to their plights. He and Jimmy had ridden the rails for a couple of years after high school and had known hard times. They had lived in camps beside the rails and bummed their meals from churches in more towns than they cared to remember. He felt well qualified to salve the wounds inflicted by the Great Depression, dispensing his own brand of psychology along with the drinks he served. He always tried to offer a glimmer of hope before turning his customers out into the night.

Times were hard in this year of 1934. Dust covered the farmlands from Oklahoma to North Dakota and from Kansas to Colorado. All over the nation, broken men stood in soup lines and hoped that President Franklin Roosevelt's New Deal would cut them a better hand. But it had been five long years since the market crash of 1929, and that many days of struggle could test the will of any man. To the men riding the rails or driving their beat-up trucks out of the Dust Bowl, Kansas City was an oasis in the desert of the Depression. It meant good times and infinite possibilities real or imagined.

If they could get to Kansas City, surely better days lay ahead. It was the premier city leading west, where anything could happen and often did. Its reputation was like that of no other city, with the likes of Jesse and Frank James, the four Younger brothers, the Dalton gang, Buffalo Bill Cody, and Wild Bill Hickok once roaming the streets. And in 1886, when Big Jack Hannon came from St. Joseph, Missouri, and walked across the Hannibal Bridge into Kansas City, Missouri, the boss system of government was born that gave every working man a fair shake, regardless of his birthplace or religion.

Last year—when the gangsters Adam Richetti, Vernon Miller, and Pretty Boy Floyd had gunned down four law enforcement officers at Union Station, while trying to free Frank Nash from federal agents—added another element of mystery and lawlessness to the mystique of Kansas City. The good-time reputation of the city had even survived prohibition and once again 12th Street was booming. Walter took a last drag on his cigarette, feeling very thankful to be a part of it all, and headed back inside the bar.

❧

Lizabeth sat in the living room with Eileen and her mother. She had spent several months trying to get her new venture off the ground without much success. She had managed to take in some sewing from the neighbors, but not enough to make a living.

"I'm going to have to venture farther away from home," she said. "The people in this neighborhood are doing their own sewing. They can't afford to send it out to a seamstress."

"Well, you can't continue to knock on doors," Mira said. "It is unseemly behavior for a young lady. The neighbors must think we are poor beyond belief."

"No, Mother. They admire me for starting my own business and would support me if they could afford to."

"What do you have in mind?" Eileen asked.

"I'm going to start leaving my card at the fashionable homes on Ward Parkway and in Mission Hills. Father said that I could use his car to make sales calls. I was wondering if you would help me."

"I will do anything for you, except knock on doors," Eileen replied. She had put her failed attempt at marriage behind her. She wasn't one to dwell on things, so after a week of moping around, she was back on the dating scene. However, she knew that suspicious eyes from her wary family kept track of her every move.

"You've worn my casual dresses around town, but I was wondering if I made you some clothes that were really special, if you would wear them to work," Lizabeth continued.

"Why would that matter?"

"Because you would make my clothes look beautiful."

"Flattery will get you nowhere. What are you thinking?"

"That the Harzfeld's buyer might like the look and ask you where you bought the dress. And if customers like the dresses, you could send them my way."

"I can do the first, but not the last. It would be unethical and would take business away from Harzfeld's."

"Sorry," Lizabeth said. "I didn't think of that."

"Here's what I can do. If I get some favorable comments about what I'm wearing when I'm on my lunch hour, then I can hand out your cards."

"Would you? That would be wonderful." Lizabeth gave her sister a hug.

"I don't know why you can't be like most young women and be satisfied with sewing for the family," Mira said. "Cam, Walter, and your sister are making enough money to keep us solvent until things pick up for your father."

"It wouldn't be right. I have to do my share," Lizabeth answered. "If you don't mind my asking, I was wondering how you think Father is doing. He seems so depressed, and he only leaves the house to take his daily walk."

"Now, don't you worry about your father. He has some down days, but that is to be expected. After all, there are millions of men in the same predicament. I'm afraid the Depression, combined with your father's advancing age, has been a lethal combination in finding work."

"He's only fifty-five years old," Lizabeth replied.

"Yes. But there are hundreds of younger men applying for every job opening."

"But he has the experience," Eileen said.

"That seems to be working against him. Employers say he is overqualified, but what they really mean is they see more energy and future possibilities in a younger man. The hardest thing for your father is that after supporting his family all these years, he is reduced to standing in unemployment lines like a beggar. He is a prideful man and it crushes his spirit."

It confirmed for Lizabeth that her father must be having an extremely hard time, because it was not like her mother to be so supportive. She was a pragmatist, and making excuses for anyone was not part of her agenda. There had been a chill in the house after her father's affair, and she was sure some bitterness lingered from his indiscretions. Her mother was too proud to put on anything but a brave face in front of her children. Any cracks in the relationship would always be dealt with behind closed doors.

"What can we do to help?" Lizabeth asked.

"You are doing all you can. Your father and I appreciate all you do to support the family. He never says so, because it is hard for him to acknowledge that he is dependent on his children."

"We are all in this together, so it doesn't matter who brings in the money," Lizabeth said.

"I'm afraid that your father and I don't see it that way. He should be supporting the family."

"We will just have to hope that he finds something soon," Eileen said.

Lizabeth worked hard in the months ahead, making sales calls on small dress shops and creating dresses that she thought would appeal to the modern woman. She managed to get a few orders from women in the neighborhood who knew her work, but they seemed more like sympathy orders than anything else. The women were rewarding her for the initiative she was showing in starting her own company. She had received a few orders from women who had admired her dresses on Eileen, but it was still not the volume she needed to establish herself in the world of fashion.

She had spent hours assessing her work. She read fashion magazines and made countless trips canvasing the fashion departments at Harzfeld's; Emery, Bird, Thayer; and Kline's. She had emulated the latest fashions from Paris and New York. Her creations were long, while highlighting a slim waist, and deemphasizing the hips. The actresses of the day influenced her work. She created the puffed sleeve and broad-shouldered look of Greta Garbo and Joan Crawford. Crawford especially, because everyone knew the actress had been an elevator operator at Kline's in Kansas City. Lizabeth had even reproduced the broad-shouldered wrap dress that Crawford had recently made popular.

Lizabeth thought that if she could just get some exposure, her fashions would be a hit, so she worked up her courage and asked Eileen if there was any way she could get her an appointment with the buyer at Harzfeld's. The buyer was Gloria Wilson and she owed Eileen a favor. Lizabeth set up the appointment for two weeks out, so she could arrange every detail and leave nothing to chance. Eileen and Mira helped her decide which of her fashions to take to the appointment. They picked five spring dresses, an evening dress, and several skirts and blouses. Mira and Eileen thought they were the best of her designs.

The day of the appointment, she was a nervous wreck and her confidence was waning. And she wondered why she had ever talked herself into going through with the appointment. Walter and Jimmy had agreed to drive her downtown for the meeting and to help her carry the garments. Walter noticed her hands shaking.

"You have got to calm down, Lizabeth," he said. "Don't let them see you sweat."

"I'm having a nervous attack," she replied.

Walter took out his flask. "You want a drink?"

That made her laugh and broke the tension, because she knew he would never let her touch alcohol.

When they arrived on Petticoat Lane, the tall buildings were intimidating and seemed to be closing in on her. She followed Walter and Jimmy into Harzfeld's and they took the elevator up to the fourth floor, where women's fashions were displayed.

A woman approached her. "May I help you?"

"I am here to see Miss Wilson."

"One moment, please." A few minutes passed. Lizabeth could hear her heart beating.

A woman she assumed was Miss Wilson came out of the office. She was dressed in a chic blue skirt with a matching jacket that covered a white blouse and was accentuated by a light blue tie. Lizabeth guessed that she was in her early thirties. She was the most fashionable-looking woman Lizabeth had ever seen.

She put out her hand. "I'm Gloria Wilson. This is my assistant buyer, Miss Davenport."

Lizabeth shook hands with both of them.

"I'm Lizabeth Braden. This is my brother, Walter, and my friend, Jimmy."

"Nice to meet all of you. Eileen said that you had some things to show me."

"Yes."

"Follow us." They walked to the backroom and hung the garments on some empty racks.

"We'll go get a cup of coffee," Walter said. "It was nice meeting you both."

"It was nice meeting you too," Miss Wilson replied.

Lizabeth watched them go, feeling very much alone. However, it was now or never, so she gathered her courage. "The purpose of my visit is to see if you would be interested in purchasing some of my designer clothing," Lizabeth said.

"We will be glad to look," Miss Wilson replied.

Lizabeth took a deep breath and started her presentation. She went over the entire line, explaining the uniqueness of each item of clothing and why she thought it would appeal to Harzfeld's customers. She took her time so that she would not miss any of her talking points. When she was finished, she felt pleased that it was a good presentation and waited for Miss Wilson's reaction.

"I have to be frank with you, Miss Braden. You have some talent for design, but we have sophisticated customers here at Harzfeld's. Would they want to buy a dress from Coco Chanel or Madeleine Vionnet of Paris, or would they want a dress from Lizabeth Braden of Kansas City? What every buyer on Petticoat Lane will tell you is that in our business, perception is everything. Paris and New York are the holy grails of our industry. We do not even have vendor codes for anything coming out of the Midwest."

Lizabeth tried to put on a brave face, but she was crestfallen. "Then why did you see me?" she asked.

"We met with you as a courtesy to Eileen, of course. I will give you some advice, Miss Braden. If you're serious about design, then go to New York and spend a few years learning the trade. It will do you a world of good."

Lizabeth could not hide her disappointment, because all her future plans were dashed.

"Thank you for the advice. It was kind of you to see me." She shook hands with both women. "I'll go get my brother."

"Of all the nerve," she heard Miss Davenport say to Miss Wilson as she left the office. Lizabeth felt her face flush with embarrassment.

On the way home, Walter tried to cheer her up. "You can't expect good results your first time out, Lizabeth. Harzfeld's isn't the only store in town."

"That's what is so discouraging," she replied. "All of the stores want dresses from well-known designers. How am I going to compete with that?"

"You will just have to make a name for yourself."

"Kansas City isn't exactly the mecca of fashion."

"No place is until someone makes it so."

"Liz Braden's designer clothing from Paris on the plains," she said, mocking him.

"And I thought our big brother had the market on sarcasm," Walter replied.

She sighed. "I'm sorry, Walter. It's just that I'm so discouraged."

"I know you are. You just have to keep trying and maybe something will turn up."

CHAPTER TWO

WALTER AND CAM WERE PLAYING in the Kansas City match play championship at Swope Park golf course. The match with their two opponents had swung back and forth all afternoon. It was a beautiful day with a slight wind from the south. The dogwood, Bradford pear, and crabapple trees were blooming and made a colorful contrast to the green fairways and light blue sky.

Jimmy was caddying for Walter, while Cam carried his own bag. They were dressed in brown slacks, white shirts, ties, and two-tone brown and white golf shoes. Cam birdied the 16th hole, and he and Walter were one up with two holes to play. Walter took his flask out of his golf bag and took a swig. He handed it to Jimmy who also took a swig.

"Quit nipping at that flask, or you will cost us the tournament," Cam said angrily.

"You worry too much," Walter shot back. "I can handle my liquor."

"Sure, you can. That's why you just put your eight iron in my bag."

"An honest mistake," Walter said, as he and Jimmy snickered.

On the 17th hole, Walter put his drive down the middle of the fairway. There was an oak tree center right of the green but it was no obstacle to Walter attacking the flag for his third shot on the par five.

"I bet I can hook the ball around that tree and onto the green," Walter said to Jimmy.

"Quit clowning around," Cam ordered. "My ball is in the rough, and we need you to hit the green."

"Where's your sense of adventure?" Walter shot back. "Don't you think I can hit the shot?"

"We are two holes away from defending our championship. I think the alcohol is fogging your brain."

"Oh, how little faith ye have," Walter said, as he took out his six iron. He took his stance and put a hook grip on the club. "I watched Walter Hagen hit this shot on a newsreel at the movies."

"I've got news for you. You're not Walter Hagen, you're Walter Braden, and we are going to lose this match."

"You can do it, Walter," Jimmy encouraged him.

"Think positive," Walter said, as he waggled the club in preparation of the shot. When he was ready, he made as smooth a swing as the alcohol would allow, and the ball shot toward the right of the tree. However, Walter had misjudged by a few yards, and the ball hooked into a branch with a loud thud and fell straight down.

"Oh," Walter said in surprise.

"Oh, my ass," Cam said. "I hope you are happy now." They bogeyed the hole, while their playing partners made a par. The match was all square heading to number 18.

"I need to fortify myself for the final challenge," Walter said, as he took another swig from his flask.

Cam was too livid to speak. He teed up his ball and hit a nice shot down the fairway. Walter had lost his sense of rhythm, and the club felt like a rake in his hand. He swung and popped the ball up a hundred yards down the fairway and into a bush in the tree line.

"Nice shot," Cam said sarcastically.

"I just wanted to get out of the way so you can be the hero," Walter said. "You love the limelight, so now is your chance to shine."

"It is so nice of you to put all the pressure on me," Cam sneered.

"Would you like a drink to help you relax?"

Cam glared at him and walked to his ball.

Walter and Jimmy watched as Cam hit a nice five iron, 20 feet from the pin. Their playing partners were about 15 feet away.

"Good shot," Jimmy said. At the green, Cam lined up his putt and stroked the ball. It was on line, but the ball caught the side of the cup and lipped out.

"Too bad," Walter said. "That was a nice putt."

Their playing partners got a good read from watching Cam's putt. Walter watched as the putt was stroked, found the center of the cup and dropped in. Cam gave Walter a look that said he would like to bury a five iron in his skull. Walter heartily congratulated their opponents, while Cam gave a halfhearted handshake and then sulked off to the clubhouse.

"Now you've gone and done it," Jimmy said. "God knows how long he will pout. Why do you have to give him such a hard time?"

"He will get over it. He always does."

They met Cam in the clubhouse, where their opponents were getting their picture taken and being interviewed by a reporter.

Walter looked at Cam. "All you had to do was make that putt, and we would be in a playoff," he said. With that, Cam became so enraged that he grabbed a club out of his bag. Walter took off running out the door with Cam close behind, chasing him around the clubhouse and up the first fairway.

"It's just a game!" Walter shouted, as Cam closed in on him.

"Everything is a game to you, Walter, but that's not how it works!" Cam yelled. The other golfers were highly amused as Cam chased Walter back and forth across the fairway. The alcohol was taking its toll on Walter, and he could hardly catch his breath. He made it back to the first tee and collapsed. Jimmy stepped in front of Cam with his hands up.

"Okay, that's enough. You two have been beating on each other since you were kids. Don't you think it's time you grew up? You keep messing around and they are going to ban you from next year's tournament."

Cam had his hands on his knees, sucking in air. "I'm getting another partner for next year's tournament. I will never play golf with this idiot again!"

"You're just a poor loser," Walter said.

Cam lunged toward him, but Jimmy grabbed his arm. "It's time we headed for the car." He helped Walter off the turf, and they walked slowly to the parking lot.

"I have to get a haircut," Walter said to Cam. "Do you want to go, or do want us to take you home?"

"Are you still going to that Negro barbershop?"

"Of course, I am. I've been going for years. Why would I change now?"

"Why indeed," Cam snarled. It infuriated Cam that Walter took all of his personal business to the Negro community. Walter was for the underdog and the disadvantaged and had never liked the way Negroes were treated. His outrage began when he was 15 years old and playing baseball. Two Negro boys were denied playing on the team because of their color. They were better players than the white boys, but that didn't matter. Walter quit the team in protest and started playing sandlot baseball with the Negroes.

In recent years, there had been a number of bombings when Negroes tried to move into white neighborhoods, and the restaurants and movie houses were segregated. Walter hated the injustice of it all and taking his business to the east side of town was his way of helping right some of the wrongs inflicted on the Negro community. He was one of those unique people who could go anywhere and seemed immune from the prejudice of others. He had made a lot of friends in the Negro community, because he treated everyone with respect and was not afraid to go where others would not.

"I'll take you home," Walter said to Cam.

Walter parked his car in front of Luther Jackson's barbershop at 18th and Woodland, two blocks east of the famous Jazz District at 18th and Vine. The shop was located in the Negro community. He and Jimmy walked inside. There were a couple of men sitting in chairs against the wall. It was a one-chair barbershop, so Walter waited his turn.

He took a seat in the shoeshine stand in the corner to get a shine. A boy who looked to be about 14 years old picked up his polish and went to work. He was a nice-looking young man with light brown skin and soft brown eyes. He was thin but muscular, with long arms that he hadn't grown into. His hair was close-cropped and curly.

Luther, who was shaving a customer with a straight razor, was in his forties and was a short, stocky man with graying hair and moustache. In his late twenties, he had played catcher for the Kansas City Monarchs, part of the Negro National League, and knew his way around a baseball field.

"Hello, Luther. How is everything?'"

"It's all good, Walter. What you been up to?"

"I've been waiting for my ear to heal after you gave me my last shave." Luther smiled and the other men chuckled. The man being shaved was not amused.

"I have bad news, Luther," Walter said. "The Braden boys just lost the city match play championship."

"At Swope Park?"

"Yep."

"Did he lose fair and square, Jimmy, or did he do something stupid?"

"His brother blamed it on too much whiskey and too little effort."

"That's Walter all right," Luther said, nodding his head.

"Walter had a clear shot at the flag, but just for the hell of it, he tried to hook it around a tree. Needless to say, it didn't work."

"Maybe that's why my brother chased me all over the golf course trying to brain me with a golf club," Walter said. Luther and his patrons laughed heartily.

"Is that the truth, Jimmy?"

"It was something to see, Luther. Laurel and Hardy couldn't have done it any better."

"Did your brother get over it?" Luther asked.

"You know how brothers are. He will hold it against me for the rest of my life."

"Ain't that the truth? I hear you working for Boss Tom tending bar on Twelfth Street."

"I am indeed. They put me in charge of all things alcohol."

"Boss Tom done made a mistake there, Jimmy."

"You said that right. I'm working there too."

"Luther, when you come downtown, the drinks will be on us," Walter offered.

"I'll do that," Luther replied. But they knew that he wouldn't. Kansas City was a decidedly Southern city. Jim Crow laws that enforced racial segregation were disregarded in some Midwestern cities, but not Kansas City. Vine Street ran north and south and was the line of demarcation between Negroes and whites. Negro musicians could cross over to play the downtown nightclubs and white men could visit the bawdy houses east of Vine. And there were some Jewish merchants who did business on the east side. Walter was one of the few who ignored the rules of segregation.

"How's it looking for your St. Louis Cardinals?" Walter asked.

"This is the year they will win it all," Luther replied.

"You said that last year and the Giants won."

"I know, but with Dizzy Dean pitching, we have a great chance. And Collins, Martin, Medwick, and Durocher could all hit over three hundred."

"You going to any games?"

"No way. St. Louis is too big and too busy, and I couldn't afford it if I wanted to. I'll stay home and watch the Monarchs in person and listen to the Cardinals on the radio."

"How is business?" Walter asked.

"Could be better, that's for sure. A lot of people trying to cut their own hair these days."

"This is the worst year yet according to the papers," Walter said.

"I believe it. But we're better off than a lot of folks. We can put food on the table and have a good time now and then."

"Better off than Clyde Barrow and Bonnie Parker, for sure," Walter said. Last week the FBI had killed the notorious gangsters in a gun battle in Louisiana.

"That was one mean couple," Luther said. "I think the Barrows, Dillinger, Pretty Boy Floyd, and the rest of them were caused by the Depression. Bad times make for bad people."

"Can't argue that."

"I have faith that President Roosevelt will get us out of this mess," Luther said.

"If he thinks that 'the only thing we have to fear is . . . fear itself,' then he's not missing many meals," Walter said.

"I know he's a rich man, but we have to give him a chance. You want to go back to Hoover?"

"Not me. I'm all in for Roosevelt."

After the other patrons left, Walter looked down at his shoes. "Nice shine," he said. "When did you hire the new kid?"

"I didn't hire him. He showed up here about a month ago with his rags and polish."

"Where is he from?"

"Dammed if I know. He won't talk."

"Is he deaf?"

"Hell, no. He's stubborn. And don't try to tip him. He takes it as an insult. Just give him a dime for the shine and put the tip in the jar there. We give the money to charity."

"Where does he live?"

"I followed him one day and found him in an old abandoned house on Lydia Avenue. I fixed him a bed here in the backroom where he has a toilet and a shower. My guess is that something must have happened to his family and he hopped a train to Kansas City."

"What makes you think so?"

"I came by late one night, and he was screaming in his sleep. Something about a fire and brothers and sisters. That's how I know he can talk."

"What about food?"

"Some of the women in the neighborhood feed him. He's too proud to take a handout, so he always pays them something from his shoeshine money."

"It's good of you to take him in."

"We help each other. He gets a place to sleep, and I get some security."

"How could he help with security? He's just a kid."

"That's what I thought, but I watched three older boys try to take his shoes one evening. He cut them up just enough to let the neighborhood know not to mess with him. If they break in here, they might not come out again."

"Does he go to school?"

"No. He gets his schooling from the library. My backroom is full of books."

"So, you don't know his name?"

"All I know is that he's a shoeshine boy who acts like he's royalty."

"Well then, Vine Street has Duke Ellington and Count Basie. Maybe we should call him the Prince of Woodland Avenue."

Luther laughed. "I like that, but I'm not sure he will."

Walter looked at the boy and spoke to him. "Jimmy and I rode the rails for a while, so we know what it's like to go hungry. If I can help, give a note to Luther and he will get it to me."

The boy looked at him curiously but remained silent.

"How is your son doing, Luther?"

"He thinks he is doing great. Me, not so much."

"What's the problem?"

"He's in a jazz band. His life is music, booze, and women."

"Sounds to me like a recipe for happiness."

"I would agree to a point. But Eddie is twenty-six years old, and it's past time to start being responsible."

"What would you have him do?"

"Take a regular job and get married and have some kids. He has a good head for business, if he would just apply himself."

"That might be the life you want for him, rather than the life he wants for himself."

"That's exactly what he says. The two of you must be conspiring against me."

"It seems that way, because I am getting the same story from my father."

"And I bet that you are not listening."

"There is too much life to be lived to settle down, Luther. And while we are on the subject, have you heard anything about the new girls around the corner at Miss Lillian's place?"

"Walter, with your looks, you must have all the women you need. Why would you want to be messing around at that bawdy house?" Luther admonished him.

"There's something about the atmosphere that appeals to me. And I never have to worry about romantic attachments. I just pay the bill and go merrily on my way."

"In other words, you get to be irresponsible."

"You got me there, Luther."

"I wouldn't know about any new girls. I'm a happily married man," Luther winked at Jimmy.

Luther finished up and brushed Walter's collar. Walter paid with a nice tip, and he and Jimmy headed for the door.

"When you get to Miss Lillian's place, you be sure and ask for Ginny and Corina," Luther said with a sly grin.

Walter and Jimmy laughed and walked out the door.

Miss Lillian's bawdy house was a large Queen Anne on Highland Avenue that was painted gold and white. It had multistoried turrets, big chimneys, and a large porch that wrapped around the front. Miss Lillian had a steady flow of customers from the jazz scene on Vine Street, a block away. She greeted Walter and Jimmy at the door. She was a big-bosomed woman about 50 years old. Her hair was starting to turn white and she looked a bit worn from years in the profession. Walter gave her a hug and slipped her a bottle of her favorite whiskey.

"Walter, you spoil me," she said gratefully.

"Nothing but the finest for my best girl."

"You'll be wanting something in return, I'm sure."

"Are Ginny and Corina busy?"

Miss Lillian eyed him suspiciously. "How did you know about my new girls?"

"Because you and your girls are as famous as you are beautiful."

"You sure are one smooth talker, Walter Braden. Let me get those girls before I end up in bed with you."

Walter and Jimmy had been nipping at the flask since leaving the golf course and numbness was beginning to set in. They followed the Negro girls into separate rooms. Walter tried to get in the mood but soon realized the alcohol had taken its toll on his libido. Ginny did her best to help him function but it was no use.

"Hey, Jimmy!" he yelled. "The shaft on my putter isn't working!"

He heard Jimmy laugh, and a few minutes later, Jimmy walked naked into Walter's room. "I bet you can't do this, Walter." He was well endowed and he had his fedora hung over his erection. "When I finish with my girl, I'll take care of yours, mister limp dick." He laughed heartily and hurried back to Corina.

Walter was getting more frustrated by the minute and listening to Jimmy's success in the next room wasn't helping either. When he realized it was hopeless, he grabbed the pitcher of water off the bedstand and tiptoed quietly into Jimmy's room. Jimmy had reached the point of no return in his lovemaking when Walter poured the ice water on his backside. It was such a shock to Jimmy's system that he let out a howl that could be heard all over the bawdy house. He tumbled off the bed and started jumping up and down and cursing Walter at the top of his lungs. The commotion brought Miss Lillian's big Negro bouncer running into the room.

"Time for you boys to be on your way," he ordered.

CHAPTER THREE

August 1934

LIZABETH SAT WITH THE FAMILY at the Sunday dinner table. Sunday dinner was an important ritual, with the men dressed in white shirts and ties and the women in their finery. It was a time for everyone to catch up and to talk about local and world affairs. It was taken for granted that Mira's mother and father would be invited and so would J.M.'s brother, Ray, and his wife, Erma. Erma had no children so she enjoyed being around Ray's family.

Lizabeth loved her grandparents dearly. She called them Pop and Nana. They offered her support without the critical analysis of a parent. Her grandparents had emigrated from Ireland and met in America. Pop was slight of stature, with a narrow face, upturned nose, blue eyes and a light complexion. Nana was a short, stout woman who was constantly fighting her weight. She tempered Pop's humor and good nature with a no-nonsense view of life.

Pop could sometimes be frivolous and a romantic, so Nana gave him daily doses of realism that kept him centered, and together they had carved out a good life in America. Pop had worked as a railroad inspector for the Union Pacific, while Nana kept house and raised their two daughters.

Mira's sister, Julia, lived in Santiago, Cuba, with her husband, who worked for Cuba Power and Light. Ray worked for Tom Hannon, but no one could pin him down on just what that involved. He was a broad-shouldered, bull of a man, with a short, thick neck and muscles that rippled in his arms. He had done some prize fighting, and Walter suspected that he might be using those muscles to intimidate Hannon's opposition.

Erma had once worked as a seamstress and had taught Lizabeth how to sew. She was short and plump with green eyes and a pug nose, and she was a delight to be around. Jimmy was also there, but he kept quiet, preferring to let Walter do the talking, while he sat back and enjoyed the family.

"Walter, I heard that you boys lost the match play championship at Swope Park," Pop said. He and Walter had a special bond because they were a lot alike and fed off each other's tomfoolery.

"We didn't lose," Cam said. "We did a Walter."

"What's that supposed to mean?" Walter challenged.

"It means that clowning around is more important to you than winning."

"You're the one who missed the putt on eighteen," Walter shot back. "You need to learn how to lose."

"That's easy with you for a brother."

"Don't you two start," Mira warned. "You are not going to ruin everyone's Sunday dinner."

There was a moment of uncomfortable silence while everyone continued to pass around Mira's roast and vegetable dishes.

"How is the new job going, Walter?" Ray asked, changing the conversation.

"It couldn't be better, and I want to thank you again for getting me the appointment."

"I hear that you are doing great things at the club. Sales are up, and the patrons are happy."

Walter wondered how he knew that but did not want to put him on the spot.

"I enjoy the work and helping people forget their troubles for a while."

"They won't find the answer to their troubles at the bottom of a bottle," J.M. said. "And you certainly don't want to be a bartender for the rest of your life."

Walter took the criticism and remained silent. He had made up his mind long ago to never challenge or be disrespectful to his father.

"You could be successful like Cam, if you set your mind to it," J.M. continued. "He has been the top salesman at the dealership three months in a row." Cam had been hired at a Ford dealer and was helping with the family finances.

"That is wonderful, Cam," Erma said. Cam accepted congratulations from the group.

It was amazing to Lizabeth that her parents were not able to see the favoritism they were showing Cam at Walter's expense.

"That reminds me," Walter said. "I've sent dozens of people out to your dealership the past few months. Have you sold them any cars?"

"Of course, I have."

"Did you ever think to thank me or offer me a finder's fee?"

"Why would I do that? I sold the cars."

"Suspicions confirmed. It's all about you."

"Do you want some money?" Cam asked

"No. I don't want your money. I want you to show some gratitude."

"If you two don't stop, you are going to leave the table," Mira said forcefully. "This is no way to behave in front of company."

"We're not company," Erma said. "We are family, and this is quite entertaining."

"Well, it is upsetting my digestion," Mira said.

"Lizabeth, how is your new venture going?" Erma asked, changing the subject.

"Not well," Lizabeth replied. "I had hoped to get my fashions into one of the department stores, but they only want to display famous fashion designers."

"The snob factor is hard to overcome," Erma said. "You would think that selling fashions in a cow town would give them some perspective. You aren't giving up, are you?"

"Never. But I had high hopes and now feel totally deflated. I'm taking a step back and trying to figure out what to do next."

"You have a real talent for design, so don't let them discourage you. Let me know if you need my help."

"Thank you, Aunt Erma."

"J.M., have you thought any more about my offer of an appointment with Tom Hannon?" his brother asked.

"There is nothing to think about. I will never ask Tom Hannon for anything. He has ruined many a good man in this town."

"He has also kept thousands more working," Ray countered.

"That's true, as long as they do his bidding. There is a fine line between patronage and extortion. We are supposed to be living in a democracy, not a political system that says do for the boss and he will do for you. They call that corruption in a lot of cities."

"If he is corrupt, then why isn't he in jail?" Eileen asked. Lizabeth's sister had been quiet until now.

"Because he controls the police department and the city officials," J.M. explained. "Most of them owe their jobs to him."

"If he was that bad, he wouldn't keep getting elected as alderman in the largest district in the city," Ray replied calmly. He did not take offense at his brother's views.

"You know very well that on election day there is a turkey in every kitchen and a free bottle of booze waiting for voters when the polls close. And the men in the district know that all construction contracts they will be working on will have to be approved at Hannon's office rather than City Hall."

Walter knew that his father was telling him in no uncertain terms that he did not approve of his job with the Hannon organization.

"I give you credit," Ray said. "Not many men would stake out the moral high ground in this economic downturn."

"I'm standing uneasy on my principles," J.M. acknowledged. "I hope I can find something soon before my family has to suffer."

"A man has to take a stand on what he believes in," Pop said in support. "You are lucky to have these four, hard-working young people to help out until you find something."

"Nana, have you heard anything from Aunt Julia?" Eileen asked, trying to shield her father from further talk of unemployment.

"She is doing fine, although she is lonely for her family. In my letter, I told her we would try to visit Cuba sometime in the future."

"I would love to go in the winter," Lizabeth said. "Cuba would be so warm and exotic."

"Vacations are a luxury in this economy," J.M. said. "Maybe when things get back to normal, we can set sail for Cuba."

"A reward for surviving the Depression," Lizabeth said.

"I just hope that we can climb out of the Depression before another war starts," Ray said. "Hitler has been rearming his military forces and now that he's chancellor, the world had better watch out."

"Surely there won't be another war," Mira said. "All those millions of boys killed in the last war was horrific."

"The Germans want another shot at ruling the world," J.M. said. "And they want revenge for the harsh terms the Allies inflicted on them after the last war."

"I don't want my sons fighting to save the Europeans from one another," Mira said. "I will join every peace movement in the country to prevent that from happening."

Lizabeth was still smarting from her meeting with the Harzfeld's buyer. She had spent several months trying to figure out how to proceed with her business. Although discouraged, she was not about to give up. She was taking in sewing from the surrounding neighborhoods and designing new fashions for her line of clothing. Mira encouraged her to get out of the house and enjoy life more, but Lizabeth was possessed by her desire to become a successful designer. She enjoyed her work so much that she did not see it as an intrusion on her personal life.

In the past, she had been pursued by several young men in the neighborhood, but romance seemed frivolous when compared to her ambition. And she was not a bit envious of the romances swirling around Eileen and was more relieved than jealous that she did not elicit from men the adoration bestowed on her sister. She felt herself the equal of any man and was wary of entanglements that might make her play a subservient role or that would interfere with her future. She viewed the flowering oratory from suitors that buoyed Eileen as nonsensical blubbering from men who should know better.

It wasn't that she didn't believe in romance, but she was not about to spend valuable time in the pursuit of it. Her father had not found a job, so she felt a responsibility to help with her share of the family finances. The rest of the money was poured back into her business. She worked furiously through the summer and early fall on her fall dress line, while she tried to come up with a solution to her marketing problems.

By the time she looked up from her work, the trees in Brookside had turned crimson and gold, and there was a crisp bite to the air. October was her favorite month, so she took some of her piecework to the sunporch, where she could enjoy the birds chirping and the sounds of life wafting through the neighborhood.

Her mother was in the yard, working on her flowers. Mira was dressed in brown cotton pants with a matching top that Lizabeth had made for her. Her bonnet was cream colored, as were her gardening gloves. Mira felt that working in the yard was no excuse for not presenting herself fashionably to the neighborhood. She was busy planting daffodils and tulips for spring and bringing in the begonia and gladiola bulbs for winter storage. Mira was as passionate about her flowers as Lizabeth was about her fashions.

Eileen walked into the sunroom carrying her coffee cup and sat down.

"Why don't you stop working, and we can help Mother in the yard?" she said.

"I would love to, but I have to get these designs finished."

"I admire your work ethic, but you are not on a deadline."

"A self-imposed one, which somehow seems more demanding."

"Your obsession continues. I remember when we were kids, you would spend hours dressing your dolls because they were never quite right. And store-bought clothes for your wardrobe would never do, because they were not up to your standards."

"And your point is?"

"That you need to get out of here and get a life beyond needle and thread."

"You don't mean that there is actually more to life than sewing," Lizabeth said in mock surprise.

They both laughed.

"If you don't slow down, you will have a warehouse full of dresses and not enough customers to buy them."

"That might be true, but with every creation I learn something and that sustains me."

34

"You don't have to work so hard. Cam and Walter are doing well, and so am I."

"I know. The competition is fierce, so I'm determined to keep up."

"Sibling rivalry at its best."

"Something like that. The runt of the litter has to work harder to keep up with the competition."

"Don't say that," Eileen admonished her. "You are not a runt, and I certainly hope that you don't see me as competition."

"Of course not. You are my dear sister. Heaven knows that we have enough competition between Cam and Walter to last this family a lifetime. I'm just not comfortable having my siblings support me."

"We support one another. That's what family is all about."

"Do you think with Mother's work ethic, she would let me sit around and do nothing? Her sympathy with unemployment only goes so far." Lizabeth paused. "I've been wanting to ask if you think it's putting a strain on their marriage."

"How could it not? She is very supportive of Father in front of us, but unemployment goes against the grain of her mind-over-matter philosophy. She thinks that if you want a job bad enough there is no reason why it can't be found."

"I'm sure there are a lot of men looking for work who wished it were that easy. The mind takes a back seat to matter in this economy. Jobs just don't exist."

"We are blessed to be working," Eileen said

"Do you mind if I ask you something?" Lizabeth asked.

"Of course not."

"Have you seen anything of the man you were going to marry?"

Eileen hesitated for a moment. "He came into Harzfeld's a few times, but I told him I was going to honor my parent's wishes. It was hard for him to accept, but I haven't seen him for months so hopefully he has given up."

"Are you okay with that?"

"Yes. Looking back on it, I realize now that I was being impetuous and self-absorbed. That close call with marriage made me realize how much I enjoy my independence. Thank goodness, you and my brothers saved me from myself. I wasn't thinking clearly."

"You can thank Mother. She's the one who put it in motion. It was a scandal to be avoided at all costs."

"And I'm now paying the price with increased scrutiny of my love life."

"We have to be vigilant, because we don't know what the temptress will do next to scandalize the family," Lizabeth joked, and they both laughed.

"The scrutiny wouldn't be on me, if you would get out and date more," Eileen said.

"I'll leave romance to you."

"What about that nice-looking Allen boy? What is his first name?"

"Cory. We are friends, but he's so painfully shy that it makes us both uncomfortable."

"Perhaps you could help him with that. He walks by the house at least twice a day trying to get a glimpse of you. And you are not exactly showing him any encouragement hiding in the house. He would have to extract you from beneath your fashions to have any chance of dating you. If you are not working, you are thinking about working. You need to broaden your interests, if you are going to attract a young man."

"I'm not in the business of attraction. I'm in the business of fashion and everything else doesn't quite measure up. And please, forgive the pun."

"Said the would-be spinster, as she sewed her life away."

Lizabeth laughed. "That's me all right. An old maid at the age of nineteen."

"If you won't go on a date, then I want you to promise me that you will set your work aside and come see the new play that I'm in," Eileen said.

"What's it called?"

"Ironically enough, it is a comedy titled *The Boyfriend*, and I'm playing Polly in the lead role."

"Mother and Father are going to love that."

"That's why I'm keeping it from them for as long as possible. Will you come?"

"Of course. When does it open?"

"We rehearse for the next couple of weeks and plan to open on November first."

"I hope you are a big success."

"Thank you. It will be my first experience in a lead role, so I'm very nervous."

"I'm sure that you will be terrific. Look out Hollywood."

"Jean Harlow, here I come," Eileen laughed.

"You can be the third famous actress from Kansas City," Lizabeth said. "Jean Harlow, Joan Crawford, and the rising star, Eileen Braden."

"Thank you for promoting me to that status, but I will be happy to stay with my current theatrical troupe. Can you imagine Father's reaction if I told him I was headed to Hollywood?"

"It would not be pretty," Lizabeth replied. "To him, Hollywood is synonymous with Sodom and Gomorrah."

"It would be the bitter end and confirm my status as the wayward daughter."

"Yes. You had better store up some parental points for when you have to tell them about the new play."

"Why do you think that I'm going out to help Mother with her flowers?"

"You scheming little wench. Give me a kiss before you go."

Eileen got up and kissed her on the cheek.

The two sisters were sleeping in their double bed when Walter came stumbling into the house. Lizabeth had cautioned him to be quiet when he came home so that he would not wake their parents, but sometimes he was too drunk to realize the noise he was making. It was becoming a nightly occurrence and Lizabeth was losing sleep. She slipped out of bed and hurried down the stairs. Eileen and Cam had acquired the ability to block Walter out and were not bothered in the least by the noise. Walter was rummaging through the refrigerator.

"Hello, Lizabeth. What are you doing up?" He swayed back and forth as he poured a glass of milk. She was glad that he was sober enough to make conversation.

"Walter, you are going to wake Mother and Father!" she scolded him.

Walter put his finger to his lips and said, "Shhh." He reeked of alcohol.

37

"Have you been drinking at work?"

"No, ma'am. Get off at two a.m. and drink 'til four a.m."

"Do you want something to eat?"

"Me and Jimmy had breakfast at the all-night diner. I just need some milk to settle the tummy."

"Why do you drink so much alcohol when you know that Mother and Father do not approve?"

"Not after their approval. Cam is the approval son."

"But it doesn't have to be that way, if you would just make an effort to please them."

"Ha!" Walter shouted, and then put his fingers to his lips again. "Impossible, because I'm not the golden boy," he whispered.

"You know that's not true."

"It is, but that's okay. I enjoy my role as the secondary son and will leave it to Cam to be the anointed one."

"Why do you suppose that is?" Lizabeth asked.

"I'll tell you why when I'm sober."

"It's just that Mother sees drinking as a weakness."

"How could she not? Mind over matter, my dear girl. Where she sees a weakness, I see enjoyment."

"Two of her uncles were alcoholics, and she's afraid that you are going down that path."

"No chance of that, because I can handle my liquor as well as any man. But enough about me. How are you doing, Lizabeth?"

"I'm doing fine."

"No. No." Walter waved his finger in her face. "Don't fib to me. You are depressed about your business."

"I suppose so, but I will bounce back."

"What can I do to help? We have to stick together if we are going to keep up with the princess and the golden boy." The princess was an affectionate term that J.M. sometimes used for Eileen.

"You have been wonderfully supportive, Walter. It might be that I was too optimistic to start a business in an economic depression."

"It might seem that way. But hang on, and things might start breaking your way."

"I'm hanging on by my fingertips and afraid to look down."

"I'll be there to catch you, so don't worry about that."

"Thank you, Walter. Now go to bed and get some sleep."

Lizabeth crept quietly up the stairs and back to bed. She tossed and turned but could not get to sleep. The fall fashion season was over, and it was frustrating that her designs were not in the marketplace. Her holiday fashions would soon face the same fate. She knew her designs would be a success, if she could get them introduced to the public. It must be how an inventor felt with an invention that could change the world but for want of a patent.

She listened to Eileen's steady breathing and thought how wonderful it must be for those who did not have the burning desire of ambition raging in their breasts. Walter and Eileen could take life as it came without worrying about success or how to make their marks in the world. It must be gratifying to stay on an even keel without that little devil sitting on your shoulder asking what you have done to make something of yourself. Perhaps everyone had their own devil stalking them but had the ability to filter it out.

She fell asleep and dreamed that she was somewhere in the vastness of the cosmos, drifting past brightly shining stars. Her autumn and Christmas fashions were swirling around her. She reached out to grab them, but they kept slipping away, and she watched in shock as they vanished into the darkness of the ever-expanding universe.

November 1934

Walter was visiting with his customers at the Hi Hat club a week before Thanksgiving when Uncle Ray walked in and sat down.

"Hello, Uncle Ray. It's good to see you. What will you have?"

"Hello, Walter. A cold beer, please."

Walter pulled him a draft from the keg.

"You've been working here about six months now," Ray said.

"That's right."

"How's it going?"

"Just fine."

"Good. I told Boss Tom you were as solid as they come, but he ran a couple of tests these past few weeks to be sure."

"What kind of tests?"

"Do you remember when the manager here suggested that you could water down the drinks to save money?"

"Yes."

"And when he hinted that you deserved more of the tip money than the other employees because you are the bartender and work harder?"

"If that was a test, anyone could pass who knows the difference between right and wrong."

"You would be surprised how many times that gets blurred in this economy. We call it the disease of rationalization brought on by the Depression. Desperate men do desperate things."

"The Boss is a busy man. Why would he be testing me?"

Ray downed his beer in two large gulps and set the glass on the bar. "Meet me at Boss Tom's office in the morning at nine o'clock sharp." He got up and walked out of the bar. Walter was more than curious as to what this was about. He couldn't imagine why the Boss would want to see a lowly bartender from the Hi Hat club.

The next morning, Walter met Uncle Ray outside Hannon's office. Men were already lined up, as they waited to see the Boss about a loan, employment, or help with a personal problem. Ray said hello to everyone, as he led Walter up the stairs to the office. Boss Tom was smoking a cigar and shuffling through papers on his desk. He immediately got up from his chair and shook hands with them.

"Glad you could make it, Walter. Have a seat."

They sat in two chairs that fronted his desk.

"Did your Uncle Ray tell you what this is about?"

"No, sir."

"I'll get right to the point. We are running a dues-paying organization. I need a man who can handle collections from our business partners. A man who is honest and has the ability to get along with people."

Walter mulled that over for a moment. "Excuse me, sir. But would I be correct in assuming that some of your business partners don't want to pay?"

"You would. And that is a question you will have to resolve."

"It's good of you to consider me, but I couldn't strongarm anyone."

"We do not want to intimidate our partners into paying. We want them to feel that we are all in this together. We think you can make that happen."

"It's hard for people to part with their money in the best of times, much less in this Depression."

"I couldn't agree more. You will have to use your wits and show them the benefits of our association."

"Forgive me, sir, but what would those be?"

"Quite a lot actually. Our business partners don't have to worry about crime, because criminals fear our organization. We keep competition away from their doorstep by not issuing permits or by making it too expensive for outsiders to compete. We provide low-interest loans, and we can backload payments in extreme circumstances. We also demand that members of our organization support the businesses that support us. We provide low-cost medical care and much more. If they had to purchase these benefits on their own, it would cost them more than the benefits we offer."

"If you don't mind me asking, with all of those benefits, why are you having a problem?"

"Our relationship has frayed, because we've had collectors in the past who had no finesse and made our partners feel they were being extorted rather than being part of our family."

"I understand, sir. But why do you need me?"

"We've watched your progress at the Hi Hat club. You are good with people, and you have made a lot of friends downtown. A number of them are business owners who we are having trouble with. When they see you come through the door, rather than someone they fear, it will make all the difference in the world."

"I like my job at the Hi Hat club."

"I'm glad to hear it, but where will it lead? Men who prove themselves move up in this organization."

"You are very generous, sir. But I'm not sure collections are for me."

"We work in two-man teams, so we will put your friend Jimmy on the payroll, and we will double your salaries."

Walter smiled ruefully because he knew the Boss had him. There was no way in this depressed economy that he could refuse the offer.

"When do we start?" he asked.

Outside the office, Uncle Ray put his hand on Walter's shoulder. "I'm going to give you one piece of advice. Keep detailed records of the money you handle. That way no one can question your honesty. There are suitcases full of cash floating around this office and one day the reformers might ask where it went."

"Yes, sir. I'll do that."

The day after Thanksgiving, Lizabeth and Eileen had an early breakfast and then walked up the stairway to the attic to retrieve the Christmas decorations. It was a ritual they had followed for as long as they could remember. To have a wonderful Thanksgiving and then start the Christmas season was a joy, and the passing years had not dimmed their enthusiasm for the traditions and sparkle that surrounded the holiday.

Cam and Walter had left earlier to cut a tree on a farm south of the city. Lizabeth took each box off the shelf, being careful not to damage a family heirloom as she lifted the lids and inspected the contents. Each bauble and strand of lights told a story of Christmas past, and if they were not careful they would spend the entire morning reminiscing about their childhood.

"I remember when you were little, you would throw a fit when we put the decorations away," Eileen said. "You thought they would be unhappy stored away in the dark."

Lizabeth smiled. "I have to confess that sometimes I would sneak up to the attic and take the lids off the boxes so the decorations could see the light and be allowed to breathe. I would tell the little figurines to have sweet dreams, because Christmas was coming soon. I sometimes wonder if figurines have a life of their own or just the ones that we give them."

"Either way, they are alive to you."

"I definitely think that my fashions have their own personalities. I know instantly when they are right for someone and when they are not. Women have to be happy with their clothing, but perhaps to make an ideal match, the clothing should be happy with the woman."

"I don't think you should repeat that in public," Eileen said, rolling her eyes. "People might think that you should be designing at the funny farm."

Lizabeth laughed. "Every designer is a bit eccentric. Sometimes dancing on the edge of madness is where we find inspiration."

"Walter's car just pulled in, so we had better dance these decorations down to the living room," Eileen said.

They watched through the window as Walter and Cam took a 10-foot Douglas fir off the roof of the car and then sawed off a portion of the trunk. The girls had the stand waiting as the two men carried the tree in and placed it in front of the picture window.

"Is it straight?" Walter asked.

"A little more to the left," Lizabeth said.

Walter complied.

"Perfect!" Eileen said.

"Now you two work your magic," Cam said. "We'll surprise Mother with the tree when she gets home."

Cam and Walter never helped decorate the tree. The girls were sure-handed and much better at design and the placement of baubles and lights.

"Go have some coffee, and we'll call you in when we are ready," Eileen said.

Eileen carefully positioned the three strands of colorful lights, and Lizabeth wove the red and gold garland around the tree. When they were finished, they stepped back and admired their handiwork.

"What a beautiful tree," Lizabeth said. "It will bring joy to us and to the neighborhood."

"You can come in now," Eileen called to Walter and Cam. She held a star in her hand that she gave to Cam. He was the only one tall enough to position it at the top of the tree. Lizabeth handed Walter his personal bauble in the shape of a golf bag that he hung on the tree.

Eileen plugged in the lights, and they stepped back in awe of what they had created.

"This is our most beautiful tree ever," Lizabeth said.

"Merry Christmas, everyone," Walter said, and they hugged one another, officially kicking off the Christmas season.

December 1934

Lizabeth was in her sewing room, when her mother came up the stairs and leaned in the doorway.

"You have a visitor," she said.

"Me? Who is it?"

"The Allen boy."

"Cory?"

Her mother nodded.

"This is a surprise," Lizabeth said, as she sat her sewing aside. Curious, she headed down the stairs. Cory was in the living room pacing nervously back and forth. Lizabeth noticed the sweat on his brow. Cory had light-brown hair that had a touch of curl. He had a classic Grecian nose and light blue eyes, was of average height and weight, and muscular from working in his father's construction business. At first glance, one would think that he would be outgoing, brash, and a lady's man, but he was just the opposite. He had none of the bluster associated with some of the other boys in the neighborhood. She noticed that he was holding a Christmas gift.

"Hello, Cory. It's nice to see you. Please, sit."

Cory sat in one of the Early American, rose-printed chairs that were a gift to Mira from her parents. Lizabeth sat in the other chair and waited for Cory to start the conversation. She waited in vain. After an uncomfortable silence, she spoke first. "How have you been?"

"Okay. I hope you don't mind me stopping by. I wanted to give you this Christmas gift." He handed it to her.

"Thank you, Cory. It is good of you to think of me. Should I open it now or wait until Christmas?"

"Please, go ahead."

She untied the ribbon and unwrapped the box. Inside was a beautiful silver bracelet.

"How lovely," she said. "You shouldn't have gone to the trouble."

"I just wanted you to have something from me."

"That is very thoughtful of you."

"My pleasure." Another uncomfortable silence followed. Lizabeth remembered Eileen's suggestion that she could do something to help Cory to be less timid.

"How is the construction business?"

"It's always slow during the holidays, but it should pick up if we have good weather."

"I noticed that you are building some houses here in the neighborhood."

"Yes. We are lucky to have work. A lot of construction companies have gone under."

"How do you like construction?"

"I like it fine."

"Will it be your life's work?"

"I don't think so. I'm taking some college courses in education. I would like to become a teacher."

"That is wonderful." Lizabeth wondered how he would ever have the courage to stand in front of a classroom.

"How is your sewing business coming along?" Cory asked.

"It's going slower than I would like, but I have to persevere until the economy improves."

"You are courageous to start your own business. Not many people would risk it in a depression."

She was surprised and delighted that he felt this way. Most men wanted women home by the fire tending to their needs.

"Thank you, Cory. I appreciate that very much." Maybe there was more to Cory than she had realized. Should she encourage his interest when she had so much on her mind? Probably not, because it couldn't go anywhere. Instead she found herself saying, "Eileen is in a play and has given me two tickets. Would you like to go?"

Cory looked both surprised and delighted. "I would love to go."

"Thank you so much for the Christmas gift," Lizabeth said. She did not want to encourage him too much, but she didn't want to discourage him either. She would have to straddle a fine line between romance and friendship, so that the relationship would not interfere with her time or her career.

Snow was falling on Saturday night when Cory picked her up at the house. She wore a brown wool suit, with a matching hat and a tweed winter coat. Cory wore a gray, wool suit, with a red tie, and he carried a gray topcoat.

"You two look dashing," Mira said.

"Thank you, Mother. We will be home when the play is over."

"Take your time and enjoy yourselves," Mira said.

Cory led her out to his blue, 1930 Ford Model A roadster. He opened the door and she slid onto the seat.

She was nervous and wondered if he was.

"I like your car," she said.

"Thank you. It took me a few years to save enough for the down payment."

"Good for you." He took a blanket from the back seat and covered her legs. The roadster was not the warmest car on the road.

"Have you seen your sister in a play before?" Cory asked, as he started the car and put it into gear.

"I've seen her in bit parts, but never in a starring role."

"It's something that I can't imagine," Cory said.

"What?"

"Having the nerve to stand in front of all those people and put on a performance."

"I know. Perhaps pretending they are someone else takes away the fear."

"Maybe. But the words would stick in my throat."

"I imagine that acting is like any endeavor. The more you do it, the easier it gets."

"For you maybe. You could do anything you set your mind to."

"It's kind of you to say so, but I have as many doubts and fears as anyone."

"I don't think so. My sister says that you have resolve."

"Really? How kind of her. How is Jennie? I haven't seen her since we graduated."

"She's fine. She's going to secretarial school and looking for a job."

"And your brother, Fred?"

"He's in his last year of college. When he finishes, he will help Father in the business."

"Will you stay on?"

"No. Fred is the designated heir to the business. I can't see myself working for him."

"How come?"

"He is as demanding as Father, and I don't want to be caught in the middle of their power struggle. And you've probably guessed that I'm not built for business."

46

"You are built for whatever you set your mind to."

"I'll remember that. For now, I will look to you for inspiration, and maybe some of it will rub off."

"So, you're putting all of the pressure on me," she kidded him.

Cory laughed. "Very unfair of me and I apologize."

She was delighted that he was overcoming his shyness and contributing to the conversation.

"You are easy to talk to," he said.

"Most people are, if you give them a chance."

"Maybe. What seems natural to you is hard for me."

She reached over and touched his arm. "I understand that."

Cory stopped the car in front of a large, red barn with a wagon wheel out front. The Red Barn Players sign above the door blinked out into the gathering darkness. They followed the other patrons inside. About 80 seats fronted the stage and 40 more were in the balcony. Lizabeth looked around and could see that it was going to be a full house. It made her apprehensive that her sister was going to be exposed on stage for all to see. She wished that she could offer her some encouragement.

The lights dimmed and the play started. After the first few scenes, Lizabeth's fears evaporated. Eileen was superb in the role of Polly. Lizabeth thought it was an amazing transformation that Eileen could immerse herself so deeply in a role that she could become the person she was playing.

The play was about a young heiress who falls in love with a messenger. Parental control of Polly was not unlike that experienced by Eileen at home and must have seemed quite ironic to her. Her timing was impeccable in the comedy scenes, and her dance numbers were first rate. When the play ended, the cast received a standing ovation, but the most applause was for Eileen, who was the obvious star. Lizabeth was relieved and very proud of her sister.

She and Cory went backstage to congratulate her.

"You were wonderful," Lizabeth said with pride, as she gave Eileen a hug. She had no idea her sister was such an accomplished actress.

"Congratulations," Cory said. "I enjoyed the play immensely."

"Thank you." Eileen was flush with excitement and obviously enjoying the success of her performance.

"I was kidding about you becoming a star, but you just might pull it off," Lizabeth said.

"Don't be silly," Eileen said. "Look around you. I'm an amateur actress playing in a barn."

"You would have been great on any stage in America," Lizabeth countered.

"I appreciate your sisterly support, and I thank you both for coming tonight."

Lizabeth hugged her again. "We will get out of your way and let you bask in the adoration of your fans."

She and Cory left and headed for the car.

When they arrived home, Cory walked her to the door.

"Thank you, Cory. I had a really good time."

"So did I. Here's my first stab at being more assertive. Do you think we could do this again?"

"Of course, we can." She saw no reason why they couldn't be good friends, as long as he understood that her business came before romance.

CHAPTER FOUR

It was two days before Christmas. Cam had met a woman from Mission Hills whom he had invited to the house for tea. This was an unusual event, to say the least. Cam being serious enough about any woman to invite her home was hard to imagine. He was insistent that Lizabeth be there with Eileen and Mira. Lizabeth's curiosity was piqued, because Cam seldom spent time with Eileen or her.

Mira had set the sterling silver tea service out on the dining room table. When Cam and the woman arrived, he introduced her. Helen Rabun was an attractive woman, with short blonde hair, hazel eyes, and a radiant smile. Cam attracted women who were extroverted and could hold their own in a conversation. It allowed him to remain silent and broody and settle into his role as an observer of the human condition. When attempts were made to bring him into the conversation, he would raise his eyebrows or grunt in response, and others could interpret that as they wished. However, when he flipped his internal switch, he could be the most charming and witty man on the planet. Why and when this would happen was anyone's guess, but women flocked to him because they evidently thought his charm was worth the wait.

"How did you meet Cam?" Mira asked Helen.

"My father bought me a car for my birthday. Cam delivered it to the house, and we found that we had a lot in common."

Lizabeth wondered what that might be but did not want to be rude by asking. A car for a birthday gift in a depression was a luxury she could not begin to imagine.

"You have a lovely home," Helen said to Mira.

"Thank you."

Helen turned to Eileen. "Cam took me to your play on Wednesday night. You were wonderful and I enjoyed it so much."

"Thank you," Eileen said. "I'm sorry I missed you. Cam should have brought you backstage."

Lizabeth knew that Cam was too egotistical to let the spotlight shine too closely on anyone but him.

"Have you seen the play?" Helen asked Mira.

"No, dear. We are still getting used to having an actress in the family."

"Oh, I see. I'm sorry if I spoke out of turn."

"You did not," Lizabeth said. "It's a generational thing."

"That is my daughter's way of saying that I'm old-fashioned," Mira said. "I find it easier to be broadminded about other people's children."

"You should be proud of Eileen," Helen said. "She is a wonderful actress."

"Thank you, Helen," Eileen said.

"Where is Walter?" Cam looked at his watch. "He is fifteen minutes late."

"Walter is coming to tea!" Lizabeth said in surprise. "How in the world did you talk him into that?"

"Never you mind," Cam said. "All will be explained in due time."

"Are you related to the Rabun family that runs the shoe store chain?" Mira asked Helen.

"Yes. My father started the business."

"He has been quite successful."

"We have been fortunate, but like everyone else, we are having a bit of a downturn."

"Do you work in the business?"

"Yes. I'm a regional manager."

At that moment, Walter came hurriedly through the door. "Sorry I'm late, everyone. I was delayed at work."

Cam introduced him to Helen.

"Very pleased to meet you," Walter said graciously.

"Me too," Helen said. "I understand that you work for the Hannon organization."

"I do indeed."

"Do you work for his concrete company?"

"No. I'm in the administrative division."

Helen leaned over conspiratorially. "Is the rumor true that he buries his opponents under cement from his concrete company when he wants to get rid of them?" She winked at Walter.

Walter was impressed. Cam had found a girl with a sense of humor. "I would answer that but then I couldn't guarantee your safety."

Helen laughed. "Cam, you didn't tell me that your brother was so witty."

Cam grunted in response.

"That means he agrees with your assessment," Walter said.

"Before you and Cam start in on each other, perhaps you would like to tell us what this is all about," Mira said, looking at Cam. "The two of you having afternoon tea is enough to frighten the dickens out of me."

"Cam, this was your idea," Walter said. "Why don't you explain?"

"Here's the deal," Cam said. "Helen is moving her downtown shoe store to the Country Club Plaza, because she needs more space. The old store is located close to Kline's and Harzfeld's, and she has agreed to sublet the space to Walter and me."

"Why in the world would she ever do that?" Mira asked.

"Because we are tired of our little sister moping around here like the world has ended, and because we think she can make a name for herself in the fashion industry."

Lizabeth looked at Cam wide-eyed and speechless. This was out of the blue and totally unexpected.

"That's right," Walter said. "Instead of begging the fashion buyers to accept your designs, you can now sell them yourself. The space is located on Petticoat Lane, and customers will have to pass your store to get to the big department stores."

The thought of starting a business had crossed Lizabeth's mind, but it was so far-fetched and expensive that she had dismissed it. That her two brothers had so much confidence in her to invest their time and money was so caring and thoughtful that it humbled her. And she felt guilty that she had thought that Cam only cared about himself.

"I don't know what to say. Do you really think it possible that we could pull it off?"

"That will be up to you," Cam said. "With your talent and energy, we think you can make it a success."

"But how will I compete against the likes of Harzfeld's and Kline's?"

"Helen is the retail expert, so if you don't mind she has a couple of suggestions."

"Of course, I don't mind."

"I think the key for you is *not* to compete. You need to come up with your own niche. Give the customers something of value they can't get at the big department stores. Your designs are original and that's a good start."

"These past few months I've been giving that some thought," Lizabeth said. "With the ongoing Depression, I think that spring and summer dresses that sell for under a dollar would be a big hit. A majority of women can't afford designer dresses that sell for $2.79 and up."

"There you have it," Helen said. "You can sell seasonal dresses for the average housewife who can't afford fashions designed in New York or Paris."

Lizabeth was so excited about the possibilities that her mind raced and she had to calm down and think this through if she was going to be successful. "How will I ever convert a shoe store into a dress shop," she wondered out loud.

"It won't require much," Helen said. "You will need three or four dressing rooms in the back of the store and clothing racks, of course."

"We hope you don't mind," Walter said. "But we have enlisted Cory's help with the construction. We figure the time he spends walking back and forth in front of the house, he can spend constructing your dressing rooms. Of course, you can pay him something when you start making a profit."

"My goodness," Eileen said. "This is what you have always dreamed of Lizabeth."

"Thank you all so much," Lizabeth said. She got up and hugged Helen and then Cam and Walter. "This is the best Christmas of my life. I will do everything in my power to make the store a success and to make you proud of me."

Walter and Jimmy's first stop on the collection route was at Castiglia Produce in the City Market. Castiglia Produce sold to grocery stores and restaurants around the city. John Castiglia was a short, rotund man, with black wavy hair and dark penetrating eyes. Walter and Jimmy introduced themselves.

"How's business, Mr. Castiglia?" Walter asked.

"No good. All my customers are cutting back." Walter looked around. Trucks were being loaded and unloaded and the place was bustling with activity.

"Sorry to hear that. We are here to collect your monthly dues."

"I'm short of cash this month. How about you take some cases of produce instead of money?"

"I wish we could, but we are only allowed to accept cash."

"What if I can't pay?"

Walter expected to be tested and he was prepared. "You know that it would not be good for business to be in bad standing with the organization."

"Is that a threat?"

"It most definitely is not. Our only concern is for you to be successful, and we want to help in any way we can."

Walter had made a study of the people on his route. John Castiglia was from the old country and knew the ways of organizations like the Mafia, so he was not going to push too hard. Walter just had to nudge him in the right direction.

"You don't help me; you take from me," Castiglia said.

Walter took a slip of paper from his pocket. "This is the telephone number of a new restaurant opening next week on 10th Street. They are expecting your call. You should make enough money from this one account to pay your monthly dues. And in the future, Jimmy and I will keep our eyes out for any business we can steer your way. We are your partners, Mr. Castiglia, and we will be on call in case you have any problems with the city or with competition."

For a moment, Mr. Castiglia was stunned into silence. "This has never happened before. Are you going to raise my dues?"

"No, sir. We are going to give you better service for your monthly contribution."

Mr. Castiglia went to his cash register and counted out the money. He handed it to Walter.

"Thank you, sir," Walter said. "We will see you next month."

And that's how Walter handled all of his accounts. He treated each business as a separate entity and learned all he could about the owner's history and any problems he or she might have. He left small gifts of kosher cookies and candy for Jewish merchants on Passover and a gift for the Irish, Italians, and Poles on Catholic holidays. He made it a point to find out the birthdays of his merchants and their wives so he could leave a box of cigars or flowers.

But his main contribution was to be an advocate and steer new business to each of his merchants. He never tried to collect money, unless he left something of value in return. If he honestly felt that a merchant couldn't pay, he would pay the dues himself and allow them time to pay him back. After a few months, he had turned monthly confrontations into partnerships, where the merchants did not view him as the enemy and were more than curious as to what he would come up with next to help their businesses.

But Walter's main asset was that he was such a likeable fellow and always had a good story or a joke to tell. He had never met a person who he could not coax out of a bad mood. He had honed his psychological skills behind the bar at the Hi Hat club, and he was now putting them to good use in the business world. And he was putting into practice the philosophy of Big Jack Hannon, that if he took care of his customers, they would take care of him.

He wanted to do a good job to repay Uncle Ray and Boss Tom Hannon for having faith in him. He understood booze was his downfall, so he continued his policy of not drinking on the job. However, at four o'clock, he had that awful craving that he needed to satisfy and he and Jimmy headed to the Hi Hat club, where he would down a couple of quick shots of whiskey. They would drink beer until 12th Street came alive with revelry and then they would get serious about their drinking. Walter was one of those lucky few who could get a night's sleep and show no effects from the alcohol, so he saw no need to limit his consumption.

CHAPTER FIVE

April 1935

TWO OF THEIR BEST FRIENDS FROM the old neighborhood off 39th and Gillham Road met Walter and Jimmy at the Hi Hat club. They hadn't seen Oscar and Charles in a while and had some catching up to do. The four of them had attended Westport High School together.

Oscar Miller was small in stature, with a thin frame. He had a receding hairline and narrow, inquisitive eyes. Oscar was a whiz at math. When they were in grade school, he had a habit of drumming his fingers on his desk while he contemplated a problem. The drumming sounded like galloping horses. It was an unconscious habit, and he was always surprised when the teacher smacked his hand with a ruler. It was great fun for Walter and his classmates when Oscar yelled out in surprise. Because of his unconscious drumming habit, Walter dubbed him Drum and the nickname stuck.

Walter thought Drum would grow up to be a mathematical genius, but he took his numerical skills in a different direction and became a bookie. He ran numbers for some nefarious organizations and did some gambling on the side. He also took bets at different locations around town and kept on the move so law enforcement could not pin him down.

The other schoolmate was Charles Harvey Forest. Charles was heavyset with a round face and large, expressive eyes. He wore a bowler hat to cover his balding head. His forehead was creased with sweat, even in the winter, and during childhood he had complained of one stomach problem or another.

Walter called him Queasy. Charles outgrew the malady, but the name stuck. Queasy was also a numbers man, working as an assistant bookkeeper for the city. He and Drum shared a house in the old neighborhood.

"Walter, we heard you were a collection man for Boss Tom. How is that coming along?" Drum asked.

"It was difficult until we got to know the merchants and figured out how to help their businesses."

"I bet you handle a lot of cash at the end of the month," Drum said.

"We do indeed."

"Have you ever thought about putting it to good use before turning it over to Hannon?"

"I have, but then I pictured the two of us wearing cement shoes at the bottom of the Missouri River."

"If you put it that way, I can see your logic," Drum said.

"I thought you might. How is the action around town?"

"It could be better. There's not a lot of loose cash floating around. It's hard to imagine that men would rather feed the kids and pay the mortgage than gamble."

Walter laughed. "The world turned upside down. How are you avoiding paying dues to Boss Tom?"

"I'm small pickings and have managed to stay ahead of his wolves. I hope that you are not trying to put me on the company rolls."

"That's the job for guys with thick necks and broken noses. I hope you can outrun them."

"Thanks for the lovely thought."

"How's the city's cash flow, Queasy?" Walter asked.

"I'm not allowed to discuss that with a man of your questionable background," Queasy replied.

"City Manager Magrath is cooking the books for Hannon, so he wouldn't miss a few thousand for our trip to the Caribbean," Walter joked.

"That idea is often suggested by Drum, which proves that imbeciles are of like minds."

"Come on, Queasy," Drum said. "Who is going to miss a dollar here or there in the scheme of things?"

"You two should open a savings and loan," Queasy replied.

"Jimmy, how are you staying in shape for the Golden Gloves hanging out with this guy?" Drum asked.

"It isn't easy. I don't try to match him drink for drink, that's for sure."

"The alcohol in his sweat will make his opponents woozy and give him an advantage," Walter said. He ordered another round of beer for everyone.

"The last time we met, you two were on your way north with Cam," Drum said. "How did that go?"

"That was in March of last year. We have since referred to it as the willing widow's tour. Cam got us a job selling magazines, and the regional manager in all his wisdom sent us north to get subscriptions. We incorrectly assumed that spring had arrived in the Midwest and almost froze to death. I called our destination the North Pole, but the natives called it Minnesota."

"How did that go?"

"We hit upon a strategy that we thought was foolproof."

"What was it?" Queasy asked, intrigued.

"What was what?" Walter was losing focus from the alcohol.

"The strategy," Drum said.

"Oh. When we went into a town, we would scan the phonebook at the local drugstore and write down the address of any single woman in the directory. We figured she would either be divorced or widowed and might be charmed into buying a subscription. If not, we might be offered something to eat. Cam would take one part of town, and I would take the other. Jimmy kept the car running between us, so we could jump in and get warm. The women were very gracious and welcomed us in. The Minnesota winters are long and many of them were lonely and wanted some company. A few wanted more than company, so we did our best to be sociable."

"I'll bet you did," Drum said.

"For the first two weeks, we were the top sales team in the country," Walter said.

"I'm sensing a downfall," Queasy said. "With you and Cam on the same team, something had to give."

"It was a cold, snowy night, and we were headed out of town after working Mankato, Minnesota, when we saw this huge mansion set back off the road. It was starting to get dark, but the address was on our list, so we decided on one more sales call. Regrettably we ended up the victims of our own strategy."

"How did that happen?" Drum asked, trying to figure out what could have gone wrong.

"Cam made the sales call, and he was invited inside. After he didn't come out for an hour or so, we wondered what was going on. Two hours later, it was dark and we were running out of gas, so we went up and knocked on the door. A butler answered and led us through the mansion and out back to the guesthouse. The mansion was the most beautiful place I've ever seen, with huge chandeliers, winding staircases, and expensive-looking wall paintings. The guesthouse was also magnificent. The butler lit a fire in the fireplace and said the cook would be along shortly to fix our dinner. We looked at each other in baffled amazement, as the butler showed us our bedrooms."

"Where was Cam?"

"Who cared? We figured he had charmed the pants off her. And we found out later that is actually what happened. She couldn't get enough of him. They had breakfast in bed, and she dressed him in formal clothes for dinner, and they danced the night away in the ballroom. She called him her brooding John Barrymore."

"How long did you stay?"

"Eight days."

"Eight days! What about your subscriptions?" Queasy asked.

"Are you kidding? Our life of newfound luxury versus selling magazines door to door in the cold. It was no contest. We watched the snowfall, ate our three squares a day, and hoped that Cam could maintain his stamina."

"He obviously could not," Queasy said.

"Obviously. We wanted our creature comforts to go on forever, so it was the worst night of my life," Walter said. "The wind was howling and we were warm in our beds listening to the snow pelt off the windows, when who should appear?"

"The Latin lover himself, I presume."

"Exactly. I was hoping it was a nightmare, but it was Cam shaking me awake."

"Walter. We've got to get out of here!" he said frantically.

"Are you crazy. Leave me alone," I pushed him away.

"That woman is insatiable, and she's never going to let me go," he moaned.

"Why would you want to go? We've got it made."

"No. You've got it made. I'm the one who has to perform."

"We should all have your problem."

"If you don't get up, I'm leaving without you," he threatened.

"Maybe I could spell you until you get your energy back."

"Get out of that bed!" he screamed. "I can't take it anymore! I'm going to wake Jimmy, so get your clothes on."

"He seemed at the end of his wits, so I didn't want to push him too far. We grabbed our belongings and crept off into the night. And that, my friends, was the end of our Minnesota adventure."

"What about your job?" Queasy asked.

"We had no sales for over a week, so we were canned by the company. The widows ended up beating us at our own game."

Drum and Queasy laughed heartily. "Good for them," Queasy said. "You should be ashamed of yourselves for preying on the innocent."

"I should be so innocent," Walter said. "We retreated to Kansas City, dead broke and smarting from our venture. But the trip was worthwhile, because we had learned a valuable lesson."

"And what would that be?" Queasy asked.

"Never to cross the border into Minnesota with Cam, unless he can maintain a two-week erection."

The four of them laughed uproariously, and then drank and told stories until the bartender came over.

"Walter, you have a phone call in the backroom."

"Who is it?"

"They wouldn't say."

Walter wondered who would be calling him this late at night. He went to the backroom and picked up the phone.

"Hello."

"Walter, it's Luther."

"What's up?"

"I have a note here with your name on it."

"From whom?"

"Prince. He's in jail."

Walter remembered that he had offered to help the shoeshine boy at Luther's barbershop.

"What has he done?"

"Don't know."

"Can't you help him?"

"The police won't pay me no mind. A Negro tryin' to get another Negro out of jail is a tough sell in this city."

"I see your point. Me and Jimmy will head that way and see what we can do."

"Okay, Walter. I hope that kid hasn't killed anyone."

At the police station, they learned from the sergeant on duty that Prince had been hassled by some boys from southern Missouri who had been drinking on Vine Street. Prince had been walking by when they came out of a club.

"We had some eyewitnesses," the sergeant said. "The white boys taunted him by saying they had seen a lot of black niggers, but never a chocolate one. Your boy tried to go on his way, but they called him more names and told him to turn around when they were speaking to him. When he didn't, one of them smacked him in the back of the head and before he could get his hand back it had a four-inch cut in it. One of the other white boys got his shoulder slashed before they took off running."

"So, it was self-defense," Walter said

"You don't have niggers cutting on whites for any reason in my precinct; especially an uppity nigger like him. He won't even tell us his name so we can book him."

"That's because he doesn't talk."

"We thought he was arrogant."

"What will happen to him?" Jimmy asked.

"He will be sent to a juvenile facility, while we figure out what to do with him."

"Are those southern boys pressing charges?"

"No. When they saw blood, they decided they had seen enough of the big city."

"Why not let him go?"

"It would set a bad precedent. We need to keep a tight lid on the east side."

"That doesn't seem fair," Walter said.

"What does fair have to do with it? You let these niggers get away with stuff and God knows where it will lead."

"So, there's no way to get him out of jail?"

"Not unless you know someone."

Walter made the call to his Uncle Ray and explained the situation.

"Are you sure you want to take this on, Walter?" Ray asked.

"Not really, but I made a commitment."

"Give me the desk sergeant."

Walter handed over the phone. The sergeant listened for a few minutes and then hung up the receiver. He walked to the back of the jail and had the jailer get Prince.

"Why didn't you tell me you worked for Boss Hannon?" the sergeant asked Walter.

"I didn't know it would matter."

"It matters this time, but don't let me see this kid in here again."

Prince had some bruises on his face and a cut lip from the police roughing him up. Walter called Luther and told him they were bringing him back to the barbershop.

The lights were on when they arrived. Prince went inside and without looking at Luther headed for the backroom.

"What happened?" Luther asked.

"Some white boys from down south tried to intimidate him. It didn't work."

"I can imagine," Luther said.

"I thought you would have Prince figured out by now."

"So did I. What are we gonna do with him?" Luther asked.

"What do you mean, we?"

"You gave him the note offering to help. I'm afraid if we don't do something to straighten him out, one of my customers will piss him off and leave here without a foot."

Walter and Jimmy laughed.

"Try to keep him under control until I can figure something out," Walter said.

"Easy for you to say. You don't have a rattlesnake living in your backroom."

"Goodnight, Luther."

"Goodnight, Walter, and thank you."

CHAPTER SIX

LIZABETH HAD SPENT A WEEK formulating her business plan. She would need at least two months to design and make her line of dresses. Aunt Erma had agreed to help her without pay while she accumulated an inventory. Cory had agreed to begin construction on the dressing rooms and shelving. Walter obtained a line of credit from the Hannon organization to help with dress material, mannequins, hangers, dress steamers, a cash register, and all the office supplies Lizabeth would need. She and Erma would use their personal sewing machines to do the alterations.

After they had worked for a week at home, it was obvious to Lizabeth that she was going to need more help and more space when the store opened. She had Cory tear out a back office and make space for a sewing room where in the future she could do everything in-house. And she asked him to have his sister, Jennie, stop by. At the appointed time, she stopped work and made some tea. Jennie knocked on the door and Lizabeth greeted her with a kiss on the cheek. Jennie was a tall, slim girl with long, brown hair, high cheek bones, and soft blue eyes. She had a radiant smile and was charming in every respect.

"How have you been?" Lizabeth asked.

"Very well, thank you. Your date with Cory made him a very happy young man."

"He was charming and we had a wonderful evening. "

"It caused a buzz in our household, because we all thought he was too shy to date."

"I must admit that I was also surprised. Has he always been so timid?"

"Yes. It comes from living with two dominating males. My father and brother are extroverts and can be overbearing, so he retreated at an early age and kept to himself. He jokingly calls them Attila and Son."

Lizabeth laughed. "At least he has a sense of humor about it."

"I understand that you put him to work on your new store."

"Yes. With no pay, I'm afraid."

"He was delighted that you asked him to help. It must be very exciting to open your own business."

"I'm learning that it can be stressful too."

"I'm sure it is. What did you want to see me about?"

"I was wondering if you had your heart set on being a secretary."

"Not really. Secretarial school was something to do until I decide on a career."

"Would you consider working with me?"

Jennie looked at her questioningly. "Doing what?"

"The first few months would be making dresses for our original inventory."

"I'm afraid that I only know basic sewing."

"I will teach you all you need to know. After we open the store, you can help me manage the sales floor. You are good with people, and we would make a great team. But first, let me warn you that I can't pay you anything until the business gets going."

"That would be the same amount of money that I'm bringing in now."

Jennie had a good sense of humor that Lizabeth would sorely need in the months ahead.

"I promise you that it will be an exciting adventure, and you will share in any success that we have."

"I'll do it on one condition. If I can't learn the sewing part of the business, then you have to let me go with no hard feelings between us."

"Agreed. But you have my guarantee that I will make a seamstress out of you."

64

Lizabeth, Jennie, and Erma were in Lizabeth's sewing room with the machines humming as they turned fabric into fashion. Lizabeth was as good as her word and after a few weeks of frustration, Jennie had become an acceptable seamstress. Lizabeth worked on jackets and blouses and any delicate trim work, while Jennie and Erma concentrated on skirts and dresses. Lizabeth's two assistants got along famously and their good-natured banter carried over the din of the machines.

"When I'm working on one of Lizabeth's designs, I try to picture the woman who will be wearing it," Erma said.

"I do the same thing when I'm creating a garment," Lizabeth said. "It must be part of the process."

"My guess is that we all picture a Claudette Colbert type strolling down Petticoat Lane featuring our world-famous creations," Jennie said. "In reality, our core customer will be a housewife fighting her weight and trying to make ends meet."

"That is exactly right," Lizabeth said. "Sometimes I have to scale back and remember who will be wearing our fashions. For now, we will leave the cosmopolitan customer to Harzfeld's and concentrate on Mrs. Middle America who might be able to afford one or two dresses a year. We want to make that woman proud she shopped with us. Our goal is to make every customer who wears our garments as deserving as any movie actress or debutante."

"Speaking of Colbert, did you see her in *It Happened One Night*?" Erma asked.

"No. Was she good?" Jennie asked.

"I don't know. I was concentrating on Clark Gable. He could visit me anytime."

Jennie and Lizabeth laughed. "Uncle Ray might have something to say about that."

"I won't tell him, if you won't."

"You are scandalous," Lizabeth said kiddingly.

"What about you, Jennie?" Erma inquired. "Is anything happening in the romance department?"

"No. I'm playing the role of the neighborhood wallflower, while waiting for men to notice that I'm blossoming into the new Myrna Loy."

"You don't have to blossom into anyone else, because you are attractive in your own right," Erma replied.

"Thank you, but I'm no Eileen Braden."

"Who is?" Lizabeth replied. "Those only come along once in a lifetime."

"Speaking of Clark Gable. Two men who are just as handsome live in your house," Jennie said. "I've been trying for years to get Cam and Walter to notice me, but to them I'm just another neighborhood kid."

"I would advise you to put a damper on your ardor," Erma said. "My nephews are wonderful young men and I love them dearly, but they should be admired from afar. You stick to sewing dresses and let them sow their oats."

"At least we have sewing in common," Jennie said, raising her eyebrows seductively.

Erma laughed. "We are going to have to keep an eye on her, Lizabeth."

"Not to change the subject, but I think we should come up with a name for our little sewing circle," Lizabeth said, steering the conversation away from her brothers and back to the job at hand. "What shall we call ourselves?"

"How about the three stitches?" Jennie kidded, as she put needle and thread to a dress.

"Clever, but stooges come to mind," Erma replied. "I like the sewing sisters."

"Not bad, but the garment girls is catchier," Jennie offered.

"Not enough sophistication," Erma said.

"You must have something in mind, Lizabeth, or you wouldn't have brought it up," Jennie said.

"I think we should go with something simple, like the Designers' Club. If we are successful, we can expand the membership to others and make them feel they are part of something bigger than just needle and thread. Every member will have input on style and design and be an integral part of the business. The company might have my name on it, but we will all share in the success."

"Does that mean that you have come up with a name?" Erma asked.

"Yes. The store will be called Liz Braden's Original Designs. And in smaller lettering: your hometown fashion headquarters."

"I like it," Jennie said.

"So do I," Erma agreed.

⁓

It was early in May. Lizabeth stood outside her vacant storefront on Petticoat Lane and tried to picture how she wanted her windows displayed. She had just turned 20 years old and felt with some satisfaction that her teen years were over and she could embark on the next phase of her life. And with that came the opportunity to become a businesswoman and fulfill her ambition.

The store would have a grand opening in two weeks. The Designers' Club had produced enough inventory for the opening, and, depending on sales, enough to last a few weeks after that. She had lined up vendors for scarves, jewelry, and purses, and Eileen had pitched in and helped her purchase those accessories. She had requested the assistance of her father in planning the advertising. It was his area of expertise and he was glad to help.

Lizabeth had enough cash left to run a small grand opening ad in the newspaper, so it had to be good. They decided to highlight designer dresses at 99 cents and Liz Braden's Original Designs in smaller lettering. The customer would have no idea who Liz Braden was, but once she had made a name for herself the lettering would reverse.

The Designers' Club picked out three of their favorite dresses for the ad and hoped they would appeal to women who were getting by with a Depression-era wardrobe and wanted something special to brighten their lives. Lizabeth was getting more nervous with each passing day. How would she ever pay the money back that she owed Cam, Walter, and the Hannon organization if the business failed? She would be too far in debt to start over again. All her hopes and dreams were tied up in the store, so she was determined to spend every waking hour making it a success.

Erma and Jennie could tell that stress was taking a toll on Lizabeth. They tried to keep the lighthearted banter going so she would not become so obsessed that she couldn't function. Cory always found a reason to stop by in the evenings and help her with whatever project she was working on. His efforts to flirt with her couldn't penetrate her focus on business, but she welcomed his support.

At the family dinner table, the night before the grand opening, she was a mess and could hardly eat. She kept going over her checklist to see if there was anything she had missed. Her father was not feeling well and was resting in his room. Eileen was at a rehearsal.

"Lizabeth, eat your dinner and quit picking at your food," Mira ordered.

"I'm sorry, Mother. I'm not that hungry."

"You would be if you let your mind rest."

"My stomach is full of butterflies."

"Butterflies have to eat," Mira countered.

Lizabeth grew wide-eyed as she mentally hit a speed bump on her checklist. "Oh, my goodness!" she exclaimed. "I just realized that outside of a few requests for sewing, I have never sold anything." She looked at Cam and then Walter in dismay. "What will I do?"

"That is the least of your worries. First, you don't want to sell anything," Cam said.

"What do you mean?"

"Walter came up with this strategy when we were selling magazines. I use it in the car business and it has worked very well. Rather than trying to sell a product, you need to find common ground with your customer. You might comment on something she is wearing, ask about her neighborhood, or discuss the weather, anything you can come up with to get the conversation going. You would be surprised at the number of things that we all share. After you have made the customer comfortable, you can let the conversation take you to the merchandise."

"It's all about making the customer a friend," Walter said. "Then you can show her that special dress you have designed just for her. After the purchase, don't let her get away without writing down her address and phone number, so you can send her a thank-you note and make her part of your customer base. The idea in a nutshell, Lizabeth, is to make friends and let the product sell itself. If you try to push your customers into a sale, they will balk like a Missouri mule and you will lose them for good."

"You are telling me that the trick to selling is not to sell," Lizabeth said.

"Absolutely," Walter replied.

"It seems more psychology than selling," Lizabeth said.

"We couldn't agree more," Cam replied.

"I have a lot to learn," Lizabeth said, frowning.

"Not as much as you think," Walter said. "Just be yourself and don't get flustered. After a few days, it will become natural and you will wonder why you were ever so nervous."

"I want to thank you both for helping me," Lizabeth said.

"We will always be here to back you up," Walter assured her.

Mira stood up and started gathering the dishes. "Cam, I need to talk to you," she said. The two of them went into the kitchen.

Lizabeth waited until they left the room and then turned to Walter. "Remember a few months back when you said you would tell me what happened to make Cam the privileged son," Lizabeth said.

"I did? I must have been drinking."

"You know very well that you remember."

Walter nodded. "You were too little to remember, but it goes back to when Cam was nine years old and I was eight. He contracted polio, and Mother and Father took turns staying at his bedside. This went on for weeks until out of desperation Mother had a Christian Science practitioner come by to see Cam. From that day on, he started to get better. It was probably a coincidence but you couldn't convince Mother of that. Cam had no damage from the polio, which was amazing. It was only natural that the three of them bonded during that time. Cam was cured, I became the secondary son, Mother was sold on Christian Science, and we all lived happily ever after."

"And you don't resent his elite status?"

"Not in the least. I was very happy that he beat polio. We don't always get along, but he is my brother."

"But he does get all the attention."

"He can have it. How would you like to be in his position and have to bear the brunt of our parents' expectations?"

"I see your point."

"Whatever we accomplish will be a plus to our parents, but we will never measure up to Cam's achievements."

"Not even when I become the queen of the fashion world?" Lizabeth kidded.

"Not even then. You will always be the baby girl."

Lizabeth laughed. "I will keep that in mind when I become successful and my ego needs to be checked."

"Your success story starts tomorrow, so you had better get some rest."

"I'll do that, Walter. And thank you again for your help."

She lay in bed going over every contingency that might arise during her grand opening. She was too excited to get much sleep and was up with the dawn. They had set the store the night before, so when she arrived, she checked the merchandise one last time before opening the door. Jennie and Erma were at their stations.

"The big day has finally arrived," Erma said.

"Isn't it exciting?" Jennie said. "The culmination of all our hard work."

"Now if people will just come through the door," Lizabeth prayed.

She watched through the store window as the streetcars made their way down Main Street, stopped and let off passengers who resolutely headed in every other direction, seemingly with a destination in mind. Lizabeth was grateful that her customers were deposited right at her doorstep. Her store was located between Emery, Bird, Thayer on Petticoat Lane to the east, and John Taylor's located on Main Street to the west. Petticoat Lane was usually so busy that people were forced off the sidewalks and into the street. If she could only get her share of foot traffic, she knew the store would be a success.

Two women about Lizabeth's age came laughing through the door. They were full figured, with wide brown eyes, and they wore calico dresses that Lizabeth was sure came from the Sears catalog. "Welcome," Lizabeth said. "You two resemble each other, so you must be sisters."

"We are," they said in unison.

"There is nothing more fun for me than shopping with my sister," Lizabeth said.

"I'm Abigail and this is Grace, and we absolutely agree." Both women were scanning the merchandise, but Lizabeth held them off as she put Walter's sales technique to the test.

"Do you live in Kansas City?"

"No. Ottawa, Kansas," Grace said.

"How nice. I love small towns."

"Thank you for that," Abigail said. "It has been a tough year down on the farm, but we have been saving our money for a Kansas City splurge."

And that statement was a confirmation of Lizabeth's business plan. Her goal was to give her customers something fashionable to reward them for enduring the stress and strife of the Depression. An original dress they could wear with pride and make a statement that even in the darkest days, they could wear something beautiful that glowed with the promise of better days ahead.

"Good for you," Lizabeth said. "Would you be interested in seeing our summer dress line?"

"You bet we would," Grace replied.

Jennie helped Grace and Lizabeth helped Abigail. The sisters purchased two dresses each and got the store off to a good start.

"You are the store's first customers, so we are presenting you each with a free scarf and hope that you will visit us again," Lizabeth said.

"Thank you so much," Grace said. "We will definitely be back, and we will spread the word about you and your store."

"Thank you, ladies. We hope you have a wonderful day in Kansas City."

And that's how the first day went. They had one sale after another and could hardly keep up. Erma had to leave her alterations and help out at the cash register. It was obvious to Lizabeth that she would have to hire more people to keep up with the flow of traffic. It was gratifying to see her designs received so well by the public, and it gave her a boost of much-needed confidence that her designs would be worn on the streets of her hometown. It also gave her a great sense of accomplishment and made her swell with pride.

The first week was a blur of selling and sewing for the Designers' Club, as they struggled to keep up with demand. The 99-cent dresses were a big hit and word was spreading that designer dresses could be had for under a dollar at Liz Braden's on Petticoat Lane. Business was brisk right up until Saturday of the following week.

Lizabeth opened the door to the shop and the anticipated swarm of customers failed to materialize. By noon, the store had made a few sales, but nothing like the previous days. She wondered if there was some big local event going on that was keeping people away, so she decided to go out for lunch and check on the competition.

While walking down Petticoat Lane, she glanced at the windows of Harzfeld's and her heart stopped. There in bold lettering was a sign that read "Summer Dresses for 99 Cents." She hurried to Emery, Bird, Thayer; Kline's; and John Taylor's and was shocked to see that the competition had met her pricing. This was totally unexpected and something she had not even considered. She chastised herself for being so shortsighted.

What had she thought was going to happen? She should have known that the department stores would do everything they could to be competitive. She had been so absorbed in her grand opening that she was caught off guard. This was her first crisis of ownership and she vowed to handle it in a professional manner and not let it shake her confidence.

A meeting of the Designers' Club was in order.

"I never thought the big stores would be concerned with our little shop," Jennie said.

"Whatever will we do?" Erma asked concerned.

"We will act boldly," Lizabeth replied. "Can you find us three more dressmakers?"

"Yes. Can we afford it?"

"We can, if my plan works."

"You wouldn't care to share that."

"We are going to cut our profit in half and sell dresses for seventy-nine cents."

"And what will keep the competition from doing the same?" Jennie asked.

"Nothing at all," Lizabeth replied. "And that is what I am counting on."

CHAPTER SEVEN

WALTER AND JIMMY HAD DROPPED off their collections at Boss Tom's office and were going to lunch. "Let's head over to the Garden of Eden," Walter said. This was the area located near Central Street and 18th Street between Wyandotte Street and Broadway Boulevard. It was actually called Film Row and was the movie distribution area for all the major Hollywood studios: Paramount, 20th Century Fox, Universal, Columbia, and Walt Disney, to name a few.

Walter called it the Garden of Eden because it was the prime area in the city to pick up women. Many of them wanted to make it as actresses but had settled for secretarial work until they could make the right connections in the industry. A number of the secretaries were country girls, and the folks back home were able to say that their daughters worked for MGM or United Artists and that was almost as good as being a movie star.

"Isn't it amazing that all these beautiful women are out on the street for our viewing pleasure?" Walter remarked, as they drove up 18th Street.

"Our own little Hollywood," Jimmy replied. "Thank goodness, Kansas City lies in the center of the country, and that makes it the perfect place for film distribution."

"I wish it was part of our collections territory," Walter said. "There is no forbidden fruit in this Garden of Eden."

"As if that would stop you," Jimmy said. "You are addicted to beautiful women."

"Leave out the beautiful and you will have it right," Walter corrected him. "Beautiful women expect to get attention, but the not so beautiful appreciate it more and will show their appreciation by sharing their affections."

"But a beautiful woman can be worth the effort."

"If you have the time and the money. But I will take the average girl over Betty Grable any day of the week."

"You are going to eat those words, because take a look at that." Jimmy pointed at a beautiful brunette with a curvaceous body walking down the sidewalk on the opposite side of the street. Walter looked her over, made a quick U-turn, and pulled up beside her. She was wearing a brown skirt and a tight, cream-colored blouse that accentuated the swell of her breasts.

"Would you like a ride, miss?" he called to her. She ignored him and kept walking. "If you will hold on a second, I just want to introduce myself." With a withering glance in his direction, she ducked into a restaurant. Walter was transfixed and could feel the rapid beating of his heart. He stopped the car and hopped out.

"Where are you going?" Jimmy asked.

"After her," Walter said.

"So much for not chasing beautiful women!" Jimmy shouted after him.

Walter was ignoring his instincts. This woman was too beautiful to be anything but trouble, but it didn't matter because he was hooked. He had never felt such a strong attraction. The restaurant was cafeteria style, so he grabbed a tray and got in line behind her. He paid no attention to what he was putting on his tray because he kept his eyes on her. She paid for her food, and Walter watched as she moved her hips seductively, weaving her way through the tables to the back of the restaurant. He followed her to an empty table.

"Do you mind if I sit with you?" he asked. "All the tables seem to be full."

She looked at him with round, hazel eyes that reminded him of soft, glowing emeralds, but she said nothing. He put his food on the table and sat down.

"My name is Walter Braden, and you are?"

"I'm not going to give my name to someone who tries to pick up women off the street," she replied curtly. "You are wasting your time."

"Talking to a beautiful woman is never a waste of my time."

"Then it's a waste of mine. Why don't you find a woman who is flattered by your attention?"

"Because you make my heart skip a beat."

"Really? How poetic. I've heard better lines from amateur actors."

"So, you work in the film industry."

"None of your business."

"You don't give a guy much of a chance."

"There are plenty of women on Film Row who would welcome your attention, so why don't you leave me alone?"

The more she tried to push him away, the more he wanted to stay.

"You know you are interested, so why are you being so mean?" he asked.

"When all else fails, the male ego asserts itself," she said. "Try getting it through your head that I am not interested."

"Why don't you let me take you out to dinner?" Walter said. "There will be no strings attached. If you don't want to see me after that, then I won't bother you again."

"Nice try, but no thanks."

"You win this time, but I want you to know that I am not going to give up," Walter said.

"It's a free country. Do what you like."

Walter watched as she took a few more bites of food, but he had obviously upset her appetite. She stood and, without looking at him, headed back the way she had come. Walter walked outside and waved to Jimmy, who had taken over the wheel, to the curb. He got in the car and they followed her at a discreet distance. They watched as she went into the office of Universal Pictures. Jimmy stopped the car and Walter hopped out and walked up to the guard at the door. He slipped him a dollar bill.

"What's the name of the woman who just went inside?"

"Can't tell you that."

Walter gave him another dollar.

"Her name is Terri Lawson."

"What does she do?"

"Film editing."

"Thank you."

Walter went back and jumped in the car.

"She must have shot you down if you had to follow her back to work," Jimmy said.

"I admit that she won the first round, but I'm not giving up. I will heal my wounds and plan my strategy. In the meantime, take me over to Carol's place, where you can have a beer while she entertains me."

"You've been seeing a lot of Carol lately. Is she your girlfriend?"

"Hardly. The thing I like about Carol is that she meets my needs without the obligations of romance or commitment."

"So does a trip to Miss Lillian's place."

"True, but there is no element of friendship in a whorehouse. Carol is a lonely widow, and she looks forward to my visits."

Jimmy drove over to the Argentine district on the Kansas side of the city and stopped the car in front of a weathered, one-story, brown bungalow that overlooked the railroad yards on the west side.

"Didn't you tell me her husband was killed in a railroad accident?" Jimmy asked

"Yes. Three years ago."

"You would think that she would want to get away from looking at the rail yards."

"She probably can't afford to move."

They walked up, and Walter knocked on the door.

Carol opened the door and greeted them with a smile.

"How have you been?" Walter kissed her on the cheek.

"Fine. Thank you, Walter." Carol was a petite brunette, with large brown eyes. Her hair was cut short, and she had a small, upturned nose. She worked as a secretary at a small accounting firm, and although she was comfortable around men, she was not the type to frequent bars or be a part of the dating scene. She was a shy girl, and it had surprised and delighted Walter that she was such a fireball in bed. Carol went to the kitchen and served them each a beer from the refrigerator.

"We were wondering why you don't move away from the rail yards," Walter said.

"I'm okay here. The neighborhood is comfortable, and I wouldn't know where else to go."

"No unpleasant memories?"

"I have some, but if I left, they would probably leave with me."

"Our baggage does seem to follow us," Walter agreed.

"I went to the grand opening of your sister's dress shop," Carol said. "She seems to be making it a big success."

"Did you tell her we were friends?"

"Of course not. We have a private relationship."

"I wouldn't have minded. I'll take you by one day and introduce you."

"That would be nice."

"Well, Jimmy. It's time Carol and I took our nap," Walter said.

"I'll wait in the car."

"No, you will not," Carol said. "You relax on the couch. And please, get another beer if you want one."

Jimmy went to the fridge. He wanted to give Walter and Carol some privacy, so he went out on the porch step and sat down and sipped his beer. He watched the trains moving back and forth in the rail yard below. They looked like miniatures and reminded him of a toy train set, as the cars moved steadily along the tracks. When the trains came to a stop, he could see hobos jumping in and out of the boxcars.

There were not as many desperate men swarming the trains as in past years. President Roosevelt had formed the Civilian Conservation Corps (CCC) and the Works Progress Administration (WPA), and other government agencies that had put men back to work. Times were still hard, but men now had hope and that made all the difference. He was thankful that he and Walter had good jobs and that their hobo days were over. His time riding the rails had made him sympathetic to those who were still suffering the indignities of no work and no place to call home. About twenty minutes later, Walter came out of the house and sat down beside him.

"What are you thinking about?" Walter asked.

Jimmy pointed at the men below, scurrying along the rails.

"I'm sure those days will stay with us for the rest of our lives," Walter said. "If not for the charity of Catholic nuns, we would have starved to death."

"That's for sure."

"The only good that came out of riding the rails was that it taught you how to fight. You got us out of many a tight spot."

"And you cheered me on," Jimmy said smiling.

"After the punch to my jaw from that cracker in Alabama, I decided that unless we were in a real pinch, I would leave the fighting to you."

"You were doing great until he hit you with that right cross," Jimmy said.

"Too bad I don't remember."

Jimmy laughed. "Those were the days, but I sure don't want to repeat them."

"Amen to that." Walter stood. "I'm going to get some shut-eye on the couch while you get friendly with Carol."

"Me? What are you talking about? She's your girlfriend."

"She is not my girlfriend, and this was her idea, so I suggest you hurry along before she changes her mind."

Jimmy stood up quickly. "You don't have to say it twice," he said.

"I will give you a word of warning," Walter said. "Don't let her size fool you, because she will wear you out. And don't forget to take off your hat."

Jimmy raised his eyebrows and hurried into the house.

Walter went in and stretched out on the couch. The hobos in the rail yard had reminded him that he hadn't made any progress on what to do about the shoeshine boy at Luther Jackson's barbershop. Luther said Prince was still doing okay, but he wasn't sure how long it would last. But Walter's main focus was Terri Lawson and how to get a date with her. If he could just get a foothold, he was sure they would hit it off. He drifted off and was sleeping soundly when he heard the sound of Jimmy's voice, through the fog of sleep, screaming for him to wake up. Jimmy was shaking him violently and pulling him off the couch.

"What's wrong with you?!" Walter yelled at him irritably.

Jimmy had a stricken look on his face as he pointed at the bedroom. "There is something the matter with Carol! I think she might have had a stroke!"

Walter got up and hurried into the bedroom. Carol was lying in the bed with her eyes closed and showing no signs of life.

"What did you do to her?" Walter asked accusingly.

"I didn't do anything!" Jimmy pleaded, "Do something!"

Walter took a washcloth from the pan of water beside the bed, wrung it out, gently laid it on Carol's forehead, and then dabbed some water on her face. Carol opened her eyes and looked around, trying to get her bearings. She saw the look of distress on Jimmy's face.

"I can see that Walter didn't tell you," she said to Jimmy.

"Tell me what?"

"I pass out when I have an orgasm. It has something to do with the blood flow."

Walter was chuckling, as he continued to rub the washcloth on Carol's forehead.

"Walter, you are one mean bastard," Jimmy said angrily, but with obvious relief.

"The look on your face was priceless," Walter said.

"One of these days your twisted sense of humor is going to give me a heart attack."

"I hope this didn't scare you too much," Carol said. "I want you to come back and see me."

"Of course, he will," Walter said reassuringly. "The three of us are the best of friends. If you need anything, just ask and one of us will come running."

"Thank you, Walter. I do value your friendship."

Walter kissed her on the cheek. "You get some sleep, dear girl, and we will let ourselves out."

Terri Lawson was still very much on Walter's mind, so for the next week on his lunch hour, he waited in his car outside Universal Pictures so he could approach her again. But to his disappointment, there was no sign of her. He knew she would not respond to a message, so he had tried following her. She left at odd hours, and he was never there at the right time.

When he had been at Carol's place, she had mentioned Lizabeth's dress shop and that had given him an idea. He did not want Terri to feel that he was stalking her so he would enlist Lizabeth's help in getting to know her. He drove to Petticoat Lane and parked the car. Lizabeth was busy with a customer, so he waited in the backroom where the Designers' Club was busily sewing garments.

"What are you up to, Walter?" his Aunt Erma asked.

"Just checking to see how you and Lizabeth are getting along."

"That is kind of you, Walter, but seeing you on Petticoat Lane in the middle of the day raises my suspicions."

Walter smiled. "I'm here because I need help with a woman."

"And who might that be?" Lizabeth said, as she walked into the room.

"Her name is Terri Lawson, and I'm trying to get a date with her."

"I assume she has turned you down."

"Yes. And I can't get her to come out of hiding."

"Now there is a smart woman," Erma said. "I can't imagine how Lizabeth can help, but I can hardly wait to hear."

The rest of the girls in the Designers' Club were listening intently.

"I was thinking that you might create a special coupon that would be too good for her to pass up. You could make it fifty percent off from ten to twelve on Saturday morning. I will make up the difference in price so you don't lose any money."

"How will you get it to her?"

"The guard at Universal is a friend. I'll have him give the coupons to Terri and the girls on either side of her desk, so she doesn't get suspicious."

"You must really be smitten to go to all this trouble," Erma said.

Walter just raised his eyebrows at her.

"I owe you, so, of course, I will do it," Lizabeth said. "I'm not comfortable with the deception, but I'll have the coupons made up and you can pick them up tomorrow."

"This could be a lot of fun," Erma said. "We can watch Don Juan meet his match right here on Petticoat Lane. What happens if she puts two and two together and smells a rat?"

"I'm hoping that she can't add and will think this is a chance meeting," Walter replied.

"She might be too smart for that, Walter," Erma said. "This could go badly."

"That's a chance I'm willing to take."

Walter picked up the coupons the next day and had them delivered to the guard at Universal. On Saturday, he was at the dress shop by 10 a.m. and waited expectantly in the backroom. Erma and the rest of the Designers' Club were working on garments, but they kept one eye on Walter and wondered how this was going to turn out. Lizabeth and Jennie were on the sales floor ready to play their parts in Walter's romantic drama.

Walter paced the floor in the backroom and peered out onto the sales floor every few minutes. An hour went by and then another half hour, and Walter figured his scheme had failed. But at 11:30, Terri Lawson came into the store with two of the other women who had received the coupons. Lizabeth and Jennie went to greet them.

"Welcome to our store," Lizabeth said. "How can we help you?"

"We received these coupons and wondered if they were for dresses or other merchandise," Terri said. Lizabeth knew right away that she was the woman Walter was after, because she was gorgeous.

"You can use them on whatever you want," Lizabeth replied.

Walter was watching from the backroom, with Erma peering over his shoulder.

"What now?" Erma whispered.

"I'm working on it."

"You'd better work fast." The other girls Lizabeth employed gathered at the door to see what would happen next.

Terri and her two friends were ready to pay for their merchandise when Walter walked into the room.

"Oh, hello, Terri." He acted like this was a chance meeting and that he was surprised to see her.

She looked at him questioningly, trying to piece together what he was doing in a dress shop.

"This is my sister, Lizabeth Braden. I help her out sometimes on Saturday mornings."

"Pleased to meet you, Terri," Lizabeth said.

"Me too," Terri replied, as she composed herself. "You have a lovely shop."

"Thank you."

Terri looked at Walter. "How do you know my name?"

"The guard at Universal," Walter confessed.

"You have a hard time taking no for an answer."

"And you have a hard time saying yes to a dinner date."

Terri turned to Lizabeth. "I get it now," she said. "How many of these coupons did you send out?"

"Three," Lizabeth said, not wanting to lie and compound the dishonesty.

"Are lies and deception the way you attract most of your women?" Terri asked Walter.

"Most women give me a chance, and I don't have to resort to this," Walter replied.

"I'm sorry that you put your sister to all this trouble," Terri said. "The answer is still no. And we couldn't possibly accept this merchandise at these prices."

"Oh, please do," Lizabeth said. "We put you to a lot of trouble."

"No, thank you." She turned to Walter. "You need to ask yourself why any woman would want to go out with a man who involves his sister in this kind of scheme."

"My brother is the nicest person I know," Lizabeth came to his defense. "He only resorted to this because of his attraction to you."

"I'm flattered by the trouble your brother went to, but he can't seem to get it through his head that I'm not interested."

"Why is one date such a big deal? What are you afraid of?" Walter asked.

"You're the one who should be afraid. There are things about me that you don't know."

"Then explain them to me over dinner."

"No. I can't. It was nice meeting you, Lizabeth. I wish it could have been under better circumstances." Terri and her friends left their merchandise on the counter and walked out of the store.

Erma came on to the sales floor. "That went well," she said.

"This isn't over," Walter said.

"How much punishment can you take?"

"The more she dishes out, the more I want."

"So, what's the plan?" Lizabeth asked.

"I don't know."

Walter had always been supportive of her, so she wanted to help him. "Are you sure that you want to continue this?" she asked.

"Absolutely."

"Okay, then. You had the right idea using the coupons to flush her out. You just had the wrong sister."

"What do you mean?"

"You mentioned that she works at Universal Pictures, so she is probably interested in film and in the theatre. A couple of comp tickets to the Red Barn Players might be in order. Of course, it would only be a coincidence that your seat was next to hers. If you want to impress her, have Eileen greet her after the show."

"That is brilliant!" Walter said, as he thought of the possibilities.

"I might buy a ticket myself so I can see Walter go down for the count," Erma said.

Walter kissed his Aunt Erma on the cheek. "Thank you for your help, ladies, and wish me luck."

"You are going to need it," Erma said.

Lizabeth cut the prices on her dresses below the competition and hired three more seamstresses so she could keep her inventory at a high level. She hoped that her plan worked before she ran out of money. As expected, the four department stores reduced their prices to meet hers and the price war was on. She managed to sell enough inventory to meet her payroll, but it was tough, and she knew if her plan didn't work, she would have to call it quits. It took all the courage she could muster to go up against the big department stores, but if she didn't take the initiative and stick with her plan, she knew that all would be lost.

"You are losing weight," Erma said to Lizabeth one afternoon when they were on the sales floor. "Are you getting any sleep?"

"Some," she said.

"You know this venture isn't worth losing your health."

"I'm fine, Aunt Erma."

"Said the girl with dark circles of exhaustion under her eyes."

"If everything falls into place, this price war should only last another week."

"And if it doesn't?"

"That's why I'm not getting any sleep."

"Do you want me to lay off some of the girls?" Erma asked.

"No. It is critical that they make as many dresses as possible."

"We have so much inventory now that we can hardly find a place to store it."

"Good."

"We have confidence that you know what you are doing, Lizabeth. But piling up inventory in the face of slow sales goes against all conventional wisdom."

"I'm aware of that. You will just have to trust me."

"I can certainly do that. I'm just trying to point out things that you might have missed."

"And I appreciate that."

"If it's more inventory you want, then it's more inventory you will get," Erma said, as she went back to work.

Lizabeth was anxious and worried through the rest of the week, as she waited for the four, big department stores to break out their ads. She had purposely not run an ad of her own. She went out to get the paper early on Thursday morning and brought it to the sunporch. She took a deep breath and opened the paper to the fashion ads.

In bold lettering, the ads revealed that all four department stores had cut their summer dress line to 69 cents, undercutting her pricing by a dime. For the first time in weeks, she felt that a burden had been lifted off her shoulders. She went into the kitchen where Walter was drinking a cup of coffee at the kitchen table. She handed him the paper. "Do you want me to fix you some breakfast?"

"No, thanks. Coffee is all I need."

Eileen came down the stairs. "Good morning, you two."

"How did the play go last night?" Lizabeth asked, as she poured her sister a cup of coffee.

"Very well. We seem to get more polished with each performance."

"Did you get my tickets?" Walter asked.

Eileen took two from the pocket of her robe and handed them over.

"I sent the other two in her name to Universal Pictures in a Red Barn Players envelope. The note said that we are trying to attract new patrons."

"Thank you very much."

"And what is my role again in this drama that you have cooked up?" Eileen asked.

"I need you to come out after the show and let me introduce you to a couple of women I will be sitting next to."

"And that's it?"

"Not exactly," Lizabeth said. "One of them is a woman Walter is trying to date, but so far she has eluded him. You are the latest bait that he is putting out."

"If she has you on the run, brother, then I can't wait to meet her."

"You are the two best things I have going for me," Walter said. "I want her to see that I'm from a well-bred, established family."

"If you are resorting to flattering your sisters, this must be serious," Eileen said.

"It might also be helpful to you," Walter said. "She's a film editor at Universal Pictures. If she likes the play and sees how talented you are, she will probably pass that on to her coworkers and to anyone who might be looking for new talent."

"You and Eileen will both have to put on your best performances," Lizabeth said.

"Where are Mother and Father?" Eileen asked.

"Father took some pills and went back to sleep. Mother had an early morning emergency with one of her patients," Lizabeth said. "I had better get to work myself."

"You don't seem as stressed this morning," Eileen said.

"Indeed, I am not," Lizabeth said. "It looks like it will be a beautiful day, and I can hardly wait to get to work. Walter, would you and Uncle Ray set up a meeting this week for me with Tom Hannon?"

Walter was taken aback for a moment. "What for?"

"I have a business proposition for him."

"I don't know, Lizabeth. How can I say this politely? You are a bit delicate for an association with the likes of Tom Hannon."

"Let me worry about that."

"Okay," Walter replied, unconvinced. "I will meet with Uncle Ray and see what we can do."

There was a lot of concern on the faces of Lizabeth's employees. The women of the Designers' Club had seen the ads and suspected they would soon be unemployed.

"Should we suspend production? "Jennie asked.

"Not on your life," Lizabeth said cheerily, as she was putting the 99-cent dress sign back in the window.

"We want to increase production while we have the chance."

"Have you gone mad?" Jennie asked.

"Possibly, but bear with me for a few more days and all will be explained."

Lizabeth kept the sewing machines humming through the rest of the week. There was a trickle of customers coming through the door, but nothing like the flood of women who were shopping the 69-cent dresses at the four, big department stores.

Walter and Uncle Ray had set up the appointment with Tom Hannon. Although she was nervous, she felt well prepared to meet him. It might mean the survival of her business. She rode the streetcar to Hannon's office building, where she met Walter and Uncle Ray. They escorted her up the stairs. When they walked into the office, she caught her breath. Tom Hannon was even bigger and more intimidating than she had imagined. He stood up immediately and took her hand, putting her at ease.

"It is a real pleasure to meet you, Miss Braden. Ray and Walter have told me that you are an industrious young lady."

"The pleasure is mine, sir. I want to thank you for taking the time to see me."

"Not at all. What can I do for you?"

"You are aware that I own a dress shop on Petticoat Lane."

"Yes."

"I have recently been in a price war with the four, big department stores. When I lower my prices, they follow suit with reductions of their own. This past week I held firm on my pricing, and they dropped theirs to an all-time low."

"Do you think they are conspiring to put you out of business?"

"Possibly. But it doesn't matter. I baited them into taking the latest price cut, and now they are in a price war with one another. I've sent shoppers in to canvas their stores and gather information, and I know that by the end of the week, they will be out of inventory. I've checked the vendors in New York, and they have switched their production to the fall line. No other chain store will give up their profit to ship their remaining summer dresses to Kansas City to be given away. My seamstresses have been busy piling up inventory. With six weeks to go in the summer selling season, we will be the only store in town that has summer dresses."

Big Tom smiled and looked at Walter and Ray. "And there you have it, gentleman. One clever Irish girl takes on the biggest stores in the city and wins. You have my total admiration, Miss Braden. Now, how can I help?"

"I want you to back me with a low-interest loan, so I can hire more people. And I want to be a dues-paying member of your organization, so that my employees have health insurance. I now know what it feels like to be alone in the business world, and I need your support. And I must admit that I want to sell my dresses to your members. I think it will be beneficial to both of us, because I get your protection and you get access to the world of fashion. You will get to share in the growth of my business."

"I'm flattered that you want to join our club, Miss Braden. This city needs entrepreneurs like you. You have a plan and the will to succeed. How could I not back you? Walter will get you signed up and if you ever need anything, my door will always be open to you."

"I hope that I'm not being rude, but there are a couple of other things," Lizabeth said.

Walter and Uncle Ray looked at each other and rolled their eyes, not wanting her to ask too much of Boss Tom.

"I'm listening," Tom said.

"To kick off our partnership, I wonder if it would be possible to block off Petticoat Lane for a couple of hours next Saturday so that I can have a fashion show."

"That will be a tough sell at City Hall, young lady. It has never been done before."

"That's the very reason it would be a sensation. We won't block the flow of foot traffic on the sidewalks. We just want to use the street so the models can mingle with the public and let customers follow them into the store."

"You have some big ideas, Miss Braden."

"And you have the power to make them happen."

Tom grunted. "And the other thing that you wanted."

"I would like your wife and daughter to be my honored guests at the fashion show. It would give stature and credibility to the entire proceedings."

"I'll see what I can do, Miss Braden. Walter, you had better get her out of here before she decides that she wants my job," Tom said in jest as he grinned.

"Thank you, sir." Lizabeth stood and shook his hand.

The next Saturday, Jennie and Erma came hurrying into the store.

"You won't believe this," Jennie said to Lizabeth. "We went by all our competition, and no one has summer dresses in their windows," she said in puzzlement.

"And what does that tell you?" Lizabeth asked.

"That they've given up the fight," Erma answered.

"And why would they do that?"

"I don't have a clue."

"Because, my dear girls, the stores have run each other out of inventory!" Lizabeth said with delight.

"You clever girl!" Erma said. "Yippee doo dah day!"

The three women held hands and then started dancing around the store and whooping at the top of their lungs. The rest of the girls came out of the backroom to see what was going on.

"We are summer dress headquarters for the rest of the season!" Lizabeth shouted at them, and they joined in the celebration.

"After work tonight, we will have a party," Lizabeth said. "And next Saturday, we are going to block off Petticoat Lane and have a fashion show to end all fashion shows."

"How exciting," Erma said. "How did you pull that off?"

"With the help of Walter, Uncle Ray, and Boss Hannon," Lizabeth replied. "Erma, you will have to hire a couple of sales-girls and Jennie can hire six models for the fashion show. We will spare no expense, because this will be our introduction into the world of fashion in Kansas City, and we want it to be an extravaganza the city won't soon forget."

CHAPTER SEVEN

Walter waited until the lights were turned down at the Red Barn Players before taking his seat beside Terri. Jimmy sat next to her girlfriend. Terri glanced at Walter but did not recognize him in the darkened theatre. There was no intermission, so he was safe until the play ended. He felt comfortable sitting next to her, like they had been friends forever. He was enchanted by the hint of perfume that she wore. She had been so serious and guarded around him that it was good to hear her laughter, as Eileen worked her magic on stage, and it was nice to know that she had a softer side and could enjoy herself.

He wondered, with all the women available, why he had fallen for this one. But there was no kidding himself, she was the woman he wanted and he would do anything to get her. She could keep rejecting him, but he was determined not to give up. Eileen kept the audience spellbound with her performance and Terri and her girlfriend were enjoying the play immensely. Walter had no idea what Terri's reaction would be when she discovered him sitting next to her. He would have to talk fast to keep her from leaving the theatre until Eileen arrived to meet her.

When the play ended and the lights came on, the actors received a standing ovation and two curtain calls.

"That was a wonderful play," Walter said.

Terri looked his way. "You have got to be kidding me!" she said in shock and surprise.

"It's nice seeing you again too," Walter replied.

"Don't try to sell me on another coincidence."

"No. This is definitely another set up."

"How did you manage this one?"

"I can't tell you that."

"But I do owe you for the tickets."

"It would be polite if you introduced me to your friend. This is my friend, Jimmy Dolan."

"I'm sorry," Terri said. "Once again you have me flustered. This is Peggy Bowers."

Jimmy shook hands with Peggy.

"Nice to meet you, Peggy," Walter said. "Terri and I are old friends."

Terri rolled her eyes in exasperation. "How am I going to get rid of you?"

"That's easy. Agree to a dinner date."

"I've told you that isn't possible."

"Then you will have to get used to seeing me wherever you go." Walter could see Eileen working her way toward them through the sea of well-wishers.

"It was nice meeting you, Jimmy," Terri said. "It is getting late, and we have to be going."

Walter was afraid she was going to get away, but Eileen arrived as they were leaving the row of seats.

Walter slyly pointed at Terri as Eileen approached her.

"I hope you enjoyed the show," she said.

Terri was surprised that the star of the play had taken time to speak with her.

"It was brilliant," Terri said. "And your performance was wonderful."

"Thank you so much," Eileen said beaming at the praise. "I'm glad that you could come tonight. My brother has told me so much about you."

"Your brother?" Terri asked in confusion.

"Yes. Walter is my brother. I thought you knew."

"I'm sure that I should have. After my experience at your sister's dress store, the last name should have registered."

"I hope you will forgive him for putting you in these awkward situations," Eileen said. "His heart is in the right place, even if he is unconventional."

"He is that," Terri agreed. "I want you to meet my friend, Peggy."

"It was a wonderful performance," Peggy gushed.

"Thank you, Peggy. I'm glad you both enjoyed yourselves. Have a pleasant drive home." Eileen's fans caught up with her, and she was swept away.

Terri turned to Walter. "You are full of surprises."

"I hope this one worked because I am all out of sisters."

"Okay, you win," Terri said. "I will have one dinner with you, and then you have to promise to leave me alone."

"I promise," Walter said.

⁓

Terri would not let him pick her up at her house, so they met at a restaurant on the Country Club Plaza. Walter wondered if there was something going on in her personal life that she was trying to hide. She wore no wedding band, so he ruled out a husband and children. She wore a green skirt with a white blouse that was covered with a sleeveless gray and white vest. Her hair was pulled up into a curl, and a small, green hat adorned the top of her head.

"I'm glad you came," Walter said.

"You promised me that this will be our only meeting," Terri said

"I will keep that promise if you answer some of my questions," Walter replied. "Why would a beautiful woman like you be so mysterious and afraid? You should be having the time of your life."

"Are you sure you want to know?"

"Of course."

"I apologize for being so rude to you, but it was for your own good. Six months ago, I went out on a blind date that was arranged by a business associate. The date turned out to be with a man who didn't know how to take no for an answer. I found out later that he was a local hoodlum, and I refused to go out with him again. However, he was enamored with me and I couldn't get rid of him. He told me that if I wouldn't go out with him, then I wouldn't be going out with anyone. He has one of his henchmen watching me all the time. I've had two dates since he threatened me, and both men were beaten up and told to keep away. There is nothing the police can do, because there were no witnesses to the assaults and he hasn't personally committed any crime against me. I don't want to see you get hurt, Walter."

"That's a relief. I thought you didn't like me."

"A relief? Didn't you hear what I said? Look at the man sitting at the table next to the window. He has been watching us since we sat down."

"Who is he?"

"He works for Sal Marconi. Have you heard of Sal?"

"Yes. He's a lieutenant for Boss Bianco in the north end. Bianco has a hard time keeping him under control. Marconi likes to intimidate people with the same methods he's using on you."

"I live with my mother. I've thought about taking her and leaving the city."

Walter took her hand. "Don't do that," he said. "You need to give me some time to come up with a plan."

"I don't want to be responsible for you getting hurt."

"You won't. I know some people who might be able to help us."

After dinner, Terri walked over and stalled the man, while Walter slipped out the back door of the restaurant. He knew they would be after him, so he would have to find a solution quickly.

At the Hi Hat club, he met with Jimmy, Drum, and Queasy and explained the situation.

"We could get some Irish guys in my neighborhood and take them on," Jimmy said.

"They have too much muscle for that," Walter replied. "We need to come up with something that doesn't get anyone hurt."

"Good luck on that idea," Drum said. "That is the roughest bunch in the city. It would be a lot easier to give up the girl."

"That's not going to happen," Walter replied.

"Maybe we could hit him in his wallet where it hurts," Queasy said.

"How so?" Walter asked.

"Sal is in the produce business. You know most of the merchants who he does business with. Find a way to take away his livelihood."

"That's not a bad idea, Queasy. The majority of his business is in my district, so I could call in some favors and have my business owners cut off his orders."

"His reaction will be to strongarm his customers," Drum said.

"Those business owners are under the protection of Tom Hannon, so I don't think that will happen," Walter said.

"Sal is one sadistic sonofabitch," Drum said. "He won't take kindly to you messing with his livelihood, so he might come after you."

"That is a possibility."

"I hope you won't be upset if I take out a life insurance policy on you," Queasy said. "Your death might be the answer to my carefree retirement."

"Don't forget that it was your idea," Walter reminded him.

"I never thought that you would take me seriously."

"Jimmy and I will put your plan in motion on Monday morning, so wish us luck."

"You are going to need more than luck," Queasy replied.

Walter met with each business owner in his district. With some trepidation, they agreed to order produce from other suppliers. Walter assured them they would be under the protection of the Hannon organization. He had helped them grow their business, so they were glad to do him a favor.

He waited until the end of the week, when he knew that Sal was feeling the bite of no sales and a backed-up inventory. He and Jimmy went to the City Market and parked in front of the Marconi Produce sign. When they walked inside, the lack of business was evident. There were men sitting around with little to do.

Walter asked to see Sal Marconi, and two large, heavyset men pointed at the top of the stairs. The men followed behind, as Jimmy and Walter headed up to the office. Sal was sitting at his desk with an unlit cigar hanging from his lips. He was a huge man with a large head. His shoulders and arms bulged against his shirt. He had coal-black hair and bushy, black eyebrows. He looked as mean as his reputation. He stood up and shook their hands.

"What can I do for you?"

"The question is what can we do for you?"

Sal raised his eyebrows. "Meaning?"

"You don't seem to be doing much business," Walter said.

"What would you know about that?"

"I know plenty. I work for Tom Hannon, and I'm here to make a deal. When you and your men decide to leave Terri Lawson alone, I will restore your business."

Sal looked perplexed for a moment and then chuckled to himself. "We've been wondering what was going on. I give you credit. No one else in this city would have the balls to put the squeeze on Sal Marconi. Was this your idea or Hannon's?"

"Mine alone."

"You get the girl, and I get my business back. Is that the idea?"

Walter nodded. He was congratulating himself on how simple it all was when Sal lunged across the desk and punched him in the side of the head. Everything went dark for a moment as Walter slumped to the floor. The two thugs grabbed Jimmy in an armlock, and Sal moved around the desk and punched Jimmy a couple of times in the face and stomach. Walter was grabbed by the neck and dragged to the top of the stairs where Sal kicked him in the butt and sent him tumbling down the stairs. Jimmy followed close behind, and they landed in a heap on the concrete floor with blood flowing from their heads.

"You restore my business or you won't survive our next meeting," Sal threatened from the top of the stairs. "Take these pansies back to Hannon and leave them as my calling card." The two big, Italian henchmen punched and kicked Walter and Jimmy all the way to Walter's car and threw them in the back seat. When they pulled up in front of Hannon's office, one of the goons grabbed Walter, put him in the front seat, and leaned his head against the car horn. It was the last thing Walter remembered.

He woke up in the hospital emergency room. Jimmy was on a gurney next to him as doctors and nurses hovered over them. He hoped that Jimmy would be okay. He saw Uncle Ray standing off to the side and wondered what he was doing here. His head pounded and his stomach and ribs hurt badly. He tried to speak to his uncle, but everything went dark again. When he woke up, he was in bed in a hospital room. Uncle Ray sat in a chair against the wall.

"How's Jimmy?" Walter asked.

"He's going to live."

"What happened?"

"That's what we want to know."

It all came back to Walter, and he took his time as he told his uncle everything.

Uncle Ray shook his head in disbelief. "Your plan might have worked if you had been dealing with a sane person. Interfering with Sal's business was a bad idea. I'm surprised that you are still alive."

"Thanks for the confirmation that I am alive," Walter tried to inject some humor through his pain.

"Your pain isn't the worst of it, Walter. You are in some serious trouble with Boss Tom. If there is one thing he hates, it's for these miniwars to break out."

"It's not a war; it's a dispute between Sal and me."

"It was, until they dropped you off at party headquarters. Sal is sending us a message that he wants a bigger piece of the action. And he's showing us that he is not afraid to attack our people. You gave him the excuse he needed by going after his business. And all because of a woman. I thought you knew better."

"So did I, but things got complicated."

"How else could it get with a woman involved?"

Walter had no answer for that. "What do we do now?" he asked.

"The hospital should release you in a day or two, and then we will figure it out. You can stay with Erma and me until your face looks better. There is no use stirring up J.M. considering the way he feels about you working for Hannon."

"That's for sure. I'm sorry about this, Uncle Ray. I know this puts you in a bad position."

Uncle Ray got up from his chair. "Don't worry about that. You heal up while I make a plan for Sal Marconi."

CHAPTER EIGHT

THE NEXT SATURDAY, AT THE advertised hour of the fashion show, both sides of Petticoat Lane were jammed with people. At Lizabeth's request, the police officers holding back the crowd made sure that the ladies were given places in front to watch the proceedings. Tom Hannon's wife and daughter had a prime spot, just outside the store in the shade of an awning. Lizabeth had provided cushions on their chairs and snacks ready for their enjoyment. She had it timed where there would be three models in the street at one time, about 50 yards apart, while the other three would be changing outfits and hurrying back to the head of the street. The models would change garments and reappear numerous times over the next hour.

The Petticoat Lane department stores were not happy with the street being blocked off and having their businesses interrupted, but somehow Tom Hannon had managed to pull it off. Lizabeth, Erma, and Jennie worked frantically getting each model ready before wrapping them in a cape and sending them out the door. Two police officers, courtesy of Tom Hannon, escorted them to the head of the street.

Lizabeth had hired a jazz band, and with the rattle of drum rolls and a blast from the trumpet section, the models threw off their capes and started walking smartly down the middle of the street, wearing the only summer dresses available in Kansas City. It was a raucous crowd that showed their enjoyment with whistles and applause as the models passed by.

"This is an amazing turnout," Erma said to Lizabeth, as she worked to get another model ready. "I think you hit a nerve with the public. They have been looking for something to celebrate that will take their minds off their troubles."

"If we can make people happy and sell some dresses, it will be a great day," Lizabeth replied.

"With this fashion show coup, you are well on your way to becoming a force in the city. There is no way they can stop you now."

"We don't want to get too carried away. We are one, small store going against the giants of the fashion industry."

"Yes, but after today, you will be someone to be reckoned with. They now know that you are not going away and that you will fight to keep your customers."

"We'll see what effect the fashion show has on our business. But regardless, we won't be able to let our guard down for a moment. Our competitors won't take losing business lightly, so we will have to be creative in every aspect of store operations."

The models smiled as they moved down the street, stopping occasionally to make a spin or pose for the spectators. Per Lizabeth's direction, they made friendly eye contact with the ladies in the crowd, and a few times they walked near the potential customers to let them see the dresses up close.

In the last hour of the show, Lizabeth dressed the models in her fall fashion line to give the audience a preview of the coming season and to let them know that she was more than a summer dress shop.

Outside, the applause alerted them that a model had finished her run, so they sent another freshly dressed model out the door and swarmed the model who had returned. All was bedlam as they worked frantically to get her ready to go out the door again. After an hour, the entire staff felt like they were caught in a revolving door that was never going to stop.

And then with a large roar and sustained applause from the crowd on the street, the show ended. Tom Hannon and his wife and daughter came through the door, got Lizabeth, and escorted her out into the middle of the street, where she received an ovation and continuous cheering. Tom Hannon put his hands up for quiet, so Lizabeth could speak.

"I want to thank Mr. Hannon and the mayor for making this fashion show possible. I sincerely thank you for your support and your enthusiasm," she said. "You are a wonderful audience and make me proud to be from this great city."

A huge cheer erupted along with more applause until Hannon once again put his hands up for quiet so he could speak.

"This young lady is a prime example of the can-do spirit of our city. She is a hard worker with a keen mind and entrepreneurial spirit. Her doors are now open. So, ladies, it is time to start shopping."

And with that, Lizabeth's store was swamped and people had to line up outside the store and wait to get in.

At the end of the day, the ladies of the Designers' Club had their shoes off and were sprawled across the floor in exhaustion. It had been quite a day, and they had given their all.

"I want to thank each of you," Lizabeth said. "We moved more inventory today than I thought possible. For the first time, I feel that we are on our way in the fashion industry."

"More than on our way," Erma said. "This fashion show was a statement they won't soon forget. You stamped the Liz Braden brand on the minds of the public and made the big department stores take notice."

"We will see how it plays out in the days ahead," Lizabeth replied. "Now, all of you get out of here and enjoy your Sunday off. And thank you again for your support and your hard work."

Night had fallen over the city and streaks of lightning lit up the darkness as Walter met Uncle Ray at Hannon headquarters. Four, burly men with a sinister presence about them stood in a corner of the room measuring a thick rope and talking in whispers. Uncle Ray took a large leather harness that he was carrying over to them and they attached the rope to the harness and then they all headed down the stairs. The brawny guys jumped into the back of a delivery truck. Uncle Ray slid behind the wheel and Walter jumped in beside him.

"What's going on?" Walter asked.

"Sal Marconi time," Uncle Ray replied.

"What are we going to do?"

"Walter, to be successful in this business, you have to know your opposition. Tonight, with the lightning, the thunder, and the rain, Sal is going to face his greatest fear."

"And that is?"

"Water."

"Water?" Walter questioned with surprise.

"Yes. When he was a kid, he and three of his friends were playing too close to the river over on the north side. It was at flood stage, and they were swept away. Sal luckily grabbed a log and held on, but he almost drowned several times before a passing boat pulled him out of the water. His three friends drowned. Since that time, he has had an obsessive fear of water. He won't even cross the bridge to go to North Kansas City, and he hates to be out in the rain. He has such a phobia that he won't even drink the stuff. He sticks with booze and soda pop."

"So, what's the plan?" Walter wondered, as streaks of lightning flashed around the truck and thunder rumbled through the buildings.

"In due time, my boy. In due time."

When they arrived at Marconi's Produce, the four men got out of the back of the truck. When the lightning flashed, Walter could see they were armed. He was scared, recalling his last encounter with Sal, and wanted to be as far away from this place as possible. The lightning cast an ominous, eerie glow off the buildings of the City Market, and Walter wondered what he had gotten himself into.

A few minutes later, he heard cursing and a scuffle next to the truck and when the lightning flashed again, he saw the enraged, monstrous face of Sal Marconi as the rain pelted down on him. Uncle Ray's four men had a rope tied around Sal, and they heaved him into the back of the truck. One of the men held a gun on two of Sal's bodyguards, keeping them at bay as he jumped into the truck.

"Where are we headed?" Walter asked. The menacing face of Sal Marconi scared him half out of his wits.

"The Liberty Bend Bridge. It is the closest bridge to the place where Sal went into the river when he was a kid."

"What are you going to do?" Walter was fearful of Sal taking revenge.

"You'll see, my boy."

Uncle Ray drove the truck to the center of the bridge. A construction truck pulled in behind them, and a crew got out and put flares in the road to warn motorists that the lane was closed. Walter and Uncle Ray got out of the truck and watched as the construction crew took a winch out of the truck and secured it to the railing of the bridge. Sal was pulled, kicking and screaming profanities, out of the back of Ray's truck and wrested into the leather harness. Walter thought that an enraged gorilla would be easier to handle. The crew attached the winch rope to the harness and to the rope tied around Sal.

Uncle Ray grabbed Sal by the hair above his forehead and with help from the lights of the truck looked into eyes.

"Nice night for a swim, huh, Sal?"

"No!" Sal let out a terrified scream that pierced the night. He braced his feet against the railing of the bridge and fought frantically as the four, burly men hoisted him over the railing of the bridge.

"Bon voyage," Uncle Ray yelled, as the winch slowly lowered Sal toward the mighty Missouri River. They could hear his screams, as the thunder rolled and the lightning flashed.

"This is cruel," Walter said.

"Ain't it just," Uncle Ray replied.

"Stop his fall just above the water and let him dangle for a while!" Uncle Ray ordered. The construction crew put a floodlight on Sal, so they could judge how far he was above the water. Walter could only imagine the psychological toll that this was taking on Sal, to be soaked in rain and thrust into the horror of his childhood nightmare. Walter had never heard such screams of anguish.

"Dunk him in the water!" Uncle Ray ordered.

Walter watched as Sal went in up to his neck before they pulled him out.

"Do it again!"

Sal went in once more, and then Uncle Ray ordered him to be hoisted back to the bridge railing. Sal was a whimpering mass of exhaustion when he came over the railing.

Uncle Ray grabbed him by the hair again. "Here's the deal, Sal. You stay away from my nephew's girlfriend, and you make no more incursions into our business interests. If we have to do this again, you go into the river and you don't come out. Capisce?"

Sal nodded his head. "Capisce," he said. He was a beaten man and Walter knew he would cause no more trouble for him, Terri, or the Hannon organization.

~

Walter was jubilant as he met Jimmy, Queasy, and Drum at the Hi Hat club. He explained to them what had happened.

"That is impressive," Queasy said. "I will reluctantly cancel your life insurance policy. Who would have guessed that the most vicious gangster in town is afraid of water? And now you get to claim your reward from the fair maiden."

"Absolutely not. A gentleman expects no reward for doing the right thing," Walter said with a wink.

"That's fine for a gentleman, but what about you?" Queasy countered.

"So, that's your strategy?" Drum asked. "You want to play the gentleman role, while knowing that she will see you as her hero and protector. If she's smart, she will keep a lock on her zipper."

"I hate to disappoint you, but this is more a matter of the heart than of sex."

"Very admirable, until you are locked in mortal combat and your balls invade your brain," Queasy said.

"You are looking at a man in total control of his impulses."

"What if I take your beer?"

"I will break your arm."

Queasy laughed. "I rest my case."

"I see nothing but good things ahead, my friends. I'm back in the good graces of the organization, Sal Marconi has been neutralized, and I've found the girl of my dreams."

"I would not rest easy," Drum said. "Trouble is always lurking where you're concerned. Hannon has had to bail you out, and I'm not so sure that Sal Marconi will let you slide so easily. He has a reputation to uphold, and you've made him lose face in the Italian community."

"No chance," Walter said. "Sal is a beaten man, and he won't risk going into the drink again. "

"We have to give you your due, Walter," Queasy said. "You emerged triumphant against the worst the city has to offer. It is our own David versus Goliath story and will henceforth be known in Kansas City lore as the Dunkin' Dago Caper."

That got a laugh out of all of them. Walter had every intention of going to Terri's house with the good news, but he could not tear himself away from the booze, and he became too drunk to present himself to Terri. Later that night, his three friends poured him into the car and drove him home to Brookside.

⁓

The next day was Sunday, and Walter drove to Hyde Park to pick up Terri. She lived at the end of Janssen Place in an antebellum home done in the Greek Revival style. It was red brick with four large columns in front and would not have been out of place in Charleston, South Carolina, or Savannah, Georgia. A carriage house in back matched the main house. Walter was impressed. The housekeeper answered the door.

"I'm Walter Braden. I'm here to see Terri."

"Just a moment, please."

Walter looked around the inside of the mansion. From his vantage point, he could see into the parlor. It featured a Victorian couch and cushioned chairs. They were covered in a red and black pattern that he guessed might be the family crest. There was a stone fireplace, a grand piano, and several early American, landscape paintings. Off to the side, he could see a staircase leading upstairs.

"Nice house," he said, when Terri arrived.

"Thank you. Would you like to come in and meet my mother?"

"I would love to."

"Come, sit in the parlor and I will be right back."

Terri came back into the room holding her mother's arm to steady her. Walter stood up and took her hand. She was an attractive woman and looked to be in her fifties. Her hair was gray, and she appeared to be frailer than her years.

"Walter, this is my mother, Charlene Lawson."

Walter took her hand. "I'm pleased to meet you."

"I'm pleased to meet you as well, Walter."

Terri helped her mother sit.

"Rheumatoid arthritis, in case you were wondering," Charlene said. "It came on with a vengeance when I turned fifty."

"Is there a cure?" Walter asked.

"I'm afraid not. The doctors are trying to stabilize my condition, without much success. I was hopeful that I could get back to teaching, but my bones won't cooperate."

"You were a teacher?"

"Yes. I taught special education in the public schools."

"Do you miss it?"

"More than anything. I tried going back to work several times, but it was too painful. I never dreamed I would be a prisoner in my own body."

"I'm sorry," Walter said.

"Enough about me," Charlene said. "I understand that you might be the answer to our problems with Mr. Marconi."

"I am indeed. You won't have any more trouble with Sal Marconi."

"Walter, that is wonderful news!" Terri said. "How did you do it?"

"I managed to persuade him that leaving you alone would be in his best interest."

"I can't imagine how you did that, but thank you so much."

"You are welcome. I thought that you might like to celebrate by coming to Sunday dinner today at the Braden's."

"Don't you think it's too soon for me to be meeting your parents?"

"No. I just met your mom, and she is wonderful. I hope you have the same experience with my parents."

"Thank you, Walter," Charlene said.

"And you can see what you are getting in to. You have already met my sisters, so that will make it easier for you."

"Meeting the expectations of others can be tricky, especially with parents and their sons."

"Not to worry. My parent's expectations are reasonable where I'm concerned. They will see you as a positive influence in my life."

"Perhaps you should explain the negatives."

"Not a chance, here in front of your mother. You will have to find those out on your own."

Terri and Charlene laughed.

"I suspected that you were trouble when you first accosted me on the street."

"I had to. I had never seen anyone so beautiful."

"He is full of it, Mother," Terri said.

"He is also charming, so watch yourself," Charlene warned.

Walter and Terri laughed.

Walter stood up. He leaned over and kissed Charlene's hand. "It was so good to meet you, and I hope we see a lot more of each other."

"Me too, Walter. And thank you very much for solving the problem with Sal Marconi."

On the ride out to Brookside, Terri looked over at Walter. "I'm nervous about meeting your family."

"No reason to be. You have to admit that everything has gone well so far."

"Yes. But, then again, it is early in the relationship."

"It is good of you to confirm that we are in a relationship."

"You tricked me into that."

Walter laughed. He stopped the car in front of the house and then leaned over and kissed her on the cheek. "Relax. I'm sure that my family will be as taken with you as I am."

"Easy for you to say. You don't have to pass inspection." She walked arm in arm with him and entered the house.

The family was gathered in the living room, and Walter introduced Terri to everyone. Helen was there with Cam, as were Walter's grandparents, Uncle Ray, Erma, and his sisters.

"Walter, you have outdone yourself," his grandfather said. "Where did you find this beautiful and charming young lady?"

Terri beamed with pleasure. "Thank you, sir."

"Everyone calls me Pop and you can too."

"I followed her to work one day and made such a pest of myself that she finally agreed to have dinner with me," Walter said.

"Well, good for you."

"I can't believe you pulled it off," Erma said. "After the debacle at Lizabeth's store, we thought that she would never go out with you."

"Well, thanks to Uncle Ray and with the help of my sisters, I managed to redeem myself."

"Helping one another is what family is all about," Uncle Ray said with a wink.

Mira came out of the kitchen, and Walter introduced her to Terri.

"I'm so pleased that you could join us," Mira said. "Now come in and sit down, everyone."

J.M. took his place at the head of the table. Mira offered a short prayer, and then Walter stood up and offered a toast.

"I speak for all of us when I offer hearty congratulations to Lizabeth. Through perseverance and hard work, you started a successful business. We are proud of you, and we wish you continued success. And to you, Aunt Erma, for your efforts on her behalf. She could not have done it without you."

"I want to thank all of you," Lizabeth said. "We could not have made it happen without your support."

"To have the Braden name on Petticoat Lane is a big deal," Eileen said. "Your idea of a fashion show in the street was brilliant."

"Thank you." Lizabeth didn't want to shine too brightly. Cam was the anointed carrier of the Braden banner, so she deflected the praise. "This was all made possible by Cam and Walter's confidence in me, so I owe it all to them," she said.

"You've done well, Lizabeth," J.M. said. "I just wish you could have done it without forming an alliance with Tom Hannon. I'm uneasy with two children and a brother in the Hannon camp."

"I know you have concerns," Lizabeth said. "But Mr. Hannon has been very supportive. I wouldn't have been able to have the fashion show without his blessing."

"Just remember, there is usually a price to pay when you get involved with Hannon."

"Terri, I understand that you are in the entertainment business," Uncle Ray said, changing the subject.

"Indirectly. I work behind the scenes as a film editor for Universal Pictures."

"With your looks, you should be in front of the camera," Pop said.

Terri smiled. "Thank you for that, but I will leave the stage to Eileen. It takes a lot of courage and confidence to perform for an audience."

"I'll take that as a compliment, so thank you very much," Eileen said.

"You are welcome. How long is your current play running?"

"It was extended for another week."

"A Universal executive is coming to town next week. Do you mind if I bring him to see you perform?"

"Of course, I don't mind. What evening will you be coming?"

"I'll keep that a secret so you don't feel any extra pressure."

"Did I not predict this would happen?" Lizabeth said. "Hollywood, here she comes."

"Don't be silly," Eileen said, although she could feel the flush of excitement at the prospect of being discovered.

"I wouldn't even think along those lines," Terri said. "For every successful actress, there are a thousand more, serving hash in Los Angeles roadhouses."

"But it certainly doesn't hurt to dream," Lizabeth countered.

"No, it does not. Dreams built the movie industry."

"Acting is fine for a hobby," J.M. said. "But I would prefer that Eileen seek another career."

"She should do what she's good at and what she loves," Erma said.

"I don't disagree," J.M. replied. "I just hope that it's something besides acting."

"Terri, are you a Kansas City girl?" Mira asked, changing the subject again. She knew that insecurity over unemployment was causing J.M. to react unreasonably in trying to control his children. But the more he tried, the more they were slipping away.

"I am indeed. My father owned a plumbing supply business downtown before he passed away. My mother has a home in the Hyde Park area, and I live there with her."

That upscale neighborhood let Mira know that Terri's family was well off. "I'm sorry about your father." She paused as Terri whispered a thank you. "How did you get involved in the film industry?"

"I answered an ad in the paper and was hired as a secretary.

When my boss left, I was given his position. I enjoy the work and would eventually like to become a documentary film producer."

"Good for you," Erma said. "These days women have to make their place in the world. The Depression has turned a man's world upside down. We need to be prepared to take care of ourselves."

"What about being a mother and homemaker?" Mira asked. "Doesn't that count for something?"

"Of course, it does," Lizabeth said. "You provide the stability that we need in this crazy world."

"Perhaps, but I don't see any of you young ladies wanting to emulate me."

"It's just that times are changing," Erma said. "And besides, you have your work as a practitioner, ministering to the sick, that takes you outside the home, and that is certainly more worthwhile than anything we are doing."

"It does give me a lot of satisfaction," Mira said. "Although sometimes I feel the breeze from the women's movement passing me by."

"There are more options for women today," Nana said. "When I was a young woman, the expectations were that I would get married and raise a family. It never occurred to me to have a career. Most of my generation only worked until we found a husband."

"There is no right or wrong in the matter," Terri said. "Each woman has to make that decision for herself."

Lizabeth knew what her decision would be. There was no way she would trade the excitement of the fashion industry and owning a business for marriage and motherhood. She now knew what she was capable of and her confidence was growing with each passing day. She also knew that Cory had become more enamored with her, and it was something she would have to deal with in the days ahead. There was no way she was going to get herself romantically involved at the expense of her business. Minor flirtations were one thing, but a serious commitment was out of the question.

"How is the car business, Cam?" Uncle Ray asked, moving the conversation away from women's issues.

"Very good," Cam said. "I've talked several more banks into loosening their credit qualifications. They have a hard time with the concept that to make money in a depression, they must make it available to the consumer."

"It's human nature," Uncle Ray said. "Banks want to hold on to their money, when they should be spreading it around."

"Exactly. Helen faces the same thing in the shoe business. Instead of using their money to buy a new pair of shoes, her customers keep patching the old ones."

"That's true," Helen said. "Lizabeth hit a niche with the ninety-nine–cent dresses. But there is not enough margin in shoes to do that."

"I think we've seen the worst of it," Uncle Ray said. "The economy should continue to get better."

"It's always good inside the machine," J.M. said. "Hannon has money coming in from legitimate and illegitimate businesses. There is no depression at Hannon's headquarters."

"You are too hard on the boss," Ray said. "He is keeping the city running in good shape in the worst of times. When things improve, we should have a booming economy. Walter is a good example of what can be done working within the organization. He has been quite successful in helping expand business downtown."

"Good for you, Walter," Lizabeth said.

"I will call it a success if the two of you stay out of jail," J.M. said.

Uncle Ray smiled. "You forget that we run the police department."

"But for how long?" J.M. said. "Hannon won't be able to keep the reformers and the press at bay forever."

"Maybe not. But the Hannons have been in control of the city for fifty years, so I'll take my chances."

Mira suggested that Lizabeth and Eileen keep visiting with the guests, while she and Erma cleared the table and took the dishes into the kitchen.

"A lovely meal, as always," Erma said.

"Thank you. Our guest list keeps growing. I don't know what we will do when the girls start inviting their friends. We can't afford a bigger house."

"And what about when the grandchildren start arriving?"

"I hadn't even considered that."

"It will happen before you know it."

"And I thought I was tired now."

Erma laughed. "Not to worry. I don't see Walter and Cam marrying any time soon. Eileen might be susceptible, but Lizabeth is dead set on having a career."

"You never can tell," Mira said, as she washed a dish. "All you can predict about people is that they will be unpredictable."

"Walter seems enamored with his new girlfriend."

"Yes. She is a lovely girl. With the first blush of romance, she doesn't realize what she is getting into. He has a drinking problem and a wild streak. And, like his father, he has an eye for women."

"You surely don't think that J.M. is still chasing other women," Erma exclaimed.

"It doesn't matter, because his affairs changed everything in our marriage. When we were young, the core of our relationship was something I could cling to in the worst of times. Now I'm grabbing at air. There are some things in a marriage that you can forgive and forget and others that hang on like a curse."

"I thought that your faith might help you with forgiveness."

"I thought so too, but infidelity pops up when I least expect it." Mira sighed.

"You might be suffering from depression."

"No. I'm suffering from resentment. I'm angry that my husband betrayed me."

"Have you talked with J.M. about it?"

"What is there to say? That he is sorry doesn't do justice to the damage."

"You are taking it personally, and you shouldn't. It's the way men are," Erma said.

"Sorry, but I don't buy the gender excuse for a lack of morality. There are lots of men who remain faithful to their wives."

"I thought that you had put this behind you years ago."

"I've found that unlike wine, infidelities fester as they age."

"You're surely not thinking of leaving him."

"Of course not. Holding the family together is the most important thing in my life. Sometimes I must vent or I will burst. Thank goodness you are here to listen."

"I will always be here for you, and I hope you can work through your feelings."

"So do I."

"How is it going with J.M.'s job search?" Erma asked.

"Nothing has turned up. I'm glad that Lizabeth has hired him to do advertising. It will give him something to do while he is looking."

"Too bad he won't join the Hannon team."

"Yes. It would be a solution. However, I won't ask him to do something that goes against his principles."

"He seems to be selective in his principles," Erma noted.

"I can't argue that. His problem with Hannon is that he invested some money in several construction projects that Hannon halted because they were not up to his version of meeting code. Hannon stalled the projects until he could replace the contractors with his own people. J.M. lost quite a bit of money in the deal."

"J.M. should have known that it was foolhardy to go up against Hannon. Nothing goes forward without his approval."

"I know. He had the mistaken idea that this was a free country and not a dictatorship."

"Be that as it may, in the game of politics, Hannon controls the ball. People must accept that, if they want to play in this town."

"J.M. found that out the hard way," Mira said, ending the discussion. "Now let's get back to our guests."

The two women returned to the table and began serving coffee.

CHAPTER NINE

New Year's Eve 1935

SALES FOR LIZ BRADEN DESIGNER dresses had been steady during the summer and given Lizabeth enough cash to fund her fall and holiday lines of clothing. Those two collections had also surpassed her expectations and left her eagerly awaiting the new year to show off her spring fashions. She would have a full year of experience selling all four seasons of fashion and that would be invaluable in calculating trends and inventory. She was excited and could hardly wait for the new year to begin.

She and Cory were on their way to Union Station, where they would meet her siblings and their dates for an evening of dining and dancing. She had decided to wear a belted, black, satin dress with puffed sleeves and a collar that was festive but conservative.

"It's hard to believe that it is going to be 1936," Cory said.

"I know. It has been such a busy year that time has flown by."

"We haven't been able to see each other as much as I would have liked," he said.

"The demands of a business are many."

"I thought things might be different once the business was up and running. I hoped you would slow down."

"Then I wouldn't be me. I suspect that you knew what you were getting into."

"I did to a degree. But I wanted more time for us."

And there it was, Lizabeth thought. The inevitable tug of war between the demands of a business and those of a relationship.

"If I don't devote myself to the business, it won't be successful for long."

"I understand that, and I'm not complaining. I just want to see you more often."

"And I appreciate that, but I can't be successful if I'm feeling guilty about giving more time to my business than to you."

"I would ask which is more important, but I'm sure I wouldn't like the answer."

She remained silent, watching the explosion of fireworks being tested over the city.

"Perhaps you should date other women," she finally said.

"I would just be wishing that I was with you."

She slid over close to him and wrapped her arm in his. "This is a night for celebration and here we are getting serious," she said.

"How right you are. What could be better than bringing in the new year together?"

"Nothing at all."

Cory parked the car in front of Union Station, and they walked into the building. Lizabeth loved the grandeur of the station. Construction began in 1911, and it opened in 1914. It had three, huge, arched windows on the south wall that bathed the Grand Hall in sunlight. The floors were laid with marble and a semicircular ticket office with bronze grillwork was the focal point. People were lined up at each of the windows buying tickets.

When Lizabeth was a child, the immensity of the station had made her feel small and insignificant. Three giant chandeliers, each weighing 3,500 pounds, hung from a 95-foot-high ceiling. She would look up at the glistening prisms and pretend they were lights on a glass carriage that would carry her into a land of make believe.

But now she was all grown up and brimming with confidence from her fashion success. She weaved her way through hundreds of revelers moving around the Grand Hall. There were waves of travelers pushing their way under the clock and into the North Waiting Room, where they waited for their trains to be announced.

Kansas City's location in the middle of the country made it ideal for the railroads to move passengers to the east and west coasts. With so many trains passing through Union Station, it was one of the largest terminals in the country.

She and Cory hurried through the crowd toward the giant clock that had been the meeting place for Kansas Citians since 1914. She saw Walter waving his hand above the crowd, and they joined him and the others beneath the clock.

"Happy New Year!" Walter said. There were hugs and kisses all around. She could tell from his breath that he had been celebrating early.

"Where's Jimmy?" Lizabeth asked.

"He is watching a Golden Glove fight and will be along later."

Lizabeth was pleased to see that her brothers' girlfriends both wore her fashion designs. Terri looked stunning in a black, lace dress with fringe at the bottom. Helen wore a form-fitting, blue, halter dress that accentuated her shoulder blades and her back.

"You ladies look lovely tonight," Lizabeth said.

"Thank you," Helen answered. "Would you like the name of our designer?"

Lizabeth laughed. "You two are the best advertisements I could have."

"I love your black, satin dress," Terri said to Lizabeth.

"Thank you."

"Let's head for Harvey House and get some dinner," Cam suggested.

"Too early for that," Walter said. "Take a drink from my flask."

"You had better slow down or you won't see the new year," Cam suggested.

"What's it to you?"

"I don't want to carry you home tonight."

"Who asked you to? And don't lecture me on my drinking."

"That's enough, you two," Lizabeth said. "You are not going to ruin everyone's evening with your bickering. You should make a resolution to treat each other better in the new year."

"Fat chance," Walter said.

"We should walk on over to Harvey House and confirm our reservation," Lizabeth suggested. "We can get some appetizers and drinks." They walked across the station to the entrance of the restaurant.

At the large, round table, they settled in and through the window watched the crowd of revelers moving back and forth across the Grand Hall.

"Where is Eileen?" Terri asked.

"She is starring in a play and should be here soon," Lizabeth answered.

"What band is playing tonight?" Cory asked.

"Jimmy Dorsey and his orchestra," Walter answered.

"Good," Helen said. "I love swing music, and I could dance all night."

"You had better get another partner," Walter said. "Cam falls asleep at ten."

"Walter!" Lizabeth warned.

Duly chastised, Walter took another sip from his flask.

"You had an extremely successful year," Helen said to Lizabeth. "You should be proud of all you accomplished."

"Thank you for leasing the building to my brothers. It has been a family success story."

"We did very little. You and your crew made it happen with your designs and promotions. And to run your competition out of inventory was pure genius."

"There was quite a bit of luck involved," Lizabeth said.

"In an economic depression, you make your own luck," Helen countered.

Lizabeth turned to Terri. "Have you heard any more from that producer who saw Eileen's play?" she asked.

"No. He has her photo and résumé. If something turns up, I'm sure he will contact me. She might be better off where she is. The competition in Hollywood is brutal."

"Is that why you didn't pursue being an actress?" Helen asked. "With your looks, you certainly fit the profile."

"Thank you. I'm not comfortable in front of the camera and prefer being behind the scenes editing film."

"Any thoughts of making a film of your own?" Helen asked.

"Yes. My goal is to make documentary films."

"About what?"

"Films that document the human experience. My latest one is on Black Sunday, about the devastating dust storm that covered the Midwest this past April."

114

"I remember that," Lizabeth said. "We were sweeping dust out of the house for weeks. How did you manage to film the storm?"

"We were in Oklahoma, covering the effects of the Depression on farm families, when this enormous black cloud covered the horizon and kept creeping toward us. I thought it was how the end of the world might look. We were mesmerized until we realized what an opportunity we had and started filming the monster storm. When the wind and the dust hit, it was like a black blizzard, and we ran for our lives. Later, in the studio we found that we had managed to capture a good portion of the storm. I want to use the film to show what effects the dust storms had on the lives of farmers in the Midwest."

"I bet the newspapers would love to have that footage," Helen said.

"Probably, but I'm saving what we captured to help jump-start my career as a filmmaker."

"And so you should," Lizabeth said. "You made the film and you should get the credit."

From out of the crowd of revelers came Queasy and Drum.

"Happy New Year, everyone!" Queasy and Drum said in unison.

"Happy New Year!" Walter replied, glad to see them because he knew they would liven up the party. The two men knew the rest of the group but he introduced them to Helen and Terri.

"Pleased to meet you, ladies," Queasy said. He sat down across the table from Terri and took her hand.

"I can see now why Walter risked life and limb to win your hand," he said.

Terri looked questioningly at Walter, but he turned away.

"You mean Walter didn't tell you that he ended up black and blue from a beating by the worst criminals in the city? This takes chivalry to a whole new level."

"You didn't mention that you were hurt," Terri said.

"It was nothing." Walter gave Queasy a look that said to leave it alone.

But Queasy was in his cups and not about to. "It is a miracle that he isn't hanging in Sal Marconi's produce locker instead of spending a few days in the hospital."

"You never mentioned that you were in the hospital," Lizabeth said with concern.

115

"We didn't want to rile up J.M., so I stayed with Aunt Erma and Uncle Ray after leaving the hospital," Walter hesitantly admitted.

"We will talk about this later," Terri said.

"Don't be too hard on him," Drum said.

"How many men would risk death for the woman they love? And besides," Queasy said, "scolding Walter would be fruitless. I've known him since he was five years old and all attempts at molding him into a decent human being have been futile."

"I kind of like him the way he is," Terri said.

"My dear, I'm surprised that a woman of your quality would set your sights so low."

"I think you are making it up as you go," Terri said.

Queasy laughed.

In the Grand Hall, Jimmy Dorsey struck up the band and revelers started dancing.

"Cam, may I borrow Helen for a dance?" Drum asked

Cam grunted his consent. Helen and Drum walked to the dance floor. Lizabeth and Cory joined them.

"Aren't you going to ask Terri to dance?" Cam asked Walter.

"What's it to you?"

"She might want to have some fun before you can't get out of your chair."

"Very funny. You let me worry about Terri."

"You two take brotherly love to a new low," Terri said.

Walter took her hand. "Let's go dance and leave him here alone. He loves his own company best."

Cam grunted, satisfied that he had annoyed Walter.

Cory danced with Lizabeth across the Grand Hall.

"I'll bet you have already made your list of resolutions for 1936," he said.

"You think you know me that well?"

"Am I right?"

"You are, indeed."

"I was hoping that you might slow down in the new year."

"Then I wouldn't be me."

"Are you at all interested in a closer relationship?" he asked.

Lizabeth froze for a moment. This was getting awfully close to a commitment and making her uncomfortable. She wondered how long she could hold Cory off without promising something more permanent. Was it fair of her to keep playing the dating game when he wanted more?

"Something more permanent might be the end of my hopes and dreams," she said. "It wouldn't be fair for me to make a commitment to you and then not give you the time and devotion you deserve. I'm consumed by my business, and I don't see that changing anytime soon."

"I thought that's what you would say, but it never hurts to ask. I want you to know that I am not going to give up."

"I don't want you to. We can have a wonderful relationship without tying each other down."

"It's not as much as I had hoped for, but things might be different in 1936."

Not likely, she thought, as he spun her around the Grand Hall. It would be many years, if ever, before she would even consider anything that might jeopardize her career. The music ended, and they headed back to the table with the rest of the group.

"What are your parents doing tonight?" Helen asked Lizabeth.

"They are having a quiet New Year's Eve at home with my grandparents, and with Uncle Ray and Aunt Erma."

"I wish they could have joined us," Terri said.

At that moment, the crowd parted and they heard whistles of appreciation from the men surrounding the table. Eileen made her entrance in a red, silk, bodice-cut dress that clung to her body in all the right places and did not leave a lot to the imagination. She took off her gold cape and put it on the back of a chair. Her friend, David, was her escort. Lizabeth recognized him as one of the men she often dated who were not focused on women. She dated them because they were fun loving, and she did not have to worry about fighting for her virtue.

"Happy New Year!" Eileen said, as she hugged and kissed everyone and introduced David around the table.

"That is a beautiful dress," Queasy said.

"Thank you. My sister's design and by far the most beautiful dress that I have ever owned."

"How was the play?" Lizabeth asked.

"As always, Eileen was the star of the show," David said. "I tried to upstage her in several scenes, but she won the day as Kansas City's most popular actress. The rest of us are reduced to performing in her shadow."

"I brought him along because he is also my press agent," Eileen kidded.

"And which one of these lovely ladies is the Universal film editor?" David asked.

"That would be me," Terri said.

"Watch out, Terri," Eileen said. "He will try to butter up anyone in the business who might further his career."

"How could you possibly question my motives?" David gasped, holding his chest in pretend shock that made everyone laugh. "It's just that you never know when a film editor might become a producer, or a director, and remember that charming actor back in the day at Union Station."

"If I ever reach that exalted status," Terri said, "I promise to pluck you out of the actor's pool and put you on the road to stardom."

"You are the girl of my dreams," David said.

"My, how quickly I am trampled under your ambition," Eileen said.

David took Eileen's hand. "I can see the wolves gathering, so you had better give me the first dance." He and Eileen headed out into the Grand Hall.

Lizabeth sat back and watched the couples move across the dance floor. She paid close attention to what the women were wearing. The dress of choice seemed to be bias cut, although halter style, and low-back dresses were not far behind. She had to stay abreast of what women were wearing and also keep up with the fashions coming out of New York and Paris if she wanted to be a serious player in the industry. It was hard to predict what would be popular in the future. Would ruffles and high-cap sleeves be in fashion for 1936, and would silk and lace continue to be popular?

The one great advantage she had was that she was not sitting on a ton of inventory, and because she made her own garments, she could manufacture into a trend rather than be caught with dresses that were out of date. It was a guessing game for large department stores that often missed the mark when the fashion world changed direction. However, she was confident in her ability, and rather than copy other designers, she wanted to set trends of her own.

Jimmy showed up at the same time as Eileen and David returned to the table.

"Happy New Year, Jimmy," Walter said, shaking his hand.

"Happy New year to you and everyone," Jimmy said.

"How was the fight?"

"Great. The boxers were a couple of middleweights who I'm scheduled to fight."

"Can you whip them?" Walter asked.

"If I didn't think so, I would hang up the gloves."

"You should quit before you get hurt," Eileen said. Jimmy was like a third brother, and she did not want him to fight.

"I couldn't give up fighting any more than you could give up acting," Jimmy said.

"At least we don't have anyone beating on our heads," Eileen replied.

"You have obviously not performed in a clunker," David said. "I was once in a play where beer cans showered the stage. I aged quicker than the play."

That got a laugh from everyone.

"I have a suggestion," Lizabeth said. "We are edging closer to midnight, so each of us should share our resolutions for 1936. I read somewhere that for goals to keep, you have to say them out loud."

"Then you start us off, Lizabeth," Eileen said

"My resolutions are to dedicate myself to my business and to make myself worthy of my friends and family. What about you, Eileen?"

"Mine is to improve my acting skills and my relationships."

"Walter?"

"Why are women always better at this than men?" Walter asked, trying to think of something through an alcoholic fog. "To enjoy life and to help out where I can," he finally said.

"What about you, Terri?" Lizabeth asked.

"Walter gave me my life back, so I resolve to never again take it for granted."

"Helen?"

"Lizabeth inspired me with her business acumen. I'm going to take more chances and try new things."

"Your turn, David."

"I resolve to never again upstage Eileen."

"That is the first resolution to be broken," Eileen scoffed.

David held up his hand. His fingers were crossed and everyone laughed.

Cam was dozing, so they passed him by. It was Cory's turn and Lizabeth held her breath, afraid that he might say something about their relationship.

"My resolution is to keep working toward a teaching degree."

"Jimmy?"

"Mine is to take better care of my granny and to try to keep up with Walter. What about you, Queasy?"

"No public pronouncements for me," Queasy said. "Last year my resolutions followed me around like dogs, nipping at my heels. Thank God, they died with the new year, and I now have a clear conscience."

"No way I can top that," Drum said. "I just want to wish you all the best in the new year. And thank you for letting us be part of the Braden family."

"It's almost midnight, so let's go out into the Grand Hall where we can see the clock," Lizabeth said. They woke Cam and headed that way.

At the stroke of midnight, as fireworks boomed outside the station, they hugged and kissed, threw confetti in the air and tooted their horns. From somewhere in the crowd, the haunting sound of "Auld Lang Syne" began and they joined in the song: "Should old acquaintance be forgot, and never brought to mind?" The song echoed around the Grand Hall and made Lizabeth tear up. She was thankful for all the past year had brought her and she was excited to see what this new year of 1936 would bring.

When she awoke the next morning, sunlight was shining through the bedroom window and a cold north wind tugged at the eaves of the house. She snuggled closer to Eileen and pulled the covers around her. Last night had been so special and romantic. When Cory had kissed her goodnight, she had wondered for a moment what a family and kids might be like. But just as quickly, she dismissed the thought as being starry eyed from the New Year's Eve celebration. One of her resolutions was to be more industrious in the new year, and here she was sinking into the mattress and clinging to her pillow.

She could hear someone downstairs rummaging around the kitchen, so she pulled herself away from Eileen and gently slid out of bed. The house was cold, so she left on her granny gown and put on a robe. She went downstairs, where her mother was in the kitchen cleaning up from last night.

"Good morning, Mother."

"Good morning. You managed to sleep in for a change."

"I was exhausted. How was your party?"

"Low key. We had dinner and played some cards."

"I missed seeing Nana and Pop. I will call and wish them a Happy New Year."

"That would be nice. How was the party at Union Station?"

"It was wonderfully romantic. One of those nights you wish would never end."

"It must have been fun. The boys did not get home until dawn."

"Where's Father?"

"He's in the back office, working on your ad."

"Maybe I should go see how he's doing."

"No, you will not. You are going to spend the day completely away from the fashion business and get some rest."

"That won't be easy."

"That's the very reason that I am insisting on it. You will have to live with the guilt of being leisurely for one day of the year."

Eileen came down the stairs.

"I hope I didn't wake you," Lizabeth said.

"No. The smell of Mother's coffee came drifting up the stairs, and I couldn't resist for a moment longer."

"I'll get you a cup," Lizabeth said.

"I thought you would be in your designing room," Eileen replied.

"Mother has me under house arrest."

"Good for her. You need a day off."

"Why do I feel like I'm in the third grade and you two are conspiring against me?"

"Just remember that we always know best," Eileen said, batting her eyelashes.

Lizabeth laughed. "Where are Walter and Cam?" she asked.

"They might have had a rough night," Mira answered. "I imagine they will sleep until noon."

"We left them at two a.m. at the Hi Hat club," Eileen said. "I'm glad they made it home safely."

"You know what they say about the Lord watching out for the inebriated," Mira said.

The saying was watching out for drunks, Lizabeth remembered. But her mother would never associate that word with her son's behavior.

The girls ate their breakfast and went upstairs to dress and to read for a while. When they came down later, Walter was at the kitchen table, nursing a cup of coffee. His hair was disheveled, and he was holding his head. His robe was on inside out.

"Happy New Year," Lizabeth said.

Walter looked up. "Please, never utter those three words again," he said. "They make my stomach do somersaults."

Lizabeth would have laughed, but she could see that he was in pain.

"You could have quit while you were sober," Mira said.

"In hindsight, that is perfect advice. However, it was hard to turn down drinks offered by my friends."

"I'm sure it was difficult for you," Mira said, with a hint of sarcasm.

"Did you get Terri home okay?" Eileen asked.

"I think so. I called her a cab, because she wanted to leave and I wanted to stay at the club."

"Walter, you didn't!" Eileen admonished him.

"What's the big deal?"

"The most romantic night of the year is the big deal. You don't send your date out into the night alone so you can stay and party with your friends."

"It seemed to make perfect sense at the time. Now, not so much."

"You must call her today and apologize," Eileen said.

"I will, after I finish my coffee."

This was a perfect example of why Lizabeth worried about Walter. The alcohol was clouding his judgment, and it seemed to be getting worse.

Cam came into the kitchen. He had cleaned up and looked immaculate. His vanity would not allow him to be seen any other way. He looked at Walter.

"Nice robe," he said.

Walter looked down and saw that his robe was inside out.

"Maybe Lizabeth could design a line of clothes for backward people," Cam continued. "You could be her model."

"The ladies were kind enough not to mention it."

Cam scoffed and then poured a cup of coffee.

"How was your evening?" Mira asked him

"If I had come home after the celebration at the station, it would have been a wonderful evening. Instead, I let Walter talk me into taking Helen to the Hi Hat club."

"I don't remember twisting your arm," Walter said.

"You don't remember much of anything."

"It was New Year's Eve, for criminy's sake! What have you got against having some fun?"

"Nothing, as long as it is within reason. You, Drum, and Queasy would be sobering up at the police station if Jimmy and I hadn't carried you home."

"It couldn't have been that bad," Walter said

"Trust me. It was. And no, I'm not going into any details."

"Did you get Helen home okay?" Eileen asked.

"Yes. She was worn out from dancing."

"You all look worn out," Mira said. "I've declared a day of rest for Lizabeth, and it won't hurt the three of you to join her. You can spend the day reading and playing cards."

"That sounds like fun," Eileen said. "It will be just like when we were kids."

Walter took a knife from the table and acted like he was plunging it into his heart. It cracked up Lizabeth and Eileen.

"I saw that, Walter," Mira said.

"I'm going back to bed," Walter said. "I'll join in the fun later." He rolled his eyes, then pulled his robe tightly around him and headed for the bedroom.

"Don't forget to call Terri," Lizabeth shouted after him.

The day turned out to be more enjoyable and relaxing than Lizabeth could have imagined. When Walter got up, they played hearts for a while and then read until it was time for their radio shows. Through trial and error and without too much grumbling, they had set a schedule so that everyone could hear their favorite show. J.M. started out at 6:45 with Lowell Thomas and the news. At 7:00, Walter loved the comedy of *Amos 'n' Andy*. At 8:00, Cam tuned into the crime drama, *Manhunters*, and at 9:00, Eileen listened to Bing Crosby and the Stoll Orchestra. The radio was reserved at 10:00 for Lizabeth and her mother for the comedy of *Fibber McGee and Molly* and it always sent them to bed in a cheerful mood.

Lizabeth looked out of her bedroom window before climbing into bed and saw snowflakes drifting down on the street. The weather might slow shopping on the second day of the year, but it would allow her time to work on the designs that had been parading through her head. This day of rest had been wonderful, but she was still anxious about what the first few shopping days of 1936 would bring.

"Are you coming to bed?" Eileen asked.

Lizabeth left the window and climbed under the covers.

"Did Terri call Walter back?" she asked

"I don't think so."

"I hope they work it out."

"Me too. Now get some sleep."

The tick, ticking of the clock that was soothing for Eileen, sounded like drumbeats to Lizabeth. Not even the snow softly gathering on the window ledge could induce sleep. It was after midnight when she finally drifted off.

She hadn't been asleep long when the ringing of the downstairs phone woke her, and she tried to get her bearings. She wondered why Terri had waited so late to call Walter back. She heard him answer the phone. As the conversation continued, he sounded frantic and agitated. She hoped they were not arguing.

124

"Okay! We will be right there!" Walter shouted.

When she heard him running up the stairs, she sat straight up in bed with her heart racing. He burst into the room. "Lizabeth, get up! There's a fire on Petticoat Lane!" The ramifications of that were so dire, that for a moment she was in shock and could hardly breathe.

"Hurry!" Walter shouted.

She and Eileen dressed quickly and ran down the stairs. Cam was at the door with their coats and they hurried to Walter's car. There was hardly any traffic as they headed downtown. Walter ignored the red lights and kept moving at a fast clip through the snow.

Lizabeth tried to calm down. Petticoat Lane was a large retail area and perhaps the fire had been held in check before it reached her store. Eileen put her arms around her sister. Lizabeth was shivering from the prospect of losing her store more than from the cold.

When they reached the top of the Main Street hill, they could see the glow from the fire downtown but could not tell the exact location. Walter half slid and half drove the car down the hill as they headed toward the fire. When they arrived, Petticoat Lane was blocked off at Main Street and also blocked at Walnut Street. Walter parked the car and they jumped out and ran as close as they could get.

Smoke billowed out of buildings on the north side of the street where Lizabeth's store was located. Fire hoses caked in ice were soaking the buildings from every direction as firemen fought the blaze in the swirling snowstorm. Walter was acquainted with the fire chief and some of the firemen, so they let them move around the corner and view the fire from the south side of Petticoat Lane.

Lizabeth felt so helpless. All her hopes and dreams were in the store, and there was nothing she could do to protect it. For a while, it seemed the firemen were winning the battle against the flames, but when they died down, another flame spurted up from somewhere else. The fire seemed to be fighting back and would not die.

Walter stared at the flames. He would never forgive himself, if he had brought this disaster down on his sister. Queasy and Drum had warned him that Sal Marconi might retaliate, but he had been too full of himself to listen. If it turned out to be true, there would be all-out war in the city. Tom Hannon had a stake in Lizabeth's business, and she was part of his team.

For a while, it looked like the driving snow would help put out the fire, but something in the building kept fueling the flames. The firemen kept a steady stream of water on the buildings and finally the fire seemed to be receding. For a moment, Lizabeth was hopeful that things would turn out okay, but then she heard a rumble deep in the building and suddenly the windows in her storefront blew out. The flames darted out of the window casings and reached hungrily for the street. At that moment, she knew that all was lost, and she slumped to her knees in the cold, wet snow.

Walter picked her up. There was nothing he could say to make her feel better, so he held her close.

"What about insurance?" Cam asked.

Lizabeth was too numb to speak. She wanted to cry but she was in shock.

"I know Helen has a lease on the building, so you don't have that to worry about," he continued. "Do you have insurance on the contents?"

She nodded that she did.

They wanted to give her a pep talk about starting over, but now was not the time. There were a lot of her original designs that had been destroyed, and she would need some time before trying to motivate herself to recreate what she had lost. Uncle Ray came out of the crowd of firemen gathered on the street. He was Hannon's eyes and ears in this part of town and the fire chief had probably called him first.

"I'm so sorry, Lizabeth," he said, as he put his arm around her. "It is a bit of bad luck to be sure."

More than a bit, Lizabeth thought.

Walter pulled Uncle Ray aside. "Was it arson?" he asked. "I hope it's not the work of Sal Marconi."

"No worries there," Uncle Ray said. "The Italians don't operate that way. We'll find out the cause in a few days."

That was a great relief for Walter. There was no reason to stay, so he drove his siblings home. When they arrived, Mira and J.M. were waiting inside the door. They looked to Cam for answers, and he shook his head, letting them know that all was lost. Her mother put her arms around Lizabeth, and that was when she let go and finally allowed herself to cry.

It was dawn by the time she crawled into bed, and it seemed like hours passed before she fell asleep. She slept all day until nightfall, woke briefly, then fell asleep again. The weight of her loss was debilitating, and she could hardly get up to go to the bathroom. Her mother came into the room as she was falling asleep again.

"Are you awake?"

"Barely," she said, not wanting to be bothered.

"Erma and the girls of the Designers' Club came by to say how sorry they are that you lost your business. And your grandparents and Cory came by to check on you."

She was so tired and depressed that she did not respond. Her mother closed the door, and Lizabeth fell back into a fitful sleep. Eileen left her alone and came and went as quietly as possible. This went on for another two days until her mother had had enough. She came into the room and pulled up the blinds.

"Get up, Lizabeth!" she said.

"I'm too tired. Let me sleep," Lizabeth begged.

"This isn't a request. It's an order. You are going to get out of this house and help me on my rounds."

"I'm too exhausted," she pleaded.

"No. You are depressed, and you need something to eat." Mira pulled the covers off the bed. "Now get dressed and come downstairs."

Lizabeth knew there was no point in arguing. Her mother had an iron will that tolerated no resistance. She tried to move, but it felt like a heavy hand was holding her in the bed. With great effort, she sat up and tried to move her legs around to the floor. They felt heavy and lifeless.

"You will start feeling better if you get on your feet and get the blood flowing," her mother said.

Why get up when there was nothing to look forward to, she wondered. She dressed slowly and went downstairs, thankful there was no one else in the house because she was not up for conversation. Her mother put eggs, bacon, and toast in front of her, along with a hot, steamy cup of coffee. The coffee tasted wonderful, and she slowly began to eat.

After breakfast, she rose from her chair. "Now can I go back to bed?" she asked.

"Your bed is made up. I want you to dress warmly and come downstairs in ten minutes."

"But—"

"No buts about it."

She did as she was told and met her mother at the front door. She handed Lizabeth a Bible and another book, *Science and Health with Key to the Scriptures*.

"Where are we going?" Lizabeth asked.

"To see a family on Wornall Road—a widow with a daughter about your age." She handed Lizabeth the car keys.

It was freezing outside, and Lizabeth pined for the warmth of her bed. Her mother remained silent on the drive, and Lizabeth knew that she was going over her plan for the patient. Several years ago, Mira met the requirements to become a Christian Science practitioner. She had been instrumental in three successful healings and attended the classes given by the church. The religion's belief was not focused on providing a cure as much as showing the afflicted the path through Jesus Christ that resulted in spiritual healing.

Mira and Lizabeth arrived at a brown, California bungalow with an enclosed porch and a brick chimney. It was a newer home that looked comfortable and cozy. Lizabeth parked on the street. They went up and knocked on the door.

A woman with blonde hair tied in a bun opened the door. She was neatly dressed in a white blouse and gray skirt; a gray broach highlighted her neckline. Lizabeth guessed that she was about 45 years old. "Come in, Mrs. Braden. It is good to see you again."

"Thank you. This is my daughter, Lizabeth. Lizabeth, meet Mrs. Buckley."

Lizabeth shook hands with her. "You have a lovely home," Lizabeth said.

"Thank you. Would you like some coffee or tea?"

"It is kind of you to offer, but no, thank you," Mira said.

Lizabeth would have loved the warmth of some tea, but she did not want to interfere with her mother's routine.

"Is Margie ready to see me?"

"Yes. Come this way." They followed her past Victorian furniture, adorned with floral-patterned cushions that were obviously family heirlooms. Lizabeth guessed the furniture had been passed through several generations who were reluctant to give it up. Mrs. Buckley knocked on a bedroom door and entered before getting a response.

"Mrs. Braden is here, Margie." Mrs. Buckley led the guests into the bedroom, and then quietly slipped out and closed the door.

Margie sat in a chair beside her bed. She had brown hair that was shoulder length and big blue eyes. Lizabeth could see a brace on one of her legs, almost certainly the result of a bout with polio that had afflicted so many. There were rolls of yarn on the bed and several crochet hooks of various sizes.

"Hi, Mrs. Braden," Margie said, with a welcoming smile.

"This is my daughter, Lizabeth."

Lizabeth walked over to Margie and clasped her hand. It was warm to the touch, and she squeezed it gently.

"I see that you crochet," Lizabeth said.

"Yes. Mother says that it keeps me busy and out of trouble."

"How old are you, Margie?"

"Eighteen. I just graduated from high school."

"Central?"

"Yes."

Lizabeth almost asked what her future plans were, but, with the brace, thought better of it.

"I've told your mother that I'm a big fan of yours," Margie said. "The newspaper story on the fashion show was amazing. I am so sorry about the fire."

"Thank you, Margie."

"How have you been feeling, Margie?" Mira asked.

"Okay. Sometimes I feel trapped by the cold weather and miss sitting on the sunporch, but I guess that happens to everyone."

"Indeed, it does," Mira said. "I miss my flowers and working in the yard. Have you been working on keeping a positive attitude through prayer?"

"I do try, but sometimes it's hard when I'm struggling with my leg brace."

"I'm sure it is," Mira said. "Just remember that God is with you and understands what you are going through."

"I wonder if my leg will ever heal," Margie said.

"I don't know," Mira replied. "We will continue searching for a path to spiritual enlightenment that allows God to heal you."

"Your visits do help," Margie said. "They make me feel better."

"When you get depressed, I want you to remember that the holy spirit is within you and God's love will never let you down."

"I often wonder why God let this happen to me in the first place," Margie said.

"I wish I could answer that, Margie. Just remember that the Lord is with you in your struggles, and I will help you learn to feel his power."

Lizabeth knew that her mother's power lay in friendship and persuasion rather than in physical healing. It was more about the whole person than any specific ailment; letting the patients know they were not alone and had a friend they could count on.

Mira read several passages from the Bible that she tied in with guidance from the *Key to the Scriptures*. It had been a long time since Lizabeth had called on a patient with her mother, and it had made her feel better. Mira finished the last prayer and Lizabeth was free to speak.

"Margie, do you have any samples of your work?" she asked.

"Of course." Margie grabbed a crutch from the corner and rose to her feet. She walked slowly, dragging her brace, and Lizabeth followed.

"I specialize in sweaters and shawls," Margie said. She took a sweater from the closet and showed it to Lizabeth.

"That is exquisite," Lizabeth said.

"Thank you. That means a lot coming from Kansas City's most famous designer."

"I'm certainly not that, but thank you, Margie. When I get back in business, would you let me include your work in some of my designs?"

Margie brightened and then just as quickly became somber and bit her lower lip. "I wouldn't want you to do that because . . . you know."

"I guarantee you, Margie, if your work wasn't first rate, I would not have brought it up."

Margie's excitement returned. "Then, yes, that would be wonderful. I've always dreamed of doing something in the fashion world."

"Okay. I will be in touch, and we will work out the details."

Mrs. Buckley came into the room to escort them out.

"Mother! Miss Braden is going to include my work in some of her designs," Margie said, bursting with enthusiasm. Mrs. Buckley looked questioningly at Lizabeth.

"Your daughter has real talent," Lizabeth said. "I would be honored to have her join Liz Braden's Original Designs."

"That would be wonderful. Thank you both for helping Margie."

Mira drove them home. Lizabeth wiped tears from her eyes with a lace handkerchief. She looked at her mother. "You didn't set that session up for Margie; you set it up for me. I've never felt so ashamed in my life. I've been pouting in bed like a two-year-old, so you showed me a young lady with real problems. I'm just sorry you didn't do it sooner."

"You needed some time to grieve."

"I should have been a rock for my family and the employees, instead of falling apart."

"Recognizing where you failed will make you stronger."

"It turns out that I continue to need you as much as I ever did," Lizabeth said. She leaned over and kissed Mira on the cheek. "Thank you, Mother."

She had been physically debilitated by the fire, but that hadn't stopped her mind from spinning with possibilities for the future. Perhaps the fire had been a blessing, in that it allowed her to explore a new path going forward. It would be risky and put everything on the line, but she had proved to herself that with a firm resolve and hard work, nothing was impossible.

There would be no waiting months to get back in business. The time to act was now and she could hardly wait to get started. The comment from Margie about her being Kansas City's most famous designer had given her the boost she needed. It might not be true, but she was going to do everything in her power to make it so.

∽

A week after the fire, Lizabeth called a meeting of the Designers' Club at her home. The girls were more than curious about the future of the business.

"I want to apologize to you for not being available when you came by to offer your support. I was so devastated by the fire that I couldn't think clearly."

"That was perfectly understandable," Erma said. "Everything you worked for went up in flames."

"That seemed to be true, but now I'm not so sure."

"What do you mean?" Jennie asked.

"I'm still formulating my plans, but I can tell you that we are going ahead with our spring fashion designs. Luckily, I had most of the drawings in my sewing room here at the house. And we have enough insurance money to pay your salaries for the next three months, and also money for new sewing machines. Here is a voucher that you can use to pick up your machines from the Singer downtown store." Lizabeth passed them around.

"We didn't think you would be down for long," Jennie said.

"Thank you for your confidence in me."

"It's not going to be easy," Erma said. "John Taylor's and Emery, Bird, Thayer had some smoke damage, but they will be back in business in thirty days. Harzfeld's and Kline's had no damage at all. They can continue to do business, while we have to start over."

"It won't be any different than when we first started," Lizabeth said. "We just have to find a way to keep our brand in front of the public."

"And how will we do that?" Erma asked.

"That is the plan I'm working on. You will have to be patient until I figure it out. Meanwhile, I need you to make as much inventory as possible in a short period of time. You can work at home until we get back in business."

The meeting of the Designers' Club adjourned with a spirit of hope for the future. They were excited that Lizabeth had recovered from the devastating loss, and they were confident that Liz Braden's Original Designs would come back stronger than ever.

CHAPTER TEN

THE DAY AFTER THE FIRE, Terri had stopped by the Braden house to offer her support. Walter had apologized for abandoning her on New Year's Eve. She had accepted his apology, but Walter noticed a coolness in her demeanor that hadn't been there before. He invited her to help him look for a warehouse for Lizabeth, and they were talking as Walter drove downtown.

"What is your sister up to now?" Terri asked.

"Hard to tell, knowing Lizabeth," Walter answered. "I think she needs some space to build her inventory until the store reopens."

"The fire was heartbreaking for her. How is she doing?"

"She was depressed for a couple of days, but you can't keep Lizabeth down for long. She has plenty of determination."

"Good for her. You two have a special relationship. She relies on you a lot."

"I guess so. Cam and Eileen have always been the stars in the family, so that gave us common ground. And we found out that living in the shadow of our siblings is not a bad place to be. The expectations and the demands are less. Although lately, Lizabeth has outshined us all."

"Like it or not, you are in a competitive family. You need to realize that life is not a contest."

"Tell that to our parents. They are supportive, but they let us know when we are not meeting the mark." Walter looked over at her. "I'm not meeting my mark with you, am I?"

She met his gaze. "This is too early in the relationship for me to start setting conditions."

"I'm not so sure. Like my parents, you have certain expectations, and I can tell that I'm not meeting them."

"How so?"

"They blow in on a cool breeze from the north."

"You are more perceptive than I've been giving you credit for."

"Was it because I messed up on New Year's Eve?"

"Look, Walter. The quickest way to end this relationship is for us to start judging each other. If you don't want to recognize your problem, there is nothing I can do that will help. You will think that I am trying to change your lifestyle, and that will lead to resentment. And I certainly don't want to play the role of the nagging girlfriend."

"But you do think that my drinking is a problem."

"You seem to be missing the regulator that most people have. Once you start drinking, you can't stop."

"I have good intentions, but then everything seems to slip away. I can't quit drinking, because it helps me relax. It is part of who I am."

"There is nothing wrong with drinking. The problem is the excess. You need to get it under control, because Lizabeth is worried about you."

"Did she say something?"

"Of course not. I can tell by her demeanor when she sees you drinking too much. She thinks the world of you, and I'm sure she is concerned about your health."

"I appreciate both of your concerns, and I will try to do better."

"That is all we can ask."

He pulled the car over to the curb and leaned over and kissed her. "Now you can warm up that cold wind from the north."

She smiled. "I will do that."

⁓

Walter found a vacant warehouse at 18th and Baltimore, a couple of blocks from Boss Tom's office. It was a one-story building, with adequate heating and room for expansion. It was owned by a member of the Hannon organization, so Walter negotiated a fair monthly rent.

When Lizabeth saw it, she was delighted and thought the building was perfect for her needs. Walter was happy for her and glad that she was back to her old optimistic self. He hoped that her new plan worked, because back-to-back blows might be hard for her to take.

Uncle Ray was waiting for Walter when he arrived at work on Monday. "Boss Tom wants to see you."

"What about?"

"You'll have to hear it from him."

Walter followed his uncle up the stairs, wondering if his New Year's Eve escapade had gotten back to Boss Tom. Like his brother, the big Irishman was a teetotaler and frowned on excessive consumption of alcohol. It mattered not that he owned saloons. He stood behind any man who would take the pledge to give up drinking.

Boss Tom motioned for them to take a seat, and they sat. He lit a cigar, inhaled, and blew the smoke to the side of the room.

"You have been doing a great job in your downtown district, Walter. The business owners have nothing but good things to say about you."

"That is nice to hear," Walter said, wondering what this was all about.

"I have no doubt that you can handle some additional responsibility. As you know, this is an election year. I'm going to need your help."

Walter breathed a sigh of relief that it wasn't about his drinking. However, he knew nothing about politics.

"We are running against a reformer from the west side who has the support of the *Kansas City Star*. Every vote will be critical in this election."

"You have the support of my district," Walter said.

"And I appreciate it. My understanding is that you have a special relationship with the Negro community. You can venture where a lot of white men are afraid to go."

"I don't know about that. I do take my business there and try to get along with everyone."

"You do more than that. Over the years, you have built up some trust with the Negro leaders on the east side. I need you to take your goodwill and my capital and find out how we can help that district."

Walter knew this was about buying votes. The boss read his expression.

"Walter, our organization was built on tit for tat. We help our friends, and they help us. There is nothing crooked about that. We have neglected that district for quite some time, because the people don't have adequate representation. We are prepared to put some community activists on the payroll and also identify some of the public needs, such as better schools and parks."

"What the people in that district need are jobs," Walter said.

"Then you need to identify those areas where we can put them to work. You will control the money that goes into the district, so start some public works projects that will help the unemployed. There will be some pushback from the white community about awarding jobs, but let me worry about that."

"This is a big step and a huge responsibility," Walter said. "I don't have the experience to bid out construction jobs."

"You identify the needs, and we will take care of the nuts and bolts. We will also raise your salary twenty dollars a week and give Jimmy ten."

"How much money are we talking about for these projects?" Walter asked.

"You spend until I tell you to stop," Boss Tom replied.

Walter and Jimmy drove to Luther's barbershop, where Luther had set up an afternoon meeting with community leaders.

"I hope you don't think this is going to be easy," Jimmy said. "Any way you cut it, this is still a southern city. There is not a lot of love lost between Negroes and whites."

"I know. This will be about trust."

"Good luck on that one."

When they arrived, they saw that Luther had brought in some chairs and made a place for Walter to stand and speak. Prince was shining a man's shoes at the shoeshine stand. Luther introduced Walter and Jimmy to two ministers, Reverend Walker and Reverend Washington, and three community leaders named Jackson, Mason, and Thomas.

"What's this all about, Walter?" Luther asked.

"First, thank you all for coming. Jimmy and I are here representing the Hannon organization."

"Hold on to your wallets," Luther said, and everyone laughed, including Walter.

"I'm going to give it to you straight," Walter said. "We need your help in the next election."

"Now there is something new," Reverend Washington said derisively. "The white man wanting something from us. You do the taking and we do the giving." There was a murmur of agreement from the men.

"I know what you are thinking, but this time we intend to earn your support."

"And how are you going to do that?" Thomas asked.

"You decide the needs of your community, and we will fund the projects."

"That will last until after the election. Then we will be stuck with no way to complete what you started."

"I know that has happened in the past, but not this time. We will sign contracts to that effect."

"Is Boss Tom going to put his name on the contracts?" Mason asked.

"He will, indeed."

"Here's what happens on these do-gooder projects," Luther said. "White workers get the jobs; white leaders get the credit for helping the poor, destitute Negro. We get the shaft until the next election rolls around."

"These projects will be given to Negro construction firms and will only have Negro workers," Walter said.

"We are not questioning your good intentions, Walter," Luther replied. "But what happens when 'the man' shows up at a construction site and fires all the Negro workers and replaces them with whites."

"I am 'the man,'" Walter said. "I will handle all problems in that regard and I answer to Boss Hannon."

"For real?" Luther asked.

"For real," Walter confirmed.

"How much money are we talking about, Walter?" Jackson asked.

"I would guess about a hundred thousand."

There was stunned silence in the room.

"That kind of money in a depression attracts the wrong type of people," Reverend Walker said.

"We will put Luther on the payroll. He knows the community and will recommend construction firms we can trust."

"I'll be glad to help out the community," Luther said. "But I need to keep barbering to make a living."

"Not a problem. You can barber and work for us. Now, what is the first project going to be, gentlemen? We have some serious money to spend."

"We need a couple of new grade schools," Reverend Washington said. "How about we test your commitment there?"

"I'll get the projects started," Walter said. "Thank you all very much, and I look forward to our new partnership." He and Jimmy shook hands all around.

They waited until the men had left to talk to Luther. "I need you to recommend a good accountant who serves the Negro community."

"That would be my accountant. Her name is Delores Johnson. She is honest, God fearing, and a whiz with numbers."

"Can you set up a meeting?"

"I could, but her office is at the end of the block."

"It would be better if you made the introduction."

Luther led them down the street to a small office on the corner. In blue lettering, the window read: Delores Johnson, Accountant. Inside, there was a place for consultation with two, worn, green chairs and a small table with some magazines.

"Delores, you got a minute?" Luther called.

Delores came out from behind a glass partition. She appeared to be in her early forties, and she was black as night. Her hair was neatly trimmed, and her matching gray blouse and skirt were immaculate.

"Delores, this is Walter Braden and Jimmy Dolan."

"Nice to meet you," Delores said. "How can I help you?"

Walter explained about the work they were going to do in the Negro community. "Luther will be our coordinator, but we need someone to handle the money and pay the bills."

"How much money are we talking about?"

"It could run two to three thousand a week."

Her eyes widened in surprise. "You need a big accounting firm for that kind of money."

"What I need is someone I can trust. This is Boss Hannon's money, and there are people downtown who don't want it spent in the Negro community. I need you to account for every dollar and verify every check that goes out."

"I can do that easy enough, but I don't want any trouble."

"I'll take care of the trouble. You take care of the money. How much will your weekly charges be for accounting services?"

"I will have to see how much work there is, but I would guess about twenty-five dollars a week."

"Make it fifty, and we'll kick in a bonus if things go well."

"Fifty dollars! Don't you know that we are in a depression?"

"Do we have a deal?"

Delores stuck out her hand, and Walter shook it. "We have a deal," she said.

Walter, Luther, and Jimmy walked back to the barbershop.

"Did you ever get this kid to talk?" Walter asked, looking at Prince.

"Nope."

"How old is he now?"

"Must be about fifteen or so."

"How much does he make?"

"Not more than a dollar on a good day."

Walter looked at Prince. "Are you ready to put your shoeshine kit away for good?"

Prince just looked at him.

"You are going to be my second hire, doing some maintenance and providing security for Luther, the accounting office, and the project sites where we will be working. Your salary will be five dollars a day, and you will be paid every Friday by Delores Johnson."

For a moment there was a glimmer of gratitude in Prince's eyes.

"Five dollars a day!" Luther said. "I'll quit barbering for that."

"I'll be sure he earns it. Delores will have his assignments every Monday. Thanks for setting up the meeting, Luther."

As he left the barbershop, Walter felt good about this new turn of events. It gave him a chance to do something worthwhile for the city and to help the Negro community. Perhaps it would improve the race relations that were badly strained. Negroes had a hard time getting jobs and that was magnified in the Depression where jobs were scarce and would always go to whites, regardless of qualifications.

Walter vowed to do all he could to right some of the wrongs inflicted by segregation and the Depression. However, he wasn't kidding himself. There would be trouble over this from men who thought Negroes were second-class citizens and not worthy of jobs that should go to white men. It was hard to overcome ignorance in the best of times, much less in an economic crisis. He had hired Prince to get him started in a good job and because he had an idea that it might get him back to functioning in society.

"I guess you've figured out that we're in a bad place," Jimmy said. "The boss has put us right in the middle of a jobs war that could easily turn into a race war."

"I'm afraid you're right. We will have to be prepared for anything."

On the way home, he stopped at Terri's house in Hyde Park. Terri came to the door. "Walter, I wasn't expecting you."

"I'm sorry. I should have called. I wonder if I could speak to your mother."

Terri looked at him curiously. "Of course. Come in." She motioned for Walter to enter the house, and they went into the parlor.

"Walter, what a pleasant surprise," Charlene greeted him. "What can I do for you?"

"This is a long shot, Charlene, but I'm going to take it," Walter said. "Because you are a teacher, I wonder if you would take on a project for me. It concerns a young Negro boy who experienced some kind of trauma that won't allow him to speak. He appears to be a bright, young man, but he has his own set of rules that he lives by." Walter explained about the tip money and Prince paying for his meals. "He has had some violent episodes in his past when anyone tried to bully him."

"I don't think Mother should be around anyone who is prone to violence," Terri said.

"If I thought he would harm your mother, I wouldn't be here.

I've hired the boy as part of my security detail for projects in the Negro community. Before your mother agrees to help him, I will bring him here for an evaluation."

"There is no need for that. If you have confidence in him, Walter, that's enough for me. I've been wondering what I would do with myself for the next few months. It will be a blessing to be able to contribute again. Bring him by, so we can meet, then we can discuss how much time I will need to help him get better."

"Thank you, Charlene."

CHAPTER ELEVEN

March 1936

ARMED WITH HER SUCCESS AS a designer, Lizabeth had considered making another appointment with the buyer at Harzfeld's, but now that she had made a name for herself and was the owner and president of Liz Braden's Original Designs, she decided to go right to the top and see Mr. Harzfeld. She called and made an appointment for the following Tuesday. She would dress the models in her best spring designs and take them along to make the presentation.

It was important for her to make a good impression, but she was not about to go begging. She saw herself as equal to anyone in the fashion industry, and she would conduct herself with confidence, knowing that her fashions were popular with the public.

On Tuesday, she walked into Harzfeld's, trailed by her models, and went directly to Mr. Harzfeld's office, where she announced herself to his secretary.

"He will be with you in a moment, Miss Braden," the secretary said pleasantly.

Lizabeth was pleased, remembering how dismissive she had been treated on her first visit with Miss Wilson, the buyer. She was even more pleased when Mr. Harzfeld came out and personally ushered her into his office. He was 68, with white hair, and a receding hairline. He had a rotund face, with expressive brown eyes, and was smartly dressed in a double-breasted suit, starched white shirt, and a blue tie.

"It is good to meet you, Miss Braden. I was terribly upset about the fire. We are a community first and competitors second, and we have to support each other."

Lizabeth could tell that he was sincere, and it gave her the opening that she needed.

"Thank you for being so considerate, Mr. Harzfeld. It was a tragedy that might end up being a blessing, and that is the reason I'm here."

He looked at her questioningly.

"The reason I went into the retail clothing business was because none of the department stores would take a chance on my original designs. The consensus was that women would only want to buy clothing from big name designers. By any measure, I have proven them wrong. I have a strong customer base, and my sales have far surpassed my expectations."

"You are to be congratulated. This is a competitive business, and you have carved quite a niche for your designer clothing."

"We were successful, because there is an untapped market for stylish designer dresses at a reasonable price. The average housewife can't afford a dress created in New York or Paris, but she can afford a designer dress made in Kansas City."

"I concede that you have proven that, Miss Braden, so what is your point?"

"I would like for Harzfeld's to start selling Liz Braden's Original Designs. I would much rather be your supplier than your competitor, and I'm sure my designer clothing would increase your sales."

He looked at her, mulling over the possibilities.

She could tell he was intrigued, so she sprang into action, and brought in her first model. She was wearing a green, spring frock, made of broadcloth, suitable for home or play. Lizabeth proceeded to march each of her models past Mr. Harzfeld and gave a running commentary of each of her designs and why they would appeal to the Harzfeld's customer.

"If you stock my designer clothing, it will show that you care about the average housewife and the sophisticated customer, and it will open up a new market for your business."

She could tell that he was seriously considering her offer, so she gave him one last incentive.

"I think a lot of goodwill will come your way if we can strike a bargain. It won't be lost on the public that you are helping a hometown girl get back in business. I will give you an exclusive contract for the first sixty days, and I won't solicit any other department stores during that time. You will have a head start at making Harzfeld's the headquarters for Liz Braden's Original Designs."

He tapped his fingers on the desk as he pondered her offer, then rang his secretary. "Please have Miss Wilson come to my office."

Lizabeth was hopeful, but she kept her composure and did not want to appear overly excited. A few minutes later, Miss Wilson came into the office. She looked surprised to see Lizabeth, but she covered it with a smile and a handshake. "It is nice to see you again, Miss Braden."

"The pleasure is all mine," Lizabeth said, and meant it.

"Miss Wilson, we are going to be the first store in Kansas City to carry Liz Braden's Original Designs," Mr. Harzfeld said.

Lizabeth wanted to shout for joy, but she remained calm and professional.

"I want a full-page ad announcing our new partnership, and I want her designs displayed in a prominent place in your department."

"Yes, sir."

"And I want you to work closely with Miss Braden and use her input on how to promote her designer clothing."

This was more than Lizabeth could have hoped for. "Thank you, Mr. Harzfeld, and thank you for your faith in me. I promise to make our partnership profitable for you."

"I'm sure you will, Miss Braden. Thank you for considering my store for your designs."

Outside the store, Lizabeth unleashed her shout for joy, startling some shoppers on Petticoat Lane. She thanked each of her models for their help and promised more work for them in the months ahead. She could hardly wait to tell her family and the Designers' Club the good news.

Lizabeth greeted everyone as they arrived for Sunday dinner at the Bradens' home. She was about to burst with the news of her success at Harzfeld's, but she waited for the right moment to tell everyone. Terri, Eileen, and Walter separated themselves from the group and were whispering conspiratorially in the other room. She wondered what that was all about. Helen and Cam were there, and so were her grandparents, and Aunt Erma and Uncle Ray. Mira called everyone in to be seated, and the table was soon buzzing with conversation.

"How is your project on the east side coming along, Walter?" Uncle Ray asked.

"So far, so good. We are going over the bids for a couple of new grade schools."

"Since when did Hannon take an interest in the east side?" Cam asked.

"It's not out of the goodness of his heart," J.M. said. "He needs the votes."

"Indeed, he does," Uncle Ray said. "But he is not twisting any arms. He does good things for the Negro community, and he hopes they will vote for him. That's how politics works."

"In other words, the guy with the most money to spread around wins."

"That is usually the case," Ray acknowledged.

"How did Walter get involved?" J.M. asked Ray.

"He runs our most profitable district downtown, and he is respected in the Negro community."

"Are you going to run for mayor of the east side?" Cam teased.

"Why would you care? You're afraid to venture east of Main Street."

"Dodging gunfire is not my idea of a good time."

"That is an exaggeration," Walter said defensively.

"No, it's not. There is so much carnage on the east side that the newspapers refuse to report it."

"They are a lot like you. They don't care what happens to poor people."

"You had better be careful, Walter," J.M. warned. "The Negro community is always on the edge of exploding. The Depression and lack of jobs makes it even more dangerous."

Terri tapped a spoon on her glass, to get everyone's attention and to rescue Walter.

"Excuse me, but Eileen has an important announcement to make," she said.

Lizabeth wondered if Eileen had found out about her new alliance from someone at Harzfeld's.

Eileen stood up. "One of the producers who saw my performance in *The Boyfriend* has invited me to Hollywood for a screen test," she said excitedly. "He contacted Terri two days ago, and she gave me the news."

Lizabeth was stunned for a moment, trying to absorb the unexpected announcement.

"What wonderful news!" she said joyfully, getting up from her chair and hugging her sister, as everyone offered their congratulations. Lizabeth was not about to usurp her sister's news, so she would wait for another time for her own big announcement.

Eileen was beaming with pleasure from the responses, but she cast a wary eye at her father, sitting in silence at the end of the table.

"How will you get to California?" he asked.

"She will take the train," Terri said. "The studio is picking up all expenses."

"And what about a chaperone?"

"She's a grown-up girl, J.M.," Uncle Ray said.

"She's an impressionable young girl, and she is not going to Hollywood on her own."

Eileen was pleased that he hadn't said no to the trip. She, Terri, and Walter had prepared for this eventuality.

"Terri has to spend several weeks at Universal's home office in Hollywood, so she has agreed to accompany me," Eileen said.

"We will room together, and I know the inner workings of the studios," Terri said. "She won't have much time on her own." Terri knew that some of J.M.'s concerns were justified. Many would-be starlets ended up on casting couches in return for a chance at stardom.

"What about your job?" J.M. continued. "You don't want to lose it chasing a dream."

"Harzfeld's has agreed to give me a leave of absence."

146

"What happens when Terri comes home?" J.M. asked.

"The chances are that I will leave with her," Eileen said. "I just want to see firsthand what Hollywood is all about. I'll be back at the Red Barn Players before you know it." She hoped not, but she had to convince her father otherwise.

"When will you leave?" Lizabeth asked.

"March fifteenth."

"Oh, my," Lizabeth said. "That is much too soon. What will I do without my big sister?"

"You'll be fine. I'll probably be back before you open the store."

"I want you to have your chance at acting in films, but I will miss you terribly."

"I'll write every day and let you know how I'm doing and when I'm coming home."

"Please keep in mind that it is only a test," Terri said. "Ninety-nine times out of a hundred these screen tests don't work out." In reality, Terri felt that given the right break, Eileen had a good chance at making it in the movies. She was made for the camera and her acting skills were first rate. But she wanted to keep the family's expectations low, so there wasn't a lot of pressure on Eileen.

"If you meet Clark Gable, please give him my phone number," Erma said, breaking the tension and making everyone laugh.

"Your father and I support you," Mira said. "But we are concerned about you taking time from your job for something as frivolous as acting, especially during these hard times."

"There is a lot of money to be made in acting," Terri said, coming to Eileen's defense. "There are millions of people going to the movies every week for entertainment and to forget their troubles. Record attendance is being set at box offices all over the country."

"Watching movies gives people a chance to laugh and let off steam," Walter said. "They are cheaper than seeing a psychiatrist."

"And movies set the trend for fashion," Lizabeth said, in support of her sister. "Women are more influenced by what an actress is wearing, than what is coming out of New York or Paris."

"We need a movie star in the family," Pop said. "Eileen, you have the support of your grandparents."

"Amen to that," Uncle Ray said.

"Thank you all so much," Eileen replied gratefully.

"I can see that your mother and I are outnumbered," J.M. said. "We reluctantly give our approval, because we don't want to stand in the way of your happiness. But be advised, that we will not be disappointed if you fail and return home."

Her father could make that statement, but she knew very well that her parents would be disappointed, because they expected nothing less than success from their children. "Thank you both very much for your consent," Eileen said, ready to prove to her parents she would be successful.

"I will design some special dresses for you for the screen test," Lizabeth said.

"That would be wonderful. You can show those Hollywood designers a thing or two."

"It is all so very exciting," Helen said. "I wish you nothing but the best." Cam even grunted his approval.

"Is this strictly business, Terri, or will you shop your documentary about Black Sunday to the studios?" Helen asked.

"I'm going to see what kind of response I get. My goal is to learn all I can about producing documentaries, so that I can produce them myself."

"Self-reliance is the key in this economy," Erma said. "Lizabeth is proof of that. She is now the role model for a lot of women trying to make it in their own businesses."

The compliment made Lizabeth blush. "Thank you, Aunt Erma."

"She certainly is motivation for me," Eileen said. "When the offer came from Terri, I thought I had better take it, if I'm going to keep up with my baby sister."

"I remember you saying that we were not in a contest," Lizabeth said.

"No, we are not. But I do look to you for inspiration."

"The feeling is mutual," Lizabeth said.

When the dinner party ended, Lizabeth said good night to everyone. Eileen's exciting news had set the tone and it had been a joyful evening. When Eileen had gone to bed, Lizabeth went into her parent's bedroom. J.M. was reading in bed, and Mira was at her dressing table. Lizabeth remembered when she was younger, how safe it felt to plop down between her parents in the big double bed, with soft, colorful comforters and an antique headboard. She liked tugging at her pigtails while reading a book, and, more often than not, she would fall asleep and J.M. would carry her to her own bed.

Sadly, the double bed had faded with her childhood and two twin beds now symbolized her parent's frosty relationship. She wished there was something she could do to help but knew better than to try. Her parent's marital problems were too personal to ever be bridged with their children.

"Hello, Lizabeth," J.M. said, putting down his book.

Mira turned around. "Hello, dear. It was a nice party."

"And wasn't Eileen's news exciting?"

"Yes, it was. Your father and I hope that she knows what she is getting into."

"I'm sure she does. Terri will take good care of her."

"I have some good news of my own, and I wanted you to be the first to know."

Mira stopped brushing her hair. "What is it, dear?"

"I'm not going to reopen the store. I met with Mr. Harzfeld yesterday, and he has agreed to carry my original designs. After a few months, I plan to offer the line to all the stores in the city."

Mira was surprised but tried not to show it. "That is exciting news; but I thought that you loved your store."

"I did, but I have to stick to my goal of becoming a nationally known designer. I only went into retail out of necessity."

"Do you have somewhere to set up shop?" J.M. asked.

""Yes, Father. Walter has found a warehouse downtown on Baltimore Avenue."

"What about financing?"

"The insurance money will keep us going, and when we start selling the garments, we'll be fine. Advertising will be an important part of the business, so I hope you will continue to help me."

"Of course, I will. What kind of shape is the warehouse in?"

"It's bare bones but has plenty of space for the girls to sew and Cory is working on the existing office space."

"You and Eileen are full of surprises," J.M. said. "This has been quite an evening."

"A lot to take in," Mira agreed. "We wish you every success, Lizabeth. But we hope you and your sister are not taking on more than you can handle."

"We'll be fine, Mother."

"We are proud of you both, but I must admit that we miss those two little girls who used to sneak into our bed at night."

Lizabeth went over and put her arms around her mother. "I miss them too. We will always be here for you and Father, no matter what."

Mira hugged her tightly. "I know you will, dear. Forgive me for getting nostalgic. Time and life are moving much too fast for me."

"I understand, and I'll try not to be too busy for my family." Lizabeth pulled away and gave her mother a good night kiss, and then did the same with J.M.

"Why don't we wait a few days before telling the others about my new venture?" Lizabeth suggested. "Eileen deserves the spotlight, while she is preparing to leave for California."

"That is considerate of you," Mira said.

"I don't want her to go," Lizabeth replied.

"We always imagined that we would lose our sons to ambition and keep our daughters, but the reverse has happened. We are coping by taking it a day at a time and supporting you and Eileen as best we can."

"Your support means everything to us," Lizabeth said. "Sleep well and I will see you in the morning." She closed the bedroom door and went across the hall to her room.

Mid-March came much too quickly for Lizabeth, and before she knew it, she was gathered with friends, family, and actors from the Red Barn Players in the North Waiting Room at Union Station. They were there to say goodbye to Terri and Eileen, as they prepared to catch a train to Los Angeles.

Walter took Terri aside.

"Promise me that you will come back."

"Of course. Why would I not?"

"Because you are a beautiful woman, and there will be a lot of offers coming your way."

"I've dealt with the Hollywood crowd. There is not much they can offer that I haven't heard before."

"I'm glad to hear it. Eileen will need your help in determining what is real, and what is Hollywood."

"I will help with that distinction and try to keep her grounded."

"I will miss you," Walter said.

"Me too."

He kissed her, and they went to join the others.

Eileen was as excited as a young woman could be. The porters had taken their bags down to the train waiting beneath the station. Eileen and Terri said goodbye to everyone.

"Good luck on your road to stardom!" her friend David yelled above the noise of the crowd. He ran up and kissed her on the cheek.

Eileen held it together until she got to Lizabeth. "I'm going to miss you, little sister," she said tearfully as she hugged her.

Lizabeth started to sob. Who would she talk to when she was in bed looking out at the starry night? "I'll miss you terribly, but it will help knowing you will be doing what you love. And don't worry about anything here. I'll watch out for Mother and Father and keep you posted on all the family matters."

"I know you will. And good luck with your store."

Lizabeth would write to her in a few days about the new business venture. Over the loudspeaker, their train was called. Eileen and Terri waved goodbye one last time and headed down the stairs, leaving Lizabeth with a knot in her stomach from the loneliness she would have to endure. Fashion design had always been her antidote to despair, so she would dedicate herself to her work.

Later that week, she met with the Designers' Club at her home in Brookside. She had also included Margie in the meeting. She had served everyone tea and they were looking at her expectantly, wondering about their jobs, and the fate of the business.

"Lizabeth, we are about to burst with curiosity, so please tell us what this is about," Erma said.

"I will be glad to. Thank you all for your patience." She went over her meeting at Harzfeld's and what it meant for the company.

"I'm surprised, to say the least," Erma said. "We were doing so well with the store."

"I'm disappointed also, but it would take us a long time to get the store up and running again, and it was the only outlet for our designer clothing. If we work at the wholesale level, and get established with Harzfeld's, we can sell to every store in the city and beyond."

"Where will we work?" Jennie asked.

"Walter found a building downtown that will be perfect for our needs. Cory is doing a quick remodel, and we can move in next week."

"What is your plan?" Jennie asked.

"Erma will be in charge of the manufacturing end of the business. I will continue to focus on design, and you and I will be our sales force. I gave Harzfeld's a sixty-day exclusive contract, but after that, we can sell to every department store in the city. We want our clothing in as many stores as possible for the spring and summer seasons."

"What an exciting turn of events," Jennie said. "Today Kansas City, and tomorrow the world. The possibilities are endless."

"Exactly," Lizabeth said. "And it is up to each of us to make it happen." She had to sound enthusiastic, although she was far from sure of herself. With this different approach, she needed something special to insulate her from downturns in the fashion industry and give her time to establish her brand. It would have to be a product that would separate her from other designers; something that sold all year round, rather than seasonal, so she could survive if there was another disaster. But at the moment, she didn't have a clue as to what that special something might be.

∽

It was April by the time Walter bid out the two grade school projects to Negro construction firms. Over the next two weeks, foundations were laid, and the walls went up. He and Jimmy visited the construction sites daily to be sure everything was going okay.

They were at one of the sites, when a truck full of white workers showed up. Their leader was a big, muscular man with a thick neck and dark brown hair, which matched his beard. His nose was flat, like that of a brawler, and several of his teeth were chipped. Some of his men tried to take shovels from the Negro workers, but they resisted.

Walter confronted the man. "What's going on?"

"We are here to take over this project," the man said.

"Where did you ever get an idea like that?" Walter asked.

"It's just the way things are. Whites get first pick on any construction jobs."

"That might be true in the white community, but this is a Negro construction site."

"There ain't no such thing in this city."

"There is now, so I suggest that you and your boys move along, so my men can get back to work."

"You got that backward. It's my men and your boys. We are taking these jobs."

The Negro workers were intently watching the confrontation, wondering how it would play out. Walter knew that he was in a bad spot. If things got violent, these Negroes would be blamed for attacking the white men, and there would be jail time and repercussions for the Negro community. Kansas City justice always fell in favor of the white man. It wasn't fair, but it reflected how life was in the city. He wondered what he would do next, as the big man took a shovel away from a Negro worker.

"Take the shovels away from these niggers," he said to his men. It was then that Jimmy stepped forward and, without warning, hit the man in the jaw with a solid right cross that spun the man around and knocked him back into the dirt. The big man shook his head and felt his jaw.

"You hit me, you blond-headed bastard!"

"Yea. And I'm about to do it again."

The man jumped to his feet and came after Jimmy. But Jimmy was fast on his feet and stayed out of his range. He knew if the bruiser got in a solid punch, it would be over. He gave the man a couple of left jabs that bloodied his nose, and then danced out of range. The man was out of shape, and Jimmy was trim and well-toned from prize fighting. They sparred around the construction site, with each man looking for an advantage. Jimmy wanted to keep the man moving, so he would wear down and drop his guard. The man was getting more winded by the minute, so Jimmy waited for the right moment, and then charged in with a flurry of punches that sent the man to the ground, where he fought to catch his breath.

"That's enough," Walter stepped in and stopped the fight. "Now you take these men and get out of here," he ordered. "If you want to make more out of this, you can take it up with Boss Hannon. These men work for him."

"You haven't seen the last of us," the man said, although he did not try to resume the fight. He rose to his feet and motioned for his men to get in the truck.

Walter and Jimmy watched as they drove away.

"Do you think they will come back?" Jimmy asked.

"Maybe. They are looking for trouble. I'm glad you stepped in. I was running out of options."

"Sometimes a punch to the jaw is the only answer."

"You saved the day, so tonight the beers are on me. Let's stop by Luther's barbershop and talk things over."

When they arrived, Prince was there painting a wall, in accordance with his maintenance duties.

"You're getting your money's worth, Walter," Luther said. "That boy never stops working."

"I might have to pull him away to keep an eye on our job sites."

They told Luther what had transpired at the construction site, and he was plenty worried.

"I was afraid this might happen," he said. "When men are desperate for jobs, the fairness of it don't matter. They are going to take what they want."

"Jimmy beat up the ring leader and scared them off," Walter said.

"Not for long. When something like this happens, they always strike back to keep us down. I predict that we will get a visit from the men in white sheets."

"The Ku Klux Klan?" Walter asked in surprise.

"Yes. The burning crosses and the white robes have quite an effect on Negro workers. They stay home out of fear and to protect their families. That gives the white workers time to take over the job sites."

"What can we do?" Walter asked.

"That is the question Boss Hannon expects you to answer."

"Lucky me," Walter said derisively.

"I can tell you this, Walter. The men in this community have had enough. They are not going to give up their jobs without a fight. The Depression has put them in a bad place, with hunger and hard times. If the Klan comes marching in here, they are going to get their heads busted. The Negro workers have nothing left to lose, and this time, they are going to fight. And for you, that means every Negro arrested is a lost vote for Hannon."

"That's what I'm afraid of," Walter said. He wondered how he had managed to get himself involved in this mess. He should have had the good sense to realize that Hannon had put him in a no-win situation. If the Klansmen were attacked, his Negro workers would be going to jail and his goals for the district would be going with them. He doubted that Hannon had much sympathy for his predicament. He had sent Walter here to shore up votes from the community, not knowing or caring that it might involve a race war.

"Luther, I need you to keep me posted if and when the march is going to happen."

"I can do that, but there won't be any ifs about it. The Klan will put the word out to scare people. They want as large an audience as possible, and they want police protection. I imagine it will be Friday or Saturday night. That will give you a few days to come up with a plan."

"Is there any way you can help me with that?"

"I wish I could, Walter. But this fight is a lot older than us. If there were easy answers, we wouldn't be living in a segregated city. It's too bad that you are caught in the middle, because I know that you are trying to help."

"Okay, Luther. You know my motto. When trouble comes, drown it in alcohol. I'll let you know if I come up with anything."

He and Jimmy went straight to the Hi Hat club, where they met with Drum and Queasy. Walter explained his predicament in hopes that his friends might come up with a solution.

"Walter, how do you manage to get yourself bogged down in one mess after another?" Queasy asked.

"Don't you see trouble stamped on my forehead?"

Queasy laughed. "I'm not much help since the failure of my Sal Marconi plan, so I'm going to take a pass on any suggestions."

"Your Uncle Ray got you out of the last jam," Drum said. "Maybe he could help."

"Not this time. It would cost too many white votes. And besides, I have the feeling they are testing me to see if I can handle this on my own."

"Do you think they might have bigger plans for you?" Drum asked.

"It hardly matters, because I'm drowning in a race war."

"We promise to attend the funeral," Queasy said.

"You're much too good to me," Walter replied.

"Not to change the subject, but what have you heard from that gorgeous girlfriend of yours. Has she wised up and left you for a movie mogul?"

Walter took a sip of his beer. He had to admit that he was worried. He had received one letter from Terri over the last two weeks that was long on substance, but short on romance.

"I can see by the look on your face that you're concerned," Queasy said.

"No way. Terri and I are doing fine."

"When is she coming back?"

"I don't know."

Queasy raised his eyebrows questioningly.

"I assure you that she is coming home soon. Now let's get back to my problem and see if we can figure it out."

"No one in this town is going to side with the Negro community," Drum said. "The police will side with the Klan, because they want to keep a lid on the east side. They don't want trouble spilling over Vine Street into the white community. The more Negroes they can arrest, the less trouble for everyone."

"What about arresting the KKK?"

"That's not going to happen. Maybe Jimmy should have thought twice before using his fists."

"Jimmy did the right thing," Walter said. "We are not going to be intimidated by a bunch of thugs. We made a commitment to the community that we intend to keep."

"Be careful of the promises you make," Queasy said. "If Hannon loses the Negro vote, he could lose the election and there goes your job."

"Thank you for adding to the pressure."

"That's what friends are for," Drum said.

Walter had to smile. He was glad to have friends who saw the

156

humor in any situation and would not let him take himself too seriously, even in the direst circumstances.

"Have you run this by J.M. or Cam?" Queasy asked.

"No way. They both warned me to stay away from the Negro community."

"But you were too hardheaded to listen."

"Obviously."

"Walter, you've always championed the underdog, but sometimes doing the wrong thing is more justified than doing the right thing," Drum said.

"I'm not drunk enough to make sense of that."

"Okay. What if I turned down every bet that I knew had no chance of winning? It would be the right thing to do, but I would go broke. You have taken on the cause of the Negro workers, which is the right thing to do, but, in the process, you are going to get your balls busted by the Klan. Staying out of it would be wrong, but it would be the right thing to do."

"Your warped sense of logic is making my head spin."

"No use trying to make sense of it, Walter," Queasy said. "You think you can right the wrongs of the city. We thought you might have learned your lesson with Sal Marconi, but now you want to take on the Klan."

"I just want to be left alone to build a couple of grade schools."

The bartender walked up to Walter and handed him a note. "A Negro boy left this for you a few minutes ago."

"Okay. Thanks." Walter opened the note. It was from Luther, and it said the Klan would be marching this Saturday night. That gave him three days to come up with a plan.

"What is in the note?" Jimmy asked.

"My obituary notice," Walter replied.

～☺～

It was late when he arrived home. He had wanted to drink himself into a stupor, but somehow the worry had outweighed the need for oblivion, and he was in complete control of his faculties. Mira and J.M. were in bed, and so was Cam. Lizabeth was cleaning up the kitchen.

"You're up late," Walter said.

"One of the pitfalls of starting a new business," Lizabeth replied. "Too much on my mind to sleep."

"I know the feeling. What have you heard from Eileen?"

"Sit down, and I will fix us some warm milk." As Lizabeth heated the milk, she told Walter about the latest letter she'd received. She poured the steaming liquid into two cups and sat across from Walter.

"She seems to be enjoying the glamour of Hollywood, but so far nothing has come of her screen test," she said.

"Did she mention anything about Terri?"

"Just that she's shopping her documentary around to the studios. Hasn't she written to you?"

"One letter, and it didn't explain a lot."

"I'm sure she must be busy with her job and trying to get Eileen acclimated to Hollywood."

"I guess so, but I thought she would write more often."

"Have you written to her?"

"I answered her letter."

"Maybe you should take the initiative. Women like to be missed."

"I will take it under consideration," Walter said as he sipped his milk. "How is the warehouse working out?"

"It couldn't be better. We delivered our first order to Harzfeld's, and sales have been great. After sixty days are up, we will be going into Peck's, John Taylor's, and Kline's."

"Good for you. It took courage to start over after the fire with a new business. You didn't stay in the dumps for long."

"Thanks to Mother. She only tolerated so much before she gave me an attitude adjustment."

"She can be formidable. I try to stay out of her way."

"How is life with Tom Hannon?"

"Not so good. We are building two grade schools in the Negro community, but the work has come to a halt."

"How come?"

"It's a long story. And you wouldn't be interested."

"Try me."

"It's too complicated."

"Who helped you get your first date with Terri?"

Walter smiled. "That would be you."

"Exactly, so let me see if I can help."

Walter explained what he was up against, with the Klan and the Negro workers.

"You're saying that if the Negro workers fight back, they will be identified and taken to jail."

"Yes. Hannon controls the police force, so we will be perceived as helping the Klan, and there goes the Negro vote in the next election."

Lizabeth leaned back in her chair and pondered the problem for a moment. "Okay. You finish your milk and give me fifteen minutes to work on something."

Walter watched her walk away, wondering what she was up to. He had gone over and over his predicament and was no closer to a solution. He sipped his milk, knowing Saturday night would come much too quickly and with it a confrontation that might end his career. He was deep in his thoughts, when Lizabeth came down the stairs. He looked up and was so startled, he spilled his milk and almost went backward over the chair.

"My God! You almost scared me to death!" She was wearing a black hood that covered her head and fell to her shoulders. Her eyes and mouth were all that could be seen.

"Do you think you could identify me?" she asked.

"Not in a hundred years." He steadied himself and his mind raced with the possibilities. "How can I ever come up with all the hoods that I will need?"

"Someone you know has access to the best seamstresses in the city. Can you get money for the material?"

"You figure up how much you need to make a profit and tell your girls if the hoods are ready by Saturday morning, they will get a bonus, courtesy of Tom Hannon."

He jumped out of his chair and hugged Lizabeth. "You are brilliant, and you have saved my life!"

"We will do the Klan one better," Lizabeth said. "They wear those bulky white sheets that have no definition. We will make medium, large, and extra-large hoods that are formfitting and have some style. They will be something your Negro workers will be proud to wear. How many will you need?"

"At least a hundred and fifty."

"Okay. I'll buy the material in the morning and have it sent to the warehouse. The girls will start working on them right away."

"What about the disruption to your business?"

"We are caught up with our inventory, so we can give you first priority."

"Please tell your girls to keep this confidential," Walter said. "We don't want this to get out and hurt your business."

Lizabeth had honored her word, and, early on Saturday morning, Walter and Jimmy carried the hoods into the backroom of Luther's barbershop. Luther had recruited some of the biggest and meanest Negroes in the community. They gathered at the barbershop to meet Walter. Some of the men were construction workers, and others had criminal records.

Luther had picked the leader well. His name was Ezra Cross. He was black as night, with yellow tinted eyes that were scary and formidable. He was six feet four, with broad shoulders and muscles that rippled with every move. Originally from Louisiana, he had run north away from some unspecified trouble with the law. He had been in the city less than a year and was unknown to Kansas City police. His reputation was assured in the Negro community, when he had singlehandedly cleaned out a bunch of toughs in a 31st Street pool hall brawl.

Walter passed around the hoods and the men tried them on. The hoods were intimidating in the daylight, so he could only imagine what they would look like at night. There was no way the men could be identified by the police in the darkness.

Luther explained the plan.

"The Klan will be parading down Troost, and then turn east on Eighteenth Street," he said. "They want attention, so they will cross over The Paseo and into the Jazz District on Vine. We let them come halfway up the block, and then our first line of defense will step out of the alleys and block the street. These will be our most intimidating fighters, led by Ezra. There will be a second and third line behind them. If a fight starts, we will have men, hiding in the Gem Theatre and in the bars on either side of the street, who will hit them from the sides. We don't want to kill anyone, but we want to send a message that there will be no more Klan marches in our neighborhoods."

"What about weapons?" Ezra asked.

"Clubs, ball bats, chains, brass knuckles, but no knives or guns."

"We are hoping the Klan will back down when they see what they are up against," Walter said. "If they start a fight, the plan is to hit them hard, and then fade into the night before the police can get their hands on any of our men."

"So, you're in this with us?" a man asked.

"Jimmy and I will be there, but we can't get involved in the fight. We have to remain neutral, if we are to complete the projects for your communities. We represent Hannon, and he can't be involved, because he needs the white vote. If he is not reelected, we can't keep the money flowing your way."

"Any other questions about tonight?" Luther asked.

There were none.

"If there are any injuries, we will have a doctor at a safe house on Prospect Avenue," Walter said. "The police will be looking for you, so going to the hospital is not an option. Each of you take a bundle of hoods and pass them out to your best men. When night falls, we will see you at the prescribed meeting place. And good luck."

Walter took Luther aside. "I don't want Prince involved in this. The police have warned him to stay out of trouble."

"I'll do what I can, but he is hard to control."

"The last thing we need is for someone to get stabbed. Can Ezra order him to stay away?"

"Ezra won't do that."

"Why not?"

"Because Ezra knows who not to mess with."

"Ezra is twice as big and as mean as they come."

"Not when he's staring at a switchblade."

"Do you think Prince would stand up to Ezra?"

"No doubt in my mind. That boy won't back down from anyone."

"Okay. I've been meaning to tell you. I have Prince lined up with a special education teacher. Maybe he can be with her when this goes down."

"You sure you know what you are doing with that boy, Walter?"

"No, but I'm going to give it my best shot anyway."

161

CHAPTER TWELVE

WALTER WAS APPREHENSIVE AS HE drove Prince through the gate of the Hyde Park neighborhood. Prince looked at the mansions in awe and wonderment. Walter parked on the street in front of Charlene's house. They went to the door and were ushered into the parlor by Millie, the housekeeper.

Charlene appeared, and Walter introduced her to Prince.

"Why don't you have coffee in the kitchen, Walter, and give us some time together?"

"Are you sure?"

"Yes."

It took about an hour for Charlene to meet with Prince. Walter wondered why it took so long when she was the only one doing the talking. He was concerned that Prince would be distressed about what Charlene might say.

When Walter returned to the parlor, Prince seemed calm and not upset in the least.

"Why don't you wait in the car, Prince?" Walter said.

"We can't do that, Walter," Charlene said. "We will have no discussions about Prince unless he is in the room. It's a matter of trust."

Walter thought about that for a moment. "Okay. How did it go?"

"It went well."

"How do you know, when he won't talk?"

"There are other means of communications. It's all about reading the signs."

"What is the plan?"

"Initially, I would like to see him three times a week for a couple of hours. I know you are busy, so I will have my driver pick him up and take him back to the barbershop."

"I can pay for that."

"No need. My driver is on a weekly salary. In addition, I know a psychologist who I have worked with in the past that Prince has agreed to see this evening. She does some charitable work for the school district."

"He agreed to that?"

"Yes."

"Congratulations. You have managed to get more out of him in an hour than the rest of us have in two years."

"We will know progress is being made when he decides to talk."

"Okay, let me know if you need anything from me. Thanks again, Charlene." He kissed her on the cheek and motioned to Prince that it was time to leave.

Later that evening, Walter and Jimmy sat at a table outside a bar on Troost Avenue waiting nervously for any sign of Klan activity on the street. Darkness was slowly enveloping the city.

"Do you think they will show?" Jimmy asked

"Luther thinks so, and that's good enough for me."

"What's your plan?"

"We'll stay off to the side and follow the Klan into the Jazz District. The main thing is to not get caught up in the fight."

"Getting sandwiched between Ezra Cross and the Klan would not be my idea of a good time," Jimmy replied.

"We would stand an excellent chance of getting our heads busted by both sides," Walter agreed.

"These Sal Marconi flashbacks are making me sweat," Jimmy said.

Walter laughed. "Sorry," he said. "I had a picture of us tumbling down the stairs at Sal's place."

"You have a warped sense of humor, and I had the bruises to prove it. Have you thought about what will happen if the Klan wins the fight?"

"I'm not letting myself go there."

As night fell, and the streetlamps started to flicker on, Walter and Jimmy watched as several cars and a pick-up truck pulled to the side of the street and parked. More cars and trucks followed, until there was a line of them several blocks long on both sides of the street.

"I didn't think they would have this big a turnout," Jimmy said.

"Neither did I."

The members of the Klan pulled white sheets over their heads before getting out of their vehicles. It was a well-orchestrated gathering, as everyone seemed to know their places. They fell into line behind their grand wizard, who wore a decorated cape and an elaborate pointed hood. Some of the Klan lit torches and one carried a drum. Two others flanked the grand wizard with American flags.

There was a lot of commotion, as the men greeted one another with handshaking and welcoming shouts, like they were members of a select fraternity. Walter guessed there were over 200 of them. After a few minutes, the grand wizard put up his hands, and the Klan grew quiet. He turned and waved them forward, as a drum beat a slow and steady cadence.

The drumbeat and the commotion brought people out of the restaurants and bars. They watched as the Klan members marched by and noticed that many of them were carrying clubs. Walter and Jimmy followed along on the sidewalk, as the Klan turned off Troost and headed east on 18th Street toward the Jazz District. Walter's heart raced faster as the Klan crossed over The Paseo, the parkway in the center of the city. The businesses along the route were shuttered, expecting trouble, and the only sound was the eerie rhythm of the drumbeat.

The fire from the torches that the men carried cast a sinister glow off the hooded mob, as they marched unwaveringly into the Jazz District. Walter spotted a couple of police cars behind the parade, keeping watch on the proceedings. Suddenly, about 50 yards ahead, a line of black hooded men materialized out of the night and lined up, blocking the street. In the center of the line stood an imposing figure, whom Walter knew to be Ezra Cross. The rest of the men carried clubs and bats.

The grand wizard put up his arm, bringing the Klan to an abrupt halt. Walter could tell they were gauging their next move, because they had never faced opposition before. The front line of the Klan huddled together for a few minutes, before the grand wizard moved them slowly ahead. He stopped in front of Ezra and raised his club.

"Move out of the way, boy, before I give you this," he said, shaking a club in Ezra's hooded face. Ezra did not move. The wizard turned to his clan. "We have us a big nigger here who doesn't hear very well." The men of the Klan laughed nervously. "It's time we taught these niggers a lesson."

He made a move toward Ezra, but Ezra stepped back and with all his pent-up anger, swung the bat hard into the side of the grand wizard, shattering his arm. He screamed in agony and fell to the pavement.

The rest of the Negro line tore into the Klan with clubs, chains, and bats. White robed men were falling to the pavement in droves. There was a pile of them around Ezra, as he swung his bat with a vengeance. Some of the Klan fought back, but then more black hooded men flooded out of the bars and the theatre and tore into the side of the crowd, causing more men to go down. The Klan collapsed and those who were able started to run away.

The police started moving cautiously into the melee. Ezra blew a whistle and his men broke off the fight, picked up their wounded, and ran into the alleys, where they vanished into the night. Sirens sounded in the distance, as the police called for backup and ambulances. Walter and Jimmy slipped quietly away to Walter's car, and headed to the Hi Hat club.

Lizabeth was in quandary. She had received a letter from Eileen that said she and Terri were staying longer than planned but did not give a timeframe. Her sister had taken a role in a B movie that Hollywood produced to accompany the main feature. These were low budget films in the horror, Western, or gangster genres. That was good news for Eileen, but it meant that she would be staying at least long enough to make the film, and that would be several months.

What worried Lizabeth most was the news that Terri had taken a screen test and had been offered a contract. Lizabeth was certain that Walter knew nothing about it. Eileen had asked her to check on Terri's mother, and that was something that Walter should be doing. Walter had cut back on his drinking and was doing well on his job, so she did not want this kink in his romance with Terri to upset him or the progress he was making. However, there was no way to keep it from him, so she waited until he came home from work to have a discussion.

Their parents were in their bedroom and Cam was seated at the kitchen table having a snack before going to bed. He looked up when Walter came in the door.

"Here he is," Cam said. "The mastermind behind the Eighteenth Street brawl." Cam had heard the details of the confrontation from his Uncle Ray. "Did you manage to get through the day without causing a riot?"

"Good evening to you too," Walter said, as he sat across from Cam.

"I hear they are going to make you an honorary Negro."

"Did you stay up to give me a hard time, or are you just being your normal sarcastic self?"

Cam grunted and continued eating.

"How did the hoods work out?" Lizabeth asked.

"Amazingly well. We would not have been successful without them."

"I'm surprised that you would involve your sister," Cam said.

"He certainly did not," Lizabeth said. "The hoods were my idea."

"How was your day in the fashion world?" Walter asked.

"It was very good. I'm thinking about hiring some more seamstresses to keep up with demand."

"Good for you. Have you ever thought about hiring some from the Negro community?"

"I hadn't, but I will give it some consideration."

"Are you trying to ruin her business?" Cam asked Walter. "That would not set well with her customers."

"They would be sewing, not selling," Walter responded. "And

later on, it might give her some connections if she ever wanted to sell to the Negro community."

"Lizabeth Braden's Negro fashions," Cam said sarcastically. "You need to think that through."

Lizabeth kept waiting for Cam to leave the table, so she could talk to Walter, but he showed no signs of going to bed.

"I received a letter today from Eileen," she finally said to Walter.

"Oh. What did she say?"

"She and Terri are staying longer than planned." She told him what was in the letter.

"And she asked you to go by and see Terri's mother?" Walter inquired.

"Yes," she answered.

"I thought Terri was adamant about staying behind the camera," Cam said.

"So did I. Someone must have convinced her otherwise."

"There's no use in stewing about it," Lizabeth said. "Why don't you make a phone call to Los Angeles and speak to her directly?"

A long-distance phone call was expensive, but he was concerned about Terri and their relationship.

"I'm going to do just that."

Walter went to the phone in the living room and placed a call to Terri's hotel in Los Angeles. The front desk rang her room, and he was surprised when she answered right away.

"Hello." The sound of her voice made him miss her all the more.

"Hello, Terri."

There was a momentary silence on the other end.

"I can tell that you are ecstatic to hear from me."

"I'm sorry. You just took me by surprise."

"How are things in Hollywood?"

"Okay."

He could tell that her responses were guarded.

"I miss you. I thought you would be home by now."

"I know. Things got hectic and spun out of control."

She said nothing about missing him, and he was getting angry. "Lizabeth tells me that you have been offered an acting contract. Are you going to sign it?"

"I'm still thinking it through."

"What happened to the girl who hated being in front of the camera?"

"With some coaching, I'm getting more comfortable."

"It's the coaching that worries me."

"What are you implying?"

"That whatever is happening there became more important than what is waiting for you here."

"I might not get another chance like this."

"And why are you sending a message through Eileen to have Lizabeth check on your mother? You might have asked me to do that."

"I thought Lizabeth might do better in assessing her needs."

Lizabeth and Cam had followed Walter into the living room and caught the gist of the conversation. She whispered in his ear, "Stop accusing her."

He nodded, but she could tell that he was angry.

"What about your job at Universal?"

"I'm doing a lot of the work at the offices here, so it isn't a problem. They have given me time to see what develops."

"That means you have no idea when you might be coming home."

"I wish I could tell you more, but the movie business moves at its own pace."

Walter was beginning to wonder if she was coming home at all. He had to get off the phone or he was going to say something he would regret.

"Tell Eileen we said hello, and that we miss her."

"I will. Give everyone our best."

Walter hung up the phone. Terri had not given him any encouragement and he guessed there must be another man involved. He felt sick to his stomach, and he was consumed with jealousy.

"That went well," Cam said.

"Mind your own business."

"You should have realized it would only be a matter of time before she dumped you for someone who doesn't get boozed up every night."

All the frustration of the past few weeks boiled over, and Walter exploded with anger and charged into Cam. He took him backward over the couch, and they landed with a loud thud against the wall.

They scrambled to their feet and squared off.

"Stop it!" Lizabeth screamed. But Walter hit Cam in the jaw with a right cross. Cam took the punch and hit Walter with a left jab in the right eye that snapped his head back and drew blood. Walter charged again and tackled Cam into the wall, which resulted in glass shattering and pictures falling to the floor.

Lizabeth kept screaming for them to stop, but they were consumed with anger as they wrestled on the floor, each trying to gain an advantage. Walter jumped to his feet, and Cam followed with a punch to Walter's ribs that buckled his legs. Walter recovered and hit Cam above the eye, which instantly swelled. Lizabeth was frantic, trying to get them to stop. They circled each other, trying to find an opening for a punch. But before they could continue, Mira and J.M. hurried into the room.

"Stop it this minute!" Mira said. "That you would disrespect our home with this kind of behavior is unconscionable! What in the world is the matter with you two? You are acting like adolescent boys instead of grown men! We are supposed to be a family, not a pack of wild animals!"

Cam and Walter backed away from each other and came to their senses.

"Sorry, Mother," Cam said.

"Who started this, Lizabeth?" J.M. asked.

Lizabeth remained silent, not wanting to take sides.

"I want this place cleaned up, and you both are going to pay for any damages," J.M. said. "And stay away from each other until you can behave like decent human beings." He retreated to his bedroom.

"I hope you are both happy that you upset your father," Mira said. "You will apologize to him in the morning. Walter, you can sleep on the couch tonight."

Lizabeth wondered why Cam didn't have to sleep on the couch. She knew there would be no apologies in the morning. Everyone would go about their business as if nothing had happened. These fights had been going on for as long as she could remember, although this was the first time it had happened inside the house. Her brother's fights had become ingrained in the family dynamic. They would not hold a grudge or be resentful to each other, and the cuts and bruises would be ignored by everyone. If the behavior was not acknowledged, it was as if it had never occurred. She felt bad for Walter. He would get over the cuts and bruises, but she was concerned about the emotional damage inflicted by Terri. Cam retreated to his bedroom.

"You had better let me put something on that eye," she said to Walter.

"No thanks, I'm going out for a drink."

She was fearful that he might start drinking heavily again. She wished that her mother allowed alcohol in the house, so she could fix him a drink and send him to bed.

"Do you want me to go with you?"

"You get some sleep. You have a business to run." With slumped shoulders, he headed out the door.

On the way to the Hi Hat club, he tried to think of where he had gone wrong with Terri. There was no way that he could have prevented her from going to Los Angeles. He had wanted to support her in every way that he could, but he should have known that a beautiful, talented, woman would get lots of offers from the men associated with the movie industry. His mistake was in thinking her ties to him were strong enough to withstand the offers.

Walter had believed Terri when she said there was not much Hollywood could offer that she hadn't seen before. That was obviously not true, because he was getting the brushoff, and he guessed it was because she had met someone else. His mistake was in allowing himself to fall in love with her. He should have known better. His former position behind the bar at the Hi Hat club had allowed him to observe the fallout from countless failed romances, and it was ironic that he had let it happen to him.

It was late, and there were few patrons at the club. He settled in at the bar and knocked down a couple of whiskeys before switching to beer. The booze helped to numb him and dulled the pain he was feeling about Terri. Why should he care anyway? There were plenty of women who would be glad to have him. The more he drank, the more he deluded himself into thinking he could get along without her. He had risked his life for her, and this was a fine way for her to show her appreciation.

170

"Thank you, Terri Lawson," he said out loud.

The bartender looked his way, then went back to talking to a customer. Walter polished off five more beers and asked for another.

"Don't you think you've had enough, Walter?"

"No, I do not."

"Do you have someone to drive you home?"

"I can drive perfectly well."

The bartender gave him another beer and then went discreetly to the phone and called Ray Braden. Later, when Ray arrived, the bartender pointed at Walter who had his head down and was asleep at the bar.

"What brought this on?" he asked the bartender.

"Don't know. The only thing he said was, 'Thank you, Terri Lawson.'"

"That's all I needed to know. I appreciate you calling me."

Ray bent over and picked Walter up and threw him over his shoulder. He took him to the car, and then back to his house, so J.M. and Mira would not see him in this condition.

The next day, Walter woke up with a tremendous hangover. He looked around, trying to get his bearings and realized he was in bed in Erma's sewing room, where colorful spools of threads and various garments were strewn over her sewing table. He didn't remember much about the past evening, but he did remember his conversation with Terri. He put on his pants and a shirt and went downstairs to the kitchen, where his Aunt Erma and Uncle Ray were having breakfast.

"That's quite a shiner," Ray said looking at his eye. "I thought you stayed out of the fight with the Klan."

Walter sat down. "I did. This is a token of affection from my brother."

"How does he look?"

"A couple of cuts above the eye, but he will be fine."

"I'm surprised you two haven't killed each other," Erma said. "Do you want some coffee or tomato juice?"

"Coffee, please. And I want to thank you both for taking me in."

"What happened with Terri?" Ray asked.

"How do you know about that?"

"You were muttering about her all the way home."

"Oh. I was given a frosty reception when I called her in Los Angeles."

"Not that it's any of my business," Erma said, "but I told you she was trouble when she first came into the store."

"You did, but I was too smitten to listen."

"I thought you two were tight after you rescued her from Sal Marconi," Ray said.

"So did I. We were both wrong."

"Do you want some breakfast?" Erma asked. "It will make you feel better."

"Coffee is all I can handle."

"Walter, don't let this stop the progress you are making with the organization," Ray said. "I've watched many a good man drink himself into oblivion over a woman, and I don't want it happening to you. Boss Tom was mighty impressed with the way you handled the delicate situation with the Klan, and he can assure your future. He has helped men become judges and state senators, so imagine what he could do for you."

"I'm not interested in politics, but I'll keep that in mind."

"Maybe you can win Terri back once she's away from the Hollywood crowd," Erma said. "When is she coming home?"

"She couldn't give me an answer on that."

"Maybe you should go out there and see her," Erma said.

"After she brushed me off on the phone, I wouldn't give her that satisfaction. She knows where I am."

"Is it better to suffer in silence than seek a solution?" Erma asked.

Walter shrugged.

"If you ever need to talk, we are here to listen," Erma said.

"I appreciate that, and I want to thank you both again. Now, I had better pick up Jimmy and head to the east side, so I can check on my school projects."

⌒

Every morning, Lizabeth would take a walking tour of her warehouse facility, before heading out for sales calls. Business was brisk, and she had put five more seamstresses on the payroll. In anticipation of the end of her exclusive contract with Harzfeld's, she had reached out north to St. Joseph, and west to Topeka and

Wichita. She had also made some contacts in St. Louis and was excited about the possibilities that city offered. Jennie was helping her make the out-of-town sales calls.

Cory had finished the offices for Lizabeth, and he installed fans and ventilation for the upcoming summer season. She knew what it was like to sew in a hot sewing room, so she wanted her employees to be as comfortable as possible. She had her own sewing station on the floor, where she designed her fashions, made the patterns, and then passed them on to the seamstresses. Her dedication to the business and her willingness to be a seamstress created a team spirit among her employees, because they could see that she worked harder than anyone. They also knew that she would look out for their welfare.

Margie's crochet items were doing well, and she had her own work area in a section of the warehouse. Lizabeth paid her a wage, plus a percentage of the items she created and sold. Cory had struck up a friendship with Margie and always stopped by her station when he came to see Lizabeth. Cory was naturally shy, and Margie was reserved because of her disability, so they had that in common. Lizabeth was glad that Cory had not put any more pressure on her concerning a closer relationship. He seemed content with their arrangement, and it allowed her to continue focusing on the business.

She still had not come up with that special item that she would need to stabilize her business during the downturns in the fashion industry. She was making enough money to glean a nice profit, but not enough to propel her where she wanted to go, and that was to sell her fashions nationwide. The Hannon organization would lend her money, but she did not want to burden her business with debt payments. When she made her breakout nationally, it would be because of her own initiative.

Today was an exciting day, because she had received a letter from Eileen announcing that she was finally coming home. Lizabeth would pick her up Saturday at Union Station. Eileen had not made it clear if she was going back to Hollywood. She did say that Terri would be coming home to visit her mother. Walter had remained steadfast in his decision not to contact Terri, so Lizabeth gathered that their romance was over.

It was regrettable, because she liked Terri and thought she was a good match for Walter. He had been drinking more after his blowup with her, but from everything Uncle Ray said, he was doing a great job and was primed to move up in the Hannon organization.

~

J.M. sat on the screened porch with his brother, Ray. Mira was in the yard working on her flowerbeds. The first buds of spring were sprouting on the trees and Mira's perennials were poking through the ground. A scattering of robins hopped around the yard, eyeing worms brought to the surface from overnight rains. A couple of blue jays were noisily scolding each other in the maple tree.

"The sun sure feels good after a long winter," Ray said, basking in the glow.

"It does indeed," J.M. replied.

"How is your job with Lizabeth going?"

"Fine. Although I never thought I would be employed by one of my children."

"She's lucky to have you."

"I wonder if she needs me, or if she's just being charitable."

"Of course, she needs you. You've been a big help to her."

"I'm not sure Lizabeth needs anyone. She's quite resourceful."

"That she is, but you helped get her business started, and I'm sure she is grateful."

"The job is only temporary until I find something more permanent."

"You might have to look for something outside of advertising, J.M. It was hit harder than most sectors in the Depression. It will be slow to come back."

"You have summed up my predicament."

They watched as Mira, on her hands and knees, planted some colorful flowers near the street.

"She's breaking her cardinal rule of not planting before May first," J.M. said. "She's grasping for spring after a long winter."

Ray was worried about his brother. J.M. seemed depressed, and Ray had learned from Erma that his relationship with Mira was not going well. He knew to tread lightly, because J.M. wasn't one to share his personal life.

"How is everything working out for you and Mira?" he ventured.

J.M. sighed and was thoughtful for a moment. "There's no doubt that we have traded romance for civility. I wonder if that is a natural progression in marriage or a result of something that I've done. But we have definitely grown apart."

"Erma tells me that Mira is still very angry about your lapses in judgment."

"That's an interesting way of sugarcoating my affairs."

"You could apologize."

"That would be hypocritical. I went into the affairs knowing exactly what I was doing. To beg for forgiveness would be demeaning for both of us."

"You've always had a weakness for the ladies. When we were kids in school you were constantly chasing pigtails."

"I've always been fascinated by women. I only wish that I had been more discreet."

"Mira can be unforgiving."

"Don't I know it."

"Where does that leave the marriage?"

"Suspended in a state of frosty limbo."

"You will have to face each other when the young people leave."

"It's something we will deal with when it comes. Marriage is a constant series of compromises, and we've managed to work our way through the things that would have destroyed our relationship."

"Where is the happiness in all that?"

"We have our moments. Our children are a joy and keep life interesting."

"You can't live through your children."

"No, but they are a welcome distraction when things get too intense in the marriage. Mira would never upset the family dynamic. She would always protect her children from the scandal of divorce."

"Would you have left her for the waitress at the Harvey House?"

"Possibly. She was a wonderful girl. If I had met her before Mira, we would have been married."

"When you met Mira in high school, she was the girl of your dreams."

J.M. thought about that for a moment. "That's true, but life came along, and there were other nights and other dreams."

"You can't recapture your youth in the pursuit of women."

"There's some validity in that, although my actions were more physical than mental."

"Have you satisfied them?"

"I've lived too long to make predictions about anything. But at the moment, there are no plans in that regard."

"Erma and I hope you and Mira work it out, and that you can be happy for the rest of your life together."

"I hope so too."

CHAPTER THIRTEEN

LIZABETH WAITED FOR EILEEN AND Terri to arrive at Union Station. She was so excited to see her sister and to hear all about her experiences in Hollywood. She glanced around the North Waiting Room in the station to see if Walter had changed his mind and come to greet Terri. But there was no sign of him. After a fifteen-minute wait, Eileen and Terri came up the stairs into the North Waiting Room. Lizabeth ran to meet them and hugged Eileen tightly to her.

"Hello, sister. I am so happy to see you."

"I've missed you these many months," Eileen said. "I can't wait to hear about how things are going with your new business venture."

Lizabeth turned and greeted Terri. Eileen and Terri were smartly dressed and looked every inch like the movie stars they hoped to be.

"The movie business has been good to you," Lizabeth said. "You both look beautiful."

"Thank you, Lizabeth," Terri said. Lizabeth could see Terri glancing discreetly around the station to see if perhaps Walter had come to greet her. She couldn't tell whether that would have made her happy or uncomfortable. Lizabeth directed the porter carrying the luggage into the Grand Hall of the station.

Above the circular ticket station, Walter looked down from the Western Union office to the floor of the Grand Hall. He watched as the three women followed the porter across the hall, toward the exit. Terri was stunning in a brown camel suit, and he felt that same flush of excitement that had happened when he first saw her on Film Row. The question was what to do about it. If he tried to contact her, it would look like he was desperate, after the way she had treated him on the phone. Maybe Eileen would know where he stood with Terri, and if there was any future in their romance.

Outside, the porter loaded the bags into Lizabeth's Ford Phaeton. It had a convertible top, was light gray in color, and sported poppy red wheels.

"What a beautiful car," Eileen said.

"Cam sold it to me last week. It's the one extravagance I've allowed myself."

"Good for you. I am so happy for your success."

"Did you sign that movie contract, Terri?" Lizabeth asked.

"Yes. I start working on my first film next month."

"Congratulations!" Lizabeth said, trying to sound excited, although her heart wasn't in it. She knew that Terri's success might spell the end of her relationship with Walter.

"How long are you both going to be here?" Lizabeth asked.

"Two weeks for me," Terri said.

"I'm not sure," Eileen said. "I'm going to get some rest and then decide."

Lizabeth wondered if things had gone well for her in the movie industry.

"It will be wonderful to have you home," she said.

They dropped Terri off at her mother's home in Hyde Park and then headed home to Brookside.

"Walter is worried that his romance with Terri might be over," she said to Eileen.

"He has every right to be. Terri has been dating the movie producer who offered her a contract."

"That explains a lot."

"I didn't want to see Walter get hurt, so I kept quiet."

"You were in a difficult position. Terri should have leveled with him from the beginning."

"How are Mother and Father?"

"About the same. They are officially together but seem to be leading separate lives."

"That's too bad. I was in hopes they had warmed to each other."

"They will be glad to see you. It will be fun to be under one roof again."

"How is Walter doing with his drinking?"

"Not good. This business with Terri has him in a downward spiral."

"I'm sorry to hear it. And how is Cam?"

"Still thinking that he is the center of the universe. He and Walter had a row, and Cam has stitches over his eye."

"Will they never grow up?"

"The debate continues." They both shook their heads at the absurdity of their brothers continuing to brawl.

"Is Cam still seeing Helen?"

"Yes. I think he has his eye on being heir to a shoe store fortune."

"I hope not. Helen is a good fit for him and he should realize that without thinking about the money she will inherit."

"Tell me about your adventures in Hollywood."

"Let me get settled first. We can talk about it tonight, when we are in bed and the lights are out."

"Perfect," Lizabeth said. "Just like we've been doing since we were kids."

⁓

Mira had fixed a special dinner for Eileen's homecoming, and the family had treated her like a queen. However, Eileen had not been forthcoming about her experiences in Hollywood, and Lizabeth knew there was something wrong. When they retired for the night and were in bed listening to distant thunder, she tried to get her sister to open up.

"I take it the movie business was not what you were hoping for," Lizabeth said.

"No. It wasn't."

"What happened?"

"It was a combination of things. I missed my home, my family, and my friends. And there is an undercurrent of expectations by producers and directors if you want to be a successful actress."

"What kind of expectations?"

"Use your imagination."

"Oh. I had no idea. I guess Father was right about the movie business."

"It is not a big deal for most actresses. They see it as just another price to pay for bright lights and big salaries."

"I can imagine how uncomfortable it was for you."

"I'm no saint. I had visions of letting go of my inhibitions when I left home, but home followed me to Hollywood."

"That was Mother whispering in your ear," Lizabeth said.

"Her values stayed with me, that's for sure."

"Are you going back?"

"I haven't decided. If I don't, it will look like I failed, regardless of the circumstances."

"Your happiness is much more important than what people think."

"It's funny how life works out. The career I always dreamed of is there for the taking, and now I'm not sure I want to make the sacrifice."

"It's not worth it if you can't live with yourself."

"My family and friends had such great expectations for me."

"It's your life. Don't get bogged down in what other people want."

"Do you think Mother and Father will be disappointed?"

"No. They just want you to be happy. What about the movie you were in?"

"We finished shooting last week. It was a terrific part, and I enjoyed making the film."

"But not enjoyable enough to go back for more."

"No. I'll be content with the Red Barn Players."

"When will the film be distributed?"

"Not for six months. I wonder if Harzfeld's held my job for me."

"Why would they not? You were one of their top salespeople. There is only one reason why they won't take you back."

"What would that be?"

"Because you are coming to work with me. I need your sales expertise, and you will also be my number one model."

Eileen was stunned for a moment, because this was totally unexpected.

"Can you afford to hire me? You are already employing Father and Aunt Erma."

"I can't afford not to. The Braden sisters will be formidable in the fashion industry."

"You are doing this because I need a job."

"You know me better than that. My priority is my business, and if I didn't think you could contribute, I wouldn't be making the offer."

"I would love to work with you."

"Then it is settled. What about your obligations in Hollywood?"

"I will call my agent and let him know that I'm not coming back."

"Good. Now get some sleep, and we will talk more in the morning."

Walter had finished his grade school projects and he was now building a recreation center in the Negro community. His stature had risen dramatically after he had helped put down the Klan in the battle of 18th Street. If everything continued to go well, Tom Hannon would win the upcoming election in a landslide. It had been almost two weeks since Terri had come home, but even though Walter was desperate to see her, his pride stood in the way.

He and Jimmy had checked in at Hannon's office and were meeting Queasy and Drum for drinks and dinner at a Film Row restaurant. Drum waved to them from the bar.

"We've been waiting for those ill-gotten gains from Hannon to buy a few rounds," Queasy said.

Walter threw some money on the bar. "As if you care where the money comes from. You would accept a drink from the devil himself."

"Not me. But the devil in me might."

"What trouble have you managed to get into this week, Walter?" Drum asked.

"All is good, and it's making me nervous," Walter replied.

"Are those bruises above your eye?" Queasy asked.

"They were received in the natural order of things," Walter said.

"Your brother, Cam?"

"Exactly."

"You need to teach him how to defend himself, Jimmy," Drum said.

"He does okay. You should see Cam."

"Your brother is the least of your worries," Queasy said. "Word is that the Klan knows about the part you played in helping the

Negroes during the march across Eighteenth Street. You are a marked man."

"I invited you to dinner because I knew you would cheer me up," Walter replied.

Queasy laughed. "You must know that Hannon put you in an untenable position. He gave you the north end and the east side to manage. That puts you squarely between the Italians and the Negroes, two groups of people who detest each other."

"That is true, but I see no scenario where the two would have to merge."

"What about in an election? You've taken the heat for Hannon in the Negro community, so the north end isn't a problem for him, but now it is for you."

"I'm not running for anything."

"Not yet, but Hannon might have other ideas."

"Have you heard something?"

"No. But it seems logical that he is grooming you for bigger things."

"He can groom away because I'm satisfied where I am."

"Oh, yea," Queasy said. "Just like you were satisfied as a bartender and then satisfied as a manager in the north end. Boss Tom has a way of bending you to his will."

Walter took a swig of beer. "Not this time. From now on, I'm my own man."

"Sure you are, Senator Braden," Drum teased him, and everyone laughed. "You have Harry Truman junior plastered on your back. You just can't see it."

"No way that I'm going into politics. It's too sordid for a man of my gentility."

"Said the man with a black eye, swigging a brew," Queasy scoffed.

"How are things at City Hall?" Walter asked. "Which set of Magrath's books are you manipulating this week?"

"That is such a crude accusation," Queasy pretended to be hurt. "You have to quit reading those editorials in the *Star*."

"We both know that Boss Tom controls the coffers at City Hall," Walter continued. "It is only a matter of time before the reformers swarm down on Magrath. You had better distance yourself from him and from his creative accounting."

182

"There is nothing to fear. Our books will stand the test of time."

"Time in Leavenworth, maybe."

"If Hannon and McGrath go down, it will be every man for himself."

"That brings to mind rats scurrying from City Hall. Just be sure you are insulated from any potential investigation."

"I recite the Fifth Amendment with my nightly prayers."

"Are we going to eat, or are you two going to keep clucking like a couple of hens?" Drum asked. "I'm starved."

They took a table in the back of the restaurant, and everyone placed an order except Walter.

"Not hungry?" Drum asked.

"No. I don't want to lose the buzz from my beer."

"I'm glad to hear Eileen is home. How is she doing?"

"Very well. She has decided to forget Hollywood and go to work for Lizabeth."

"Good for her," Queasy said. "Although I had hoped to see her on the big screen. That girl has talent."

"There were extenuating circumstances beyond her control." Lizabeth had told Walter about Eileen's discomfort with the demands of producers and directors who could make or break an acting career.

"How is Cam doing?"

"The Ford Motor Company is putting him in charge of its Midwestern dealerships. He was selling more cars than anyone, so they promoted him to district manager."

"That's great," Queasy said. "Offer him our hearty congratulations when you see him next."

"I will."

"And be advised that for Cam to be successful, you will have to quit using his face for a punching bag."

"Your concern is duly noted."

They had finished dinner and Queasy was into his second dessert when suddenly Drum said, "Uh-oh."

"What are you groaning about?" Walter asked.

"I believe someone you know just walked into the restaurant."

Walter turned around and there she was, walking to a table with a middle-aged man who was dressed in an expensive blue suit. Terri had on a brown ensemble that matched her hair and she looked so beautiful that Walter was mesmerized. He assumed the man must be the producer that Lizabeth said she had fallen for. He was probably here to accompany her back to Hollywood.

"I hope you are not going to embarrass us by making a scene," Queasy said. "She is huddled with her date, so we can slip by without being noticed."

"That sounds like a plan," Walter said. "Let me finish my beer, and we will be on our way."

He took the last swig, rose unsteadily to his feet, and followed his friends through the restaurant. As they were walking by Terri's table, Walter thought about giving her a pass, but he was too frustrated and too angry to let it go.

"Hold on, fellas," he said. He turned and faced Terri. She had a look of both shock and surprise.

"I believe we have a celebrity here!" Walter announced to the room. "It's Terri Lawson, the movie star! Can we have your autograph?" The restaurant had quieted, and the patrons were watching to see what was happening. Terri was red in the face with embarrassment.

"Is this necessary?" she whispered.

"It seems to be. I've been wondering how long it took you to forget your friends when you signed that movie contract."

Queasy grabbed him gently by the arm. "Come on, Walter. You don't need to do this."

Walter pulled away. Terri's date stood up to intervene.

"Sit down," Jimmy said. "Unless you want your nose busted." The man sat.

Walter stared at Terri's date. "Do you see this?" he asked drunkenly, pointing at his black eye. "It's a minor wound from being trampled by Miss Lawson's ambition. The other wounds go much deeper."

Drum tried to move him along, but he was too drunk to be rational.

"My sister was going to be a movie star," Walter continued loudly. "But she decided not to compromise herself for a shot at stardom. Too bad we can't say the same for you, Miss Lawson."

"Okay. That's enough, Walter," Drum said. He and Jimmy each took an arm and escorted him from the restaurant.

Queasy stayed back. Terri was in tears. "I'm sorry, Terri," he said and then left to catch up with his friends.

Walter stepped outside with Drum and Jimmy. He was feeling total remorse for what he had just done to Terri. His friends let go of his arms and he steadied himself. He took a deep breath and looked around. He could feel the warm May breeze against his cheek and see a fingernail moon floating above the building across the street. From somewhere up the block, he heard a car start and come racing down the street. If he had not been consumed by Terri, and by alcohol, he might have had his wits about him and things might have turned out differently.

He heard a pop, pop, pop, as the car raced past, and he wondered why anyone would be shooting off fireworks in May. In that instant, a bullet hit him in the shoulder, tore the flesh away, and knocked him to the pavement. In a daze, he was aware that Jimmy and Drum had both cried out in pain and had fallen into the street. It took a moment for him to realize what had happened, and then a wave of pain hit him, and he groaned. Queasy had run out of the building and was standing over Walter.

"Where are you hit?"

"Left shoulder," Walter said through the pain. Queasy quickly checked Jimmy and Drum. Jimmy had lost half his ear and Drum had been shot in the thigh. Queasy ran back to the restaurant. He burst through the door, knocking a waiter with a tray to the floor, with a loud crash that got everyone's attention. "Get me the police and an ambulance!" he shouted frantically.

Terri bolted from her table and followed Queasy outside. Jimmy was up on his knees holding a handkerchief to his right ear. Walter and Drum were flat on their backs. In the glow of the streetlight, she could see blood staining the sidewalk. Her heart was pounding, so she took a deep breath and tried not to panic. She checked their wounds and then took a scarf from around her neck. "Tie this above Drum's leg wound, Queasy." She took a handkerchief from her skirt pocket and used it as a compress on Walter's shoulder wound.

Walter looked up at her. He wanted to apologize for what he had put her through, but he couldn't form the words. He felt everything slipping away.

"Hold on, and we will get you to the hospital," Terri said. In the distance, she could hear the sirens from the police cars and ambulances growing louder.

⁓

Lizabeth was at the kitchen table going over sales figures. Her parents were in bed, and so was Cam. The phone rang, and she wondered who would be calling this late at night, as she picked up the receiver.

"Hello."

"Lizabeth, this is Terri." Terri's voice was strained, and Lizabeth sensed that something was wrong.

"What is it, Terri?"

"Walter has been shot!"

Lizabeth felt her heart in her throat.

"Don't panic," Terri said, as calmly as she could. "He is going to be okay. I'm at Research Hospital, and you need to get here right away."

Lizabeth hung up the phone. She was shaking so badly that she had to get control of herself. For a moment, she wondered if it was some kind of a lover's quarrel involving Terri, but it hardly mattered, she had to see Walter. She ran into Cam's room.

"Cam, wake up!" She shook him. Cam sat up in bed.

"What is it?" he said irritably.

"Walter has been shot!"

"What! Where? Is he okay?"

"Terri said he was going to make it. I don't have any details. I'm heading to Research Hospital. You have to tell Mother and Father." Lizabeth hurried to her car.

⁓

Ray Braden knocked on the door of the Hannon mansion on Ward Parkway. It was a few minutes before Boss Tom opened the door. He was dressed in his robe. The Boss knew it must be urgent, because no one had the nerve to knock on his door late at night.

"What happened, Ray?"

"Walter, Jimmy, and one of their friends were shot outside a restaurant on Film Row."

186

Boss Tom's eyes widened with surprise, and Ray could tell his mind was churning.

"Will they survive?"

"Yes. Unless there are complications."

"Any idea who pulled the trigger?"

"Not yet. If I had to bet money, I would say either Sal Marconi or a member of the Klan."

"You get the police chief out of bed and have him here in twenty minutes."

Ray made the call, and the chief arrived quickly. He had already received a report on the shootings.

"I want every available police officer on this," Hannon said. "Spread the word to every crime boss in the city, except Sal Marconi. You tell them if I don't have a suspect in custody in forty-eight hours, we will start jailing anyone even remotely suspected of committing a crime. This is an attack on our organization and a personal attack on me, and it will not be tolerated," Hannon fumed. "Do you understand?"

"Yes, sir," the chief replied.

"Ray, you contact our man inside the Klan, and keep me posted on how Walter and Jimmy are doing."

Terri was in the waiting room when Lizabeth arrived at the hospital. It was chaotic with medical personnel and the police scurrying through the hallways.

"How is he?" Lizabeth asked.

"He was shot in the shoulder. They removed the bullet and are treating the wound and stitching him up. The doctors assure me that he is going to be okay, but he will have to spend some time in the hospital."

"What happened and why were you there?" Lizabeth asked accusingly.

"We just happened to pick the same restaurant for dinner," Terri said. "Walter was shot leaving the restaurant."

"I'm sorry," Lizabeth said. "With what has happened between you two, I assumed the worst."

"The relationship has been stormy, but I haven't resorted to gunfire."

"I thought Walter might have been shot in an act of jealousy."

"I was not involved in any way."

"Then please, accept my apology. Did the doctors say when we can see him?"

"They should be out to visit with you in a few minutes. Now that you are here, I am going to leave."

"Why? Walter will want to see you."

"I don't think so." Terri told her what had happened inside the restaurant before the shooting.

"Your relationship was going so well," Lizabeth said. "What happened?"

"Like you, I want to live my dream."

"My dream?"

"Yes. You haven't let anything get in the way of your career, including your relationship with Cory. My dream is to make it in films. It will be demanding, and there is no way that Walter would tolerate the amount of time we would have to be apart. It was not an easy decision, but one I had to make."

It pained Lizabeth to be the role model for Walter's unhappiness.

"You could have told Walter how you feel rather than start a relationship with another man."

"I'm not in a relationship. I have gone to dinner with a few friends I've met in Hollywood."

Terri saw Cam, Mira, and J.M. coming up the hallway. She did not want to get involved with Walter's family because uncomfortable questions were sure to follow. When Lizabeth went to greet them, Terri opened a side door and slipped quietly down the stairway.

⁓

Walter was on pain medication and not fully alert for a couple of days. When he awoke the evening of the second day, Uncle Ray was standing by the bed.

"Awake at last," Ray said. "How are you feeling?"

"Sore, but much better. How are Jimmy and Drum?"

"Jimmy lost part of his ear, but he will be fine. The bullet missed the bone in Drum's leg. He will be on his back for a while, but no lasting damage."

"Any idea who fired the shots?"

"Yes. The Boss put the fear of God into the city's crime lords to come up with a suspect. I was certain it was going to be Sal Marconi's men, but I was wrong. Our man inside the Klan found out the hit was ordered by the grand wizard and carried out by some of his men. Somehow it was leaked that you were the brains behind their defeat at the Eighteenth Street brawl and the Klan wanted revenge."

"What happens next?"

"The grand wizard and the two shooters will stand trial. The police have a confession, so you probably won't have to testify."

"That was a quick confession."

"They decided to talk after the boys busted them up a bit. They will have plenty of time to heal in the big house."

"How are my folks taking this?"

"Not good. This incident confirmed the doubts J.M. had about you working for Hannon."

"Any chance we could keep this from going public? I don't want them to be embarrassed by a scandal."

Ray picked up a copy of the *Kansas City Star* off the foot of the bed and held it up. The headline read, "TWO HANNON LIEUTENANTS SHOT IN AMBUSH."

"Could it get any worse?" Walter asked.

"It could. Your mother was worried about you going to war and you end up getting shot on the streets of her hometown. You can imagine how distraught she is."

"I'm trying not to."

"They are going to pressure you to find another line of work."

"Thanks for the warning. What does Hannon think about the publicity?"

"You took a bullet for the organization, so you are in solid with him."

Lizabeth came into the room carrying some flowers. She was followed by Eileen and Cam.

"Is he behaving himself, Uncle Ray?" Lizabeth asked.

"Not likely. The nurses have their hands full. Where are J.M. and Mira?"

"They will be along later."

"How are they handling this?" Walter asked.

"They are happy that you are okay," Cam said. "But that is tempered by people driving by and staring at the house where the

189

notorious Walter Braden lives. They've spent a lifetime avoiding scandal, and you laid it on their doorstep."

"Maybe I should move out."

"No way," Eileen said. "We have to keep an eye on the infamous black sheep in the family."

"How is the job with our sister coming along?" Walter asked her.

"It couldn't be better. We love working together and Lizabeth is teaching me the wholesale end of the business."

"She's a natural," Lizabeth said. "She has a flair for selling fashion."

"You two make a terrific team," Walter said.

Jimmy walked into the room. He had a bandage on his head to hold what was left of his right ear in place, but he was smiling and moving around okay.

"I heard you had company," he said to Walter, as he greeted Lizabeth and Eileen.

"How are you feeling?" Lizabeth asked.

"I'm good, and very thankful the bullet wasn't a few inches to the left."

Walter was thankful too. He had never dreamed that trying to help the Negro community might put others in danger. He felt responsible for what had happened to his friends, and he vowed not to let it happen again.

"How long are you in for?" Cam asked Walter.

"I should be released to recover at home by the end of the week."

"You will be in Mother's domain," Eileen said. "Her *Key to the Scriptures* and mind-over-matter philosophy should have you up and around in no time."

"Maybe I can stay here for a few more days."

"We will have none of that," Lizabeth said. "If you can face a bullet, you can face Mother."

"I'll leave on that note," Uncle Ray said, and Jimmy said he'd be going too. They bid them goodbye, and Walter visited with his siblings for another half hour until his eyes started to close.

"Walter, you look tired," Eileen said.

"Yes. I can't seem to control when I'm going to fall asleep."

"You need your rest, so we are going to leave," Eileen said. She and Lizabeth kissed him on the forehead.

"Please stop by and see Drum," Walter said.

"We were planning to, and we will see you tomorrow."

"Lizabeth, could I talk to you for a minute?" Walter asked. She stayed behind as the others left the room.

"I thought Terri might come by to see me."

"I'm sorry, Walter. She had to get back to Los Angeles."

"Oh. I see."

"I don't think you do. She helped stop the bleeding on your shoulder wound and rode to the hospital in the ambulance. She stayed with you until the family arrived and waited until she knew you were going to be okay before she left."

"What did she say about us?"

"She is not in a relationship with anyone. She was afraid you would be resentful of the time it would take for her to become an actress, so she put you off."

"She could have given me that explanation."

"She didn't think you would understand."

"Perhaps not. Her ambition seems more important than romance."

"Maybe something will work out for you later."

"Perhaps," he said. For now, he was still angry that she had chosen Hollywood over him.

"You need to get your rest, so don't dwell on it. I will see you tomorrow." She kissed him on the cheek and left the room.

When the commotion died down and the family had left the hospital, Luther and Prince came into the room.

"Hey, Walter. How you feeling?" Luther asked.

"Not too bad, considering the Klan used me for target practice."

"I heard that. A lot of us feel responsible for you getting shot."

"Sometimes things happen that are out of our control. How did you get Prince here?"

"He handed me a note saying he wanted to come."

"Are your meetings with Charlene going okay?" Walter asked.

Prince nodded that they were.

"Do you like the psychologist?"

Prince nodded again.

"I'm glad to hear it. I'll go by and see Charlene when they release me."

Walter stopped to take a sip of water. "Luther, you and Prince will have to keep an eye on our projects while Jimmy and I are laid up."

"We are taking care of that, so don't you worry."

"Prince should be making enough money to get out of your backroom and into an apartment."

"That's what I said, but he won't go. He likes to keep his door open and hear what's going on in the barbershop. We're the only family he's got."

"That's okay, as long as the lies you and your customers tell don't corrupt him."

That got a laugh out of Luther and the trace of a smile from Prince.

"We'll let you get to sleep, Walter. We're glad you're okay. Get well, and we will see you when you're back at work."

"Thanks for coming," Walter said.

Luther and Prince walked out the door, and Walter fell into a deep sleep.

CHAPTER FOURTEEN

July 1936

LIZABETH WAS HELPING EILEEN AND her mother prepare Sunday dinner. Walter was in the living room visiting with the family. It had taken a couple of months for him to recover from his wound. He had lasted a week under Mira's watchful eye, and the prodding from J.M. to switch jobs, before deciding it would be mentally beneficial to get back to work.

Jimmy's ear had been reconstructed by a surgeon. It was a bit shorter than the ear on the other side. However, it was a conversation piece that he could point to when the Film Row ambush came up; how a few inches made all the difference between losing an ear or taking a bullet between the eyes.

Drum had recovered from the leg wound with only a slight limp that the doctor said would go away in a few months. He kiddingly announced that he and Walter were still friends, but that he would be declining any future dinner invitations.

Lizabeth's business was in bit of a downturn. The country was still struggling to get out of the Depression, so new clothing was a luxury that most could not afford. And the Midwest was experiencing a major heat wave that sapped the energy of consumers and kept them seeking shade rather than shopping for clothes. She was fortunate that her designs were merchandised in enough stores to carry the company through these difficult times.

Eileen's return home had been a blessing. She was Lizabeth's number one salesperson, because she was so likable and could dress the part. There were few fashion designs that did not look good on Eileen. The first few weeks she was home, Lizabeth thought Eileen was depressed about not making it in films, but soon she was back acting with the Red Barn Players and seemed to be putting her Hollywood adventure behind her.

Lizabeth went into the dining room and started taking the plates out of the china hutch to set the table. Her mother had fans circulating in the dining room and the living room. The men's concession to the heat was the removal of dinner jackets and the loosening of ties.

"I don't believe it's ever been this hot in July," Pop said.

"Not that I can remember," J.M. confirmed.

"If it is over a hundred degrees now, can you imagine what August will be like?" Uncle Ray asked.

"I try not to," Cam said.

"What did you think of the Louis and Schmeling fight, Jimmy?" Ray asked. In New York, Max Schmeling had knocked out Joe Louis in the twelfth round of the world championship held at Yankee Stadium.

"I was shocked that Schmeling won," Jimmy replied. "I thought it would be the other way around."

"Everyone did," J.M. said. "Hitler is boasting that Schmeling's win is an example of the superiority of the Germanic race. Now that Hitler has occupied the Rhineland without a whimper of protest from England or France, the world had better start preparing for war."

"I don't think we will be suckered into another European war," Ray said. "President Roosevelt has promised that we will not get involved."

"I doubt that he will have much choice," J.M. countered. "Germany is out for world domination and eventually it will be coming for us."

"If it's that obvious, then why can't England and France do something?" Cam asked.

"Collective denial," J.M. answered. "Both countries lost millions of young men in the last war, and they can't believe that Germany would start another one."

"I can't believe it either," Pop said. "How much misery can one country let loose on the world?"

"I'm afraid we're going to find out," J.M. said.

The talk of war was unsettling for Lizabeth, because of the implications for her brothers, so she finished setting the table and joined the women in the kitchen. Her mother had long ago given up on keeping her kitchen clear of company. Perhaps it was the smell of food or feminine curiosity that made it a natural gathering place. Mira had learned to work around everyone, doing three things at once, and picking up just enough of the conversation to join in when something was directed her way. Lizabeth and Eileen were old hands in the kitchen and anticipated most of her moves, but Mira was a stickler for precise measurement, and no one could help with her recipes.

Helen, Erma, and Nana stayed out of her way as best they could, without relinquishing their share of the kitchen.

"How do you think Walter is doing?" Nana asked.

"I think he has recovered nicely," Mira replied. "He was up and about sooner than expected. I'm not sure whether it was good care or too much mothering that put him back on his feet."

"You did your best," Eileen assured her.

"I thought he might try another line of work," Nana said.

"J.M. and I try our best to convince him to leave Hannon, but he just ignores us. I'm afraid if we keep nagging, we will drive him away."

"Walter is not one to be intimidated by what happened," Erma said. "Ray says that he is very good with people and with community organizing."

"Then why are people shooting at him?" Helen asked.

"His work in the Negro community made some Klan members angry. With their leader in prison, there isn't much chance of that happening again."

"It seems to me that he is still in a vulnerable position," Mira said, as she checked the roast in the oven. "Trying to improve race relations in this town is a thankless task."

"Walter has always stood up for the underdog," Lizabeth said. "I'm proud of him for what he has accomplished in the Negro community. He has built two grade schools, and a recreation center, and created a lot of goodwill."

"Yes. But is it worth taking a bullet?" Mira countered.

"Has he heard anything from Terri?" Helen asked.

"I don't think so. She is too busy trying to make it in Hollywood."

"I miss her," Helen said.

"Yes. We all do," Mira said. "I'm grateful that she helped Walter when he was wounded, but disappointed that she chose a career over him."

"Maybe something good will happen for the two of them," Eileen said.

"You've always been the optimist in the family," Mira replied. She put her hands on her hips and looked around. "Now where did I leave my oven gloves? This dinner would be done twice as fast if I could remember where I put the things that I need."

Lizabeth stared at her mother for a moment, her mind churning with possibilities. "Oh, my goodness!" she said excitedly. "Say that again, Mother!"

"Say what again?"

"What you just said about the dinner."

"What in the world has gotten into you, Lizabeth? I said the dinner would be done twice as fast if I could remember where I put things."

"That's it! That's it!" Lizabeth hugged her mother, bursting with excitement.

"What are you so worked up about?" Mira asked, looking at Lizabeth like she had gone mad.

"The product that I've been searching for all these months." She grabbed a sheet of paper off the kitchen counter and started sketching, as everyone gathered around to watch. She made some swift strokes with a pen and held it up for everyone to see.

"It's an apron with enough pockets to hold your gloves, utensils, and anything else that you might need. We will call it the Liz Braden

196

Home Helper apron. It will be a product that women can use year-round, and we can sell it in all types of stores."

"It's a great idea, but are you sure it will sell?" Erma asked.

"I've never been surer of anything in my life. Would you buy one?"

"Indeed, I would."

The commotion brought Cam and Walter into the kitchen.

"What in the world is going on?" Walter asked.

"A new product design," Lizabeth answered. "Do you think you could have three seamstresses from the Negro community come by next week for Erma to interview?"

"That I will gladly do."

"Good. We will start production on the Home Helper apron immediately, and we will need all the help we can get."

The next three months were a whirlwind for Lizabeth. J.M. had designed ads for the major department stores: Harzfeld's, John Taylor's, Kline's, Peck's, and Rothschild's, for a test market on the Home Helper apron. Lizabeth was ecstatic when the stores sold out and were clamoring for more of the product.

She hired the three Negro seamstresses Walter had sent for the interview. They were dedicated employees and a good fit for the Designers' Club. She made a sales trip to St. Louis to sell the apron to leading department stores. Eileen did the same in Chicago, and Jennie was covering Des Moines, Wichita, and the smaller cities in the Midwest. The Home Helper apron was a huge success and orders were coming in from all over. She had to hire ten more seamstresses to keep up with the demand.

The warehouse Walter had found for her was bulging at the seams and sewing machines were humming all through the work-day, and she still couldn't keep up with the orders. She did not rest on her success, because she knew that complacency would be the death knell for her business, so she designed the apron in different styles and colors. Some had striped patterns, and others were floral prints. Lizabeth insisted that each apron be feminine, so bows and frills were part of every design.

The apron was so popular that she had J.M. create a catalog that she sent to department stores in every major city in the country. Orders were pouring in, so she had to hire more employees to run the catalog department. She sold the apron to retailers at six dollars a dozen, so they could sell them for under a dollar and make a tidy profit.

She knew that her business was vulnerable to cheap knockoffs, so she had her attorney patent the apron, and she would not sell to any store that would not give her an exclusive. The Liz Braden Home Helper apron was very much a product of Liz Braden's Original Designs and she was proud of the quality her name represented. But the biggest surprise was that her original business model of designing dresses was turned upside down.

She had planned for her fashions to lead the way into new accounts, but retailers were having such success with the apron, they were also ordering her fall fashion line and holiday designer dresses. With this kind of success, she was so busy that she had no personal life. Cory was being considerate and making no demands on her time, because he could see how busy she was. When he showed up at the warehouse, he would greet her and then go visit with Margie, or his sister, Jennie.

Margie's part of the business had also expanded, and Lizabeth had hired two women to help with crocheting. Her father was also a big help in expanding the business. Lizabeth appreciated that he stuck with advertising and did not try to make suggestions about how to run the company.

A lot of men would have tried to take on that role, because they felt women should be subservient, but J.M. stayed in the background. Lizabeth knew that he was proud of her success. When there was a decision to be made on advertising, he always deferred to her wishes. She hoped his title as advertising director for Liz Braden's Original Designs was enough to heal any wounds inflicted by the Depression, and that he would not leave her for something more prestigious.

With money pouring in, she paid top wages and furnished lunch for her employees in addition to lemonade, coffee, and tea breaks. Erma let the employees decide when they needed to rest. It seemed that the more freedom and benefits the employees received, the harder they worked, and production was soaring. To show her appreciation, Lizabeth designed a blouse with a Designers' Club logo, which her employees wore with pride. It gave them a sense of belonging to something more than working for a paycheck.

She had Cam to thank for a tremendous increase in production. He had gone to Dearborn, Michigan, to observe the workings of the Ford Motor Company. He suggested that she consider mass producing the apron, using a technique that Henry Ford had perfected to speed assembly. She assigned each employee a specific part of the apron to work on and did the same for dresses. Her employees caught on quickly and became experts at their assigned task before passing the item down the line for completion. The process had doubled production.

The entire staff had worked so hard that at the end of October she called a meeting at quitting time, and they gathered around her.

"I want to thank you for the hard work you have put in over the past few months. You have made the company a huge success, and I want to show my appreciation. We have been going at such a frenetic pace, that it is time to slow down and have some fun. Tomorrow, we are going to work from eight until eleven, and then have a Halloween party from eleven until four. That will give you time to get home to be with your families. Eileen and I have always had great fun greeting the ghosts and goblins at our door in Brookside, and I'm sure you want to do the same in your neighborhood. It is not mandatory, but you might want to wear your Halloween attire tomorrow, and we will have prizes for the most original costumes."

There was a collective murmur of excitement from the group. "Now go home and work on your costumes and try not to scare anyone too badly when you ride the streetcar to work in the morning."

Her employees got into the spirit of the Halloween party, and the next day all sorts of monsters, skeletons, and ghosts came parading through the warehouse door. Lizabeth couldn't tell anyone's identity, so there was great fun when they peeled off their masks and revealed themselves. She had dressed as a clown, and the staff got a charge out of squeezing the round, red nose.

She was grateful for the friendliness displayed by the staff for the Negro employees. They were respectful of the Negro women's tendency to stick together and not get too friendly. Lizabeth knew that although her company was integrated, decades of segregation could not be easily set aside.

When the Negro employees stepped outside Liz Braden's Original Designs, they faced challenges unknown to white employees. She was thankful that every staff member had put on a costume, because it made her feel like they respected the camaraderie she was trying to establish in the company. At noon, they ate a catered lunch and played games until three o'clock, when Lizabeth was going to announce the costume winner and two runners-up. She had let the staff vote on their favorites, and she and Erma were tabulating the results.

"Okay! Quiet, everyone! It is time to announce the winners of the costume competition." She looked at the tabulated results. "The grand prize winner is Sarah, for her loveable hobo costume." That got applause from everyone, as Lizabeth handed Sarah a card with some cash. "Second place is Kayla's friendly ghost." More applause, as the Negro employee received her card with cash. "And third place goes to Margie's fairy princess." Lizabeth went to her and handed her the prize as everyone cheered. "Happy Halloween to you all," she said. "Now go home and let the fun continue."

She and Eileen were at home in Brookside when darkness fell, and a big harvest moon lit up the neighborhood. They took their stations at the front door. Eileen had donned a cape and a scary Dracula mask to offset Lizabeth's friendly, painted-on clown face. Mira came into the living room to see what they were up to.

"I'm convinced that you two have more fun than the kids," she said. She looked at the candy dishes. "My word! You are giving out Hershey candy bars in a depression! The neighborhood kids will be spoiled beyond belief. Most of them are happy with a stick of gum."

"We decided they needed a special treat this year. Something they can enjoy and won't soon forget."

"They will probably camp out on our doorstep for years to come."

"We have the money, so what better way than to share it with the kids."

"Well, then, trick or treat," Mira said. The girls handed her a candy bar and laughed with her as she went back into the kitchen.

The first group of kids came to the door and was welcomed by Lizabeth's friendly clown face. They watched in awe as she put a candy bar in each of their bags.

"Thank you," they muttered in complete astonishment. And just when they least expected it, Eileen jumped out from around the corner, threw up her cape and screeched through her Dracula mask. It scared the wits out of the kids, and they ran screaming from the porch.

"Happy Halloween," Lizabeth called after them. The sisters repeated their routine throughout the evening and soon realized that the candy bars were drawing two and three visits from some of the ghosts and goblins. But they didn't mind and were thankful the candy lasted until the last trick-or-treater faded into the night.

Lizabeth took off her rubber clown nose and plopped down on the couch.

"I'm beat," she said. Eileen sat down beside her. "What a day. The Halloween party and the trick-or-treaters have worn me out."

Mira brought in some tea and cookies.

"Thank you, Mother," Eileen said. "This is so kind of you."

"Your reward for surviving another Halloween. I liked the way you lured the poor darlings with the candy bars, and then scared the wits out of them with Dracula."

"I'm sure the candy bars were worth the fright," Lizabeth said. "Hopefully the parents won't have to stay up all night reassuring them."

"I remember when you two were holy terrors in the neighborhood, running from house to house, trick or treating like you were afraid the candy would run out. You would fill your bags three and four times, and I would have to limit how much candy you could eat."

"We stashed some away in our secret hiding places, but you always managed to find it," Lizabeth said. "It was terribly distressing when we went to retrieve our stash and found that it was gone."

"You should be thankful that I saved you from a life of sugar dependency. You've both had a busy day, so as soon as you finish your tea, it's off to bed." She kissed them both on the cheek and retreated to her bedroom.

"Nothing has changed since we were kids," Lizabeth said. "We are still taking orders from Mother."

"Yes, and I think it's something we've both grown to cherish. She's our safety net."

"She is indeed, so let's follow orders and call it a day. You take the bathroom first, and I will meet you in bed."

Later, they were both so keyed up from the Halloween excitement that it was hard to sleep. It was Lizabeth's favorite time, because she could have Eileen all to herself.

"What would you think of us getting a place of our own?" Lizabeth asked.

"Why pay rent when we can live here for free?"

"I mean to buy a home."

"We are in a depression. Where would we get the money?"

"If business continues at this pace, we could buy a home and pay if off in a couple of years."

"Really?" Eileen was surprised. "You are doing that well?"

"No. *We* are doing that well. The Home Helper apron has been a godsend for us."

"It might be heartbreaking for our parents."

"Maybe not. I've heard there is something to be said for empty nesting."

"I have a feeling that Walter and Cam will be leaving soon. If we moved out, our parents would have to face each other. Who knows where that would lead?"

"Perhaps to reconciliation." Lizabeth wanted to be optimistic.

"Not likely. Haven't you felt the chill in the room when they are together?"

"They might warm to each other if they're left alone. And besides, we can't live with our parents forever."

"I know, but now is such a happy time that I don't want it to end."

"Does that mean you have recovered from your adventure in Hollywood?"

"I still have pangs of regret."

"In March, you said that your movie would be out in six months. It should be out now. Have you heard anything from your agent?"

"I don't expect to. It was going to be distributed on the East Coast, where most B movies have a short life and disappear quickly.

But it doesn't matter, because we are having such fun working together that I am gradually putting it behind me."

"We are, aren't we? The Braden sisters taking on the world of fashion. How could it possibly get any better than that?"

"If your feet were warmer, it would help."

Lizabeth laughed and snuggled closer to her sister. "Get some sleep, because tomorrow our adventure continues. We are shipping our first batch of holiday aprons."

November 1936

Tom Hannon won the November election, with help from the Negro community and his base in the first ward, which included the merchants and friends whom Walter had cultivated downtown. The Boss had closed off two blocks of Main Street and the victory party was in full swing when Walter and Jimmy arrived at party headquarters. Tom came over and handed them each a beer.

"Congratulations on your win," Walter said.

The Boss grabbed a glass of lemonade and held it up for a toast.

"Thank you, but it was our win. That was a fine job you and Jimmy did in the Negro community. My strategists tell me you put us over the top."

"I'm glad to hear it. The money you put into the community made the difference more than anything we did."

"I don't buy that. It was a matter of winning their trust, and you came through. And it wasn't lost on the Negro community that you and Jimmy each took a bullet for your actions against the Klan."

"What happens now that the election is over?" Walter asked, hoping the money flowing into the community would not be cut off. Uncle Ray walked up and joined the conversation.

"That's what I wanted to discuss with you. The second ward is two-thirds Negro and one-third Italian. The reason no money flows back into the Negro community is lack of representation on the city council. The Italians always win the seat."

"Why? There are more Negroes than whites in the district."

"Intimidation," Ray said. "There have been forty Negroes murdered in that district the past few years. The Black Hand keeps the Negroes in line, much the same way the Klan does the Negroes."

"The Italian vigilante group," Walter said, acknowledging the covert operation.

"Exactly so. They are a vicious, clandestine bunch of gangsters. Many of them learned their trade in the old country. They blanket the polls at election time, and their presence alone keeps the Negroes away. The Negroes have to weigh voting against having their homes burned down."

"I see your point. Can anything be done about it?"

"Not until now," Tom said. "I've needed a man who has the respect of the Negro community before making a change, and that's where you come in."

"Hold on," Walter said. "We fought the Klan, but we are not taking on the Black Hand."

Tom smiled. "That's not what we are asking of you. I'm incorporating some of the first ward into the second ward and creating a new third ward, so the Negro community can stand alone."

"How is that going to set with the Italian community? Won't they lose revenue?"

"The spoils from the first ward will more than make up for the loss. I've squared this with Joe Bianco, the second ward boss. There is a strict rule that ward bosses don't infringe on any other ward, so you don't have to worry about the Black Hand."

Walter thought that separating two ethnic groups that didn't get along was a master stroke.

"Where do I come in?" he asked.

"I want you to be ward boss for that district."

Walter was stunned and speechless for a moment. "I'm flattered, sir, but there are several reasons that won't work. I'm too young, too inexperienced, and I'm not a Negro. And if that's not enough, I'm no politician."

"It's true that you will be my youngest ward boss, but you have plenty of experience working with the business community downtown. And more important, you have the respect and admiration of the other ward bosses. None of them have taken a bullet for the organization. You have the respect of the Negro community, and you have proven that you can get things done. If you walk away now, all the progress you've made comes to a halt. The money dries up, and you will be abandoning the friends you have made. And for your last concern, being a ward boss is not a political appointment."

Walter thought about that for a moment. "You must have a reason for creating a new ward."

"There is no secret agenda. I want to solidify my base for future elections. The more we can make that ward prosper, the more votes for me in the next election. And I want a Negro appointed to the city council to represent the ward the way it should be represented."

"If I take the job, would you consider making a Negro the ward boss sometime in the future?"

"The timing would have to be right. But, yes, I would consider it."

Walter felt like he would be walking away from his responsibility to the Negro community if he turned down the offer.

"If you think I can do the job, I'll give it my best." Walter tried to sound more confident than he really was.

The two men shook hands.

"Ray will explain how things work. Now, you and Jimmy enjoy the party." Tom disappeared into the sea of well-wishers.

"What is this ward business all about, Uncle Ray?"

"You will be responsible for collecting money from merchants and any underground businesses, like gambling establishments and houses of ill repute. Hannon takes his percentage of the spoils in all the wards, but everything else is yours to spend as you see fit. The Italians were milking the Negro community and keeping the money for themselves. You should have enough money to continue your goodwill projects."

"Does that mean the funding from Boss Hannon is coming to a halt?"

"The organization will kick back enough money to pay you and Jimmy a nice salary and money for three staff members. The community projects will have to come from your collections."

"Why does he need a ward boss? He has people who can make collections."

"That's true, but then he has to control the ward. This way he just has to control you."

"What's the secret to getting everyone to pay?"

"That will be up to you. The Italians used intimidation."

"That's not my style."

"You found a way with the merchants downtown, and the Boss is confident you will do the same on the east side."

"It would probably be a good idea if we kept this news away from my parents," Walter said.

"I couldn't agree more, so I will offer my congratulations here, rather than in front of the family." He shook Walter's hand and then left to join the party.

"We have to get in touch with Luther and set up a meeting of business and religious leaders," Walter said. "And we will have to set up an office on the east side."

"Boss Braden has a nice ring to it," Jimmy said, giving Walter a playful dig.

"Don't even go there," Walter replied.

The meeting was held at the new community center. The room was packed and noisy, as everyone wondered what this was about. On stage with Walter sat the imposing figure of Ezra Cross, who had led the 18th Street brawl. Sitting next to him were Delores Johnson, the accountant, and Jimmy. Prince was in the background, watching.

Walter held up his hands for quiet. "Thank you all for coming tonight. We have some important announcements to make. First, your vote put Tom Hannon back in office, so to show his appreciation he is going to make this district independent, and you will no longer be part of the second ward." That stunned the crowd into silence.

"You mean we will have our own ward?" a man asked.

"That's right."

"What about the money we have to pay Boss Bianco?"

"There will be no more Bianco. Instead of the money he extorted from you and spent in the Italian district, you will now be making those payments into a fund for yourselves and this community."

"What about payments to Hannon?" asked a man seated in the front row.

"Hannon will still get his percentage of the dues. That is a fact of life in all of the wards."

"Who will be the new ward boss?"

"That would be me."

"You? You're too young to be a ward boss." Several people shook their heads in agreement.

"My sentiments exactly."

"Why does Hannon want the ward controlled by a white man?"

"My appointment is temporary, until we see how things go."

One of the religious leaders stood up. "How do we know that you will put the money back into the community?"

"Take a look around you at this new community center. We also kept our promise on the two grade schools. Many of you know Delores Johnson. She is the newly appointed accountant for the ward, so I will let her speak."

Delores went to the podium. "We have decided the best way to handle your payments will be by check. We don't want any loose cash floating around. Walter is insisting on transparency, so you are welcome to check the books whenever you wish."

"Which set of books will you show us?" a man asked. That brought laughter from the gathering.

Delores remained composed. "There will only be one. I am a God-fearing businesswoman and God says, 'thou shalt not bear false witness.'"

That quieted the crowd, because they could tell she was sincere.

"Thank you, Delores."

Delores nodded and sat down. Walter pointed at a man with his hand raised.

"How much money will you be taking for your cut of the action?"

"My staff and I will continue to be paid by the Hannon organization."

Another man stood up. "Bianco's thugs made the collections. Who will be making them now?"

Walter pointed at Ezra Cross.

"Ezra led our defeat of the Klan and he will head our collections. We no longer want this to be contentious. If you have a problem making payments, please come and see us, and we will try to work things out. However, if you are trying to dodge your responsibility to the community, you will find Ezra to be a very impatient man."

Luther stood up. "I've known Walter for years, and there is no reason for us to question his integrity. He helped us fight the Klan, and he was shot for his efforts. He is providing us a great opportunity to help our community, and we should be thankful. What else do you need us to do, Walter?"

"The leaders of the community should appoint someone to the city council to represent the third ward, and then you should decide what projects to spend the money on that will best serve the community. Please let me know when you have a plan in place."

After shaking hands with a few people, Walter and Jimmy left the meeting.

"Thank goodness, that is out of the way," Walter said, as they got into his car. "It went better than I expected."

"It will work, as long as we don't stay in charge too long. At some point, they will want a Negro running the ward."

"And so they should. Once we smooth things out, we will turn it over to them. I give it about a year, and then it will be time for us to go."

"Hannon might not agree with that."

"He won't have a choice. The Negroes hold the power, because they hold the votes. He won't take a chance on losing an election due to maintaining a white ward boss."

"What will we do when our job here is over?"

"I haven't worked that out yet. But enough of business, let's get a six pack and head to Carol's house."

"I've been wanting to talk to you about that."

Walter looked at him questioningly. "What's up?"

"I've been going out with Carol."

Walter thought about that for a moment. "You mean like dating?"

"Yes. I like her a lot."

"Well, good for you. She is quite a girl, and I wish you both the best. You must bring her to Thanksgiving dinner next week, so she can meet the family."

"She was your girl first. Are you sure you don't mind?"

"Not in the least. I'm happy for you. Now let's head to the Hi Hat club and celebrate a new beginning for the Negro community and for us."

The next day Walter decided that even though he and Terri were not getting along, there was no reason not to go by and see Charlene to see how Prince was doing.

Millie, the housekeeper, directed him to the parlor where Charlene was seated. "Hello, Charlene." He kissed her hand. "How have you been?"

"Just fine, Walter. How is your shoulder? I was so sorry to hear that you were wounded."

"I'm fine. Thank you for the card that you sent. It meant a lot to me."

"You are very welcome."

"I wanted to stop by and see how Prince is doing."

"With the help of the psychologist, we are making progress."

"Can you be more specific?"

"Yes. His name is Marcus Taylor."

"That means you are getting him to talk."

"We are."

"That's great news. Have you found out anything about his background?"

"He is from Detroit. His father left the family when he was an infant. He was raised by his mother and grandmother until his mother became hooked on drugs and left town. He has no idea where she might be. His grandmother took over, and she was the sole provider for Marcus and a younger brother and sister."

"Any idea what caused the trauma?"

"The family lived in a tenement apartment. Marcus was out early on his newspaper route when a fire broke out. He lost his grandmother and his two siblings."

"That's heartbreaking," Walter said.

"Yes. That traumatic experience, and the realization that he was all alone, caused him to stop talking. He lived on the streets of Detroit for a while, getting by on his wits, and an ability to defend himself."

"How did he get to Kansas City?"

"He was sleeping in an alley outside a jazz club when he heard some musicians talking about Vine Street. It sounded enticing, compared to how he had been living. He hopped a freight train to Kansas City and made it to Vine Street but was unable to find work, so he drifted a few blocks east to Luther's barbershop. He knows you were having a bit of fun when you gave him that moniker, the Prince of Woodland Avenue, but it made him feel special. He thinks that he would have ended up in a bad way if you and Luther hadn't taken an interest in him. He is a very loyal person. He got his sense of honor from his grandmother, who taught him not to take what he hadn't earned. That's why he turns down the tips."

"You've made amazing progress, Charlene. I want to thank you and the psychologist."

"Don't thank us yet. He still has a lot of anger issues. It won't take much to set him off."

"If you and the psychologist can keep working with him, Luther and I will try to keep him busy and out of trouble."

"Of course, we will. It might take some time for him to start talking anywhere else but here, so I wouldn't push him."

"Okay. We will follow your instructions. Let us know if there's anything else we can do."

"Now, for the important question," Charlene said. "What is going on with you and my daughter?"

Walter paused and met her gaze. "Beats me. She was amazing when I was wounded. She stopped the bleeding and rode with me to the hospital. After that, she hasn't been in contact and doesn't seem to have any interest in continuing the relationship."

"She is focused on her career, and ambition might be winning out over romance."

"I gathered as much."

"You need to give her some space and some time, and maybe it will work out."

"I had better be going, Charlene. Thanks again for all you are doing for Prince. Although I guess I should start calling him Marcus."

"Keep calling him Prince. The name Marcus takes him back to a place he doesn't want to be."

"Okay. I'll do that."

⁓

The day before Thanksgiving, Lizabeth and Eileen were at home with the family. The two of them, along with Jennie, had become quite a successful sales team. Lizabeth rewarded them by paying a percentage of the business they brought in. The Home Helper apron had given the company a huge boost in sales, and production was at an all-time high. She and Eileen worked so well together that she was thinking about making her a partner in Liz Braden's Original Designs. They were at the dining room table, going over fashions for the spring season. Mira was in the kitchen, polishing silverware for Thanksgiving dinner, and J.M. was reading in his den. Cam was due in from a road trip, and Walter was out for the evening.

Lizabeth showed Eileen one of her drawings. "I think we should manufacture a line of colorful frocks for women to wear around the house. Something that is stylish, yet comfortable, and can even be used for maternity wear. We can also make specialty frocks for artists and for those who work in situations where they need something to wear over their good clothes."

"They would be great for our employees, because they would be comfortable and functional for sewing," Eileen said.

Their meeting was interrupted by a knock at the door. Lizabeth went to answer. The November air had turned cold and a man carrying a briefcase stood shivering on the stoop. He was dressed in a fashionable gray suit with a matching striped tie. His face was tanned from the sun, and he had wavy, black hair. He was immaculate from head to toe and looked out of place in a cold Midwestern neighborhood. Lizabeth wondered what he was selling out of the briefcase.

"May I help you?"

"Yes. Is this the home of Eileen Braden?"

"It is. Come inside before you freeze to death."

"Thank you. I left California yesterday and didn't expect it to be this cold."

Lizabeth wondered why people from warm climates expected their weather to travel with them.

"Eileen. You have a visitor," she called, and Eileen appeared at the door.

"Max? What are you doing here?" Mira and J.M. heard the commotion and came to the door.

"This is my agent, Max Abrams."

Max shook hands with J.M. and nodded at Mira.

"Come and sit in the living room," Mira said.

Max followed them in and sat on the couch. "To answer your question, Eileen, I'm here to try to convince you to give Hollywood another try."

"We've been through that, and I'm not interested. What made you think I might change my mind?"

Max opened the briefcase and dumped a pile of letters onto the coffee table.

"Your movie is a big hit on the East Coast and these letters are just a fraction of the fan mail the studio has been receiving."

Eileen looked bewildered. She picked up a letter and scanned the contents. It was full of superlatives about her acting performance.

"I thought the movie would be out of circulation by now."

"So did the studio executives. Now they're clamoring to get you back. I know you were not comfortable with the exploitation in Hollywood, but with the success of the movie, you will be in charge of your career. Now Hollywood wants you, rather than you wanting it."

"I'm flattered by the response to the movie and by the fan letters, but I'm enjoying working for my sister's company."

"I understand that. I told the studio executives that they would have to come up with a good offer to get you back."

"What are they offering?"

"Five hundred dollars a week, plus expenses."

"Five hundred dollars a week!" J.M. was incredulous. "Don't they realize we are still in an economic depression?"

"I appreciate your dismay, Mr. Braden. It seems that Hollywood is making more money than ever and is insulated from the effects of a depression."

"Money isn't everything," Lizabeth said. "You have to be happy." She did not want her sister to leave again, especially because their future together looked so bright.

"I agree with my sister," Eileen said. "No amount of money is worth being away from my family and friends and being unhappy."

"With the money you will be making, you can bring your family to Hollywood, or come home when you are not making a picture. You will have the star power to do whatever you want. And think what that money could do to help your family."

"Thanks to Liz Braden's Original Designs, my family is doing just fine."

"I believe you have a personal stake in this, Mr. Abrams," J.M. said.

"Yes, sir. The studio pays me a percentage of the earnings, but I try to do what's best for my clients. Your daughter has the talent to become an A-list actress, and I would be remiss if I did not do everything in my power to make that happen."

"It's all so confusing," Eileen said. "I had put Hollywood behind me and now this happens."

"You had better think it through," Mira said. "We want you to be happy, so be sure you won't regret your decision if you turn it down."

Eileen's agent stood up. "I want you to do one thing for me and then if you are still undecided, I will get on the train to California and you will never see me again."

"What is it?"

"My car is outside. I want you and your sister to ride downtown with me and let me show you something."

Lizabeth and Eileen looked at each other, wondering what this was about.

"Why not?" Lizabeth said. "You can decide about the movie business once and for all." She couldn't imagine what Eileen's agent had in mind, but she was sure that she was ahead in the competition for her sister.

As they drove downtown, Eileen and her agent made small talk about what was happening in the movie industry. Lizabeth looked out of the car window at some of the homes and businesses that were testing Christmas lights. It was a Thanksgiving tradition in Kansas City to not turn them on until Thanksgiving night, when the entire city would be lit with colorful displays. When they arrived at 11th and Main downtown, Max stopped the car at a red light.

"Okay, I want you to close your eyes," he said.

"What for?" Eileen asked.

"You said you would play along."

Lizabeth and Eileen closed their eyes.

Max drove another block and then parked the car along the curb.

"Now open your eyes and look to the left," he said.

213

When Lizabeth opened her eyes, she knew she had lost Eileen to Hollywood. Across the street, shining out into the darkness, the bright lights on the marquee of Loew's Midland Theatre shone with the bold lettering of the current release. It read: "Jean Harlow Starring in RIFFRAFF." Below that the marquee read: "Coming Soon—*A Country Afternoon* starring Tom Morgan and Eileen Braden." What actress could resist having her name up in lights for all the world to see? And it seemed to Lizabeth that it was Eileen's destiny to be a star, because Jean Harlow, the other actress on the marquee, was also from Kansas City.

"If you sign a contract," Max said, "the studio will pay for a Kansas City Christmas premiere showing of *A County Afternoon*. You can invite your friends and family, and I will invite the dignitaries. We will make it the event of the year."

Eileen turned away from the marquee and looked at Lizabeth.

"I know what you are thinking," Lizabeth said. "I release you from your commitment to me and to Liz Braden's Original Designs, because we both know this is the opportunity of a lifetime, and you can't turn it down."

"I feel like I would be deserting you."

"Don't be silly. I would hate myself if I kept you from living your dream."

"Then it is settled," Max said. "I will contact the Kansas City newspapers about the premiere and have you available for interviews. Your life is going to change dramatically, so be ready for a wave of publicity."

That night Lizabeth lay in bed listening to Eileen's steady breathing. Her sister could sleep through anything, even the realization that she was on the verge of stardom. Life was going to be difficult without her sister, especially because things were going so well with the business. However, her experience with the fire had taught her that with every setback comes opportunity. There was something about tonight's events that was eluding her, so she tossed and turned, trying to figure it out.

Tomorrow was Thanksgiving Day, with friends and family, and she wanted to be at her best. She went over a checklist of what she would wear for the occasion. Suddenly, she sat straight up in bed with her heart pounding. Eileen's movie premiere would be the perfect vehicle to promote the Liz Braden line of formal dresses. She would bring in the wives of the dignitaries for a fitting and not charge them for the dresses. She would do the same for friends and family. It would be the best publicity she could get for her fashions, and it would be free.

She wanted Liz Braden's Original Designs to be associated with the premiere because women identified with the movies. If they couldn't be a star, they could dress like one. She would hire an emcee and get Max Abrams to let the emcee handle the red-carpet interviews. And, of course, the emcee would ask each of the women what designer they were wearing. Liz Braden's Original Designs would be front and center at Kansas City's biggest event of the year. After her initial surge of excitement, exhaustion took over, and she fell asleep with designs of formal dresses parading through her dreams.

CHAPTER FIFTEEN

THE DAY BROKE RAINY AND COLD, but nothing could dampen Eileen and Lizabeth's excitement for the announcement that would be made at the family gathering. Eileen wanted her father, as head of the family, to tell everyone the good news. He gathered everyone in the living room. There were some new faces in the group. Jennie was there, and Jimmy had invited his friend, Carol. Max Abrams was a mystery guest, who would soon be revealed by J.M.

"Happy Thanksgiving, everyone. We are glad you could join us to celebrate this joyful occasion. We received some news last night that makes the day even more special. Our out-of-town guest is Max Abrams. Max is Eileen's Hollywood agent, and he has brought some good news. It seems Eileen's movie is a big hit on the East Coast, and she will sign a movie contract with MGM."

There were cheers of delight from the group and many hugs of congratulations for Eileen.

"My two daughters will tell you the rest of the story."

Eileen spoke first. "Max and MGM have arranged to have a Christmas premiere of the movie at Loew's Midland Theatre. It will take place in two weeks, and you are all invited." There was a buzz of excitement in the room.

"And for this very special occasion," Lizabeth said. "Liz Braden's Original Designs will make the dresses for the wives of the dignitaries, and also for you ladies, at no charge. You will need to come in tomorrow and get a preliminary fitting, because we have a lot of dresses to make, and we will be short of time. And that includes you, Carol." Carol beamed with delight. "Now Max wants to say something."

Max moved to the front of the room. "First, I want to thank J.M. and Mira for graciously inviting me to join you on this special occasion. And I want to thank Eileen for signing a contract. Most actresses would have jumped at the chance to become a star, but Eileen was very reluctant to leave her family for a chance at stardom. That is a good indication of the values she was raised with and they will hold her in good stead as she begins her movie career. The movie premiere will be Kansas City's entertainment event of the year, perhaps of the decade. Think searchlights, limousines, red carpets, waves of photographers, and Eileen's costars, sent by the studio to attend the special event. And it will be heavily publicized in newspapers and on the radio. MGM is pulling out all the stops to show Eileen how much it values her as an actress. I hope you all can attend. It is a pleasure to be with you today."

The men stayed in the living room and the women were drawn to the kitchen where the smell of turkey and dressing hung invitingly in the air.

This was such a special occasion that Walter went against his mother's alcohol ban and discreetly removed a bottle he'd hidden and fixed everyone a drink.

"To Eileen's success in the movies," he said, holding up his glass.

The men drank to that as they nodded in agreement.

"Max, you said the movie industry was isolated from the effects of the Depression," J.M. said. "How is the rest of California doing?"

"Not so well. We are being inundated by a mass migration of desperate people from the Dust Bowl. There are shanty towns springing up outside most agricultural communities, where workers wait for any type of labor that might help feed their families. With winter approaching, the migration has slowed a bit, but there are still plenty of jalopies, loaded with family possessions, chugging along the road to a promised land that holds little promise for anyone. That is the shocking reality to those who make the trip and end up worse than when they started. The communities do what they can to help, but there are just too many people who think the road to California is paved in gold, when it's actually paved in misery."

J.M. thought about Eileen's five hundred dollars a week. "But gold keeps flowing into Hollywood," he said.

"There is no denying the movie moguls are making millions. However, they do spread the wealth around by hiring thousands of people, and they have set up funds to help the poor and destitute."

"The movies do a lot of good," Walter said. "What would people do if they couldn't go to a movie and dream about a better life and happier days ahead?"

"With FDR elected to his second term, I'm hopeful we will work our way out of this mess," Max said.

"We are all hopeful," J.M. said. "These are difficult times, but looking at the rest of the world, it doesn't seem so bad. Stalin is purging his citizens by the millions; Germany and Italy are police states bent on war; and this year, five million people have starved to death in China."

"I agree," Pop said. "I would rather be in America in the worst of times, than anywhere else in the best of times."

"I'm afraid the rest of the world will be coming for us," J.M. said. "The Allies are showing nothing but weakness, so Hitler will be emboldened to keep expanding the Fatherland."

"I have some relatives in Germany," Max said. "We are trying to convince them to leave. Hitler has started his own purge and sending those he feels are a threat to the Reich to concentration camps."

J.M. guessed that Max was Jewish, but it would be impolite to ask.

"FDR has promised to keep us out of war," Cam said. "I hope he is as good as his word."

"Don't count on it," Uncle Ray said. "When the going gets tough, they will call on us to bail them out again. What the Europeans start, we have to finish."

Lizabeth came into the room. "Mother is ready to serve, so please be seated at the dining room table."

Mira set an exquisite Thanksgiving table. Her sterling silver service was polished to perfection and set beside Wedgwood china.

The drinking glasses were thin crystal and so delicate they were only used at Thanksgiving and Christmas. Her tablecloth and napkins were white linen, matching the white candles in the silver candelabras, and at each plate was a china turkey figurine. J.M. sat at the head of the table and Mira sat at the other end.

"Please, bow your heads," Mira said. "Dear God, we thank you for the food we are about to receive and for the blessing of having our friends and family together on this day of Thanksgiving. In Jesus name we pray. Amen."

"Amen," echoed the guests.

J.M. started carving the turkey that had been basted in butter as it cooked for most of the day. Mira passed around the side dishes. Each bowl contained food from old family recipes that Mira had treasured through the years. She was the guardian of Thanksgivings past and felt it was a way of keeping alive those relatives who had gone before and were no longer here to share the bounty. Her Thanksgiving meal was traditional. The sweet potatoes were fluffy, topped with butter and brown sugar. The stuffing held the fragrance of steamed chestnuts, and a hint of oranges gave a touch of citrus to the cranberry sauce. Each plate was passed to J.M. for a generous serving of turkey. The guests were aware they were in the presence of cooking greatness, so they savored each bite and kept the conversation to a minimum.

After a while, Max put down his fork and took a sip of water. "This has to be the best meal that I've ever had, Thanksgiving or otherwise."

"Thank you," Mira replied. "Everyone leave room for pumpkin pie or pecan pie."

At the end of the meal, Lizabeth and Eileen removed the dinner plates from the table. They served freshly brewed coffee while Mira was taking requests for homemade pie.

Cam stood up. "I propose a toast. We've been celebrating Eileen, and rightly so, but we have been ignoring the other success story in the family."

Walter thought it was kind of Cam to toast Lizabeth's success.

"To my brother, Walter, who has been appointed by Tom Hannon as boss of the third ward."

There was dead silence at the table. Walter looked at Uncle Ray, who seemed as dumbstruck as Walter. He could feel his father's eyes boring into him.

"Is this true, Ray?" J.M. asked his brother, shifting his contempt away from Walter.

"Yes. It's true." Ray did not meet his brother's gaze. "Walter has done a fantastic job with that ward, and he deserved the promotion."

"I thought we had agreed that after two stays in the hospital, Walter would be pulling away from the Hannon organization."

"With all due respect," Walter said, "that was something you suggested, but there was no agreement."

"I guess being beaten up and then shot was not enough to convince you that you needed another line of work," Mira said.

Max was wide-eyed with curiosity. What had been a peaceful dinner was now an acrimonious standoff. To his understanding, ward boss plus being shot equaled gangster.

"We should all be more appreciative of Walter's accomplishments," Cam said. "He will be getting kickbacks from every business in that ward."

"That is not true," Walter said, defending himself against Cam, who was enjoying Walter's discomfort. "All the money paid in dues goes back into the community."

"I thought hiding money went with the territory." Cam smiled smugly.

"You thought wrong."

"Jimmy tells me that Walter is doing great work in that ward and improving race relations," Carol said.

"Thank you, Carol," Walter replied gratefully.

"You had better be careful," J.M. warned. "Tom Hannon has been using public funds for his own ends for decades. Word is that over the years he has lost more than a million at the racetrack, and the reformers will be tracking that money. When he falls, a lot of people are going to fall with him."

Lizabeth felt bad for Walter. She was sure he missed having Terri here, and now he was once again occupying the family hot seat.

"Congratulations on your promotion, Walter," she said. "My Negro employees tell me you are doing great things in that district. A lot of people owe their jobs to you, including my employees."

"That might be," J.M. said. "But being a white boss in a Negro ward has to breed resentment. Not only will you be ostracized by the white community, you will be a target for every militant Negro who doesn't want a white boss. Where you see benevolence, they see an overseer."

"And don't forget the enemies you have made in the north end," Cam said, keeping the heat on Walter. "I'm sure Sal Marconi still holds a grudge, and the rank and file of the Klan haven't forgotten that you toppled their leader."

It had not occurred to Lizabeth that her brother might still be in danger, and it worried her.

"I understand the implications," Walter said. "I've met with community leaders and told them that I'm only there for the short term. As soon as we get the ward running smoothly, we will appoint a Negro ward boss."

"What is your timeframe?" J.M. asked

"Less than a year."

"I think this conversation needs to take place at a later date," Ray said. "It does not do justice to this wonderful meal and to the spirit of the holiday."

"I second that," Erma said. "We need to be discussing our plans for Eileen's movie premiere."

Walter was glad his aunt and uncle had come to his rescue.

Pop spoke up. "I would like to say that Nana and I are very proud of our grandchildren. The four of you have achieved success in this Depression, and that shows a lot of moxie. In an uncertain world, we have to keep supporting one another, even when we disagree. Now it's time to stop talking and start enjoying Mira's wonderful desserts."

December 1936

Max Abrams was as good as his word. The movie premiere was dazzling. Rotating searchlights flashed through the darkness above the Loew's Midland Theatre. The theatre was completed in 1927 in the Renaissance Revival style at a cost of four million dollars. The exterior featured a four-story arched window above a marquee containing 3,600 lights. Inside, 500,000 feet of gold leaf was displayed throughout the theatre, along with five, huge, hand-cut, crystal chandeliers and precious artwork and antiques. All of the seats were booked for the evening premiere. The street was packed with movie fans, as the limousines pulled up to the curb and deposited the dignitaries and movie stars in front of the theatre.

The governor, the mayor, Tom Hannon, and all of the ward bosses were in attendance. A brass section from the Kansas City Philharmonic greeted each arrival, and they walked on a red carpet, which led to the theatre entrance. The evening was cool, rather than cold, and allowed women to wear a shoulder wrap, so their dresses could be seen. Lizabeth had made sure that no one would outshine her sister on this auspicious occasion.

She had designed a form-fitting, gold satin, evening dress with a matching cape that made Eileen look every inch the movie star. She was escorted by Max Abrams, who led her to the various interview and autograph stations, where she received cheers and applause. Lizabeth wore a black net, beaded-sequin gown that was formal but not overly glamorous. Walter, looking very debonair in a classic tuxedo, was her escort.

She had insisted that Cory escort Margie to the event, so he could help guide her through any uncomfortable situations. Lizabeth had appointed Jennie to be the emcee, because Jennie knew the Liz Braden inventory better than anyone but herself. Jennie was vivacious and not overly impressed with celebrity status. And that allowed her to stay focused and describe the details of the formal dress fashions as they came down the red carpet. The main attraction of the evening was Eileen, but it would also be a big night for Liz Braden fashions.

Queasy and Drum met Walter and Lizabeth in the theatre lobby.

"Look at you two," Walter said. "I never thought I would see you in tuxes."

"We are putting on the dog for Eileen," Queasy said. "We saw Cam out front with Helen talking to the news media. He looked every bit the movie star."

"He is in his element," Walter said. "He wants to soak up as much of Eileen's celebrity as he can."

"Where are your parents?" Drum asked.

"They will be here with my grandparents and with Aunt Erma and Uncle Ray."

"A night for the Bradens to shine and a night to remember," Queasy said. "It looks like the theatre is sold out."

"Tickets are hard to come by," Lizabeth said. "I had to talk Eileen's agent and the theatre owners into a matinee performance tomorrow for my employees. They are so proud of Eileen and want to see her perform."

"A movie star and a fashion czar," Queasy said. "Your sisters are putting us on the map."

"They are at that," Walter said. "And I couldn't be prouder of them."

Another half hour passed, and the lights in the theatre dimmed, causing a rush to be seated. The Bradens and friends had their own row of the best seating in the house. The seats for Eileen and her costar, Tom Morgan, were vacant. Lizabeth suspected Eileen would be too nervous to watch herself perform and it was probably old hat to an established star like Tom Morgan. Lizabeth wondered why actors worked so hard to get on screen and then refused to watch the finished product.

The MGM lion let out a roar and quieted the theatre. *A Country Afternoon* was a delightful comedy. Eileen's role was much like the one she had as Polly in *The Boyfriend*. She was a natural in that her timing was impeccable, and the audience could tell that she didn't take herself too seriously, and that made for an endearing performance. There was lighthearted laughter throughout the movie, and Lizabeth could tell it was going to be a hit.

When the movie ended, the audience rose to their feet and gave a standing ovation. Eileen and Tom Morgan came out onto the stage, and the audience went wild with enthusiastic applause. They received three curtain calls and that closed the evening. Tears of happiness and dismay ran down Lizabeth's cheeks. She was happy for her sister but sad that she would be losing her to Hollywood. Walter handed her a handkerchief and she wiped her eyes.

"Eileen is a homebody, so you will still be seeing plenty of her," he said. "And we can catch a train to Hollywood any time you want."

Lizabeth nodded. Walter was trying to make her feel better, but she had lost her business partner and her roommate, and she knew that nothing would ever be the same again.

The family went backstage, and Lizabeth gave her sister an enthusiastic hug. "You were marvelous, and I know that you are going to be a big star."

"I have a going-away present for you," Eileen said.

Lizabeth looked at her questioningly.

"I had it written into my contract that I will wear your fashions in my movies. That way you will get the publicity and we can stay in contact."

"That is wonderful. How did you manage it?"

"Star power." Eileen winked at her, and they both laughed.

"Remember when you predicted that I would be the third big star from Kansas City?"

"I wish I had predicted that you would be vice president of Liz Braden's Original Designs."

"It's going to be okay," Eileen said. "We will find a way to make it work."

It had dawned on Walter that maybe Max Abrams knew Terri's agent. He grabbed Max by the arm and moved him to a quiet corner of the backstage area.

"I was wondering if you know the agent for Terri Lawson?"

"I do. That would be me."

It made perfect sense, Terri and Eileen had gone to Hollywood together.

"Can you tell me how she is doing?"

"Not so well. She has all the qualities of a good actress, but none of her charisma transferred to the screen. It happens more often than not, and I have never figured out why."

"What is she doing now?"

"She is under contract, so the studio is assigning her bit parts, and she also works as an extra."

"Sounds like you have given up on her."

"Not entirely. She is taking acting lessons and sharpening her skills. She might get a shot at a starring role, but I told her it's not something she should count on."

"Do you have any idea what she will do when her contract expires?"

"No. She is interested in producing documentaries, but she doesn't have the funding."

"Can I have your telephone number?"

224

Max gave Walter his business card.

"Thank you, Max. Is it okay if I contact you?"

"I look forward to it. I gathered from the conversation at Thanksgiving dinner that you are leading a very interesting life here in Kansas City. Would you would be interested in telling your story to a writer? It has all the elements for an interesting script."

"That is a definite no. One family member in the movie business is enough. And I'm sure my parents don't want my exploits on the screen for all to see. Where you see excitement, they see embarrassment."

"I understand. If you change your mind, let me know."

"I will. And thank you for all that you are doing for Eileen."

Two days after the premiere, it was time for Eileen to depart. She had said her goodbyes to her father the night before, and to Cam and Walter before they left for work. Eileen was dressed for her journey, and her suitcases were taken to the front door. Mira had fixed her two girls their favorite breakfast of oatmeal, topped with brown sugar, and a side of cinnamon toast. Max would be picking up Eileen and driving her to Union Station. Lizabeth was glad her sister was leaving from home, because she could not bear another tearful goodbye at the train station. This way she could pretend this goodbye was nothing out of the ordinary.

"Should I pack you something to eat on the train?" Mira asked.

"No, thank you, Mother. The staff on the train will feed us."

"Are you exhausted from yesterday's matinee?" Lizabeth asked Eileen.

"No. I'm still running on adrenaline."

"My employees enjoyed it so much. Somehow you managed to give every employee an autograph. They now feel very much a part of your success."

"I'm going to miss them."

"Where will you live when you get to California?" Mira asked.

"Max has rented me a home in Beverly Hills. I won't be there long, because in a week we are leaving for Monument Valley in Utah to shoot a Western."

"That sounds like a John Wayne or a Gary Cooper movie," Lizabeth said.

"I hope not. I will be intimidated enough without working with a megastar."

"You can hold your own with anyone," Lizabeth encouraged her.

"When I get discouraged, I will think of the resolve of my mother and my sister and quit feeling sorry for myself. You two are my inspiration."

Max showed up at the door, and they let him in.

Lizabeth embraced her sister, and they both started to cry. "I will leave our room just the way it is. When you come back, nothing will have changed," Lizabeth said, as they continued to cling to each other.

Mira never let emotion get the better of her. "Break it up, girls. We don't want Eileen to miss the train." Eileen kissed her mother on the cheek.

Max took Eileen's suitcases, and they moved quickly out the door and into the car. Lizabeth could feel an attack of melancholy coming on, so she grabbed her car keys, said goodbye to her mother, and headed out the door. Her antidote for depression had always been hard work. She would be doing a lot of it in the days ahead.

Walter knew his father was right. No matter how well intentioned, the Negro community would never fully accept him. He had decided to let someone else be the face of the ward while he worked behind the scenes. He also knew that his job could end with a Hannon defeat in the next election. And there was always the possibility of an indictment.

He had to plan for the future, so he called a meeting at the East Side Club, where he would meet with Luther; Luther's son, Eddie; Queasy; and Drum. Jimmy would also be there. The club was at 19th and Vine and catered to a mostly Negro clientele. The marquee announced the Ragin Cajun Jazz Band that Luther's son was a part of. Walter scanned the vacant buildings on either side of the club.

Some of the businesses on the street had made a halfhearted attempt to put up Christmas lights, but they added nothing to a neighborhood that looked old and tired. Inside the club, the only acknowledgment of the holiday season was a small Christmas tree lit up at the side of the stage. There were couples at some of the tables and a few people at the bar. Queasy and Drum were seated with Luther at a table in the back. Luther waved Walter and Jimmy over. The band took a break and Eddie came over to meet Walter and the others.

Luther introduced his son to the group. Eddie was more mulatto than black, and he reminded Walter of the Jamaicans they had met when he and Jimmy were riding the rails in Florida. Eddie had close-cropped hair and expressive brown eyes that were inquisitive, yet friendly. Walter guessed from his demeanor that he had a good sense of humor. Walter shook his hand. "Your father told me you were the only man in Kansas City having more fun than me, so I wanted to meet you."

Eddie laughed and sat down next to Walter. "Don't believe anything he tells you. He's leading a conspiracy to tie me to a life of mediocrity."

"You're confusing mediocrity with normalcy," Luther said.

"Is it natural to trade wine, women, and song for marriage, diapers, and nine-to-five?"

"We don't want to gang up on your dad, Eddie. But I'm on your side," Walter said.

"Well, then, we are off to a good start. What can I do for you?"

Walter had not discussed his plan with anyone. He wanted to give it to them all at the same time and get their reactions.

"This is a lot to digest, so think about what I'm going to tell you before giving me an answer. I'm considering buying this club and the adjoining properties and turning them into a nightclub, with gambling, a supper club, music, and dancing. There are quite a few cabarets and gin joints on the Vine Street corridor, but nothing on the scale I am planning. They either cater to a white or a Negro clientele. This club is located on the border between the two communities, and I think it's time for an integrated nightclub."

"That's not the craziest thing I've ever heard," Luther said. "But it's in the top three. Are you lookin' for ways to cause yourself trouble?"

"It's what he lives for," Drum said.

"It's not as crazy as it sounds. I think it will work, if given the chance. We will make it an upscale operation that will appeal to people of both races. Money doesn't know color, and neither should we. Whites will see it as a bit dangerous and living on the edge and Negroes want something better than taking their girlfriends to a strip bar or a gin joint. We will have a dress code and make it first class in every respect."

"Tell us more," Eddie said

"We would have to pay our dues to the community fund. The rest of the profit would be split between the five of us—Eddie, Drum, Queasy, Jimmy, and me. Eddie would be the face of the operation for the Negro community and head our entertainment. Drum is the expert on gaming, and Queasy would handle the money. Jimmy would be in charge of maintenance and security, working with Ezra and Prince.

"Why did you pick me?" Eddie asked.

"Your dad said you have a good head for business, but the main reason is that you know the nightlife in this ward, and you are someone the Negro community can relate to."

"I've always dreamed of having a place of my own, but I could never come up with the financing. This joint ownership would be the next best thing."

"It's not a bad idea, but I don't think I could handle working two jobs," said Queasy.

"One of the reasons I'm doing this is to get you away from downtown," Walter replied. "The rumors about corruption at City Hall grow louder every day, so you need to exit the Magrath machine before you get caught in a scandal. You will be better off counting our money than hiding his."

"Is Hannon behind the financing?" Drum asked.

"No. I'm using my savings and working on getting the rest of the money. If we accept Hannon money, we will be taking a chance on the reformers crying foul and closing us down. We have to run a legitimate business and operate under Hannon's protection for as long as we can. That will keep the police off our backs and discourage any competition from trying to move in on us."

"What kind of gaming are we talking about?" Drum asked.

"Craps, roulette, poker, and all the games of chance. You know the odds, so you know what to feature. We might take some losses, but my cardinal rule is to run an honest nightclub. We want to establish a first-class operation, so no drugs will be allowed, and no prostitution. We will leave that business to the bawdy houses and cabarets."

Walter paused and let them mull it over. "Well, what do you think?"

"What's not to like?" Eddie said. "I continue with my current lifestyle, with the chance to make some big money."

"I'm in," Drum said. "Instead of running all over town taking bets, my customers can come to me." Walter was gratified that Drum had accepted his offer. He felt responsible for Drum being shot and for his loss of income while he recovered.

"It's not that I don't appreciate the offer," Queasy said. "But we all know that whatever Walter is involved in, trouble is sure to follow."

"Come on, Queasy. You know you can't wait to see what will happen next," Walter chided him. "Where is your sense of adventure?"

"It's muted by thoughts of burly Italians chasing me through the streets and the Ku Klux Klan measuring me for a rope."

"Ezra, Jimmy, and Prince will be handling security, so that should make you feel better."

Queasy had heard the stories of the 18th Street brawl and the role Ezra had played.

"That is some comfort. It's against my better judgment, but count me in," he said.

"Good. I'm looking forward to working with all of you. Construction will begin as soon as I get my financing."

"What will be the name of the nightclub?" Drum asked.

"I was going to keep it as the East Side Club, but that denotes one part of the city. To make it more inclusive, we will call it the Kansas City Club."

They shook hands, and Walter said he and Jimmy would give Luther a ride home.

On the way, Luther spoke up from the back seat. "Walter, I appreciate you setting my son up in business. It gives him a chance to make some real money."

"You are welcome," Walter replied.

"Now, tell me what you want from me."

"What makes you think that I want anything?"

"I've lived long enough to know when I'm being set up."

"It's hard to get anything by you, Luther."

"Then you should give it to me straight."

"Okay, here's the scoop. I need a man who knows the workings of the community and has the respect of the leaders on the east side."

"What for?"

"To be my deputy ward boss."

"That's a big job. Who do you have in mind?"

"You."

"Me?" Luther said skeptically.

"I want you to take the job, with the expectation that you will take over as ward boss sometime in the future."

"You can't be serious! What do I know about being a ward boss?"

"About the same as I did when I took the job."

"You have to quit drinking, Walter. You are having delusions. I'm happy running a barbershop."

"There's not a lot of difference between running a barbershop and being a ward boss. You listen, you learn, and you give advice. You have the respect of the neighborhood, and that is half the battle. They will listen to me, because they have to. They will listen to you, because they want to. When you feel you are ready, I will step aside."

"I don't know, Walter. I don't mind listening to people's problems but trying to solve them is something else again."

"Think of all the times you wished you were in charge, so that you could right some of the wrongs inflicted on your community."

"I can't see myself wearing a suit and working out of an office."

"I can't see that either. You can keep holding court out of the barbershop. If you need to have a private meeting, we will keep an office next door. All I'm asking is for you to give it a try to see how it goes. If it doesn't feel right, you say the word, and I will get someone else."

Walter kept quiet and gave Luther time to think.

"You are a hard man to say no to, Walter. You got the Klan off our backs. You are creating jobs and giving my son a chance in business. I owe you, so there is no way that I can say no."

"Good. We will start our partnership on Monday morning."

∽

The sewing machines were humming and there was a flurry of activity when Walter entered Liz Braden's Original Designs warehouse and walked back to Lizabeth's office.

Lizabeth rose from her desk and greeted him with an embrace.

"How are you getting along without Eileen?" Walter asked.

"It is difficult, to say the least. I miss our morning and afternoon powwows to help me sort things out."

"You are lucky to have Aunt Erma and Jennie."

"That's true, but they are not my sister."

"It will get better with time."

"I'm counting on it."

Walter looked around. "You seem to be outgrowing this warehouse."

"Yes. I'm looking to move to an eight-story building close to Union Station."

"Congratulations. I'm glad you are doing so well."

"Better than I ever thought possible. We are moving five hundred dresses and six hundred aprons through here every day and the orders keep coming in."

"That is amazing."

Lizabeth knew that he wasn't there to visit, so she got right to the point. "Did you need something?"

"I'm starting a business, and I was wondering if you would introduce me to your banker."

"I would be glad to. What type of business?"

"A high-class nightclub on the east side."

Lizabeth wondered if it would be a good idea for him to have a business that would exacerbate his drinking problem, but there wasn't much she could do about it. "If you don't mind my asking, what do you need from a banker?"

"I need a five-thousand-dollar loan to help with construction."

"That hurts my feelings."

"Why? For heaven's sake."

"You helped get me started in business and now you won't let me help you."

"That was different."

"Why?"

"Taking your money doesn't seem right."

"Then consider me an investor. You can pay me the interest you would pay a bank."

"Do you have five thousand dollars?"

"I do, so please let me invest in you." Lizabeth opened the top drawer of her desk, took out her checkbook and wrote Walter a check for the full amount.

"You invested in me, and now I'm investing in you," she said, handing him the check. "Good luck with your new venture."

"Thank you, Lizabeth. I will pay you back as soon as I can."

He was uncomfortable borrowing money from his sister, but he was gratified that he didn't have to go begging to a banker. Owing money to Lizabeth would make him work all the harder so he could pay her back.

July 1937

It was well into the summer when Lizabeth could assess her business. The first few weeks without Eileen had been difficult, but as the months went by, she remained focused on her goal of making Liz Braden's Original Designs a force in the industry. Eileen was busy filming the starring role in a Western, and from the letters she had received, Lizabeth knew that she was happy with her decision to be a film actress.

Lizabeth had moved the company to an eight-story building at 22nd and Central that had previously housed an envelope company. The building fit her needs and gave her plenty of room to expand. From her top-floor office, she could look out over Union Station to the south, and downtown Kansas City to the north. The location allowed her easy access to ship her goods by rail across the country. It had given her immense pride to put the Liz Braden's Original Designs sign on a building of such magnitude and made her feel that she was a real player in the business world.

The country was still fighting its way out of the Depression, but there were signs that the economy was picking up. She felt extremely fortunate the public had embraced her fashions, and she was making more money than she had ever thought possible. She was thankful the business was doing well, because so many had not survived the Depression. She was very sympathetic to those who had lost everything. Her charitable giving included supporting soup kitchens and she gave away a lot of clothing. But her main contribution was to keep people working. She never laid off anyone, even during downturns, and made sure her employees took precedence over profits.

The Home Helper apron was still the core of her business, and the profits had allowed her to branch into women's accessories, like belts and hats. Her line of women's fashions still consumed her. She kept up with the latest trends and had hired two more designers to assist her in creating new fashions for work and for play. But the thing she enjoyed most was creating fashions for Eileen to wear in the movies. She had never considered making Western wear, but it was a challenge, and gave her business exposure to a new line of women's clothing.

It was gratifying that her family was doing so well. Cam was successful with the Ford Motor Company. Walter's nightclub was almost finished and would open this weekend. Eileen was making a name for herself in the movies. Her mother and father were in good health, so she felt that life couldn't get much better. Her thoughts were interrupted by a knock on her office door.

"Come in," she called.

Cory walked through the door. "Can I talk to you?"

"Sure. I can spare a minute or two."

"You are always so busy."

"I hope you are not going to lecture me about more time for us."

"No. I've given up on that speech."

"How can I help you?" Lizabeth asked, ignoring his remark.

Cory appeared to be very nervous and was looking away from her out the window. "I hadn't meant for this to happen, but we haven't seen much of each other the past six months, and I've grown very fond of Margie."

"I know. We all have. She is an endearing person."

"You are making this very difficult."

"What?"

"There is no easy way to say this, so here goes: I'm in love with Margie, and we want to get married."

Lizabeth felt like her heart had stopped. She was in shock for a moment, and then her heart started to race. She thought back to all the times she had seen them together, but it seemed natural because they were both shy and protective of each other.

"I don't know what to say. Isn't this rather sudden?"

"No. It's been going on for a while, but you have been too busy to notice."

She struggled to get her bearings. She had always been the focus of Cory's attentions, and she never even considered that he might fall in love with someone else and leave her. It was true that she had taken him for granted, but that happens in relationships. She now realized that she had gone too far.

"We want you to know that we both care for you and value your friendship. Margie has a lot of guilt because you have done so much for her. She won't marry me without your approval."

Lizabeth had always known that she would choose business over romance but believed that eventually she and Cory would have a life together. He had always been there for her and had never denied her anything. She felt lost, knowing that he would not be there for her in the future.

"Are you sure this is what you want? Marriage is a big step to take."

"I know. But, yes, we want to build a life together. We have a lot in common. We like the quiet life and being with each other is enough."

"You are saying that it would never be enough for me."

"We both know the answer to that."

"I never dreamed that I would have to choose."

"Margie doesn't want this to change her business relationship with you."

"It won't. Not in the least."

"I'm glad. We want to remain a part of the Liz Braden family."

"Of course." She walked around the desk and squeezed his hand. He put her hand to his lips and kissed it, and then he quickly left the office.

She was numb from his announcement. A moment ago, she had been on top of the world and felt like she could accomplish anything. Now she felt empty, alone, and abandoned. The hard part was knowing that through neglect, she was responsible for losing him. How many times had he asked for a closer relationship, only to be rebuffed because of her time constraints? She rubbed her eyes and tried to get her bearings. Her office walls seemed to be closing in on her. She grabbed her purse, closed the office door, and rode the elevator down to the second-floor workroom. Erma saw her and came over.

"I'm leaving early," she said.

"You. Leaving early? Are you not feeling well?"

"There are some things I need to do."

"You look pale. Is there anything I can do?"

"No. I need some time to myself. Take care of things here, and I will see you in the morning."

When she made it home to Brookside, her mother was waiting at the door.

"Erma called me. She was concerned about you." Mira could see that Lizabeth was about to cry.

"Come into the kitchen and I will make us some tea." Mira worked slowly, giving Lizabeth time to speak.

"Cory informed me that he is going to marry Margie," she finally said.

Mira was taken aback for a moment. "Oh, my. I can understand why you are in shock."

"It was totally unexpected. I'm not sure what to do."

"There is not much you can do. I wish I had an answer, but matters of the heart are very difficult."

"I blame myself. He wanted me to make a commitment and give more time to the relationship."

"And why didn't you?"

"I thought that I couldn't take that much time away from my business."

"And now you are questioning your judgment?"

"I guess so."

"What if you had given more time to Cory, at the expense of your career?"

"I would not be happy. I was holding out for both."

"Life goes on while we are waiting for what we want."

"I wish I were more like you and could see the practical side of everything."

"You are more like me than you realize. There was a time not so long ago when I had my heart broken."

This was the closest her mother had ever come to discussing the relationship with Father.

"What did you do?"

"I searched for answers, but after a while I realized that it was something I would have to endure."

"How long does it take to get over it?"

"I'm not sure you ever do. You file it away and hope time eases the pain. In your case, I feel some responsibility because I introduced you to Margie."

"Margie has been a blessing. It would be easy to blame her, but I know the fault is mine."

"Your father and I are so proud of your success. Take a look at how far you have come. A few short years ago, you were creating fashions in your sewing room and trying to sell them in the neighborhood. Now, you have an eight-story building downtown and a hundred employees. You are the most resilient person in the family, and you will work through this disappointment. I want you to think back to the fire and the courage it took for you to bounce back from that disaster. You can handle this setback. You have a lot of people counting on you, and I know that you won't let them down."

No, she would not. This was going to hurt for a while, but she would stand by her decision that business always came first.

"Thank you, Mother. I don't know what I would do without you."

"Nonsense. Now, I'm going to insist that you spend the evening in bed. I will bring you another cup of tea and then you will get a good night's sleep, so you can face the morning with confidence."

CHAPTER SIXTEEN

LIZABETH DID NOT FEEL PARTICULARLY confident, but she managed to get through the next day and the day after that. She held her head high and would not allow herself to show resentment or disappointment, but she was not about to shower Cory and Margie with congratulations. They would just have to simmer on that until she had healed enough to mean it. She had lost Eileen, and now Cory, and back-to-back blows were not so easy to overcome.

She was not in a good mood when she arrived at work on Wednesday. There were two burly looking men waiting to see her. They wore suits that were well worn and too small for their frames. One man had large, black eyes, set above a fleshy nose. His chin was narrow and sported a goatee. The other had bulldog cheeks, a bulbous nose, and narrow gray eyes that were vacant and lifeless. The men looked like longshoremen and seemed out of place in the Midwest. The man with the goatee spoke first.

"My name is Duke Symanski and this is Olaf Larson." Unlike the suits, the names fit the frames perfectly. She shook their outstretched hands and invited them into her office.

"What can I do for you, gentlemen?"

"We are with the ILGWU, the International Ladies' Garment Workers' Union."

"And?"

"We want to organize your employees."

"Organize them how?"

"Bring them into our union."

"Why would they want to join your union?"

"Better wages, better working conditions, and healthcare are just a few of the things we offer."

"You obviously haven't done your homework," Lizabeth said. "I pay the highest wages in the industry. My employees have excellent working conditions, and they are provided with healthcare."

"When your employees have grievances, there is no one to bargain for them."

"I always stand up for my employees."

"You are missing the point," Symanski said, in frustration. "Your employees should have the right to representation that can only be handled by organized labor."

"No. I think you are missing the point," Lizabeth was getting agitated. "They don't need representation if they are satisfied with their employment. Have you talked to anyone who is unhappy working here?"

"Well, no."

"There you have it. The problem is solved, and now you can let me get back to work."

"If you have nothing to hide," Olaf leaned closer to her desk, and she had to back away from the bulbous nose, "you would let us talk to your employees and see if they would like union representation."

"I don't like anyone telling me how to run my company. I understand that you want to grow your membership, but this is not a New York sweatshop. Why should my employees pay dues to an organization that adds nothing to their existing benefits?"

"Collective bargaining is always advantageous for any labor force," Symanski said. "We make sure they have a voice in any negotiation with an employer."

"It might come as a shock to you, but my employees can speak for themselves."

"Why make this hard on yourself?" Olaf said. "We don't want to set up a picket line outside your building, unless you force us to."

"So now you are threatening me."

"Of course not. We just want you to see what could happen in the future if you don't cooperate."

Lizabeth was seething, but she managed to control herself. She could call Uncle Ray and have these two goons thrown out of the building, but she wanted to handle her own problems. "I will give this some serious thought and give you an answer in a couple of days."

"That is all we ask," Symanski said. The two men stood and shook hands with her, and she ushered them out of the office.

"Of all the nerve," she fumed. She and her employees had built the company and now that it was profitable, the union wanted in on the action. She didn't want to say or do something she would regret, so she went down the hall to her father's office to ask his advice.

J.M. was leaning over his desk, laying out a newspaper ad.

"Who were the heavyweights I saw go into your office?" he asked.

"Union representatives."

"What did they want?"

"To organize my employees."

"How do you feel about that?"

"I'm angry. I don't want anyone telling me how to run my company."

"I can understand that, but you must remain levelheaded. Labor unions put FDR in the White House, and he supports their agenda. The president would be a happy man if unions organized every company in the country. He champions the worker and sees these organizing efforts as a worthwhile class struggle between the haves and the have nots."

"That is odd, because he is a member of the haves."

"The Roosevelts have already made their money, so he doesn't have a business to protect."

"But we do, so what do you suggest?"

"How did you leave it with the bruisers?"

"I told them to come back for an answer in a couple of days."

"Good. We will discuss it with Ray at Sunday dinner."

⁓

On Sunday, Uncle Ray did not offer much encouragement. Aunt Erma and J.M. were in the room while they discussed the matter. Ray spoke first.

"The problem is that many of the companies in our organization are unionized, and we can't be seen as anti-union. Boss Tom built the organization with the help of organized labor and supporting you against the union would cause problems. And I agree with J.M. that politics has emboldened unions in their quest to organize the country. Roosevelt's administration has appointed the judiciary, so they will lean his way in any disputes with company owners."

"So, you think I should let them organize my employees."

"That's entirely up to you. I will say that it will be easier than dealing with picket lines and the agitation the union will surely direct your way."

"The intimidation factor is one of the things I dislike about unions. If they can't get their way, then they demonize business owners until they give in."

"If you decide to put up a fight, the outcome depends on how your customer base sees the dispute. If they side with the union, you will face a boycott. If not, you should come out okay. You've worked hard to build your company, and you need to decide if this dispute is worth putting all that at risk."

"It seems un-American to run from a fight when I feel that I'm in the right."

"There is no disgrace in wanting to protect what you have worked for," J.M. said.

"What do you think, Aunt Erma?"

"You have been very successful going with your instincts. I advise you to go with your heart, or you won't be happy with your decision."

"Even though it might cost us our livelihood?"

"Yes. Even then."

"What will the union throw at me first, Uncle Ray?"

"The union will put up picket lines and spread false rumors about the poor working conditions your employees have to endure. If the dispute lingers, then your employees could face some physical violence. The police are reluctant to get involved in these disputes, so you might have to hire security guards. The union reps know the expense of fending them off will weaken your company and ultimately bring you around to their way of thinking."

"In other words, defending my business is more trouble than it's worth."

"Exactly. The unions have been at this for a long time. They have a plan that is usually successful, so if you decide to fight, you have to counter that with a plan of your own. I understand your need for independence, but you have to think about your health. You have a heavy workload and fending off the union will require all your physical and emotional strength. I've seen strong men wilt under the pressure. The energy they needed to run their companies was exhausted in fighting the union."

"You're saying that I will be fighting a battle of attrition."

"Exactly so. And once the battle is engaged, it will create an adversarial relationship that won't bode well for future negotiations."

"Is there a chance I can win?"

"There is always a chance, but is it worth the cost?" Ray questioned.

"What do you think, Father?"

"I want what is best for you, and that might not be what is best for the company, so I'm not going to influence your decision."

"I understand. You've all given me a lot to think about, and I thank you."

That night she tossed and turned, mulling over what she would do when she met with the union representatives. She missed having Eileen to talk to. The real question was, would this be a good thing for her company and her employees? And if it was not, then she would be giving in just to keep the peace, and somehow that seemed like a cowardly way of conducting business. She had always run her company with integrity. If she gave in to the union, what would that do for her own peace of mind?

Her mother was right in that she had come a long way in a very short time. Her business would not exist if she had not been willing to risk everything. She was aware that things had changed with success and the growth of her business, and she had an obligation to protect the jobs of her employees. It was a big responsibility, and she would be putting the company in jeopardy, but she knew what she had to do. Sleep would not come, so she went to her sanctuary of the sewing room and started working on a dress design for her spring fashion line.

Two days later, Symanski and Larson followed her into her office and sat down. "I've given this a lot of thought, gentlemen, and I want you to know that I think unions are a good thing. You've helped clean up sweatshops in the big cities where women and children are working over fifty hours a week for a four-dollar paycheck. I concede there are big problems and abuses in the garment industry. But the fact remains, they are not happening in my company. Just because you want to organize my employees doesn't mean you should. All of the reforms that you are trying to gain for workers in the garment industry are already in place at Liz Braden's Original Designs. My company has set the standard for garment workers, and I am proud of it. I think your motives are less than admirable. My company is nationally known, so you want to make an example of me to help you organize other companies in the Midwest. In other words, you are not here to help my employees, you are here to help the union."

"This sounds like you won't be joining us," Symanski said.

"No, I will not."

Larson spoke up. "You don't want to make us your enemy, Miss Braden."

"I don't want us to be enemies either. That will be entirely up to you."

"The United Automobile Workers recently brought General Motors to its knees. If a big corporation can't defeat a union, what chance do you have? You could have been the showcase for our marketing efforts, but now you will be an example of what can happen to a company when it defies the union."

"That sounds very much like another threat."

"If you are allowed to remain a non-union shop, it will embolden others to challenge us and damage our credibility," Symanski said.

"Freedom of choice is what America is all about."

"A perfect thought in an imperfect world. Should we give robber barons the freedom to abuse American workers?"

"You know that is far from the case here. We are at an impasse, gentleman, so I must bid you good day."

"You have not heard the last from us, Miss Braden, and you might be facing many a sleepless night." The two men stood and abruptly left her office.

She had a momentary attack of butterflies, but she took a deep breath and held it until she heard their footsteps fade down the hallway. It was easy to talk about, but now that the deed was done, she was thinking in a defensive mentality. The union had a lot of ways they could disrupt her business, so she had to be ready for anything.

She sat at her desk and composed herself. One of her heroines, Amelia Earhart, had recently been lost over the Pacific Ocean, trying to fly an airplane around the world. Amelia had not backed away from a challenge and neither would she. But there were only so many distractions she could handle at once. She left her office and went down to the third floor, back to Margie's work area.

Margie looked surprised to see her. Lizabeth quickly said, "I understand that congratulations are in order. I hope you and Cory are very happy."

"Thank you, Lizabeth. I'm sorry about—"

"Don't be sorry about anything. We have to move forward and continue to support each other." She wasn't sure she meant it, but there could be no divisiveness in the workforce if she was going to do battle with the union. The company took precedence over her personal feelings.

She didn't have to wait long for the union to act. When she arrived at work the next day there were ten women carrying signs in front of her building. The signs read, "LIZ BRADEN PAYS SLAVE WAGES" and "LIZ BRADEN HAS POOR WORKING CONDITIONS." The women walking the picket line were showing the effects of the Depression. They wore frayed dresses and scruffy shoes. Their faces were sallow, the result of missing too many meals, and they moved slowly, trying to conserve enough energy to last the day.

Lizabeth watched them from her office window for a few hours, until she could bear it no longer. She went downstairs to get Erma and together they calmly walked out and approached the women on the picket line.

"Good morning, ladies. I'm Liz Braden, and this is my aunt, Erma Braden."

The women were defensive, expecting a confrontation.

"How much is the union paying you to carry these signs? I would guess the minimum wage of twenty-five cents an hour."

"That is correct," one of the women replied.

"How many of you can sew?" All but one girl in her late teens raised their hands. The lone dissenter was a tiny redhead with big brown eyes.

"How would you like to work for me at one dollar an hour?"

"You mean a full-time job?" a woman asked incredulously.

"That is exactly what I mean."

A job that would feed their families was a godsend that was not about to be turned down. They put down their picket signs in a show of acceptance.

"I want you to go with Erma, and she will see to your lunch and then get you dressed in our uniforms. And you will each get a new dress to mark the occasion of your employment at Liz Braden's Original Designs."

Lizabeth wasn't entirely altruistic. A huge apron order from a client on the East Coast had come in, and she needed help. The tiny girl turned away and continued walking the picket line.

"What's the matter?" Lizabeth asked. "Don't you want to work for me?"

"I don't know how to sew," she said sadly.

"What is your name?"

"Mary Kelly."

"We Irish girls have to stick together, Mary. If you put down that sign, I promise that you will be sewing by the end of the day." Mary's face lit up. Lizabeth put her arm around Mary's shoulder, and together they marched into the building.

~

Walter, Jimmy, and Ray were in Tom Hannon's office, with several other men, as Ray recounted the story. They were all laughing uproariously. "My God," Ray said. "The Garment Workers' Union is the laughingstock of the city. They put a picket line in front of Lizabeth's building, and she marched out and hired the entire lot—lock, stock, and barrel. That has never happened in the entire history of union organizing."

Ray slapped his knee in merriment and continued. "Lizabeth said that when those two bruisers came by to check on the picket line, they had the most perplexed look on their faces. They looked up and down the block and were scratching their heads in wonderment. It was as if someone had kidnapped the entire picket line, and in a way, that was correct. The union is scrambling for a way to save face. They have put homeless men on the picket line, so Lizabeth can't hire them away. The men are enduring catcalls from passing cars, asking why they are not wearing skirts and high heels."

Ray and the men laughed even harder. "The men picketing can't get their hearts into the protest, because Lizabeth brings them water and something to eat, and she always has a kind word for them. The union countered her move by slandering her in leaflets declaring that she was paying slave wages and her employees had horrible working conditions. She blew a hole in that by giving guided tours of her building to clubs and schools, allowing them to talk to her employees. Every time they make a move, she does them one better."

"That girl has spunk and a good head on her shoulders," Hannon said. "I'm not sure I would want to go up against her. Ray, you and Walter had best keep an eye on her. She has made an enemy of the union, and it is bound to keep up the pressure. That might mean violence of one sort or another."

"We are watching the situation closely," Ray assured him.

Walter was also worried. He and Jimmy stopped by to see Lizabeth on a daily basis to be sure everything was going okay, and he was never far from a phone, in case she needed him. He was at Boss Hannon's office to deliver a personal invitation to the nightclub grand opening in a couple of weeks. He had learned a valuable lesson from Max Abrams on how to have a grand premiere. He had invited every dignitary in the city and spent a lot of money advertising the event on radio and in the newspaper in the weeks leading up to the opening.

When the big night arrived, there were searchlights scanning the dark sky, valet parking, and a red carpet leading into the Kansas City Club. The press was there in force, and Walter had hired a society reporter to conduct interviews. He had constructed the building to offer a supper club on one side and a casino on the other side.

In between was the dance floor and orchestra stand. Eddie had hired Charlie Barnet and his band. It was known as the blackest, white band in the country, which was perfect for the integrated club Walter had envisioned.

He and Eddie were at the entrance greeting customers, while Drum supervised the gaming tables and Queasy kept a sharp eye on the money. As the night wore on and more alcohol was consumed, a few fights broke out, but Ezra and Jimmy quickly intervened. Ezra handled the Negro customers and Jimmy the whites, so there could be no charge of unfairness or discrimination. They didn't rough up the customers too much, because they wanted them to return. They did just enough to get their point across. Prince stayed in the background, keeping a watchful eye on everything that happened in the club. Walter had built him a room in back with a bed and a bathroom with a shower.

Walter was proud of what he had accomplished, and he wished there was someone special he could share it with. His parents would never go to a gambling establishment. Cam and Eileen were out of town, and it would be bad for Lizabeth's business for her to be seen in a nightclub, especially because the union reps had been watching her closely. They would like nothing more than to scandalize her behavior. But most of all, he missed Terri and thought how wonderful it would have been to have her by his side. He was still hoping they could find a way to be together, but their long-term prospects were not good, because they were emotionally and physically so far apart.

One of the bright spots of the past few weeks was his deputy ward boss. Luther had turned out to be a natural at getting things done and handling disputes within the community. His years of barbering held him in good stead. He had put his people skills to good use in promoting a progressive agenda. The money collected from business owners had built a couple of neighborhood parks and funded a basketball league.

Hannon was getting his share of the proceeds, so, for the moment, everyone was happy. Walter kept a low profile and let Luther and the newly appointed member of the city council handle community business. There was no doubt that Walter was getting credit for Luther's work, but that would eventually be rectified when he nominated Luther to be ward boss.

246

The arrangement had allowed him to concentrate on making the Kansas City Club the top entertainment venue in the city. Eddie had turned out to be a natural at working with people, and he had confirmed his father's observation that he had a good head for business. Walter waited until he had greeted the last of the dignitaries, then went inside to walk the floor of the club.

There was shouting and laughter in the casino, so he walked over and saw that it was coming from the roulette table. Tom Hannon must have hit his numbers, because his ward bosses were cheering him on. Walter was not overly concerned about the losses, because it was common knowledge that the boss would never quit while he was ahead. He was one of those unfortunate gamblers whose luck never changed for the good, but had convinced himself, that given time, he would become a winner. Boss Tom saw him and waved him over.

"Walter, you have done a great service to the city by opening this club. It is first class in every way."

"Thank you, sir."

"I can't remember when I've had such a good time."

"That is nice to hear. Dinner is on the house, if you would like to eat."

"No, thank you. I'm having too much fun to stop now. You need to come by the office next week, so we can discuss your future."

This is my future, Walter thought.

"We have bigger plans for you than running a nightclub," the boss said, as if reading his thoughts. "We need to get you thinking about politics."

"I know nothing about politics."

"Nonsense. You know everything you need to. As my brother, Jack, used to say, politics is nothing more than helping people, and they in turn help you on election day. There is no one in the city better at helping people than you, Walter. You have proved your merit downtown and here on the east side."

Tom's chip hit another number on the roulette table, and he was distracted for a moment. Walter slipped quietly away. He wanted no part of politics and hoped the boss would forget about making him a politician. He headed over to where Prince was cleaning up a spilled drink.

One of the best things to have happened recently was that Prince had begun to talk. It was gradual at first, as if he was trying to find his way. He was still withdrawn, but he could have a conversation if it suited him. Charlene and the psychologist had worked wonders with him.

Walter started to speak to Prince when someone tugged at his arm. He turned around and was face to face with Joe Bianco. Joe was the boss of the Italian north end. He was with his girlfriend, a buxom blonde who was half his age.

"How are you, Joe?" Walter shook his hand. Joe was not the typical cigar-smoking, beer-bellied, ward boss. In his prime, he had been a good athlete, and he kept in shape. Still, he was known to be the most ruthless of the ward bosses. Prince stood up and was listening to the exchange.

"I'm fine, Walter. I just don't like these niggers hanging around white women."

Walter knew to tread carefully. Joe could wield the Black Hand, and Walter did not want trouble, tonight or in the future.

"The club is located on the border of the Negro community, so it has to be inclusive," Walter said.

"That might be, but be glad you are under Hannon's protection."

"I thought there was an unwritten rule that ward bosses don't threaten one another."

"You have nothing to worry about as long as Hannon stays in power. If he doesn't, you might want to change your admission policy."

"I will take it under consideration. I hope you both enjoy your evening. If there is anything you need, please let me know." He walked away. Bianco would not do anything that would anger Tom Hannon, so Walter was glad he was operating under the Hannon umbrella. He left Prince and walked across the casino to where Jimmy was watching the action.

"You better keep an eye on Bianco and steer him away from any contact with Negro customers. The last thing we need is a fight between the Negroes and the Italians."

"Okay. I will mellow him out with some comp drinks and then buy him dinner," Jimmy said.

"Good idea. I'm hopeful that he won't pay us another visit."

Walter found Drum at the blackjack tables and motioned him over. "How are we doing?"

"Are you kidding? This is better than printing money, because we don't get ink on our fingers. The take at the end of the evening should be tremendous."

"What about Boss Tom hitting a hot streak?"

"More noise than action. When he wins, it's usually after a losing streak. When he hits the skids, we will be picking up his markers. How long do we keep taking his bets?" Drum asked.

"Give him a while longer, and then convince him to have dinner. We will deduct his losses from the dues we pay him."

Walter marveled at the amount of money people spent so freely. The Depression didn't seem to be affecting those at the top. Working men and women were scraping to get by, but the economic elite thought nothing of gambling money away. He would make sure that some of the profits from the nightclub trickled down to the disadvantaged, because he knew what it was like to beg for a meal.

He had hoped to get through the grand opening without a drink but running into Joe Bianco, and the pressure of the grand opening, made the bar irresistible. He downed a whiskey and soda and then had another. Jimmy walked by and shook his head, indicating not to overdo it on the booze. Walter acknowledged the warning and went back to work.

CHAPTER SEVENTEEN

LIZABETH CLOSED HER OFFICE DOOR. She had worked until nightfall after returning from a two-day trip to New York to see the latest fashions. She spoke to the night security guard, as she left the building. The picket line had dispersed for the evening, and all was quiet. The ILGWU had been persistent in its goal to unionize her company, but the efforts had been fruitless. Her sales had continued to increase.

Her customers supported her as the hometown girl being bullied by an out-of-town organization. The union was losing the battle for the hearts of the people, and that was critical if it was going to win the war. Lizabeth started her car and drove east to Main Street. She had not wanted to go to New York while being picketed by the union, but Erma had convinced her the trip was critical, if they were to keep up with the latest trends in fashion.

She turned right on to Main Street and headed south across the viaduct over the trainyard. The lights of Union Station were shining brightly in the night.

Her trip to New York had been worthwhile. She had found that straight-line designs were out, and a softer look would be in style for 1938. The trend for dresses would be form-fitting with emphasis on the waist and a hemline that came to the middle of the calf. She had also noted that puffed sleeves would still be in fashion. An actress,

Katharine Hepburn, was starting a trend wearing tailored jackets and pants, but that was a trend for someone else. Lizabeth would stick with simplicity for the average woman. It had been the key to her success, so she wasn't about to change.

Margie's specialty line would get a boost, as crochet hats would be popular for the coming year. Margie and Cory had not yet picked a wedding date. The thought of losing Cory still caused her pangs of regret, but it was getting better with time, and she couldn't let her personal feelings interfere with running the company.

She crossed Pershing Road, glancing up at the imposing tower of the National World War I Memorial and headed up the Main Street hill. She was lost in her thoughts, when suddenly a car slammed into her back bumper and knocked her forward onto the steering wheel. She was confused for a moment, and then she realized that she had been hit from behind. She tried to move the car off to the side of the road, but another car cut in front of her, and she was caught in between. The car in back had bright lights that blinded her. When she tried to stop, the car behind would bang her bumper again.

She was afraid that if she didn't keep moving, her car would be crushed. Several times, her car banged into the back of the car in front, but it kept her wedged in, so she could not turn to the right or the left. Her heart was pounding, because she realized this was no accident and someone was deliberately trying to harm her. When she thought she could make a break for it and turn onto a side street, she got slammed again. It was a mile to the top of the hill, so she hoped the cars would break away when they reached the crest. But that didn't happen, and the slamming continued on down Main Street.

She prayed there would be a police car on the east side of the Plaza, but the car behind slammed her right through the Brush Creek intersection onto Brookside Boulevard. She was trembling with fear, wondering if they were going to kidnap her or do something worse. Her back and neck hurt from the pounding. All she could do was to brace herself when she thought the next slam was coming. For a brief moment, she wondered why this was happening, but she was caught in a fight for survival and tried to keep focused. The pounding continued on up the boulevard and she felt like it was never going to stop.

When they reached the Brookside shopping center, the car in front suddenly sped away and the car behind broke off and made a U-turn. She was never more relieved in her life. She quickly turned into the shopping center and parked. She took a couple of deep breaths to calm herself, then laid her head on the steering wheel.

She did not want her parents to see her in this condition, so she decided to drive to Aunt Erma and Uncle Ray's house, a few blocks away, off Meyer Boulevard. When she arrived, she tried to get out of the car but her back had stiffened and she couldn't move. She laid on the horn and the lights came on. Uncle Ray hurried out to the car and saw she was in distress.

"What happened, Lizabeth?" he asked with concern.

She tried to speak, but for a moment nothing would come out.

Ray could see that she was traumatized.

"Sorry, Uncle Ray. I have to catch my breath."

"Your car is a mess," he said checking the car over.

She composed herself and then explained the entire series of events.

"These two cars trapped you and repeatedly hit your car?"

"Yes."

"Erma! Get out here!" Ray called. Erma heard the urgency in his voice and hurried out to the car.

"What happened?"

"Lizabeth was attacked on the way home."

"Are you injured?" Erma asked in disbelief and concern.

"My back is stiff and sore. I'm not sure I can get out of the car."

"Erma, call the doctor," Ray ordered.

Erma hurried into the house.

"You stay put until the doctor gets here. We don't want to move you and cause any damage. I'm assuming that you came here so you wouldn't worry your parents."

"Yes."

"That works for Walter, but it will not work for you. This is not something we can hide from your folks. We will call them after the doctor checks you out. Once we know you are okay, your mother can take over your care." He was afraid Mira would not call a doctor and instead rely on her prayers to heal Lizabeth.

Erma came back and got into the car to comfort Lizabeth. "The doctor should be here in a few minutes." Lizabeth was in pain, but she tried to relax, knowing she was in good hands.

When the doctor arrived, he checked Lizabeth's back and neck and then helped her out of the car. "No major damage," he told Erma and Ray. "She will be stiff and sore for a week or so. Take her home and put warm compresses on her back and neck and keep her in bed for twenty-four hours."

Erma made the call after the doctor left, and a few minutes later Walter arrived with his parents. Ray explained to them what had happened.

"Have you called the police?" J.M. asked. He was incensed this had happened to his daughter.

"We don't need the police. I've got a good idea who did this. The boys and I will take care of it."

"Do you want me to go with you, Uncle Ray?" Walter asked.

"No. I don't want you involved in this." Ray suspected this had been the work of the Garment Workers' Union. Walter was too high profile as a Hannon ward boss and could not be seen as anti-union, even if it was for revenge. Ray and his men would operate in the dark, so they would not be recognized.

Mira went to Lizabeth and held her hand. "Are you sure you are okay?"

"Yes, Mother." She didn't mention the doctor and neither did Uncle Ray.

Mira took Lizabeth's arm to steady her, and Walter took the other. They led her to Walter's car. "Don't you worry about a thing," Mira said. "I will have you up and around in no time." Mira was beginning to worry about the safety of her family. Walter being attacked was bad enough, but she had never considered that Lizabeth would be in danger.

"Thank you, Uncle Ray and Aunt Erma," Lizabeth said, before gingerly getting into the car.

"You get some rest. I will take care of everything at work," Erma said.

Ray took J.M. and Walter aside. "Rest assured we will get our point across that this criminal assault will not be tolerated. Take

Lizabeth home, and I will let you know how it goes. I will have Lizabeth's car towed to the shop."

∽

Ray and his men waited outside a bar on Grand Avenue. They had extinguished the only light in the alley. Duke Symanski and Olaf Larson came out of the bar. They were talking loudly and laughing uproariously. Ray stepped out of the shadows and grabbed Olaf by his bulbous nose. Olaf screamed in pain, as Ray pulled him into the alley.

"What are you doing!" Olaf fought to get away, but Ray had his nose in a vice grip. Two of Ray's men grabbed Symanski and shoved him against the wall of the alleyway. They started pummeling him in the stomach and ribs. He tried to fight back, but Ray's men were stronger and Symanski was too drunk to resist. Olaf was being pounded in the stomach by Ray's other man, as Ray kept a firm grip on his bulbous nose.

"Listen to this very carefully," Ray said. "We love unions in Kansas City." He paused so Symanski and Olaf could take more blows to the stomach. Olaf was turning blue, because he couldn't breathe. "We also love fair play." They were punched again. The two union men wanted Ray to keep talking because when he stopped, the blows started.

"Here's how it's going to be, boys. There will be no more attacks on Miss Braden or her employees, and you will not threaten her company in any way." The two union men waited for the hits to come, and they did.

"You will be fair in your attempts to organize her company." Olaf's nose felt like it was going to explode. "If you do not heed this warning, your union organizing days will be over, because your friends will find you both floating in the Missouri River." Ray squeezed harder on the man's nose. "Do you understand? Because we do not make idle threats."

"Yes, we understand," Olaf managed to say, before he was hit again.

"You will have a cashier's check on Miss Braden's desk tomorrow morning to pay for the damages to her car."

"We will," Olaf wheezed through the pain, and Symanski nodded in agreement.

Ray let go of his nose and Olaf moaned, grabbed his sore nose, and fell in a heap on the ground. Symanski took one last punch to the head and collapsed on top of Olaf.

"Have a nice evening," Ray said. He and his men ducked out of the alley and into a waiting car.

⁓

When the family arrived home, Mira helped Lizabeth to her bedroom. She helped her undress, put her in bed, and then prepared some hot compresses. The heat worked miracles for her neck and back. Her mother massaged her muscles between the heat treatments. Lizabeth was feeling much better, as much from her mother's touch as from the compresses.

"Who do you think is responsible for the attack?" Mira asked.

"It has to be the Garment Workers' Union trying to send me a message."

"Maybe you should listen."

"Neither of us would like me very much if I gave in to intimidation."

"I don't know about that. My primary goal is to keep you safe."

"I appreciate that but playing safe emboldens those who wish me harm."

"Be that as it may, you are going to ride to and from work with your father until this trouble subsides. This incident could have been disastrous, so we are going to start taking precautions."

"I don't think that is necessary."

"Those hoodlums could have injured you more seriously or overturned your car. If they are capable of attacking a young woman, they are capable of anything."

"If they wanted to hurt me, they could have. They just wanted to scare me to the negotiating table."

"And I assume that is not going to happen."

"If it does, it will be on my terms. When they bully me, it just strengthens my resolve."

"You are stubborn, like your father. There are times when you both should set that aside."

"We can't change who we are."

"Perhaps not, but you could be more compromising in the positions you take."

"You think after being attacked I should give in to them."

"Not in the least. Just give it some time and see if there is anything you can do to make the situation less volatile."

"Like what?"

"Perhaps you could be less rigid and give them something they want. I'm sure they have people to answer to, and would be less hostile if they could report a small victory of some sort."

"You and I are at odds, Mother. I'm thinking of the welfare of my company, and you are thinking of my welfare."

"You will always come first. I don't want to put any undue pressure on you, but the fire that destroyed your business and now this attack is putting a lot of stress on your father. He is conditioned to these things happening to Walter, because trouble has swirled around him since he was a young boy. You, however, are the one who is keeping him up at night."

For a moment, Lizabeth was speechless. "Me? I thought he was focused on Cam and Eileen."

"Nonsense. I'm not going to deny that Cam is his favorite child, but he loves all of you in his own way."

"Except for Walter."

Mira thought about that for a moment. There was no use in trying to deny the obvious. "Your father sees a lot of his own father in Walter. Your grandfather was an alcoholic and a womanizer."

"Maybe he also sees some of himself," Lizabeth said. She wondered how far she could push this before Mira stopped the conversation.

"Perhaps. They have been at war with each other since Walter was in grade school."

Lizabeth was going to push this as far as she could. "Why do the two of you celebrate Cam's success and ignore Walter's achievements?"

Mira paused for a moment, as she decided whether or not to answer. "I guess it's because we are conditioned not to celebrate his victories, because the defeats are sure to follow. We've lived through a lot of ups and downs with Walter."

"Maybe he was just trying to get your attention."

"Possibly. We were thankful when he bonded with you, because we didn't seem to be getting anywhere with him. When he has a problem, he can go to you." Mira adjusted the pillows for Lizabeth. "Now, that's enough conversation for one evening. I want you to get a good night's sleep, and we will see how you are in the morning." She kissed Lizabeth on the forehead.

"Good night, Mother. And thank you for the heat treatments."

Her mother turned off the light and closed the door. Lizabeth thought about what her mother had said and wondered if there was something she could do to ease tensions between her company and the union organizers. One thing was certain, there would be no concessions for several months. She did not want the union to think the bullying tactics had worked and that she had been intimidated. It had been an exhausting day, so she fell asleep and dreamed fitfully of crashing cars and faceless men reaching out to harm her.

She felt much better in the morning, so she dressed and went downstairs to breakfast. Her mother and father were in the kitchen.

"I see you are dressed for work," Mira said. "I thought you might take the day off."

"It's important that I show up today. I don't want the union reps to think they intimidated me."

"How is your back?"

"A bit sore, but not enough to keep me home."

"Ray called last night," J.M. said. "He assured me that you won't be harmed again. I didn't ask for any details and none were offered."

Lizabeth hoped no one was hurt on her account, and that her uncle had been able to settle things peacefully.

"Who would have ever thought that women's fashions would be hazardous to your health," Mira said.

"I'm sure that Ray is right, and Lizabeth doesn't have anything to fear," J.M. said. "I am concerned that you are well enough to work."

"I feel fine."

"If you are sure, then we need to go over our first ad for Bloomingdale's store in New York."

"My word," Mira said. "You are stepping up in the world of fashion."

"Our goal is to have our merchandise in every city in the country," Lizabeth said proudly.

"Your expansion into the big cities might run into trouble, if you don't settle this union business," Mira said.

"You are right about that. It is something I am considering in my future plans."

"You are doing very well without my advice."

"Your advice is always appreciated, Mother. This is a family business after all."

"We had better hit the road, Lizabeth," J.M. said. "Have a good day, Mira."

Lizabeth noted there were no hugs or kisses between her parents.

"Thanks again for the heat treatments, Mother."

"You are very welcome, dear. Have a wonderful day."

The news of Lizabeth's incident had spread throughout the company, and when she arrived all the employees gathered around her to be sure she was okay.

"Thank you for your concern," Lizabeth said. "I am going to be fine, and I don't want this assault to cause an adversarial relationship between our company and those people walking the picket line."

"So, you think this was an attack by the Garment Workers' Union?" Jennie asked.

"I do. But I'm just as sure the picketers had nothing to do with it. They are working for a paycheck, so we will continue to treat them with respect. I suspect the people who were responsible have paid a price for their crime, so none of us have to worry about our safety when leaving the building. In a few months, I will have a sit-down meeting with the union representatives, and I promise you that we are going to settle this issue once and for all."

"Will we have to join a union?" an employee asked.

"I suspect that sometime in the future you will be asked that very question."

"What can a union offer us that you can't?" another asked.

"If and when the time comes, that is something the union will have to answer. I can promise you without reservation that you won't be forced into anything and any decision to be made will be entirely up to you. You control your destiny and that is the way it should be. Now, we have some big orders heading for the East Coast, so we had best get to work."

Everyone dispersed, and Lizabeth went to her sewing machine that she kept on the production floor. Her workstation was in the middle of the action, and it was the happiest part of her day, because she was a seamstress like any other, and part of the engine that made her company run. She knew that it raised morale for the other seamstresses to know that she saw their work as a calling, and not something to be done for a paycheck. And it did not hurt that she was the best seamstress in the building, and that gave her employees something to aspire to.

September 1937

Lizabeth waited through the summer, to see if there would be anymore strong-arm tactics by the union, but there were none. She thought that Labor Day would be a good time to have a meeting with the union representatives and get things settled once and for all. Regardless of the rightness of her position, she did not want it perceived that she was anti-union.

The company was expanding nationwide, and she did not want this labor dispute hanging over her head. Duke Symanski and Olaf Larson were in her office. She had also called a business reporter from the *Kansas City Star* to sit in on the meeting, because it offered a good story and she did not want anything misconstrued after the fact.

"Thank you for inviting us," Olaf offered.

"Yes. What can we do for you, Miss Braden?" Symanski asked.

They were as docile as baby lambs, and Lizabeth wondered what her uncle had done to them to manage this transformation.

"I want you to meet John Reynolds from the *Star*. He is here as an observer and to report on what I am about to offer." The men shook hands.

"You've been picketing my company for months, because you think that my employees would be better off with union representation," Lizabeth said.

259

"That we do," they replied.

"Here is my offer, and it will be winner take all. You meet with my employees without any interference from me, and you present everything you have to offer. I will not counter your offer in any way. When you have finished, we will let them digest your offer for a few days and then we will have a vote, witnessed by Mr. Reynolds. If I win, you take down the picket line and there will be no more attempts to organize my company for at least four years. If you win, I will welcome the union with open arms."

"How many votes will we have to get?" Symanski asked.

"What is standard for a union vote?"

"The most votes win."

"That would give you no chance whatsoever," Lizabeth said. "I have one hundred and fifty employees. If you can get fifteen votes, or ten percent, you win."

They looked at her in astonishment. "You have got to be kidding."

"No. I am serious."

"We want to be fair, Miss Braden. Historically, we have never failed to get at least twenty-five percent of any vote."

"Then, very shortly you will be celebrating. Do we have an agreement?"

"We do indeed," Symanski said confidently. "Please set up our meeting with your employees."

After the union men left, John Reynolds made a few notes and then looked at her questioningly. "Why did you go so low in the number of votes to win? I've been at this a while and have learned that most companies have at least a twenty percent dissatisfaction rate among their employees."

"That might very well be, but I either know my employees or I don't."

"It's great to be confident, but you never know what will happen when a vote is taken. All of the hidden grievances get tossed into the ballot box along with the vote, and they always come as a shock to business owners who think they are altruistic."

"That might be true in other companies, but my feeling is that if I have created a climate that fosters a ten percent dissatisfaction rate, then I deserve to lose."

"I'll be pulling for you, Miss Braden, for purely selfish reasons. If you win, it makes for a much better story."

Lizabeth smiled. "Your selflessness underwhelms me."

John Reynolds laughed. "I will see you at the ballot box, Miss Braden."

A few days later, the union reps met with Lizabeth's employees. Duke Symanski and Olaf Larson gave a glowing scenario of life under the union banner and all it had to offer. John Reynolds was there to keep an eye on the ballot box and to get his story. Lizabeth stayed in her office so there would be no question of her influencing the vote. After the speeches and questions from the employees, the employees marked their ballots and lined up to drop them in the ballot box. Lizabeth came down from her office with her father to hear the final results. John Reynolds had no stake in the election, so they had him count the votes.

When he finished, he said, "The question you were asked to vote on was, do you, the employees of Liz Braden's Original Designs, want union representation? The totals are five votes in the affirmative, two abstentions, and one hundred and forty-three of you voted no."

A cheer went up from the gathering and everyone turned toward Lizabeth and gave her an ovation. She was grateful beyond belief, but she wondered who in the heck those five yes votes were from.

"I want to thank you for the confidence you have shown in me and in the direction you want the company to go. We harbor no ill will against the union and its representatives, and we recognize the good they do for workers who need representation."

She looked at Symanski and Larson. "Now, it is time for you to leave and time for us to get back to work." She escorted the union representatives from the building and shook their hands.

"Gentlemen, I believe per our agreement, I won't see you or any member of your organization until Labor Day of 1941."

"You have our word on it," Symanski said. "It has been interesting, to say the least, Miss Braden."

"Indeed, it has." She watched them cross the street, and, in short order, the picket line dispersed. She let out a big sigh of relief that it was actually over.

"Congratulations, Miss Braden," John Reynolds said. "The vote is an amazing affirmation that your employees hold you in high regard. A good deal of my reporting is on labor unrest, so it will be a joy to write a story about worker satisfaction. How do you elicit such loyalty from your employees?"

"I see myself as a seamstress. I know how I want to be treated and valued, and that is how I treat my employees. It is as simple as that."

"If you could pass your philosophy on to every business owner in the country, there would be no labor unrest in America. I'm sure my readers would like to know your plans for the future of your company."

"Certainly. By next year, we will have our fashions in every state in the country. The Home Helper apron has fueled the latest expansion. Our women's dress line continues to sell extremely well, and you can announce that we are going to start a women's work clothing line that we are excited about. We will call the line Work Wear by Liz Braden and we will feature work dresses, pants, and blouses that will be functional for women. I'm adding fifty more seamstresses to the company to keep up with the expansion."

"Then you don't see the Depression as an obstacle?"

"I've learned that to enjoy the best of times, it requires daring greatly in the worst of times."

"May I quote you?"

"Absolutely."

"With the rapid expansion of your business, I suspect that you have had offers to transfer your business to a larger, more populated city."

"Yes. There have been feelers to merge with companies in New York, Chicago, and St. Louis."

"And?"

"I love Kansas City and will never leave under any circumstances. I was born here, and it is home to everything I hold dear."

"Has your sister's success as an actress helped your business?"

"Immeasurably. She is the best advertisement I have. She keeps me apprised of her films and their opening dates in cities around the country. We have to prepare ahead for the rush of business that is sure to follow."

"Do you ever wish you could trade places with her?"

"I love my sister. She is a great actress, but I don't envy her. We are both doing the jobs we were born to do."

"You might see yourself as a seamstress; others would argue that you are an extraordinary designer and savvy businesswoman."

"Thank you for that compliment."

"Here is my headline: LIZ BRADEN WINS IN A KNOCKOUT. Then I will give the vote totals, the loyalty of your employees, your struggles with the union, and follow with the story of your company."

"I appreciate you doing the story."

"And I appreciate the opportunity. Goodbye and good luck to you, Miss Braden. Although I suspect you make your own luck."

"Goodbye, Mr. Reynolds." She breathed a sigh of relief as she walked away.

She felt like a burden had been lifted from her. The picket line had been a chain around her business that had caused her worry and stifled some of her creativity. She felt like nothing could stop her now, and she could hardly wait to get back to the drawing board.

CHAPTER EIGHTEEN

December 1, 1937

WALTER WAS LOOKING FORWARD TO Christmas. Eileen was coming home, and Lizabeth had solved her union problems and could now relax and enjoy the holidays. His nightclub had been very profitable, and he was able to pay Lizabeth back the money he owed. It helped that Vine Street had the reputation as the hottest jazz scene in the country. The Depression had dried up other music venues across the land and caused musicians to flock to a wide-open Kansas City.

For his support in the last election, FDR had put Tom Hannon in charge of dispensing federal funds for the area, and Boss Tom spread the money around liberally in the local economy. A lot of it ended up on Vine Street. After a few weeks in business, Eddie had enough funds to book Duke Ellington, and then Count Basie. Benny Moten and other popular bands followed. Where the hot bands went, people followed, and the money flowed.

Walter was also gratified that Luther was making progress on his way to becoming ward boss for the Negro community. Everything had gone according to Walter's plan for the ward, so Hannon was okay with the transition. His only requirement was that because of racial considerations, Walter would act as a conduit between Luther and him and sit in on meetings of the ward bosses. Walter was the face of the ward for the white community, but the Negro community would be answering to Luther.

Walter's only regret for the year was that he had been too stubborn to contact Terri. He had dated other women, but it only made him miss her all the more. He had tried everything to get her out of his mind, but nothing had worked. It was time to set aside his anger and try to win her back. He picked up the phone and called Los Angeles.

Max Abrams' secretary answered the phone and put him through.

"Walter Braden. How are you?" Max asked.

"Good, Max. And you?"

"Couldn't be better. Have you changed your mind about turning your life into a script?"

"No way, Max. I'm calling to see how Terri is doing."

"Oh. She's not doing as well as she would like, but she is holding her own with bit parts in B movies and waiting for her big break."

"Will that break ever come?"

"It's possible, but not likely. She's also shopping her documentary around to the studios, but so far there is no interest."

"That's what I'm calling you about, and I will need your help to make it work."

"Anything for the brother of my biggest star."

"I want to finance her documentary, but she needs to think it is being financed by a studio."

"How would that benefit you, Walter?"

"The studio needs to tell her that for the documentary on Black Sunday to be accurate in time and place, she will need more interviews and background shots from here in the Midwest, the area the dust storm affected. The studio should insist that she work out of its offices here in Kansas City."

"This sounds like the plan of a desperate man."

"And?"

Max laughed. "This might require calling in some favors."

"I've seen you work your magic here in Kansas City, so I know you can pull it off."

"Flattery will get you everywhere. I'm just worried about deceiving Terri."

"Getting people to believe what you want them to is what movies are all about. And since when did a bit of deception hurt when it benefits all the parties involved?"

"You are trying to get me to do something that goes against my principles as a Hollywood agent."

"I'm not sure principles and Hollywood should be used in the same sentence."

Max laughed again. "You got me there, Walter. When would you like me to put your plan into action?"

"Now would be a good time."

"Okay. I will meet with my Universal contacts first thing tomorrow. They are familiar with her work, and they owe me some favors."

"Don't mention my name; just tell them you have a private investor who wants to bankroll the project. But make it clear that Terri has to think the studio is funding the project."

"Okay, Walter. If we can pull this off, she should be coming your way in a couple of weeks."

"Thank you, Max. And happy holidays."

"You too, Walter. Please give my best to your parents. Your mother's Thanksgiving dinner was a culinary delight that I've never forgotten."

"I will pass along the compliment. Let me know how much money to send to get Terri's project underway."

"Will do. Goodbye, Walter. I will keep you posted."

"Goodbye, Max. And thank you."

⌒⌒

It didn't take Max long to complete the deal. Walter received the call three days later.

"Walter, you are one lucky man. Not only are you going to get the girl, but, as often happens in Hollywood when an investor comes forth, the studio executives think they might be missing out on something, and they want part of the action. I played hard to get, but they were adamant that Terri was their girl and will develop the project at Universal in Kansas City."

"What does that mean?" Walter asked

"It means Universal will be funding most of the project, and you will be a minority investor. The more I protested, the more the executives wanted. I let them know they were taking advantage of us, which pleased them no end. As a concession, they agreed to give you a percentage of whatever the film grosses, and they approved the film being shot in the Midwest."

"Max, you are brilliant."

"I hope you don't mind that I took a tiny piece of the action for myself."

"I would expect no less. You earned your commission."

"Terri should be coming your way a few days before Christmas. She is beyond excited about her project and wants to spend Christmas with her mother."

"It will be great to have her home again. How is Eileen doing?"

"She has been a busy girl. We have been offered enough movies to keep her booked for a few years. She is looking forward to coming home for Christmas."

"I'm glad to hear it and look forward to seeing her too. Thank you for your help, Max. It is much appreciated."

"You are welcome. Call me anytime."

Walter hung up the phone. This had turned out better than he could have imagined. Terri was coming home, and her studio would be funding the majority of the money to produce her documentary.

Walter's Uncle Ray had asked for a meeting at the club and he wanted Jimmy, Drum, and Queasy to be there. Walter had the beer ready, and they sat down.

"What's up, Uncle Ray?"

"I want to give you an update about what is going on with the organization. You know how the city works, so it will be no surprise that some of the cash Hannon takes in stays off the books. The reformers are starting to ask questions about where the cash has been going."

"Where has the cash been going?" Walter asked.

"I don't know and don't want to."

"I know where a good portion of it goes," Drum said. "Best estimates from gambling houses and the racetrack put Hannon's losses at a million dollars over the past six years."

"Wow!" Queasy said. "That's a lot of cash."

"The reformers have been trying to get him for decades and nothing has happened," Drum said. "What has changed that makes you so concerned?"

"It's different this time. The city's religious leaders want action, the *Star* is blasting him in editorials, and Governor Stanton is calling for a grand jury investigation. The governor has vowed to clean up the city. I'm here because I don't know how far the investigation will reach, and you need to be prepared. Where the reformers go, the tax man is sure to follow. I suggest you have your books in order."

"I took your advice and financed the club myself," Walter said. "And we are keeping detailed records."

"What is happening at City Hall with Magrath?" Queasy asked.

"They are putting the squeeze on him. He has none of Hannon's bookkeeping skills, so he will be the first to fall. It looks like you got out in time."

"Yes. Thanks to Walter."

"The reason I'm telling you this is because we have to protect Walter," Ray said. "If Hannon falls, they will be going after the ward bosses next, so get your accounts in order, and I will find you a good attorney."

"How will this affect Luther?" Walter asked.

"I know he's a friend of yours, so you need to keep him in the background. I wouldn't make him ward boss in the middle of an investigation. He wouldn't stand a chance facing the white man's justice."

"I am still the ward boss, and I will take the responsibility. We should be okay with the business owners. The money collected from them has been used to support the community. Delores Johnson, the ward accountant, keeps clean records."

"That's good, but you never know when they might turn on you. You are a white man operating in a Negro world and that entails a lot of resentment. Some of it is justified and some not. You have created a lot of goodwill in the Negro community, and I hope that follows you into court."

"Do you really think it is going to come to that?"

"It's the reason I'm here. I feel responsible for encouraging you to join the organization."

268

"I'm glad you did. It has been a great experience. How will this investigation affect you, Uncle Ray?"

"The reformers are following the money and my job is in security, so I should be okay."

"What are Hannon's odds of survival?" Drum asked.

"We'll see. The Boss has been in dire straits before and managed to survive. Just when they think they have him, he slips away. There's a reason they call the city Tom's town. He knows the workings of the city better than anyone."

"Thanks for the warning, Uncle Ray. We will do all we can to be prepared."

Walter gave the guard at Universal a free dinner and gambling chips at the Kansas City Club to let him know when Terri was back at work. After he received the call, he gave Terri a few days to get settled and then knocked on her door in Hyde Park.

Millie, the housekeeper answered. "Hello, Walter," she said.

"Hello, Millie. I would like to see Terri." She directed him to a seat in the foyer, and then disappeared into the confines of the house.

A few moments later, Terri came walking in, looking radiant in a lavender silk dress. Walter didn't rush to embrace her, because there had been some hard feelings between them and he wanted to see where they stood. He kissed her on the cheek.

"It has been a while," he said.

"Yes. Come into the parlor and sit down. We have a lot to talk about."

"It's nice that you could come home for Christmas," he said, pretending that he didn't know the real reason she was back in town.

When they were seated, she told him about getting the funding for her documentary.

"Congratulations. When do you begin the project?"

"After the first of the year."

He didn't sense any of the aloofness from their previous conversations. Perhaps getting what she wanted had cooled her Hollywood ambition.

"I wanted to apologize again for what happened in the restaurant," he said.

"You were drunk and angry. That can be a deadly combination."

"The fates got even with me outside the restaurant. I want to thank you for treating my wound and going with me to the hospital."

"How is your shoulder?"

"It only bothers me in cold weather."

"What about Jimmy and Drum. Are they okay?"

"Yes. The only lingering effect is the hard time they give me about having to associate with a gangster."

"Speaking of that, Lizabeth told me about your promotion to ward boss. How is that working out?"

"I'm in hopes it will be temporary. That's why we opened the nightclub."

"I heard the grand opening was spectacular."

"I missed having you there."

"You will have to give me a tour."

"Does that mean we can put the animosity of the past few months behind us?"

"I'm willing, if you are. But you have to understand that I will be busy with my work." Terri was fond of Walter, but she wanted to make sure he didn't expect too much right away.

"I won't resent playing second fiddle to your documentary."

"I promise to make as much time for us as I can." Terri reached out and took Walter's hand.

He leaned in and kissed her for real this time. They embraced and Walter asked, "Will you come to Christmas dinner?"

"Are you sure your family will want me there?"

"They will be fine once they know we are back together."

"If you are sure, then I accept. Now come say hello to Mother."

～◦

Lizabeth was delighted to have everyone home for Christmas. She and Eileen had stayed up past midnight catching up on friends and family and enjoying each other's company. On Christmas morning, the family had opened Christmas gifts while enjoying pastries and coffee. The women were now cleaning house and preparing the food for Christmas dinner. Mira had even consented to let her daughters help her with the cooking, which was a first for the Braden household.

"Walter wanted me to let you know that he is bringing Terri," Lizabeth said to her mother.

"That should be interesting," Mira replied. "I thought their relationship was over."

"They've made up," Lizabeth said.

"I'm not sure that's a good thing," Mira said. "She's an ambitious young lady, and Walter might need a steadier influence."

Lizabeth was reminded once again of Cory and herself. "I could write a book on ambition," she said.

"Sorry, Lizabeth. That wasn't directed at you."

"I know. I guess I'm still sensitive about matters of romance."

"Where are Walter and Cam?" Eileen asked.

"They left early. Cam is spending the day with Helen, and Walter had some work to do at the nightclub. If we are going to have a happy Christmas, we need to steer the conversation away from Walter owning the nightclub and his association with Hannon. Those are sore subjects with your father, and we don't want Walter to endure a double dose of lecturing on Christmas Day."

"I wish Father could acknowledge that Walter is successful," Lizabeth said. "It would mean a lot to him."

"Where you see success, your father sees trouble. He doesn't think any good can come from owning a nightclub or an association with Hannon."

"We will do what we can to keep the conversation civil," Eileen said.

"Yes," Lizabeth agreed. "Between us, we should have enough stories to keep everyone interested and shield Walter from being grilled by Father."

"Good. We have a plan," Mira said. "Now, I'm going to take a short nap before the guests start arriving."

Lizabeth and Eileen looked at each other. This was another first for their mother.

"Are you feeling okay?" Eileen asked with concern.

"I'm fine. You girls carry on, and I will be with you soon."

Lizabeth and Eileen set the table and kept a watchful eye on the pots and pans warming on the stove. They had to continually answer the door, because the neighbors, in numbers they had never experienced before, kept coming by to leave Christmas goodies. Lizabeth finally figured out that besides being neighborly, they wanted to see Kansas City's latest movie star. There was also a parade of cars driving slowly down the street from people wanting to get a glimpse of her. Eileen shrugged off the trappings of stardom and didn't seem to be fazed by the attention. She was gracious and polite to everyone who stopped by.

Pop and Nana were the first to arrive. "What's going on with all the traffic?" Pop asked.

"One of the pitfalls of celebrity," Lizabeth answered.

"Don't people have better things to do on Christmas Day?"

"Evidently not."

"How do you handle the attention, Eileen?"

"I recognize that people are infatuated with the woman on the screen. However, that isn't me; it's a character I'm playing and part of the fantasy created by the movies. The attention doesn't bother me, because without the support of the public I would be out of a job."

"Have you thought about getting a bodyguard?" Pop asked.

"Heavens no. I hope it never comes to that."

"Walter has Jimmy, and it wouldn't hurt for you to have some security."

"Thanks for worrying about me, Pop, but I'm fine."

Mira was back in the kitchen, putting the finishing touches on the feast, as everyone arrived. Eileen and Lizabeth took their guests' coats as they gathered in the living room.

When Walter showed up with Terri, there were greetings all around. Mira came out of the kitchen and greeted her.

"We've missed you," Mira said graciously.

"And I've missed all of you."

"Walter tells us you are going to be working on your documentary in Kansas City," Lizabeth said.

"Yes. I'm excited about the project and glad to be working here at home."

"I'm sure Walter is also happy about that," Pop said. "We thought he was going to let you get away."

"No chance of that, Pop. She can't shake me."

"You are a smart man," Pop said, as Terri blushed.

"How are things in the fashion world?" Terri asked Lizabeth.

"Walter told me about you being attacked on your way home from work."

"What attack?" Eileen asked, looking at Lizabeth with alarm. "You never mentioned anything about an attack."

"It's over, and I didn't want to worry you."

"The Garment Workers' Union was trying to intimidate her," Uncle Ray said. "It's all settled, so there is nothing more to worry about."

"I had no idea you were in danger," Eileen said.

"We were all caught by surprise," Walter replied.

"Speaking of danger," Cam said. "Were you and Uncle Ray surprised by the governor calling for a grand jury investigation of the Hannon organization?"

So much for keeping the conversation away from Walter, Lizabeth thought. She should have known that Cam would bring up any subject that made Walter uncomfortable.

"We are hoping it won't come to that," Walter replied.

"If they can indict Hannon, the ward bosses will be next."

"I have nothing to hide."

"There is guilt through association," J.M. said. "Once these grand juries convene, they will try to taint anyone connected to Hannon."

"We have prepared for that eventuality," Uncle Ray said.

"I tried to warn you that it would come to this," J.M. replied, warming to his lecture.

"It hasn't come to anything yet. There are a lot of rumors floating around."

"You know what they say about smoke."

"I do, but Hannon is a master at putting out fires."

"They will catch him eventually, and I'm betting that time is soon."

"We'll see."

"Does Walter have an attorney?" J.M. asked Ray.

"I do," Walter replied, trying to keep his father from talking around him.

"I hope you don't bring down a scandal on the family. We have Eileen's reputation to think about, and it wouldn't do Lizabeth's business any good either."

Lizabeth sadly noted that he did not say anything about Walter's welfare.

"I had no idea you might be in trouble," Terri said. "Is there anything I can do to help?"

"Thank you, but no. Everyone is getting way ahead of themselves about something that might not happen. If it does, we are fully prepared."

"There is never a dull moment in Walter's world," Cam said.

"If there were, you wouldn't have anything to talk about," Walter shot back.

"That's quite enough," Mira said to the gathering. "I shouldn't have to remind you that it's Christmas, so let's do more celebrating and less bickering. We have a lot to be thankful for."

"I second that," Erma said.

"Now, dinner is ready, so please join me at the table," Mira announced.

The conversation turned lighter as they sat around the dinner table. They discussed the Duke of Windsor, the former King Edward VII, and his marriage to Wallis Simpson in June.

"You can't get much more romantic than giving up your kingdom for the woman you love," Erma said.

"A selfish move, if you ask me," J.M. countered. "What about his responsibility to his people and to his country?"

"I agree," Ray said. "However, the United Kingdom might be better off. There are rumors that he and his bride are Nazi sympathizers. Can you imagine the king of England being in bed with Hitler?"

"Perhaps they are trying to demonize him for giving up the throne," Eileen said.

"What kind of life will he lead?" J.M. asked. "He will be cheered by romantics and jeered by critics."

"Where will they live?" Carol asked.

"They got married in France, so maybe they will live there," J.M. said. "He's estranged from his family, and he is viewed as a traitor by many of his countrymen. He might spend the rest of his life as a man without a country."

"A test of his commitment will be when he realizes what he has given up," Helen said.

"I agree with Aunt Erma that it is still a fairy tale story and a testament to love," Eileen said.

Cam stood up. "As we are on the subject of romance and marriage, Helen and I would like to make an announcement. We are engaged to be married in April of next year." There was stunned silence for a moment, and then Helen held up the ring on her finger that she had kept hidden.

They both received hearty congratulations from everyone. Lizabeth went around the table and gave them each a hug. Her happiness for them was genuine, but it also meant that Cam would be leaving home, and her world would be changing once again. She knew his departure would be hard for her mother and father.

"Where will you be living?" Mira asked. She put on a brave face but was less than enthusiastic about losing her son.

"Ford is allowing me to set up a regional office in Kansas City. We will get an apartment on the Plaza, and Helen will continue to work."

Lizabeth was glad for her parent's sake that Cam would be close by. However, he wouldn't be under the same roof, and that meant all their attention would be focused on Walter. She knew it was something Walter dreaded, so she couldn't imagine that he would live at home much longer. What had been a bustling household would be down to her parents and her.

Cam's announcement was the highlight of the evening and topped off an enjoyable Christmas dinner for everyone. Lizabeth was upbeat about beginning the new year. Walter was back with Terri and much happier than before. Eileen was living her dream, and Cam was making a name for himself at Ford. And she was thankful that her business had been very profitable and was continuing to expand. The only negatives were her parent's frosty relationship that was sadly becoming the norm, and her worries about Walter being caught up in an investigation.

She and Eileen were helping their mother gather the dishes and clean the kitchen.

"I thought that went well," Mira said.

"Yes," Eileen said. "Although the announcement from Cam was a shocker."

"He is such a lady's man that I never pictured him married," Lizabeth said.

"The household is breaking up much more quickly than I had planned," Mira said. "When you were all living here together, I felt like I had some control."

"Change is inevitable," Lizabeth said. "Although we certainly don't have to like it."

"The two of you are so busy that I hardly get to see you," Mira said. "I miss spending time with my girls."

"We miss that too," Lizabeth said.

"I know it will be an imposition for you both, but I'm going to make a request."

They looked at Mira questioningly.

"I want to visit my sister, Julia, in Cuba, and I want you to come with me. I know it will be a sacrifice because of your busy lives, but I want to spend some time with you both before I lose you to the world."

"When do you want to go?" Eileen asked.

"Whenever you can clear your schedules."

"Is Father going?" Lizabeth asked.

"No. I want it to be just the three of us. Your father and Erma will stay here and run the business for you."

"How long will we be gone?"

"I was thinking that ten days should be about right."

Lizabeth was apprehensive about leaving the business, but her mother asked so little of her that she didn't want to disappoint her. And she wanted to see Cuba and Aunt Julia.

"My next film starts February first," Eileen said. "The sooner we go, the better."

"We will agree to go, on one condition," Lizabeth said.

"What?"

"I will pay for the vacation and make the arrangements." It had been a long time since she had had any worries about money, and she wanted to pay her mother back for all the sacrifices she had made.

"We will split the cost," Eileen said, wanting to hold up her end of the expenses.

"If you insist," Mira said. "But it won't seem right. I'm supposed to be taking you."

"You've done plenty of that in the past, so it's time for a role reversal," Lizabeth said.

"Let's set it up for the first week in January," Mira said. "I will get a letter off to Julia and let her know we are coming."

CHAPTER NINETEEN

January 1938

IT WAS 10 DEGREES ON A cold, winter day when Mira and her two daughters left Union Station. Lizabeth had booked a Pullman sleeper on one of the new streamliner trains that could average over 100 miles per hour. They switched trains at St. Louis and then New Orleans before traveling to Miami to board a ship for the trip to Santiago de Cuba. The journey had been relaxing and allowed the three of them to bond like never before. Lizabeth thought it interesting that they could live together for years, but only skim the surface of how they felt about life and relationships and one another's perspectives on viewing the world.

She and Eileen had reached a point where they were beginning to see their mother as more of a friend than a parent. And that allowed them freedom to discuss a variety of issues they would not have been comfortable discussing with a parent. Their mother had revealed that Uncle Ralph, her brother-in-law, was Aunt Julia's second husband, but it was never to be discussed. Julia had been swept off her feet by a rogue who abandoned her after looting her checking account. Lizabeth and Eileen had remembered Aunt Julia as being too contained to be swindled by romance, so it was hard to imagine. Pop and Nana had had the marriage quietly annulled.

Lizabeth looked out at Santiago Bay as the ship slowly approached the city. She could see the domes of several churches gleaming in the sunlight. Santiago was built on a hill that sloped from the city center to the bay several miles below. Her mother and sister were with her at the ship's railing, attired in their summer dresses and bonnets, looking for Julia among the crowds on the dock. They were enjoying the warm, Cuban sun that was making the Kansas City winter a distant memory.

Julia waved excitedly when their eyes met, and they waved back. She had on a yellow dress and matching sun hat. Uncle Ralph wore a crisp, white suit and a Panama hat. Lizabeth was thankful there was no press here to meet them. Eileen's movies had not made it to Cuba, so she could vacation in peace.

When they disembarked, there were hugs and kisses all around. Julia was a heavier version of Mira. She favored Pop with blue eyes and a fair complexion, but there was no doubting that she and Mira were sisters. Uncle Ralph was medium height with a round face and narrow cheekbones. He had brown eyes and a receding hairline. He was a gracious man but contained his emotions and was not overly enthusiastic in his greeting.

"I am so excited that you are here!" Julia exclaimed. "I get to be with my sister and hear all about my famous designer and movie star nieces. It's not often we get celebrities in Santiago."

"They don't see themselves that way," Mira said. "I think you will find them grounded."

"You must be so proud of their success."

"Yes. And I'm just as proud of Walter and Cam."

"Of course, you are."

"How are Mother and Father? I'm sorry they couldn't come too."

"It would have been difficult for them to face the rigors of winter travel."

"I'm disappointed, but I do understand. Let's get you out of the sun and into the car."

They walked to the parking area and the porters followed with the bags and loaded the luggage into the car's trunk. Ralph gave them a nice tip and the ladies climbed into his large Chrysler touring car. Ralph drove away from the pier and started up the hill past

400 years of Spanish and French architecture. Many of the buildings were white with red tile roofs, gleaming under the Cuban sun.

"Cuba is so warm and exotic," Lizabeth said, as she looked around at the street vendors and people sitting outside their apartments watching the activity on the streets.

"You will have to get used to the slow pace of Cuban life," Julia said. "Work reflects who you are in America. Not so in Cuba, where the work ethic is less driven."

"Lizabeth would never fit in," Eileen said.

"You're surely not suggesting that I'm driven," Lizabeth pretended shock.

"If you set up shop here, it would change the culture," Eileen said.

"That's not a bad idea. Fashions of the Caribbean by Lizabeth Braden."

"See what I mean, Aunt Julia. There is no stopping her."

"Cuba will slow her down. It is the natural order of things."

"Cuba has its work cut out when it takes on Lizabeth."

"I want to hear all about the exciting things that have happened to you both. Your mother sent me clippings of the movie premiere in Kansas City. I wish I could have been there."

"We missed you," Mira said. "When will you be leaving Cuba and coming home for good?"

"I keep trying to get Ralph to retire, but Cuba Power and Light won't let him go, or so he tells me. I think he enjoys Cuba and doesn't want to leave."

"You would have me give up a life of luxury to freeze in Kansas City?" Ralph asked. "To say nothing of giving up our cook and housekeeper. I have to remind Julia how far we can stretch a dollar in Cuba."

"If I could get back to Kansas City and be with my family, it would be worth doing the drudgery myself."

"You will have to come home once a year and spend a couple of months with us," Mira said. "That would be a nice compromise for you both."

"I've been reading about Cuba," Lizabeth said. "How is the political situation?"

"Mostly quiet, but we have our moments. There is always talk of revolution by students and dissidents, but it doesn't last long.

Batista, our leader, keeps the lid on issues by controlling the military and appointing puppet presidents."

"One day it might boil over," Lizabeth said.

"Not likely, as Cuba is an American protectorate. The US government would send in troops and that would be the end of any revolt."

"Speaking of politics," Julia said, "how is Walter doing? I was surprised when you wrote that he was a ward boss for Tom Hannon."

"You might have been surprised, but we were shocked," Mira said. "J.M. still hasn't recovered. He thinks no good can come from that association."

"The article you sent from the newspaper was alarming," Julia said. "We wondered what Walter had gotten himself into."

"Walter goes his own way. Now he has opened a nightclub with several of his friends."

"My parents have a hard time accepting Walter's success," Lizabeth said. "He's too unconventional to their way of thinking."

"Lizabeth is protective of Walter and can't see that he might be headed for trouble. The city's reformers are closing in on Hannon and we hope Walter isn't guilty by association."

"I've always been impressed with Walter," Ralph said. "The few times we've met, he's made me feel welcome and part of the family. There are not many men with his people skills."

"We're afraid those skills might be sorely tested in the days to come," Mira said.

After driving a few more blocks, Ralph entered a street in the Tivolí neighborhood. There were French and Spanish Colonial mansions, shaded by large trees, that lined the streets. He pulled into a landscaped driveway and stopped in front of a white, stucco, Spanish home with a terra cotta roof.

"How beautiful," Eileen said.

"Thank you," Julia replied.

A neatly dressed, bronze-skinned man came out to help them with the luggage.

"This is Emil," Ralph said, and the man smiled and responded, "Hola." Ralph introduced him and then led them into the house where he introduced them to Pepi, the cook and housekeeper. She greeted them with a smile and a warm handshake. She was a short, plump woman with graying hair, dark brown eyes, and a glowing complexion. And she could speak English.

"Welcome to Cuba. How was your trip?"

"It was wonderful," Mira said. "We are happy to be in your beautiful country."

Pepi beamed. "I will be taking care of you, so if you need anything let me know. We will have tea in the courtyard in a few minutes."

"I'm heading back to work," Ralph said. "You ladies get settled, and I will see you at dinner."

Lizabeth looked around at the furnishings. The furniture was made of mesquite wood, with intricate carved designs. The chairs were covered in leather and the light fixtures were forged iron. Colorful tile was laid on the floors throughout the house.

"Your home is lovely and the furniture is exquisite," Lizabeth said to Julia.

"She is as enamored with furniture as you are with fashion," Mira said. "She is always on the lookout for a piece to add to her collection."

"I can't deny it," Julia said. "Home furnishings have always been my passion."

"Girls, when we were growing up, your grandfather had to keep a place in the garage for the furniture that Julia would scrounge from wherever she might find it. To her, every item was an orphan and needed a good home."

Julia laughed. "Every so often, Father would make me have a garage sale, because we were running out of space. It was heartbreaking to give up my furniture."

"Did you have a passion for anything?" Lizabeth asked her mother. Eileen was resting quietly on the sofa but perked up, curious to hear the response.

"She was a tomboy extraordinaire," Julia said. "We lived in the Argentine district near the rail yards and she loved to follow Father on his rounds when he was inspecting the trains. The Union Pacific supervisors relaxed a few rules to allow her in the yards, because she was so enamored with the locomotives. If she were a man, they would have made her an engineer."

"Mother was thankful when I decided to give up the rails and become a young lady. Although it did take a while."

"When she was in her teens, she turned to cooking and baking," Julia said. 'That's why your family enjoys those fabulous meals."

"I outgrew my trains, but you never outgrew your passion for interior design."

Julia nodded in agreement as Pepi came into the room to serve the tea. She placed the saucers and cups on the table, along with a plate of cookies, and then poured the tea.

"Thank you, Pepi," Julia said. Pepi turned and left the room.

"I could get used to someone waiting on me," Lizabeth said.

"I understand that you are doing well enough to have a staff of your own," Julia replied.

"I'm afraid that Mother would never permit it. We are conditioned to fend for ourselves, regardless of our circumstances."

"Indeed, I would not," Mira confirmed. "If the Depression has taught us anything, it is not to spend money on things we can do for ourselves. However, I'm glad your Aunt Julia can afford these luxuries."

"And I want you to also enjoy them. After tea and a nap, it will be time for dinner. I want to hear all about Eileen's movie career and Lizabeth's success in the fashion industry. I'm so excited to have you here that I could burst."

They drowsily finished their tea and dispersed to their rooms for naps. After a brief respite and a bath, they put on fresh clothes and gathered in the dining room. Pepi had the dinner she had prepared on the table. They started with a salad of tomatoes and avocados and then enjoyed pork chops with black beans, white rice, and steamed vegetables.

"The food is so fresh," Mira said.

"One of the benefits of living in Cuba," Julia said. "We have fresh fruits and vegetables year-round."

"Do you have a garden?" Mira asked.

"Absolutely. Pepi will give you a tour in the morning. She is an expert on growing a variety of fruits and vegetables."

"The men in the family want us to get them some Cuban cigars," Eileen said.

"Your Uncle Ralph will take you to a tobacco farm, where you can buy the best cigars available."

"Where is Uncle Ralph?"

"He had to work late, so that he can take time off for your tour.

Now enough about Cuba. Tell me about the movie business, Eileen."

"It's not as exciting as it sounds," Eileen said. "There are hours of preparation for each minute that is shown on screen. The time between takes can be boring."

"But isn't it exciting to meet the most famous movie stars in Hollywood?"

"I was starry eyed at first, but then I realized they were people, like everyone else. The thing I like most is that they share their experiences and skills. I'm learning so much from my acting partners on how to be an accomplished actress."

"It must be thrilling to be famous."

"Not so much. Celebrity is the least attractive part of being in the movies. I didn't appreciate my anonymity until I lost it."

"Don't let her go on too much about that, Aunt Julia," Lizabeth said. "She loves to see her name light up a marquee."

"I can't deny it, but sometimes I would like to put a regulator on celebrity."

"You will have your privacy here in Cuba, unless you run into tourists. We will get you some large sunglasses and a bonnet so you won't be recognized."

"Now tell me about the fashion industry, Lizabeth. You must be proud that your company has grown so fast."

"Yes. The expansion has been amazing. We managed to carve out our niche in a competitive industry."

"Mira wrote to me about the Home Helper apron. That must be your most inspired moment in creative design."

"It taught me that something simple can be as lucrative as the most expensive creation. The apron has secured the company financially, so that I can concentrate on research and design."

"Who would have ever thought that you in your little sewing room would evolve into being the largest dress manufacturer in Kansas City?"

"I know. Sometimes it feels like a dream."

"It shouldn't," Mira said. "You have built your company on hard work and dedication. You are successful because you refused to accept defeat."

"I read about the fire," Julia said. "That must have been devastating."

"It was. But Mother wouldn't let me stay down for long."

"I can imagine," Julia said. "When we were kids I was never allowed a down day. Your mother would lecture me on getting in the right frame of mind to control any illness or negative thoughts. I wasn't surprised when her philosophy led her into Christian Science."

Pepi came into the room. "Are you ready for dessert, Miss Julia?"

"Yes, Pepi. We will have it out on the terrace."

Julia led them outside where they could enjoy the warm Cuban air and look up at the moon and the stars. Pepi served them vanilla ice cream with warm chocolate sauce.

"This is a real treat, Aunt Julia," Lizabeth said. For the first time in years, she felt totally relaxed. The trip made her realize the fast pace she had been living and how much stress she had been under.

"We will have a day of leisure tomorrow, so you can relax and recover from your trip," Julia said. "Your Uncle Ralph is excited to show you the wonderful sites in Cuba. He will entertain you while your mother and I visit."

"Don't you want to join us, Mother?" Eileen asked.

"No. I want to relax and visit with my sister."

"I can hardly wait to see your corner of the island," Lizabeth said.

After a day of rest, Uncle Ralph loaded the car with a picnic basket and some wine and they were off to see the city and the surrounding area. Their first stop was at a medieval fortress above the bay, complete with a drawbridge and Spanish cannons, which in the past were used to protect the city. At the top of the fort, they could see all the way to the Sierra Maestra mountain range.

After touring the fortress, they headed to the foothills of the Sierra Maestra, where Ralph parked the car in the village of El Cobre. From there, they walked to the Basílica Santuario Nacional, the most revered church in Cuba.

"This is where Cubans make pilgrimages to pay their respects to their patron saint. They ask the Virgin of Charity to protect them," Ralph explained.

"It is beautiful," Lizabeth said, looking up at the three domes above the church. She took off her bonnet and wiped her brow, wilting in the hot sun of the tropics.

"I apologize for keeping you too long in the sun," Ralph said. "I sometimes get carried away with my love of Cuba and her historical sites. We will go back down the steps and have our lunch in a shady grove of trees outside the town square."

After lunch, they were revived and ready to continue touring. Ralph took them back to Santiago, where Lizabeth wanted to scout the stores for fashions and see if there were any possibilities for expansion.

"What are you thinking?" Eileen asked.

"I'm picturing a line of Liz Braden tropical wear."

"There is no containing her," Uncle Ralph. "This is our first day touring Cuba, and she has her mind on business."

"I'm sorry," Lizabeth said. "I can't help thinking that my summer dress line would be a natural for the tropics."

"Can't you forget about fashion for at least a day?" Eileen asked.

"Not while I'm still breathing."

"Most people want to get away from work when they are on vacation."

"Maybe I can help," Ralph said. "I know some people in the clothing business who might be able to steer you to a Cuban distributor."

"Really? That would be wonderful, Uncle Ralph."

"But on the condition that you forget about work for now and enjoy your vacation."

"That's blackmail, but I promise to do my best."

Uncle Ralph kept them busy for the next several days, touring coffee plantations, tropical groves, and a tobacco farm, where they purchased cigars for the men in the family. It was fun and educational, but they were thankful when their uncle went back to work and they could spend the rest of their vacation relaxing with Aunt Julia and their mother.

The four of them were on the terrace. Eileen and Lizabeth were basking in the sun, while Julia and Mira preferred the shade.

"Uncle Ralph is a wonderful tour guide," Eileen said.

"Yes. He knows Cuba and its history."

"He must know business also. He gave me the name of a woman I can use as a distributor," Lizabeth said.

"I'm sure he did. She's his mistress and the main reason he doesn't want to leave Cuba."

Lizabeth glanced at her mother, who did not show surprise. She assumed the two women had been discussing the infidelities of their husbands. The revelation hung in suspended silence for a moment until Lizabeth could get her bearings.

"Then I couldn't possibly use her as a representative."

"Of course, you can. The things that are shocking back home are taken for granted in Cuba. Most married men have mistresses. Ralph doesn't know that I know. He also doesn't know some things about me."

Lizabeth wondered if she meant a prior marriage or that she had a lover, but she was not about to ask. It seemed that Aunt Julia had left her inhibitions in America. What surprised Lizabeth was her mother's reaction. In the past, she would never have allowed this type of conversation to take place. It was further evidence that she viewed her daughters as equals.

Lizabeth was beginning to wonder if every marriage contained layers of intrigue and betrayal. Her mother and Aunt Julia carried on, despite the burden of infidelity. She wondered if maintaining stability was worth the price of unhappiness.

Eileen broke the silence with her own revelation. "When I first went to Hollywood, the expectations of directors and costars surprised me. I had no idea that to be successful you had to give up your dignity. That is why I left the business. If I have a relationship, I want it to be my idea."

"Good for you," Julia said. "It is not often in a man's world that a woman can control her destiny. You and Lizabeth are an inspiration, and I am so proud of you both. Your mother and I are from a generation of women who gave up their hopes and dreams to maintain the natural order of things, like supporting a man and providing a stable home."

"Are you unhappy, Aunt Julia?" Lizabeth asked.

"I would say more restless than unhappy."

"That is because you are not doing what you were meant to do."

"And what would that be?"

"Don't let her start in on you, Julia," Mira warned. "Your life will never be the same."

"The Liz Braden brand is in every state in the country, and I will soon be expanding into Europe. I want you to picture this."

Lizabeth drew an imaginary headline with her hand: "LIZ BRADEN HOME FURNISHINGS. You could get the benefit of using the Braden name and play off my success. I'm in a position to fund a startup, and we could find you a warehouse and storefront in Kansas City."

"Oh, my!" Julia exclaimed, putting her hand to her heart. "I've only dreamed of such a thing."

"Why not make your dreams come true?"

Julia looked at Mira.

"Don't look at me," Mira said. "Once Lizabeth gets an idea in her head, she will overwhelm you."

"I'm not sure Ralph would make the move."

"Maybe it's time he had to choose between you and his mistress," Lizabeth said.

Julia mulled that over. "Where would we live?"

"If you come to Kansas City with Ralph, we will find you a house," Mira said. "If you come alone, you can live with us. Cam will be leaving soon, and Walter won't be far behind."

"You've given me a lot to think about," Julia said.

"You don't have to make a quick decision," Lizabeth said. "After we leave, you can talk it over with Ralph and let me know. In the meantime, I will be scouting some locations, in case you decide to take me up on my offer."

"This might be the most important decision I have ever had to make. Thank you, Lizabeth, for your idea and giving me the opportunity to fulfill my dream."

"You are welcome."

"Now, we are going to forget about business and enjoy our last few days in Cuba," Mira said.

⁓

That came quicker than Lizabeth could have imagined. It was their last day, and they were packing. Mira was resting in bed, saving her energy for the return trip. Julia took Lizabeth and Eileen into the courtyard for their last serving of tea. They sat down, as Pepi put some finger foods on the table and poured the steaming tea into their cups.

"There is no easy way of telling you this, so I'll just say the words," Julia said. "Your mother is not well. She didn't want you to know while you were enjoying your vacation."

"If she isn't well, we will leave when she feels better," Eileen said.

"I'm afraid it isn't a short-term illness."

"What is it then?" Lizabeth asked with shock and concern. She remembered the last few holiday dinners when her mother had needed to rest, and that she had not left the house here in Cuba. She felt guilty that she hadn't picked up on it.

"There is no way to know. She won't see a doctor."

"Well, we have to convince her," Eileen said.

"Your mother will be working with a practitioner when she gets home. Her entire life revolves around Christian Science, so you will be wasting your time trying to get her with doctors and hospitals."

Lizabeth knew that to be true. If prayer and mind over matter couldn't cure her mother's illness, it would destroy her core beliefs. And she now realized that her mother had not come to Cuba for a vacation, but to see Julia, in case something happened and she wouldn't be able to see her again. It frightened Lizabeth and she was worried about what lay ahead for her mother.

Her fond memories of Cuba would always be clouded by this revelation, unless she could do something to see that her mother was cured. She vowed to do everything possible to make that happen. Her mother was the one person they all depended on for stability, and Lizabeth was fearful for the family if something happened to her.

When they left Julia's home, they thanked Pepi for everything and issued an invitation for her to visit them in America.

On the dock, there were tearful goodbyes before the ship sailed.

"Thank you for everything, Aunt Julia," Lizabeth said, as she hugged her. "And thank you, Uncle Ralph."

"You ladies have a safe journey home," Ralph said.

"I hope you take me up on my offer, Aunt Julia," Lizabeth whispered to her. "We are going to need you."

"I know. I will write to you soon."

The women headed up the gangway.

"Bon voyage, my dear girls!" Julia yelled from the dock.

On the journey home, Lizabeth and Eileen fussed over their mother so much that she sat them down for a talk. "I know you both mean well, but you are smothering me. I want you to continue leading your lives and quit worrying about me. I plan on winning this fight, and it will help me to know that I'm not a burden to you and to the rest of the family. That is the reason I don't want your father or your brothers to know there is anything wrong with me. We will carry on as we always have, and there will be no moping around. From this point on, I need to see a positive attitude and happy faces. Do you understand?"

"Yes, Mother," they said in unison. They were scared and anxious for her but tried not to let it show.

CHAPTER TWENTY

Lizabeth and her mother had said goodbye to Eileen in Miami. Eileen had to get to a movie set in Virginia for her new film. But before leaving, she asked her mother if she should take some time off to help with her illness. Mira was adamant that Eileen continue with her career. Lizabeth was glad they were able to rest in Cuba, because they arrived back in Kansas City in the middle of a political firestorm. Tom Hannon had been indicted for income tax evasion and was awaiting trial.

The ward bosses were also indicted on various charges, and Walter had been arrested and was out on bail. He was facing a preliminary hearing. If her mother's illness and Walter's troubles weren't enough, when she returned to work, a wedding invitation was lying on her desk, announcing Cory's May marriage to Margie. Lizabeth was left in a quandary. If she did not go, it would make her look jealous and vengeful, and if she did go, it would be depressing. She set the invitation aside for another time, because she had enough to worry about with her mother's mysterious condition and Walter's court date.

The Sunday headline in the Kansas City newspapers about Walter's court hearing did not bode well for a quiet, enjoyable Sunday dinner. Walter thought about skipping out, but he knew that at some point he would have to face his father, and it might as well be in front of family, where he would have some support. Lizabeth and Aunt Erma were in the kitchen with Nana, where they had prepared the meal under the watchful eye of Mira.

When everyone was seated, Mira gave the blessing. Then J.M. waded into Walter with a vengeance. J.M. looked at his brother, Ray.

"Did I not warn you both this would happen?" he said, pointing at the headline in the newspaper. "I guess Walter being shot wasn't enough of a scandal; now we have to endure this disgrace."

"A preliminary hearing is not an admission of guilt," Ray said nervously.

"Oh, really. Do you think they hand these subpoenas out like penny candy, or do you think they might have some evidence to back them up? The other ward bosses had hearings, and they were all indicted."

"They are not Walter."

"Can we save this discussion until after dinner?" Mira said.

J.M. replied, "With all due respect, no, we cannot. I have to get this off my chest. There is no doubt that Hannon will get convicted on tax evasion charges and that the other ward bosses will go to jail. Are you so naïve as to think that Walter won't suffer the same fate?"

"Whatever happened to being innocent until proven guilty?" Walter interrupted. He knew Terri was worried about the hearing, and this grilling by his father was not helping her confidence.

"How can you not be guilty when you are operating in a corrupt political machine?" J.M. asked vehemently. "The prosecutors can tie you to all the things that Hannon is involved in, and you will be guilty by association."

"Since when was association a crime?" Walter asked.

"You know what I mean," J.M. said, getting red in the face.

"When will you have the preliminary hearing?" Lizabeth asked, trying to break up the heated argument.

"Next week, on Tuesday," Walter replied.

"Do you have a good attorney?" Cam asked.

"Yes."

"Do I know him?" J.M. asked

"Not likely."

J.M. looked at him questioningly.

"His name is Henry Williams and he is a Negro," Walter said.

"He's what?!" J.M. exploded and rose to his feet, wagging his finger at Walter. "The most important event in your life and you have hired an inexperienced attorney!"

"Calm down, J.M." Ray said to his brother.

"You said that you had a good attorney for Walter!" J.M. pointed his finger accusingly at Ray.

"Walter turned him down," Ray replied.

"Henry is not inexperienced," Walter said. "A lot of this inquiry will be about my work in the Negro community. I need someone familiar with the culture."

"What you need is someone familiar with the justice system, and that system happens to be white!"

"I'll take my chances with Henry," Walter said.

"I think everyone has had their say, so let's change the subject," Pop said, trying to keep J.M. from having a heart attack.

"Amen to that," Aunt Erma agreed. "Lizabeth, tell us about your adventures in Cuba."

Lizabeth obliged, glad to take the focus off Walter and his upcoming hearing and giving her father a chance to calm down. When she finished, her grandmother spoke up.

"Do you think Julia will take you up on your offer, Lizabeth? It would be wonderful to have both of my daughters in Kansas City."

"I hope our offer of a home furnishing store was irresistible. I've been looking for a space where she can set up shop, just in case she decides to come home."

Lizabeth was praying that Julia would decide to leave Cuba, not only to fulfill her dream but so Julia could help her in caring for her mother.

⁓

The courtroom was packed for Walter's preliminary hearing. J.M. and Mira stayed home, but the rest of the family was there. Lizabeth sat with Terri, Helen, and Cam. Drum and Queasy sat with the family, along with Jimmy and Carol. Walter's Uncle Ray and Aunt Erma were also there to support him. It was a noisy, boisterous courtroom, with reporters and photographers elbowing one another for the most advantageous view of the proceedings. The Hannon indictments were the hottest news in town and no paper wanted to miss out on the story.

Walter sat with his lawyer, Henry Williams. Henry was of medium height, but very thin of stature. He wore thick glasses and sported a short goatee. His suit was a bit rumpled, but he appeared to be a man who couldn't care less about the trappings of fashion, because he had more important matters to attend to. He was in his sixties, and Walter guessed he had seen most everything courtroom proceedings had to offer.

Walter looked over at the prosecutor and his team. They seemed to be a confident lot. And rightly so, with three ward boss indictments behind them. There were a lot of smug, righteous faces, and they seemed to be impatient for the proceedings to start so they could add Walter to their collection.

The prosecutor was Clayton Hall. He was a big man with broad shoulders. He wore a fashionable gray suit, with a red handkerchief placed expertly in the small pocket by his lapel. He had wavy black hair, blue eyes, and a square chin that was clenched and ready for battle. Walter guessed rightly that in his college days he had been a football player.

The judge entered the courtroom. He appeared to be in his seventies, with gray hair, stooped shoulders, and a slight limp was noticeable as he walked to his seat behind the bench. Walter was happy to see a veteran judge, rather than someone younger who would be trying to make a name for himself. There would be no jury at the preliminary hearing.

"All rise!" the bailiff said. The spectators obeyed and then sat when the judge did.

"Case number twenty-one, ten," the bailiff said. "The state of Missouri versus Walter Braden. The charges are racketeering and extortion."

"How do you plead, Mr. Braden?"

"Not guilty, Your Honor."

"Proceed," the judge said to the prosecution.

The prosecutor hesitated for a moment, as if he had expected Walter to plead guilty like the other ward bosses. He recovered quickly.

"Your Honor, we intend to show that as part of the corrupt Hannon machine, Mr. Braden intimidated business owners into paying into a protection scheme that extorted money from them to enrich himself and Tom Hannon. He started out in the north end and was so successful at this criminal activity that he was promoted to the east side, where he continued to extort money from the Negro community. I have sworn statements from business owners in both locations that these payments were made monthly to Mr. Braden."

"Objection, Your Honor," Henry Williams stood up. "Those payments were not made to Mr. Braden. They were paid to the political organization led by Tom Hannon. Walter Braden's job was merely to collect dues from the merchants for their healthcare, business insurance, and security needs."

"Your Honor," the prosecutor said. "The defense would have you believe that Walter Braden was nothing more than an errand boy and has done nothing to enrich himself or Hannon's machine at the expense of these business owners."

"Then let us proceed and see if we can establish the truth," the judge said.

"I call to the witness stand Tommy Conti of Conti's Produce Company," the prosecutor said.

Tommy walked to the front of the courtroom, was sworn in, and took a seat.

"Mr. Conti, do you know the defendant, Walter Braden?"

"Yes."

"Did he collect a monthly fee for protection of your business?"

"Yes. Protection was included in the dues I owed to Boss Tom."

"Did you feel threatened in any way by the defendant if you did not make the payment?"

"Not by Walter; but I wouldn't want to cross Boss Tom."

"Do you have any idea what Hannon did with the money he collected from you?"

"I would guess that he bet it at the racetrack."

That got a laugh from the courtroom.

"Objection, Your Honor!" Henry said. "Where this money ended up has no bearing on the case against my client. His job was as a collection agent for the Hannon political organization."

"Sustained," said the judge.

"Let me put it another way," Clayton said. "Mr. Conti, do you feel you got your money's worth from these payments?"

"Another objection, Your Honor. My client's job was to collect money. Whether Mr. Conti was satisfied with the value of his payment is of no consequence to this case."

Walter was beginning to congratulate himself on hiring Henry.

"Sustained," the judge said.

The prosecution called three more business owners who basically gave the same story. Clayton Hall made the case that money was handed over, and that the merchants were intimidated by Boss Hannon, but so far, the prosecutor had not proved extortion against Walter.

"Mr. Williams, you may call your first witness," the judge said to the defense.

Henry called John Castiglia, the owner of Castiglia Produce, to the stand.

"Mr. Castiglia, what is your relationship to the defendant?"

"Walter collected my dues for the Hannon political organization."

"Was this done under duress?"

"Under what?"

"Did you feel threatened?"

"I did from some of Hannon's other collection agents, but not from Walter."

"What if you couldn't pay?" Henry inquired.

"I never had that problem, but I know several merchants who did. Walter would either carry it over to the next month or pay the dues himself."

"Did he charge interest for doing that?"

"No. We all tried to pay on time, because Walter was more than fair with us."

"Would you explain that?" Henry asked.

"Walter tried to bring us enough new business to offset our dues payment."

"Did he ask for a fee for this service?"

"No, he did not."

"So, you were not intimidated by Walter in any way?"

"Not only *not* intimidated, we looked forward to his visits," Mr. Castiglia replied heartily.

That caused a stir in the gallery.

"Cross-examine, Mr. Hall?" the judge asked.

"No, Your Honor." Clayton Hall had been at it for quite some time and was getting nowhere with the merchant witnesses. His frustration was showing. His team had obviously not done their homework, because they had figured this would be an easy indictment.

"We call Walter Braden to the stand."

Walter swore the oath given by the bailiff and took a seat in the witness chair.

"Mr. Braden, you had a ton of cash every month to deliver to the Hannon political machine," the prosecutor said. "And you want us to believe that you didn't keep any of that cash for yourself?"

"I don't want you to believe anything. I want you to check the records."

"And how would I do that?"

"I have a journal of all the transactions that were made by me in the north end. Every payment I collected and turned in was signed for by Hannon's secretary."

That caused a buzz from the spectators in the gallery, and the reporters were scribbling furiously. Prosecutor Hall was taken aback for a moment. He collected himself and addressed the judge.

"This journal was not made available to the prosecution by Mr. Braden's attorney," the prosecutor said, hoping to catch Walter in deceit.

"That's because my attorney knew nothing about it. I didn't know it would be important until you started this line of questioning."

"We will make the journal available, Your Honor," Henry Williams said.

Clayton Hall knew that it would be hard to tie Walter to the money as a collection agent, but everyone knew that ward bosses were corrupt. He had three ward bosses who had pleaded guilty and were awaiting sentencing to prove it.

"Let's move on to your promotion to ward boss of the east side. It seems like a big step for someone so young and inexperienced."

"I thought so too. I had always done business in the Negro community and built some friendships. Tom Hannon thought those relationships would be useful to his organization."

"And you would get to enjoy the spoils reserved for a ward boss?"

"I don't know about any spoils. All I ever received was a paycheck."

"We have a record of monthly checks made out to the Hannon political organization from every business in your ward."

"And your point is?" Walter asked calmly.

"That you were extorting money for the enrichment of you and Boss Hannon."

"Those were payments for healthcare and insurance, just like the dues payments I collected in the north end."

"Then explain why the checks were made out for much more than that."

"The excess money went into a fund for schools, parks, and a recreation center."

"You are going to have to prove that, Mr. Braden."

Walter was dismissed and stepped down from the witness stand.

Henry Williams stood and said, "The defense would like to call Delores Johnson to the stand."

Delores came forward, was sworn in, and took a seat.

"Miss Johnson, you own an accounting firm. Is that correct?"

"Yes, sir."

"And what is your connection to Walter Braden?"

"I'm his accountant for the ward finances."

"And what did you do in that capacity?"

"I collected the checks he brought me each month from business owners, made insurance payments, and paid for the projects that Walter, excuse me, I mean Mr. Braden was working on."

"What kind of projects?"

"School lunches, parks, helping the needy. Whatever our merchants requested for the betterment of the community."

"Thank you, Miss Johnson."

"Cross-examine, Mr. Hall?" the judge asked.

Delores Johnson was twitching nervously at the prospect of being interrogated by Clayton Hall.

"Relax, Miss Johnson," the judge said. "I'll see to it that Mr. Hall doesn't bite."

Delores smiled. "Thank you, Your Honor."

"Miss Johnson, it is our understanding that a lot of loose cash was floating around your political organization." The prosecutor was fishing.

"I wouldn't know about that."

"Did Mr. Braden or his associates collect the money?"

"His associates did."

"So that cash could have gone to Mr. Braden before being turned over to you."

"No, sir."

"Why not?"

"Mr. Braden insisted that all payments were to be made by check."

"Checks that he could have cashed as ward boss."

"No, sir. The checks were made out to my accounting firm, and I have a record of every deposit and where those funds went."

That exonerating evidence caused a frenzy among the reporters.

"Silence, please!" the judge ordered.

"What about the checks you made out to charitable organizations? He could have set those up to siphon money out of the political account."

"Objection, Your Honor. That is pure speculation on the part of the prosecution, and it seems they are making it up as they go."

"You don't have to answer that unless you want to, Miss Johnson," the judge said.

"I don't mind, Your Honor. We don't make any payments unless we know what the money is being used for. And I checked to make sure it was used properly. Mr. Braden is strict about accountability."

"Thank you, Delores," the judge said. He rubbed his chin. "Here is what the prosecution is getting at, Miss Johnson. Do you feel Walter Braden used these collected funds for his personal use?"

"No, sir. That would not be possible."

"Why not?"

"Mr. Braden set it up so that he receives a paycheck from the political organization, but he doesn't have access to the bank account."

That information created another stir in the courtroom.

"What about a check going to Tom Hannon, Miss Johnson?" the prosecutor asked.

"Yes, sir. I made a payment each week to the political organization. Mr. Braden said it was for administrative costs and to pay our salaries."

"It seems that Walter Braden has put a lot faith in you, Miss Johnson. What makes you so trustworthy?"

Delores looked the prosecutor in the eye. "I obey the Ten Commandments."

There was an excited buzz and some laughter in the courtroom, because the prosecutor had trapped himself into that one.

The judge had the hint of a smile on his face. "Is that all, counselor?"

"Yes," Hall said in frustration.

"You may step down, Miss Johnson. And thank you for your testimony."

"We would like to recall Walter Braden to the stand," the prosecutor said.

Walter went up and took a seat, after being reminded he was still under oath.

"Mr. Braden, last summer you opened a nightclub. Is that correct?"

"Yes."

"I imagine that was quite an expense."

"It was."

"And where did you get the funding for your operation?"

"I live with my parents and don't have a lot of expenses, so I saved my weekly paychecks. I came up short of the money needed, so I borrowed the rest from my sister. She owns Liz Braden's Original Designs."

"Are any profits going to Tom Hannon?"

"Only the dues that I pay to Delores Johnson, like every other business owner."

"Why not get a business loan from Hannon?"

"Objection!" Henry Williams said. "Where Mr. Braden gets a loan is not relative to this case."

"It is if he is using the nightclub to launder money from Hannon's illicit operations," the prosecutor said.

"Your Honor," Henry Williams said. "It is obvious the prosecution is flailing blindly through scenarios of their own making, hoping to stumble on to something damaging to my client. Mr. Braden will open his books to the court at any time of your choosing. And I ask that because the prosecution is trying to paint my client as a criminal that you would allow me to call some character witnesses."

"Go ahead, Mr. Williams."

For the next hour, Henry called a host of business owners from the east side who had nothing but good things to say about Walter. Next up was Luther Jackson.

"Mr. Jackson, how did you come to know Walter Braden?"

"I've been cutting his hair for a long time."

"Isn't it unusual for a white man to get his hair cut in a Negro barbershop?"

"It is, but Walter don't see color. He just gets along with everyone."

"The prosecution would have us believe that as ward boss, Walter Braden strong-armed business owners and took resources from the poorest people in the city."

"That would be a description of Boss Bianco. Walter turned that around as soon as he took over as ward boss. Our money is now going to parks, schools, and recreation centers. And he does a lot of things that no one hears about."

"Can you give me an example, Mr. Jackson?" Henry inquired.

"Yes. Walter kept the Ku Klux Klan from taking over our job sites. We needed the jobs, and he kept a lot of our people from going hungry. He was shot by the Klan for his efforts, so in effect he took a bullet for the Negro community. On a personal level, I have a shoeshine boy who had been living on the streets. Something bad happened to him in his past, because he wouldn't talk and he had no prospects. He got into a scrape with some white boys, and even though it wasn't his fault, he was arrested. Walter got him out of jail and has him seeing a special education teacher and a psychologist. He gave him a good job, and that boy, who was headed for a life of crime, now has a future. The thing I want you to know about Walter is that he has a good heart. On the east side, we know that he is not looking out for himself, he is looking out for us. The state should be giving him an award for community service, rather than trying to prosecute him for a crime."

Luther's testimony caused a flurry of whispers in the gallery.

The judge banged his gavel for order. "Would you like to try any of that on for size, Mr. Hall?" he asked.

"No, Your Honor."

"I think we have heard enough testimony, so here is my ruling."

Walter and his attorney stood.

"It is not often I have the pleasure of saying this, but it looks like the state of Missouri has run smack dab into an honest man. Walter Braden, please accept the apologies of this court for wasting your time. You are free to go."

The gallery erupted in a cheer, and Walter vigorously shook Henry Williams' hand. Lizabeth was in tears when she hugged him. She had no idea about all the good things he was doing for people, and she was so proud of him. She only wished that her father and mother could have been here to witness it. Walter whispered a thank you to his Uncle Ray for insisting that he keep records of his transactions.

Walter left the courtroom with Terri on his arm and nothing but good prospects ahead of him. However, when he returned home after being acquitted, J.M. did not say one word about it or offer any congratulations about Walter's innocence. Lizabeth knew that must have hurt Walter, because later that week he announced that he was moving out of the house into an apartment. The pattern of her parents not seeing the good in Walter was ingrained and seemingly impossible to overcome.

Walter rented a garden apartment near the William Rockhill Nelson Gallery of Art, which was a few blocks from where Terri lived in Hyde Park. Lizabeth was now well aware of being the last sibling at home. She did not want to leave while her mother was ill, but wondered if she could move out later without feeling like she was abandoning her parents.

Lizabeth monitored her mother closely over the next few months. A practitioner came to the house daily to pray and to encourage Mira, but she didn't seem to be getting any better. After the first few visits, Lizabeth's father and her brothers realized something was wrong. They offered Mira encouragement, but did not try to get involved with her treatment. Mira had conditioned them over the years to believe that she could defeat any illness with prayer and a positive outlook. They were not about to go over her head and seek medical treatment, because it would be betraying her and not respecting her beliefs.

However, Lizabeth felt that her mother's life was more important than any religious doctrine, so she consulted with doctors on a continuing basis, describing her mother's condition and symptoms to them as best she could. They could not make a definitive diagnosis from afar, but they guessed that it might be some type of cancer.

CHAPTER TWENTY-ONE

April 1938

IT WAS SUNDAY, AND LIZABETH was sitting on the sunporch with her mother. Mira would normally be out in the yard working on her spring flowers, and then fix Sunday dinner for the family, but she now lacked the strength. Sunday dinners would be on hold until she felt better. Lizabeth knew she would never forgive herself if she failed to get her mother to a doctor, rather than relying on the Christian Science practitioner, so she broached the subject with her.

"You've been seeing Mrs. Allman for three months now and you don't seem to be getting any better. I want you to let me take you to the hospital for an evaluation."

Her mother looked at her. "Where is your faith, Lizabeth? Prayer and a positive attitude don't work overnight."

Lizabeth wondered how she could get across to her mother that prayer wasn't working, without undermining the confidence in her faith.

"Why not seek medical treatment along with seeing a practitioner?"

"That would go against everything I believe in. I'm putting my trust in the Lord and seeking medical treatment would be betraying that conviction."

Lizabeth wondered if her mother was putting her faith into a deity that didn't exist.

"Over the years, I began to realize you were skeptical, Lizabeth. I could read it in your eyes when you were helping me on my rounds. You must remember that I never tried to convert you to Christian Science. You should give me the same respect and not try to undermine my faith with talk of doctors and hospitals."

"I'm not trying to undermine you, Mother. All I'm asking is that you take one medical examination to find out what we are up against."

"That would spark medical treatment that would spiral out of control. And it would be an admission that I was willing to betray my faith."

Lizabeth felt that her mother's life was more important than following the Christian Science doctrine, but she was walking that line between Mira's faith and the family seeking medical treatment. What if her mother started to get better? It had happened to Cam in his battle with polio. Lizabeth decided that rather than pressure her mother, she would give her more time before enlisting the rest of the family to convince her to see a doctor.

One bright spot in all of this was that Aunt Julia was coming home. It was yet to be determined if Ralph would come later. Julia could take the bedroom vacated by Walter, and she would be a tremendous help with Mira. Lizabeth had found Julia a small warehouse with a storefront for Julia's home furnishing startup business. She knew that she and Julia would be busy, and she didn't want her mother to be home alone, so she hired a housekeeper who could cook and also keep an eye on her mother.

What kept Lizabeth sane and occupied during her mother's illness was that fashion was ever-changing, and she had to stay busy to keep up with the latest trends. The 1940s would be ushering in styles for the hourglass figure, which called for broad, padded shoulders; a tiny waist; and full hips. The hemline would be moving from the calf to the knee and be a fabric saver during production. It would be the perfect opportunity to start a new line of clothing for the full-figured woman to help her achieve the new look. Most designers ignored that segment of the population, and she wanted to fill the void.

She was so deep into design and production that when she looked at the calendar, she realized the day she had dreaded was at hand. Cory and Margie would be married on the first Sunday in May. She was Margie's employer, so there was no way she could not go. She would have to set her feelings aside, put on a brave face, and attend the wedding.

∽

When Sunday arrived, Lizabeth was at home getting ready to attend the mid-afternoon nuptials. Downstairs, she heard the house-keeper answer the door. She put on her last dab of makeup and went down to the foyer, where Jennie and Erma waited for her, dressed in their wedding finery. She realized they were there because they didn't want her to face the wedding alone. It was so unexpected and such a gesture of friendship that she teared up.

Erma took out her handkerchief and handed it to Lizabeth. "Are we ready to go, ladies?"

"Not ready, but willing," Lizabeth replied, wiping away her tears.

The wedding was held in a chapel next to the Methodist church that Cory attended. Both he and Margie wanted a small wedding with no bridesmaids or groomsmen. Margie would not be walking down the aisle because of her disability, so she and Cory were seated on the front pew as guests entered the chapel.

For Lizabeth, the entire experience was surreal. A kind of numb-ness set in that allowed her to function but not fully participate in what was going on. She focused on the stained-glass windows of the chapel that showed Jesus in various stages of his ministry.

When everyone was seated, the minster motioned for Margie and Cory to join him at the altar. Cory assisted Margie, who looked beautiful in her wedding dress. She wore an ivory gown, covered with gathered chiffon. It had an illusion neckline and a sweeping skirt. A beaded headband matched the dress, and she carried a bou-quet of pale purple lilacs.

Lizabeth couldn't help but think that it should be her standing beside Cory in her own wedding dress, but knew she had traded that possibility for ambition. Any regrets would be self-defeating, so after the service, she congratulated the bride and groom and stayed at the reception in the church fellowship hall just long enough to be polite. She then gave Erma her car keys and told her she had decided to walk home.

She stepped out into the sunshine and took a deep breath of air. It was a beautiful day in May, with trees and flowers blooming under a light blue sky. With the exception of her mother's illness, she had a lot to be thankful for, with friends and family at her side and a business that was booming. There was no denying that losing Cory was a setback, but she had to concede that Margie was a better fit for him than she could ever have been.

When she made it to her street, she felt better. She stopped and visited with neighbors working in their yards. They inquired about her mother and asked if there was anything they could do. Mira was the leader of the block's yard brigade, and the neighbors missed visiting with her and listening to her expert advice on the care of flowers and trees.

Lizabeth assured them that her mother was doing fine, even though it wasn't true. She was in denial, afraid that if the truth were spoken about her mother's condition, it would be true, and she was not prepared to handle reality. When she walked far enough down the block to see the house, she scanned the sunporch for her mother, hoping she would be out on this beautiful day. It was not to be, however, and arriving home, she went to her mother's room to fill her in on the wedding.

Tom Hannon had been convicted of income tax evasion. Walter wanted to show his support by being in court for the sentencing. He stopped on the steps of the courthouse and looked up at the 22-story Art Deco building that the Hannon machine had built five years ago. Walter thought it ironic that "The Boss" would be sentenced in a building that would not exist without his hard work and dedication. He had built a vibrant downtown, where skyscrapers now defined the skyline.

Tom had no doubt broken the law, but his good works were evident everywhere in the city. Walter listened as the judge handed down a 15-month sentence that was to be served in the US Penitentiary in Leavenworth, Kansas. It seemed a mild punishment to some, but with Hannon in declining health, Walter knew it could very well be a life sentence. Two weeks later, Boss Tom Hannon, one of the most notorious political bosses in American history, would walk through the gates of the Leavenworth prison to serve out his prison term.

That evening, Walter had a few drinks at the club and then headed to his apartment to meet Terri. He was depressed about today's sentencing. Hannon had been good to him and given him the opportunity to be a force in the city. He could only imagine the shock of Tom leaving his mansion on Ward Parkway and entering a small cell, where he would be just another inmate.

The ward bosses tied to Boss Tom would be sentenced in the coming week. Walter was thankful to have been acquitted of any crimes associated with the organization. And he was thankful that everything had worked out with Terri.

He and Terri sat down to a quiet dinner of Chinese take-out.

"I'm so grateful you were acquitted," she said.

"Thank you. It would be hard to leave you and go to prison."

"I had no idea you were doing so much good in the city."

"Luther is a friend and prone to giving me more credit than I deserve."

"I doubt that. At the trial, you had testimonials from a lot of businessmen on the east side."

"I don't want any credit for doing the right thing."

"Your mother wasn't at the hearing. How is she doing?"

"Not good, I'm afraid. She won't see a doctor, so there is no way to judge her condition."

"Can't you insist?"

"Lizabeth is pushing her, but trying not to alienate her."

"That's a lot to put on Lizabeth."

"I know. She's better at diplomacy than the rest of us. If Mother's condition doesn't improve, then we will insist."

"Good."

"How is the documentary coming along?" Walter had not mentioned that he was an investor and had initiated the project, because he did not know how she would react.

"We have to do more filming in farm country to finish the film. We should start the distribution process in the next few months."

"I've been meaning to ask you something."

She looked at him questioningly.

"Would you consider moving in with me?"

"What would I tell Mother?"

"That you are moving in with me."

"That would not go over well. Mother has certain standards for me, and maintaining my virtue is one of them."

"I thought the Victorian Age was behind us."

"Not where Mother is concerned."

"There is another option."

"We are not ready for that kind of commitment. Our relationship is back on track, so let's be happy and see where it leads."

"That sounds very much like a rejection of my proposal."

"That wasn't a proposal; it was a fishing expedition."

He laughed. "I will make a more concrete offer when you feel you are ready to settle down."

"That's fair enough. You have enough to think about with the political changes that are sure to come."

"Yes. I'm now a relic of the boss system of government. All the wards will now be controlled by the city council. Luther will fill the council position for the ward, and I will concentrate on running the nightclub."

"A much better outcome than going to prison."

"Yes, I'm very fortunate."

After dinner, they listened to the radio for a while, and then Walter leaned over and began kissing Terri's neck.

"Not fair," she said. "You are playing on my weakness."

"You know what they say—all's fair . . ."

"That must have been said by a man gathering his forces."

"Maybe we should continue this discussion in the bedroom."

"What would my mother think?"

"What she doesn't know won't compromise your virtue."

"No, but it seems you plan to."

He took her hand and led her into the bedroom.

It was close to midnight when Terri drove home to Hyde Park. Walter was exhausted mentally and physically. He drifted off, but a few hours later, his sleep was interrupted by the phone ringing. He tried to ignore it, but the caller was persistent.

"Hello," he answered irritably.

"Walter, it's Jimmy." Jimmy sounded frantic.

"What's happened?"

"There's been an explosion at the club! The fire department's here and the chief says it was a bomb. The place is destroyed."

Walter cleared his head and tried to think of the implications of what Jimmy had said. Who would want to bomb his nightclub? And then he chastised himself for not remembering Bianco's threat against the nightclub if Tom Hannon went to prison.

"What about Prince? Is he okay?"

"We don't know. The firemen searched the back rooms. There was no sign that anyone was in the building. Ezra heard the blast and he's here."

Walter remembered that Prince had been there when Bianco had threatened him. He also remembered what Charlene had said about Prince's sense of loyalty.

"Jimmy, call Luther and Eddie. Have them meet me at the club right away. Tell Ezra to stay there. I'll get in touch with Drum and Queasy."

"Okay, Walter."

Walter dressed quickly and hurried to the nightclub. When he drove into the parking lot, his heart sank. The club was a total loss. The acrid smell of smoke hovered in the air, as he looked around at the charred remains of his business. He gathered the men in the parking lot after being assured by the firemen that no one had been in the building.

"Joe Bianco threatened to destroy the club if Tom Hannon went to prison. I should have put on more security, but I forgot about the threat. Has anyone heard from Prince?"

"No, but the delivery truck is gone," Eddie said.

"My guess is that he is going after Joe Bianco," Walter said. "Prince will take this as a personal attack on me, and he will want revenge."

"That would be suicide," Drum said. "Bianco never has fewer than two bodyguards, and he is so ruthless that he hardly needs any protection."

"That's why we have to find Prince. There is no happy ending here. If he gets to Bianco, it will start a war with the Black Hand that we can't possibly win."

"Prince is too street smart not to find him," Luther said. "We have to find Prince before he finds Bianco."

"I'm sure Bianco has his guard up, waiting for us to retaliate. That will make it riskier for Prince. Jimmy and I will head for Bianco's house and follow him, if he leaves. Luther, you, Ezra, and Eddie head for the north end where Bianco has an office. Drum and Queasy will check out the City Market where Bianco eats breakfast. Jimmy and I will get in touch with Delores Johnson and have her stay by the phone. Check in with her every hour until you find Prince. Stop him at all costs. He will be facing a murder charge if he kills Bianco."

Prince had been in his room at the back of the club when he heard people break in. He assumed they were there to rob the place. They evidently thought no one was in the club, because they made no effort to be quiet. Prince went to get his knife out of the drawer.

"Once I set this, we have thirty seconds to get out of here," a man said. Prince realized they were about to set off a bomb. He hesitated, because he didn't know if the man had set the timer.

"Run!" the man shouted.

Prince had moved quickly out the back door to a vacant lot. The explosion had shaken the ground, and the club had gone up in flames.

He remembered the threat that Joe Bianco had made to Walter if Hannon went to prison. He crept around to the front of the burning building. Two men were getting into a car. He was thankful that Walter had left him the keys to an old truck to be used for deliveries and for emergencies. He followed the car at a distance and when it pulled into a driveway, he parked the truck a few houses away. He was outside Bianco's home when the sun came up.

Walter had the locations right, but the wrong timeframe. In the morning, Bianco had left earlier than usual with his two body-guards. Prince had followed them to Union Station where they were having breakfast at the Harvey House. He guessed they were at the train station to pick up a member of their gang. He had learned at an early age on the streets of Detroit how to blend in with his surroundings. Joe Bianco and his men would be looking for anything out of the ordinary, and a Negro hanging around without a job would be suspicious.

Prince walked through the Grand Hall and down the stairs, searching for something that would make him blend in. He weaved through the corridors until he found what he was after. A porter's jacket and a red hat were hanging on a hook outside an office. He put them on and hurried back up the stairs, where he grabbed an empty luggage cart and wheeled it off to the side. He waited for Bianco and his two bodyguards. They paid for their meals and headed his way.

"You boy! Over here!" An elderly lady came directly at Prince, waving her cane. There was no way he could ignore her without creating a scene and alerting Bianco.

"Pick up my luggage and follow me," she ordered.

Prince loaded the luggage and followed her. She was about 10 yards behind Bianco when they passed under the clock and into the North Waiting Room. There were people everywhere, greeting arriving passengers or waiting for trains. Prince knew he had to act quickly. He had no idea how many men would be getting off a train to meet Bianco, and the numbers were already against him.

He let the elderly lady get way ahead of him. She expected her orders to be carried out and was unaware that Prince was no longer following her. Bianco's two bodyguards were standing side by side with their backs to him. He got a running start with the luggage cart and then let it go. The cart hit the two men, and they went down, yelling in pain. In an instant, Prince had the switchblade out and lunged at Bianco, but he tripped on a piece of the spilled luggage, and Bianco spun away from him and went for his gun.

Prince had missed his chance. He ran toward the entrance to the trains. Bianco aimed but couldn't fire because of the crowd. Prince hurried down the stairs, jumped over the barriers, and ran into the trainyard. Bianco could see him up ahead. He dropped to one knee and fired. The bullet hit Prince in his right hip. He yelled out in pain but did not go down. He weaved his way through the parked train cars, trying to hide from Bianco. He had to get away quickly, because Bianco's men were sure to follow and cut him off. A couple of shots pinged off the train cars as he ran north across the yard.

He was in agony from the wound, and he was getting weak from the loss of blood. He made it to the last train and knew he was out of options. He took a deep breath and looked to the heavens for help. What he saw, high on a building across the yard, was a sign that read "Liz Braden's Original Designs." He had often heard Walter talk about his sister. He took a couple of deep breaths and then sprinted as fast as he could for the building. When he made it inside, he grabbed the first garment he saw and compressed it to his hip, so he wouldn't leave a trail of blood.

Lizabeth was in her top-floor office when she got a call from Erma.

"There is a young Negro boy here who says he works for Walter. He wants to see you."

Lizabeth was instantly anxious. She had heard about the bombing on the news, and Walter had called to tell her that he was okay.

"He has blood on his hands. Do you want me to call the police?"

"No. Bring him up to my office."

Lizabeth was waiting at the elevator when it opened. She could see the pain on Prince's face, and he was holding his side. "Where are you hurt?"

He pointed at his hip. She and Erma checked the wound through his torn pants.

"Is this from a gunshot?"

He nodded.

"Who shot you?"

"Don't know."

"Do you work at the nightclub?"

"I did. The nightclub's gone"

"Is that what this is about?"

He nodded again.

"Is someone after you?"

"Yes. I saw your sign from over in the trainyard," he said, as he grimaced.

"That sign will be a beacon for anyone chasing you, so we have to hurry." She figured he must be the boy that Luther had talked about at Walter's hearing.

"Erma, take the freight elevator down and have a truck ready. Stop and get one of the first aid kits and bring Kayla back with you."

Lizabeth sat Prince on the floor and continued to press the cloth against the wound. In a few minutes, Erma was back with Kayla. She was a striking girl with smooth skin and a cropped hairstyle that accentuated her forehead and her large, brown eyes. At the age of 20, she was the youngest of Lizabeth's Negro employees, but the most dedicated, and the spokesperson for the group.

"What happened to him?" she asked, as Lizabeth and Erma cut away his pant leg and started treating the wound.

"He was shot."

"Oh." Kayla put her fingers to her lips. "What can I do?"

"You have to help us get him to safety. He works for my brother." She paused and then asked Prince, "Where can we take you?"

"Luther's barbershop at Eighteenth and Woodland," he whispered through the pain.

"Do you know where it is?" she asked Kayla.

"I do."

"Good. A white woman in that neighborhood will raise suspicion, so I need you to stay with him until I contact my brother and get him there to help."

She and Erma got Prince on his feet. He put his arm around Kayla for support and limped onto the elevator.

"There is a truck waiting at the dock. Go as quickly as you can," Lizabeth said, pressing the down button on the freight elevator. She took the regular elevator down to the work area and went to her sewing station. Her heart was beating rapidly, and she began to sew to steady herself. It wasn't long before a man boldly approached her.

"Miss Braden?"

She turned around. The man confronting her was dressed in a suit and tie that was a bit rumpled. She guessed it was from the chase across the trainyard. He looked sinister, so she averted eye contact and tried to remain calm.

"May I help you?"

"Yes. You can turn over the nigger who ran in here."

"What Negro?"

Joe Bianco smiled. He had the coldest eyes she had ever seen. "I was at your sister's movie premiere. You're almost as good an actress."

"I don't know what you are talking about." She hoped Kayla and the young man were gone.

"A trail of blood ended at your doorstep."

"If someone is hurt, then I should call the police."

"That won't be necessary. We will just have a quick look around."

"Be my guest. The person you are looking for could be anywhere."

"Not likely. The Braden name on top of your building would be too inviting to pass up."

Lizabeth wondered if these were the men who had bombed Walter's nightclub. At any rate, she knew they were dangerous, and she wanted them out of the building.

"You have ten minutes, and then I'm calling the police," she said. She had not been intimidated by union bullies, and she was not going to be intimidated by gangsters.

Bianco and his men started a search but soon came back empty-handed.

"It was nice meeting you, Miss Braden," the man tipped his cap. "You tell your brother that he will be hearing from Joe Bianco."

Lizabeth was glad to see him go, and once again she was fearful for Walter's safety.

Walter waited for an hour outside Bianco's house before realizing he wasn't home. He found a pay phone and made the call to Delores Johnson.

"Has anyone reported seeing Prince?"

"No. But something odd is going on at Luther's barbershop."

"What?"

"A Liz Braden's Original Designs truck drove around back. It looks like they are making a delivery. What could Luther be buying from your sister?"

"Thanks, Delores." He slammed down the phone and headed the car for 18th and Woodland.

When he arrived at the barbershop, Prince was lying on the bed in the backroom. There was a Negro girl with him, holding a compress to his hip.

"Who are you?" Walter asked her.

"My name is Kayla. I work for your sister."

"Oh. It's good to meet you. Tell me what's going on."

Prince explained to Walter what had happened.

"How is the hip?"

"Your sister patched it for me. Kayla has been keeping pressure on it to stop the bleeding." It still surprised Walter when Prince spoke.

"I'll get a doctor to finish the job, then we have to get you out of here. Bianco will remember Luther's testimony from my hearing, and this is the first place he will look. Kayla, thank you so much. Tell my sister that everything is okay. I will call her later."

"Take care of yourself," Kayla said to Prince.

"I will. Thanks for all you did for me." She started to go, but Prince held her arm. "I hope this didn't scare you too much. I would like to see you again."

"I would like that too. It takes a lot to scare me."

Walter realized there was something deeper going on here.

"What is your address, Kayla?" Walter asked.

"It's twenty-two, twenty-one Forest Avenue."

Walter wrote it down and handed it to Prince, who managed a weak smile. He hurried Kayla out to the truck and helped her in. "Thanks again, Kayla."

Later, when the doctor was working on Prince, Walter made a phone call to Charlene and explained what had happened. She had formed a motherly connection to Prince and agreed to let him stay in the guesthouse behind her house until he healed. His next phone call was to Lizabeth to thank her for helping Prince.

"I was willing to help your friend, but this has to end, Walter," Lizabeth said. "I don't have the energy to run a business, worry about you, and deal with Mother's illness."

"I know. I'm sorry you were involved in this. I'm going to make peace with Joe Bianco."

"Good idea. He's the most sinister man that I've had the displeasure of meeting."

After getting Prince settled at Charlene's place, he made the call to Bianco at his office.

"Joe, it's Walter Braden."

"Walter, how are you doing?" Joe sounded like he was greeting an old friend rather than an adversary. His ability to go from cold-blooded killer to acting normal was one of the traits that made him so dangerous.

"Good, Joe. How is the family?"

"Never better. Thanks for asking."

"I heard on the grapevine that you had a close call at Union Station. I called to see if you were okay."

"I'm good. I put one of my running back moves on your boy."

"You were a legend on the gridiron."

"Back in the day, Walter. Back in the day."

"I called to tell you that your close call was not ordered by me, and that it won't happen again. You can relax before going on your extended vacation at Leavenworth."

"That's good to know, Walter. I was sorry to hear about your nightclub."

"Thanks. I have decided not to rebuild."

"Good decision. It will make your life less hectic. What will you do?"

"I'm thinking about buying a bar downtown with the insurance money."

"I'll stop by for a drink, when I get back from vacation."

"You do that, Joe. Good luck."

"Thanks, Walter."

Walter hung up the phone. He was relieved to have Bianco out of his life for good. It was time to call a meeting of his business partners to see where they should go from here. They met at Luther's barbershop.

"I think it would be foolhardy to rebuild the nightclub," Walter said. "Joe Bianco can wield the Black Hand from prison, so I'm sure another attack would happen. An integrated club was a good idea, but we were probably ahead of our time with what people were willing to accept."

"What do you suggest we do?" Eddie asked.

"We can split the insurance money. You have always wanted a place of your own, so you might consider opening a bar and supper club on the east side. The rest of us can put some money in to give Ezra and Prince a piece of the action. If Drum, Queasy, and Jimmy are agreeable, we will open up a small club downtown."

"That means Bianco wins," Drum said.

"In a way he does, but he will have to enjoy his victory from a prison cell."

"I might take my share of the insurance money and open a small accounting firm," Queasy said. "A continuing association with Walter might prove injurious to my health."

"You should thank me for making your life interesting," Walter said.

"Interesting is one thing. Joe Bianco, the Klan, and Sal Marconi chasing me through my nightmares is another," Queasy responded.

Jimmy spoke up. "If not for Walter, you would be sharing a prison cell with the city manager."

"That is true. However, fear seems to be winning out over gratitude."

"All that gangster stuff is behind us, Queasy," Walter said. "We will be living the quiet life of respectable businessmen."

"Somehow quiet and respectable doesn't fit with your lifestyle."

"Are you in with us, or are you going to whine?" Walter asked.

"I'm in, although by now I should know better."

"Good. Let's start making our plans."

CHAPTER TWENTY-TWO

August 1938

MIRA HAD NOT OBJECTED WHEN Lizabeth had hired a nurse to be with her, and that concerned Lizabeth, because her mother would have normally fought any hint of medical help. It was not like her to give up on her faith in self-healing. Despite the housekeeper's good meals, Mira had lost weight and had no appetite and was experiencing a lot of pain. She slept most of the day and night. Lizabeth was afraid she might slip into a coma.

She was thankful that a week ago her Aunt Julia and Uncle Ralph had arrived from Cuba. They were living in the Braden house until they could find something to buy in the neighborhood. Ralph had evidently decided that Julia was more important than his mistress and had agreed to leave Cuba. Lizabeth and Julia were in the kitchen having tea.

"Mother seems to have accepted the nurse, so I'm bringing in a doctor to examine her," Lizabeth said.

"She's not going to like it, but it's time," Julia replied.

"I would never forgive myself if I did nothing."

"You are doing the right thing."

"Should I discuss it with Father and my brothers?"

"That would put them in the position of going against Mira's wishes, and it would complicate matters. I'm sure they will go along with whatever you decide."

"If we can get her medical treatment, she might make a full recovery," Lizabeth said hopefully.

"The diagnosis will give us the information we need to put up a fight."

Lizabeth prayed they hadn't waited too long before seeking medical help but dismissed the thought because it was too dire to consider. The Bradens had no family doctor, so Lizabeth did her research and had the best internist in the city come to their home to examine her mother. She urged him to bring in any specialist he needed to get the best diagnosis.

Lizabeth waited impatiently in the living room while her mother was being examined. The doctor finally came out of her mother's bedroom and walked down the stairs.

"What did you find?" Lizabeth asked.

"I'm going to have two gynecologists come by tomorrow and examine your mother and then I will give you my diagnosis."

"But you must suspect something."

"I do, but I want confirmation."

"Not knowing is very difficult."

"I'm aware of that. Give me one more day and then we will talk."

"Okay. Thank you, doctor." She let him out the front door and then went back to check on her mother.

"How did it go, Mother?"

"We discussed my digestive problems, and he examined my stomach and pelvic area. I badgered him for a diagnosis, but he was not forthcoming."

"He is sending two more doctors to examine you tomorrow and then we should know something."

"I warned you that once the medical profession was called in, there would be no end to it."

"I'm sorry, Mother. I couldn't stand by any longer and do nothing."

Mira took her hand. "I know, dear. It goes against your nature not to act."

෨

The next day Lizabeth and Julia waited with J.M. and Walter while the doctors examined Mira. Cam was out of town. Lizabeth nervously paced the floor with butterflies churning in her stomach. No one felt like talking. The tick ticking of the grandfather clock in the hallway broke the silence, as the time moved ominously toward a diagnosis from the doctors. Lizabeth wanted to run into the bedroom and scream at them for taking so long, but she feared what they might say, and all she could do was pace and feel the rapid beating of her heart. After what seemed like an eternity, the three doctors came out and the family gathered around them. The internist did not mince words.

"The three of us agree that Mrs. Braden has ovarian cancer."

Lizabeth went numb and felt like she couldn't breathe. She felt lightheaded and had to sit in a chair.

"What is the treatment plan?" J.M. asked.

"I'm sorry," the internist said. "There is no treatment for this type of cancer. All we can do is to try to make her comfortable."

"Surely there is something you can do." J.M. was incredulous.

"This cancer leaves us feeling helpless. There has not been a lot of research on ovarian cancer, and we don't have any methods to treat the disease."

Lizabeth was feeling guilty about the amount of time wasted before she had contacted the doctor.

"Would contacting you sooner have made a difference?" she asked.

"No. Ovarian tumors are silent, until they are large and incurable. By the time symptoms appear, it is too late to help the patient."

J.M. raised the question they were all thinking but dared not ask. "How long does she have?"

"It is difficult to say. I would guess a few weeks."

"What should we do?" Julia asked.

"I suggest twenty-four-hour care. I will give instructions to your nurses on how to keep her as comfortable as possible."

Lizabeth willed herself to stand. Her mother would not want her to be anything but gracious. She shook hands with all three doctors. "Thank you for doing all that you can for my mother," she said, as she led them to the door.

"Call us anytime, Miss Braden," the internist said.

When they were gone, she ran up the stairs to her room and collapsed on the bed, sobbing her heart out.

The next few weeks, Lizabeth was in a trance. For the first time in her life, she couldn't concentrate on her work. All she could think about was her mother's suffering and the empty spaces there would be in her life and in her heart when Mira was gone. She put her work aside and spent every precious moment with her mother. And then the day she dreaded arrived. Her mother looked at her and said, "It is time to call your sister." When Lizabeth called, Eileen went straight to the train station and was home the next day.

When they sensed it was the final day, the family gathered in the Braden home and waited. J.M. spent some time alone with Mira. Lizabeth hoped they were able to resolve some of the conflicts in their marriage and part in peace. Pop, Nana, and Julia went in and reminisced about their time together as a family. They were followed by Erma and Ray.

When Lizabeth went in with her three siblings, her mother was having difficulty breathing, but she could still speak. There wasn't much to say, so they made small talk about anything but the obvious. After an uncomfortable silence, they kissed her on the forehead, squeezed her hand, and then headed to the door to leave, so Mira could rest.

As Lizabeth stood, her mother grasped her hand. "Stay with me for a while."

Lizabeth could tell she wanted to talk, so she waited until her mother caught her breath.

"When I'm gone, it will be up to you to hold the family together," she whispered.

Lizabeth looked at her in surprise. "Why me? What about Father? If not him, then Cam or Walter."

"They are not as strong and capable as you."

"If I'm strong, it's only because I have you to back me up," Lizabeth said tearfully.

"Nonsense, you have the tenacity to persevere. You've proved that time and time again."

"Walter said that I would always be the baby girl."

"You will always be my baby girl, but order of birth is not an

320

indicator of resilience. You have spent your life looking up to Cam, Walter, and Eileen, but in reality, they have looked to you for strength and stability. You are the base they operate from, so you can't go to pieces on them."

"I can't replace you."

"I'm not asking you to." Mira squeezed her hand. "I'm passing my strength to you, to carry on for our family, and I know you won't let me down."

Lizabeth lay her head on the pillow next to her mother. Her mother stroked her hair for a while and then said, "It's time for you to go, baby girl, and time for me to sleep."

Mira passed away that evening, and Lizabeth thought she would never stop crying. In the ensuing days, she had no energy and could hardly get out of bed. She was barely functioning in a cloud of depression. The funeral was sad beyond belief and difficult for the entire family to endure, but for Lizabeth the hardest part was coming home and not having her mother there. A piece of her life was missing that could never be replaced and she wondered how she would ever fill the void.

Her mother's touch was everywhere: the trees, the flowers, the furniture, the paintings on the walls; all a reminder of her mother's essence. It was life's great puzzle, how such a dynamic person like her mother could vanish from the face of the earth.

When she and Eileen came downstairs the morning after the funeral, they were so conditioned to their mother greeting them with a smile and coffee that they could only look at each other in profound sadness.

"I'll make the coffee," Lizabeth said, drying her tears. "If we are going to make it through this, we will have to get out of here and get back to work."

"I know," Eileen said. "This all seems surreal. I will never be able to picture this home without Mother in it."

"We will have to rely on each other to make it through."

"I feel bad that I won't be here to support you."

"I will be fine. I have Father, Aunt Erma, and Aunt Julia. I'm worried about you, because you will be on your own."

"I have an entire staff following me around."

"But they are not friends and family."

"No, but I have colleagues I can rely on."

"Good. The next few months will be difficult." Lizabeth knew that healing would take some time, and to get started they had to think about the future.

"When and where is your next picture?"

"We start filming a contemporary drama next week in New England."

"You are branching out from comedy and Westerns."

"Yes, and I'm a bit intimidated."

"Don't be. With your acting skills, you can handle any role." She was honoring her mother's request about providing encouragement and stability.

"Thank you. It will certainly be a challenge."

When the coffee was finished brewing, they took a cup to their father's bedroom. J.M. was reading the newspaper.

"Thank you, dear," he said, as Lizabeth placed the cup at his bedside.

"Do you want something to eat?"

"No, thank you."

She wondered how he was holding up, but there was no way to ask without being intrusive. Her father had never been one to discuss his feelings.

"I'm keeping the housekeeper on permanently to take care of the cooking and cleaning," Lizabeth said.

"That's a good idea. You have enough to manage at work. How long do you get to stay, Eileen?"

"I'm leaving tomorrow, unless you need me."

"The best thing for you both will be getting back to your work. Your mother would not want you moping around the house."

Lizabeth started to tear up every time she looked at her mother's bed, so she and Eileen excused themselves and went back to the kitchen. Aunt Julia and Uncle Ralph came out of Walter's former bedroom. Lizabeth was overcome with emotion, because Julia reminded her so much of her mother. She put her arms around Julia and held on.

"There, there," Julia said. "It's going to be okay. We will get through this together."

"I'm sorry. I don't know why I keep falling apart."

"It's perfectly natural," Julia said. "It will take a few weeks to get your feet under you."

"I'm glad you are here to help us through this," Lizabeth said.

"Your mother will always be a part of you both. She would expect that while you grieve, you channel your energies into something positive. That is the best way to honor her and what she stood for."

"That's a wonderful idea," Eileen said. "We could fund a college scholarship or a Christian Science reading room."

"Mother would love that," Lizabeth said. "Let's think about the possibilities and then make a decision."

The holidays were subdued that fall and winter; a time to get through rather than to celebrate. The family knew it would be futile for anyone to attempt to take over Mira's role of preparing her delicious meals at Thanksgiving and Christmas. She was the end of an era, and the joy she had brought to the family would not come again. For the next few years, Thanksgiving and Christmas dinners would be at a restaurant. It would be quite some time before any sparkle came back to the holidays.

Lizabeth and Eileen had set up a college scholarship for five students in their mother's name. The Mira Braden Fund would expand to include more students each year, depending on the success of Lizabeth's business and Eileen's movies.

September 1939

The news that Germany had invaded Poland, and three days later England and France had declared war on Germany, hardly registered with Lizabeth. It had been a year since her mother died and she was too consumed with thoughts of missing her to worry about a far-off war in Europe. However, she was thankful that her mother never had to face the possibility of her sons going to war and the distress that would have caused her.

Life moved on as Lizabeth and her family continued to grieve the loss of Mira. Every day was a challenge, which brought back memories of her, but they acknowledged that Mira wanted them to be strong. They continued their careers and things got better with time.

∽

Talk of war dominated the news in 1940. The majority of citizens wanted no part of another European war, but many were afraid of being swept up in world events. In April, Germany invaded Norway and Denmark. In May, the Germans invaded the low countries of the Netherlands, Belgium, and Luxembourg. In June, the British Expeditionary Force retreated to the beaches of Dunkirk and had to be evacuated by sea.

It seemed to Lizabeth that the world was unraveling. And then in September, President Roosevelt instituted the first civilian draft for the military. It was an ominous indication of what might lie ahead for her brothers and for America. It was even more unnerving when she arrived at work one day in early October, and two military men were waiting in her office. Their Army uniforms were neatly pressed, and their shoes were shined to perfection.

"Miss Braden, I'm Colonel Harris, and this is Major Davis."

Lizabeth shook hands with the officers. "What can I do for you?"

"We're from the War Department. What we are about to discuss here is strictly confidential."

"Go ahead."

"Your company has a reputation for making quality garments at a fair price," Major Davis said. "We want you to start making uniforms for the military."

Lizabeth thought about that for a moment. "That might be possible, but why the secrecy?"

"Two reasons. There are German saboteurs operating all over the country. We don't want your company to become a target. And we don't want the public to think we are mobilizing. Seventy percent of the citizenry are against another war."

"That would include me," Lizabeth said. "And from what you just said, you are mobilizing."

"We can't be caught flat-footed," Colonel Harris said. "None of us want a war, but we have to be prepared if it happens."

"I don't want to seem unpatriotic, but I have a fashion business to run, and a lot of people to support."

"We are well aware of that, and we are prepared to give you whatever assistance you need, financially or otherwise."

"How big a project are we talking about?"

"We will require an entire floor of your building. Preferably the floor underneath this office. We don't want anyone walking in off the street and observing what you are making. You will also have to hire one hundred seamstresses in the next two weeks."

"That is an enormous operation," Lizabeth said.

"Yes. And anyone who works on the project will need a security clearance. We will take care of that part of our arrangement."

"How will we ever be able to keep this massive activity secret?"

"You should have a talk with your employees and emphasize patriotism. We don't want to threaten anyone, but let them know that any loose talk can be traced back to them and there will be consequences. We will have a guard watching the building twenty-four hours a day."

"Why my company, other than quality and price?"

"You have an excellent location. We can bring the uniforms down the back elevator and into the trainyard where railroad cars assigned to the military will be waiting to load."

"What type of uniforms will you require?"

"Your first project will be US Army combat uniforms."

"I've never made clothing for men."

"Not a problem. You've made pantsuits and workwear for women, so uniforms won't be much different. We will give you patterns with all the instructions you will need."

"What about material?"

"You will be using wool for some uniforms and heavy cotton herringbone twill for others. Wool will be used in cooler climates and herringbone in the tropics. Well, Miss Braden, do you think you are up to handling this project for your country?"

"With all due respect, gentlemen, if you didn't think I was, you wouldn't be here."

"And that is the final reason we selected you. We like your determination and your ability to get things done."

"I will do it on one condition. My military division will make a profit during peacetime. If a war starts, we will set aside any profits and operate at cost. It will be our contribution to the war effort."

"Then we have a deal," the colonel said.

"There is one other thing. I have an agreement with the Garment Workers' Union. The union has to stay away from my company until Labor Day of next year. The leaders will be back at that time to try to organize my employees."

"When you partner with the government, you will be exempt from any union-organizing efforts. The nation's security needs take precedence over the needs of labor unions."

"Then when do we start?" she asked.

"The materials will arrive in the rail yard at Union Station in two weeks. Good luck, Miss Braden."

Lizabeth said goodbye to the two officers. She was worried, because the government would not be pursuing her help and going to this expense unless it thought war was imminent. However, she was grateful her company had been picked to contribute something to aid the country. Hard work had helped her deal with losing her mother, and this new project would keep her mind occupied for quite some time. She went into her father's office.

"Who were the brass?" he asked

"From the War Department. They want us to start making Army combat uniforms."

"What was your reaction?"

"I agreed. It is time for an expansion into something new. We can grow the company and help our country at the same time."

"It confirms my belief that we will eventually be pulled into the war conflict," J.M. said. "What do you need me to do?"

"Run an advertisement for seamstresses."

"How many will you need?"

"Eighty to start."

J.M. raised his eyebrows.

"I know. It is a big project, but we can handle it."

"No doubt. But what kind of toll will it take on you? You've been under a lot of stress."

"I need the challenge. We will have a company meeting after we get everyone hired and let them know what we are taking on."

She went down to the work floor to meet with Kayla and the other Negro women of her workforce.

"We are taking on a big project in a few weeks, and I want to know if you can find twenty seamstresses from the Negro community. Attitude and work ethic will be more important than an ability to sew. We can teach them what they need to know."

"There are plenty of women looking for work," Kayla said. "When will you need them?"

"As soon as you can get them here for an interview."

"We can sure do that," Kayla said.

"Good. I'll be counting on it."

Erma took Lizabeth aside. "What's going on?"

"It's all hush hush, but in two weeks we are taking on a big project for Uncle Sam, and we need to hire a hundred new seamstresses."

"Wow! How will we ever get them trained that quickly?"

"We are going to open an in-house sewing school. It is something I've wanted to do for a long time. We will rotate our best seamstresses into the school for a couple of hours each day. It will give them a break from their regular duties and give them a chance to help other workers."

"That's a great idea," Erma said. "They can learn our way of doing things from day one."

"Father is running an ad, so we will have to set some time aside for interviews. I'll have a couple of our experienced employees help us evaluate the candidates."

For the next two weeks, Lizabeth worked long hours to get ready for the first shipment of material from the military. The seamstresses were hired, and their security clearances were in place. She purchased the new sewing machines with company profits and did not have to borrow money from the government. Her new employees were spending several hours a day in seamstress school and the rest of the day studying the practical application of the patterns required by the military. The day the material arrived from the military, Lizabeth called a company meeting of all the employees.

"First, I want to welcome our new seamstresses to the company.

We hope you will find it rewarding for you and for your families. We have discovered that job satisfaction equals profits, so if you have a problem, please come to me, Erma, or Jennie, and we will do our best to solve it. The salaries we pay and the benefits we offer are tops in the industry, because you make it possible. The Liz Braden designer logo on your shirts signifies that you are a member of our Designers' Club team, and no member is any more important than any other. We are a sorority of sisters working in a common cause to support our families and our country.

"And that brings me to our latest venture. We have been given the honor of doing some work for the government. That work will take place on the eighth floor and will be off limits to anyone not working on the project. It is only natural that you will be curious as to what goes on there, but be advised the government has designated that floor as a classified area. The work is not to be discussed between you or with anyone outside this building.

"We are now part of the national security apparatus, and we will have to work within those constraints. However, this will continue to be a happy workplace, and I have no doubt that we can enjoy our work and still keep our commitment to the government. Just remember to talk up our fashions, but never discuss our military work. Our first shipment from the military is making its way up the back elevator, so good luck. Let's show the government what we can do."

Walter and his three friends had purchased and renovated a tavern on 5th Street in the heart of the historic City Market. In the past, Walter had worked under a lot of stress. Now he wanted a place where he could gather with his friends and enjoy the quiet life and leave the revelry of 12th Street to someone else. The new place would serve food and drink. It would be an ideal place for Queasy to hold court and for Drum to continue his gambling operation. Jimmy would be a draw for the sports crowd. Walter would be a draw for those nostalgic for Boss Hannon and the days of a wide-open city.

"We are opening in a week and have no name for our new venture," Walter said. "What shall we call the place?"

"We could continue using the Kansas City Club," Drum said.

"Our friends would be expecting another nightclub," Queasy replied.

"How about Four Friends Tavern?" Jimmy suggested.

"Not bad, but we need something historic that binds us to the city," Walter said. "We need a name people can relate to and won't soon forget."

"I'm guessing that you have something in mind," Queasy said.

"I think we should call the place Tom's Town Tavern. It is historic and honors the good things that Tom did for this city. It's also a bit notorious and has the right amount of intrigue to attract people in off the street."

"It might alienate the reformer crowd," Drum said.

"Possibly. But I suspect they will be curious enough to check us out. Tom Hannon will forever be a part of our history, and no amount of reforming can change that."

"You will be honoring a man who almost got you put in prison," Queasy said.

"He also made me more than I ever hoped to be."

"When does he get out of prison?" Drum asked.

"In a few months."

"If we could get a picture of him here at the bar, having a soft drink, our tavern would become legendary," Queasy said.

"Now you are talking," Walter said. "Does anyone object to Tom's Town Tavern?"

No one did, and the name was adopted.

In the fall of 1941, Tom Hannon walked out of the Leavenworth prison as a free man. Walter gave him a couple of weeks to get settled and then invited him to a dinner in his honor at the tavern. He had invited Tom's closest friends and associates, and the place was packed. Tom ordered a soft drink at the bar and Queasy took a picture that would hang on the wall and indeed make the tavern legendary.

"Walter, your naming of the tavern makes me proud," Tom said. "I heard about it in prison and it let me know that I was not forgotten. It is an honor that I will cherish."

"The honor is ours. You have championed the working men and women of this city, and this is where we want them to come and have a good time. Now, before we have dinner, some of your friends want to say a few words. I made them promise not to be long-winded."

The assembled guests listened to a few speeches praising Tom and his legacy, and then it was Walter's turn to speak. He stood on a chair and put his hands up for quiet.

"Thank you for coming, ladies and gentlemen. Tonight, we honor Tom Hannon and also the memory of his brother, Jack. These two men built this town from muddy streets and wooden storefronts to the colossus it is today." There was rousing applause from the audience. "Through their vision and hard work, Kansas City has taken her place among the great cities of the nation and given every working man and woman a fair shake and a chance at a better life." More applause reflected the crowd's agreement.

"Tom Hannon helped my sister and me achieve our dreams, as he did for thousands of others, and we are extremely grateful. Because of his dynamic personality and his dedication to his fellow man, this city will never be known as Jesse James' town, or Buffalo Bill's town, or even Harry Truman's town, it will always be known as Tom's Town." A big cheer went up from the crowd.

"Please hold up your glasses and drink a toast to Tom Hannon, a man we will always hold in high esteem and with great affection." Shouts of "hear, hear" went up, the drinks were downed, and the party lasted far into the night.

The years 1940 and 1941 had been good for Lizabeth's business. The country was coming out of the Depression, and women were spending money on fashions. To offset the dire reality of a possible war, designers were becoming more creative in the use of glamorous fabrics and vibrant colors. Women wanted clothing that would match their interests for play and evening wear. Calico skirts, known as broomstick skirts, were popular, and Lizabeth had designed her own version with the Liz Braden label.

The Home Helper apron and her military work, along with her designer clothing were very profitable, and her cash flow was excellent. She was sure textiles would be rationed if the country went to war, so she was stockpiling fabric in a couple of warehouses. It was her responsibility to see that none of her employees was laid off because of shortages or her lack of foresight.

Margie's end of the business was booming. She had designed knitted items along with her crochet pieces, and Lizabeth bought some knitting machines to help fill the demand. Women were wearing knitted scarves, known as mufflers, with every outfit, and knitted stocking caps were all the rage for college girls. Margie and Cory had purchased a nice home in the Brookside area, and the money she was earning allowed Cory to go to college and work toward his teaching degree. Any feelings Lizabeth had for Cory were long since gone, and she could be friends with the two of them without any lingering resentments from the past.

CHAPTER TWENTY-THREE

December 1941

LIZABETH, WALTER, AND TERRI WERE having brunch at Cam and Helen's. They had purchased the apartment on the Plaza when they got married.

Lizabeth had insisted they meet the first Sunday of each month to catch up and spend time together. She had promised her mother that she would hold the family together and that was a promise she intended to keep. It was too traumatic to meet at the family home without their mother being there, so Helen and Cam had volunteered their apartment.

J.M. was having dinner with Julia and Ralph. Walter and Cam had set aside their differences after their mother passed away. Perhaps they had realized the fragility of life and that put the relationship in perspective. They still disagreed but did not intentionally bait each other into a fight as they once did.

"Father tells me you have been working twelve-hour days, Lizabeth," Cam said.

"Yes. We have taken on a large project."

"Care to elaborate?"

"I wish that I could."

"No need to explain. If you can't discuss it, that means the government is involved. We are experiencing the same thing in Detroit, where we are switching some of the assembly lines from trucks to tanks."

Lizabeth looked at him in surprise. *So much for secrecy,* she thought. "And you are allowed to talk about it?"

"We get warnings from the government about loose lips sinking ships, but it is very difficult to hide a tank. The government should quit pretending we are not mobilizing and start doing it in earnest. We won't be able to stay out of the war in Europe. England is standing in the way of Hitler's quest for world domination and if he wins the battle of Britain, then we will surely be next."

"Our president has activated general headquarters to mobilize the Army, so it seems to me the secret is out," Walter said.

"I think they want to keep a lid on war preparations, in case of saboteurs," Lizabeth said.

"I'm worried about the draft," Helen said. "I wonder if the government will be calling up anyone over the age of thirty."

"I wouldn't think so," Lizabeth said, with more hope than knowledge. Cam was 31 and Walter was 30.

"Terri has been asked to do some documentary work for the government," Walter said. "It seems they are affecting every part of the workforce."

"Was your last documentary successful?" Helen asked.

"It made enough money so that I can keep producing films."

"What will you be producing for the government?"

Terri put her finger to her lips.

"You've got to be kidding."

"Yes. I am kidding. I'll be doing some documentary work on small-town America. The goal is to unify the country and get everyone behind the war bond effort."

"How will you manage that?"

"Wrap the citizenry in the flag and promote God, home, and country."

"You sound cynical."

"Millions went to their deaths in the last war because of nationalism. And now we get to do it all over again."

"You do agree that we have to stop Hitler."

"Yes. That is why I accepted the government project."

"How was your night honoring Tom Hannon, Walter?" Lizabeth asked, wanting to get away from talk of war.

"It was good. Lots of people came, and Tom enjoyed it immensely."

"Was he okay with you naming the tavern Tom's Town?"

"He was flattered and grateful."

"Do you think we could get J.M. to stop in for a drink?" Cam joked.

Walter smiled. "That would take some doing."

Cam agreed and added, "Helen and I will come by for dinner some time."

"Please do. The food and drinks will be on me."

Lizabeth wished that Walter had opened any business but a bar. He had always had trouble turning down a drink, and now he would feel obligated to drink with his customers. She wondered what effect the drinking had on his health and on his relationship with Terri. She knew that Terri would only tolerate so much before moving on. His work in the Negro community had shown that he had a lot to offer, and it would be a shame if that potential was stymied by alcohol.

"How are your former nightclub partners on the east side doing?" she asked.

"Great. Eddie has opened a small club, and Ezra and Prince have a piece of the action."

"How is Prince doing?"

"Charlene has made unbelievable progress with him. The psychologist is also making headway with his anger issues. He is earning good money, but he still lives in the back of Luther's barbershop. Luther says it's because that's the only place that feels like home. Prince would have had no chance at anything, Lizabeth, if you hadn't rescued him from Bianco and his thugs."

"You two seem to be working as a team," Cam said to Walter and Lizabeth. "First, it was the black hoods in the attack on the Klan, and now the Bianco episode."

"I'm grateful that she was there when I needed her," Walter said.

"You and Lizabeth will never have any regrets about your lives being dull," Helen said. "The war might be anticlimactic for you."

"We've had our moments, that's for sure," Lizabeth said. "I was hoping for a respite, but with this latest project, fate has intervened once again."

"Cam and I worry that you are not leaving room for a personal life," Helen said.

"What is a personal life?" Lizabeth joked. "Thank you for your concern, but at the present time it would be too much of a distraction. I might be destined to become an old maid at the age of twenty-six."

"You are a perfect age for marriage and a family."

"You are my family. It was not a difficult decision to devote myself to my company at the expense of a romantic relationship."

"You could have both."

"Cory was proof that I can't operate that way. Either my business or my personal life would suffer."

"What about love?"

"It would complicate my plan for the future."

"And that would be?"

"I hope this doesn't sound too self-serving. I want to be the most successful designer in America."

"I knew you were ambitious, but I had no idea. That is a lofty goal."

"And to achieve it, there are things in life that I will have to give up."

"But will it be worth it?" Terri asked.

"I won't know that until the end. Regardless, my business is my life, and I can't change who I am."

"Don't bet against her," Walter said. "She has a way of making her dreams come true."

"I read in the newspapers where you are becoming involved in city events," Helen said. "You are doing a lot of speaking engagements."

"Only if they are educational, charitable, or support my business."

"What have you heard from Eileen?" Terri asked.

"We've spoken every other day since Mother passed away. She was scheduled to make a movie in Europe, but world events changed that, so they will be shooting the film in Hollywood."

"She is living the life she always wanted," Helen said.

"Yes. That keeps me from begging her to come home. I miss her a lot."

"How do you think your father is doing?" Terri asked.

"It's not like him to open up about his feelings, especially to his children. The two of us waltz around anything serious and try to stay busy."

"It will take time," Terri said. "It was years before I could deal with my father's death. He died when I was a teenager, and it was traumatic."

Lizabeth knew there was more to deal with than her mother's passing. Her father had not made peace with Walter. The two of them still clashed whenever Walter came by the house, so he eventually stopped coming. J.M. could not get over the good son, bad son perception he had formed and that was tragic.

Cam went to the house a couple of times a week and talked business with his father and that seemed to keep him happy until the next visit. Lizabeth was disappointed that not even her mother's death could change the family dynamic between her father and his sons. She was thankful that her brothers were now able to communicate without hostility. She suspected that after her mother's passing, Helen and Terri had influenced them to call a truce for the sake of family harmony.

Lizabeth's reverie about her father and her brothers was interrupted when Cam asked her a question.

"How is Aunt Julia doing with her new venture?"

"I've introduced her to several interior designers who will help her get started in commercial design and also home furnishings. She has such a passion that I'm sure she will be successful. My offices are decorated in a mess of hand-me-downs, so I'm going to be her first customer."

"What about Uncle Ralph?"

"He was hired by KC Power and Light. Julia and Ralph have found a home on Oak Street and will be moving next week." Lizabeth wondered what it would be like living at home with no one but her father. Aunt Julia had been her support system since Mira's death and had made life bearable. There would be an awful stillness in the house after she left.

The phone rang and Cam went to answer.

"What!" They heard him exclaim in alarm. "You have got to be kidding me!" He put the phone down and hurried to the radio. He scanned the dial and found nothing but music.

"What's going on, Cam?" Helen asked.

Suddenly the excited voice of an announcer broke in. "We interrupt this program to bring you a special news bulletin! Japanese military forces have attacked Pearl Harbor. Details are not available but President Roosevelt has announced the attack has been made on military bases on the island of Oahu in the Territory of Hawaii."

Lizabeth was stunned. For her, war had been a thought rather than a reality and now the full impact of the announcer's words and the dire implications of what it meant for her family and for the nation was alarming and filled her with dread.

"Has anyone heard of Pearl Harbor?" Terri asked.

No one had. Cam went to get a map and they located it on the island of Oahu.

"Is there any chance we won't go to war?" Helen asked.

"No. Not with an attack on our military bases," Cam said.

"It's hard to believe the Japanese would attack without a declaration of war," Walter said.

"Terri, you won't have to unify the country with documentaries," Cam said. "The Japanese just did it for you. This dastardly deed will anger every American."

The radio announcer broke in again and announced that President Roosevelt would speak to Congress the next day, and his speech would be broadcast live.

"We have to be with Father when the president speaks," Lizabeth said.

"Absolutely," Cam agreed.

"We will be there," Walter said.

No one felt like talking after the shock of what had happened, so they hugged one another and said their goodbyes.

The president's address was such a momentous occasion that no one wanted to listen alone. Nana and Pop were at the Braden house, along with Julia and Ralph. Erma and Ray joined them, and Walter had invited Jimmy, Drum, and Queasy. Walter had closed the tavern until after the speech and Lizabeth had shut down production, so her staff could listen to the president.

"J.M., you were right in your prediction of war," Ray said.

"I wish I had been wrong. The world never seems to learn that appeasing dictators never works. They want absolute power and will go to any means to achieve their goals."

"Do you think the Japanese will attack the West Coast?" Terri asked.

"No. There are too many people and too much territory for them to control. However, I wouldn't rule out an invasion of the Hawaiian Islands. We need to hold Hawaii at all costs as a last bastion of defense in the Pacific."

"How much damage has been done to our military installations?" Pop asked.

"I don't imagine that we will get any specifics," J.M. said. "The leaders can't let the enemy know how much damage they inflicted on our military. Germany will probably declare war on us in support of its Axis partner."

"So, instead of an isolated war," Pop said, "it looks like we are in for another world war."

"It looks that way. Hopefully we can end it quickly."

Lizabeth knew the president had a tough sell ahead of him to unite the country and move it from pacifism to war. Despite what her father thought, she was hoping against all odds for a peaceful settlement. If anyone could achieve peace it would be Franklin Delano Roosevelt. She took a deep breath, as static on the radio cleared. The voice of the president came clearly and confidently over the air. "Yesterday, December 7, 1941—a date that will live in infamy—the United States of America was suddenly and deliberately attacked by the naval and air forces of the empire of Japan."

Lizabeth listened as the president told of the attacks and that Japan had undertaken a surprise offensive extending throughout the Pacific area. Her hopes for peace were dashed when the president concluded his speech. "With confidence in our armed forces, with the unbounding determination of our people, we will gain the inevitable triumph—so help us God. I ask that the Congress declare that since the unprovoked and dastardly attack by Japan on Sunday, December 7, 1941, a state of war has existed between the United States and the Japanese empire."

J.M. turned off the radio. They were numb with the realization that the United States was at war. In that short address by the president, millions of lives would be altered, and they knew many lives would be lost. Lizabeth wished that her mother was here to support the family. Her wisdom and her faith were sorely missed. If ever a prayer was needed, it was now. She was really worried when Walter spoke up.

"What we have to decide now is which branch of service to join," he said.

"Work here will be just as important as joining the military," Lizabeth countered.

"Nice try, Lizabeth. But we need to get in the fight and pay the Japs back for their treachery."

"I vote for the Marine Corps," Jimmy said.

"Too gung-ho for the likes of us," Drum said. "Me and Queasy thought this might be coming, so we talked about it and we are joining the Army Air Corps."

"It's the Army for me," Cam said. "I've met some of the Army liaison officers when we were transitioning the plant in Detroit from cars to Army vehicles. I'll try to join their ranks."

"I think this is something we need to discuss," Helen said, obviously not happy with his decision.

"I guess it's up to me to join the Navy," Pop said, breaking the tension and making everyone laugh.

However, it was no laughing matter to Lizabeth. She had two brothers to worry about, and she was sure that neither of them realized the gravity of what they were getting into. The next step for her was to call a meeting of her employees and lay out what would be expected of them for the duration of the war.

"Erma, we had better get back to work," she said, even though she hated to break up the gathering. These moments together would be precious now, and she vowed to spend as much time as she could with her brothers before they went off to war.

At Liz Braden's Original Designs, she gathered her employees in the warehouse's vast sewing room to give them an update on the future of the company. "The president's speech called us to action for the good of the country" she began. "We are going on a war footing, and that means we will be operating under a state of war. We want to make as many uniforms as possible without sacrificing quantity for quality. Our contribution to the war effort will be to ship uniforms our fighting men will be proud to wear. From now until the conclusion of the war, there will be no profits made in our military division and we will work at cost. We have to stay united behind a common cause, and that cause is to win this war. Everything else we do is secondary."

Lizabeth paused, looking over the employees. "As part of our war efforts, we will also fund and set up a canteen at Union Station to serve coffee and sandwiches to the servicemen who will be crossing the country to their duty stations. I will volunteer for that, and I hope you will too. We should all do what we can to support these brave men. The company is forming a support group for those of you who have loved ones in the service, where you can voice your concerns and share your feelings. Most of us did not want war, but now that it is a reality, we must remember that every uniform we complete puts us that much closer to victory and an end to the war.

"I will do my best to make that happen, and I know that you will too. However, we are in business to make a profit, so to make up for the lost revenue, we are expanding our work clothes division. My guess is that women will be employed in large numbers, as they fill in for men going off to war. And war or no war, women will continue to want fashionable clothing, and we will continue to offer the best that money can buy. I hope that each of you, in every division of the company, will join me in continuing your commitment to be the best that you can be, even through the tough times ahead. Thank you."

Walter and Jimmy waited outside the Marine recruiting office in a line that stretched around the block. Walter had not discussed with Terri his choice to join the military, because he didn't want her to question his decision. He felt it was his duty as an American to help avenge the sneak attack on Pearl Harbor. He thought not joining would be cowardly, and he would be shirking his responsibility as a citizen.

"It looks like a lot of men are signing up," Jimmy said.

"I'm glad to see it. The Japs don't know what they have let themselves in for. The entire country will be mobilizing for war."

"Have you thought about what will happen to the tavern when we leave for the military?"

"We will have to bring in a manager we can trust."

"Once we join, I wonder how long it will take before we head for basic training."

"With the country on the defensive, we should be sent quickly. Have you told Carol you are joining up?"

"No. I'm going to break it to her tonight at dinner."

They waited a few more minutes and were then swept into the building for processing. There were medical people at every station. One checked height and weight, another checked eyes and hearing and another tested mobility. They had their private parts checked and were asked to cough and move on. The last tests were urine and blood.

340

It had been a long day of hurry up and wait, so as soon as they were finished, Jimmy and Walter headed to the tavern for a well-earned beer.

"That made me feel more like a number than a human being," Jimmy said.

"That might be the idea. The military sees us as a group rather than as individuals."

They walked into the tavern. "How did it go?" Queasy asked from the bar.

"We won't know for a couple of days," Walter replied.

"How did you and Drum make out with the Army Air Corps?"

"As soon as the test results are in, we should be too. The recruiter did not see a problem."

"They obviously did not require an intelligence test," Walter said.

"Why would they, when face to face with two Charles Lindberghs? They were thanking their lucky stars that we had not joined the Navy."

"Have you told your girlfriends that you are joining the service?" Queasy asked. "They might not be too happy."

"We are hoping they see it as us fulfilling our patriotic duty," Walter replied.

"Then again, they might see it as being abandoned for your military ambitions."

"As you seem to have the questions and the answers, perhaps you could tell us how to proceed."

"I could, but then I wouldn't get to see you suffer. However, I would suggest that you be well fortified with alcohol."

"Perhaps we should tell them after we take the oath. If things get dicey, we can retreat to our home in the military," Jimmy joked.

"Hiding behind the skirts of the Marine Corps is less than manly. Even Leathernecks could not weather the wrath of an angry woman," Queasy said.

"We will go forward hoping for the best," Walter said. "Now let's put our heads together and try to figure out who we can get to run this place while we are gone."

Three days later, Walter and Jimmy were back in front of the Marine Corps recruiting sergeant. They were there to get their test results and to take the induction oath. The sergeant looked up from the paper he was reading.

"Congratulations, Jimmy, you passed the physical. Walter, I regret to inform you that you did not."

Walter was stunned for a moment, trying to process what the sergeant had just said.

"What do you mean? I'm in perfect shape."

"I'm afraid not. You have chronic liver disease. Are you a heavy drinker?"

"I am. But so are a lot of people in the military."

"That might be, but they don't have your condition. How long have you been abusing alcohol?"

"I wouldn't call having a few drinks abusive."

"Tell that to your liver. You must be having more than a few. Do you sometimes have a fever and nausea?"

"Yes. I thought it was part of a hangover."

"I'm afraid it is more serious than that."

"Will you allow me to join if I cut back on my drinking?"

"No. The doctors have the last word."

"What about another branch of the military?"

"They all require a blood test. And with your health issues, even though you think you're in perfect shape, you wouldn't make it through basic training."

Walter had always thought of himself as robust, so this was shocking.

"Is there anything I can do to get in the service?"

"I would suggest that you quit drinking and see if you can reverse the disease. Try to enlist in a couple of years."

"The war could be over by then."

"That is very likely, but you never know. Would you like to take the oath, Jimmy?"

"Not yet. Me and Walter have been together since we were kids. We will see if we can get in another branch of service."

"I'll keep your records here on my desk," the sergeant said, confident Jimmy would be back.

Walter hoped this was a stringent test given by the Marines, and he could pass a test given by one of the other branches of service. Over the next week, he tried the Army, Navy, Army Air Corps, and the Coast Guard. Jimmy patiently took the tests with him, but Walter was rejected by every military branch. It was embarrassing when he had to tell Queasy and Drum that he was 4F, unfit for military service.

"It's not the end of the world," Drum said. "You can join the civil defense or any number of organizations that protect the country."

"It's not the same, and you know it. I would be carrying a whistle, while you guys are carrying guns."

"The four of us are a team," Queasy said. "We will have three out of four on active duty and one to shore up the home front. That's as patriotic as it gets."

"Thanks, guys, but there is nothing you can say that will make me feel better."

"Perhaps if you lay off the booze for a while your condition will improve," Drum said.

"I could, but more than likely I would miss out on the war and the booze."

"But your health would improve," Queasy said.

"Perhaps," Walter said. "I say we have a drink and talk it over."

His three friends looked at him and shook their heads like he was a lost cause.

Walter met with Terri that evening for dinner. He told her what had happened with his attempt to join the military.

"You said you were thinking about joining, but I thought you would discuss it with me first."

"I should have, and I apologize. I got caught up in war fever and wanting to pay the Japs back for attacking Pearl Harbor."

"I would not have been against you joining the military, if that is what you wanted. I'm sorry it didn't work out for you."

"I only have myself to blame. I should have listened to you and Lizabeth about controlling my drinking."

"It's not too late."

"Maybe not. I will find a doctor and see how long it will take to reverse my condition."

"That's a good idea. It might help if you stayed away from the tavern."

"The tavern is my livelihood. And I have to make money for my partners while they are away."

"Helping your partners contributes to the war effort."

"That's true. But I won't be happy until I can fight for my country."

"What is Jimmy going to do?"

"He will be joining the Marine Corps."

"I know it won't be easy for you with your three best friends leaving."

"I have you. That is the most important thing."

"That might not be true, but it makes up for not confiding in me."

He laughed and then leaned over and kissed her.

That afternoon, he stopped by Luther's barbershop to get a haircut.

"Where's Jimmy?" Luther asked.

"He's joining the Marine Corps, so he's spending as much time as he can with his girlfriend."

"What about you?"

"I tried signing up, but my liver didn't pass muster."

"Nothing too serious, I hope."

"It just needs some drying out."

"You taking the pledge?"

"Not yet. I need to make a plan."

"No. You need to make a commitment. The urge to drink might be too great without one."

"Are you speaking from experience?"

"I've had my battles with the bottle."

"Did you win?"

"We've gone into extra innings. Just when I think I've won, the bottle gets a base hit."

"In other words, you have to be careful."

"Every day of my life."

"What's the secret for staying ahead of the game?"

"No secret. Just don't do it."

"I'll give it my best. Is Prince still living here?"

"No. He's got an apartment over on Prospect. When he's not at the club, he's with that girl he met at your sister's business.

"Kayla?"

"That's her. He's found out there is more to life than work."

"Good for him. Eddie seems to be doing well with his dinner club."

"He's making a good living, and so are Ezra and Prince."

"Is Eddie ever going to settle down?"

"Not likely. I keep hoping the right girl will come along."

"How will the war affect his business?"

"That depends on the draft. If his number comes up, he will have to go."

"What about Ezra and Prince?"

"They don't have to worry about the draft. The government doesn't know they exist. And they both have an attitude. Asking those two rebels to fight a war for freedom when they are denied their own would be asking a lot."

"That is something every Negro has to ponder."

"That's true enough. I would join, if I could. The freedoms we have here are better than Hitler's plan for us. I can picture my neck under the jackboots of the master race."

"Can't we all? How are things at City Hall?"

"A lot going on with the war heating up. The government is always wanting this or that, and it's all top secret or top priority. It would be easier if we just let them run the city."

"Do you think the city ran smoother when Boss Tom was in charge?"

"No doubt in my mind. The only committee that works is a committee of one. How is Boss Hannon doing in retirement?"

"Not too well. He's a man without a city. The loss of control has taken a lot out of him."

"That's the trouble with being on top. It's a long fall to the bottom."

"Don't I know it?" Walter said, as he stood and paid Luther for his haircut.

"Do you miss being a ward boss?"

"I miss the excitement. Most days I was in over my head."

"You will always be revered in this part of town."

"Thanks, Luther. That means a lot."

"You take care, and let me know if you need any help with the booze."

CHAPTER TWENTY-FOUR

JANUARY OF 1942 WAS A fearful time. The Japanese had continued their conquests in Asia. They invaded Manila, the Dutch East Indies, and Singapore. The Germans ruled all of Europe and were at the gates of Leningrad in Russia. England was the only country standing between the Nazis and total domination of Europe.

The rise of fascism seemed unstoppable. The fate of America and the rest of the world depended on the hard work and dedication of the common man and woman to pitch in and support the war effort. And pitch in they did. Lizabeth could feel a renewed energy in her employees, as they worked to preserve a way of life along with earning a paycheck.

Lizabeth kept her business going at full speed, not only for her employees but to keep her mind off family matters. She was going over some figures on the expansion of the work clothes division when there was a knock on her office door.

"Come in."

Margie entered her office in tears.

Lizabeth stood up and helped her to a chair. "What's the matter?"

"It's Cory. He wants to join the Navy, and I can't talk him out of it."

"I thought he would wait to be drafted."

"I thought so too," she sobbed. "I don't understand why he is in such a rush to go."

"What can I do?"

"You can talk to him. He will listen to you."

"I'm not sure I could dissuade him, if he wants to do his patriotic duty and serve the country."

"What about his duty to me? You could convince him to wait for the draft. The later he goes, the better chance he has of coming back."

Lizabeth could appreciate how Margie felt. She didn't want Cory to go either, and she had been relieved when Walter was rejected by the military. This quandary was probably going on inside most American families. The desire to serve and protect the country but not wanting to risk the sacrifice of a loved one.

"I will talk to him, but I can't promise anything. It will be difficult if he has his mind made up."

"If anyone can do it, you can."

Lizabeth helped Margie stand and gave her a hug. "Now, you stop crying and remember that whatever Cory decides, you are not alone in this. We are all here to support you."

"Thank you, Lizabeth."

Cory came to pick up Margie after work, and she sent him to Lizabeth's office.

"You don't have to tell me why I'm here," he said, as he sat.

"It's nice to see you too."

"Sorry, Lizabeth. I was trying to stay ahead of you."

"I'll get right to the point. I shouldn't have to remind you that your wife has a disability and your first duty is to her."

"I'm well aware of that. But if every man's duty is to his wife, then who will fight for the country?"

"There are millions of single young men who can't wait to go."

"That doesn't address my personal responsibility as an American."

"In your heart, you know that leaving Margie is not the right thing to do. Your judgment is clouded because you feel a duty to your country."

"And I can't see any way around that."

"Your responsibility is to contribute in the best way you can, and that could be to continue studying for your teaching degree."

"It's not the same as putting your life on the line."

"What if you don't come back?"

"That is something every man has to consider."

"Why the rush to enlist? The war isn't going anywhere."

"We are losing the war, and I feel that I should contribute something to turn that around."

"My guess is that we are in the beginning stages of a long war. Why not wait until things get sorted out, and then you can decide what direction to take to help the war effort. If you joined now, it would be a waste of time because it would take the military a year to figure out what to do with you." She had no idea if that were true. She was just trying to sound convincing to keep him home with Margie.

"How long are you suggesting I wait?"

"At least a year, until you get your teaching degree."

"Are you sure I wouldn't be taking the easy way out?"

"I'm positive. With a degree, you might even want to apply to Officer Candidate School. I'm working with some high-ranking officers who might help you in that regard."

"You have always managed to get your way with me."

"Obviously not, or we wouldn't be having this conversation."

They looked into each other's eyes, realizing the irony of her words.

"Okay, Lizabeth. I respect your opinion. I will get the degree and then join the service."

"Good. It's the best decision for you and for Margie."

⁓

It was a winter of heartfelt goodbyes for Lizabeth. Cam had been summoned to Detroit by the Ford Motor Company. Ford had sub-contracted with Willys-Overland Motors to build thousands of Jeeps for the military. Cam would go into the Army as a first lieutenant and be the liaison officer between Ford and the Army. He might have to go overseas later to administer Jeep shipments between America and England. Helen would take a leave of absence from her job and make a home for them in Detroit.

The family had a party for them the night before they were to leave, and everyone had a chance to say goodbye.

"You take care, brother," Lizabeth said, as the party ended.

"No worries. I won't be seeing any combat."

"I am proud of you, son," J.M. said, as he shook his hand. "Let us know if you need anything."

"I will. Write to me when you can."

Walter shook his hand. "You will be dealing with some top brass, so if there is any way you can get me in the service, it would be appreciated."

"I'll see what I can do. Good luck with the tavern."

"Please send us your new address so we can get if off to Eileen," Lizabeth said.

"Cam is not much of a letter writer, so I will keep you posted on how everything is going," Helen said.

Nana and Pop said their goodbyes, as did Uncle Ray and Aunt Erma. Aunt Julia embraced him and Uncle Ralph shook his hand and kissed Helen goodbye.

"Good luck in rolling out those Jeeps," Drum said. "We will let you know where the Army Air Corps sends us, so we can stay in touch."

"When are you two leaving?" Cam asked.

"Next Monday night from Union Station."

"God help the Army Air Corps," Walter said, making everyone laugh.

They sent Cam and Helen off into the night with a sense of pride, but also of dread for what lay ahead. They knew these partings were happening in many American homes but that did not make them any easier to endure.

On Monday night, Lizabeth went with Walter, Terri, and Jimmy to the sendoff for Drum and Queasy. They gathered at the tavern and after everyone was well into their cups and speeches were made, the two friends were escorted to Union Station, where they would catch a train to Lowry Field in Denver. Queasy held court in the North Waiting Room while waiting for the train to arrive.

"We will miss you, Queasy," one of the women said from the crowd of well-wishers.

"Thank you, my dear. By now it has dawned on most of you that with our departure this burg will sink into mediocrity and linger there until our triumphant return."

"I'm sure Hitler and Tojo will surrender, rather than face the two of you," Walter said. "If the war can be won with blarney, you will be home next week."

That got a laugh from the crowd.

"You be sure and hold down our seats at the bar," Queasy said.

"We will save your places of honor and set an evening aside each week to read your letters to your friends about your experiences in the military."

"Thank you, Walter," Drum said. "It will make us feel that we are still part of the Tom's Town Tavern gang."

"You keep your spirits up, and we will keep you in our hearts," Lizabeth said. She and Terri kissed each of them on the cheek, as their train was called. Walter and Jimmy bade them farewell with a handshake and a pat on the back.

Lizabeth could tell that Walter was putting on a good front. In reality, each of these departures was taking a bit more out of him. And every time someone asked him why he wasn't in the service, it took a bit more. She knew that he was soothing his self-inflicted inadequacies with alcohol, and she feared that he might be damaging his health even more. It was killing him that he was losing his friends to the war effort and he was not allowed to participate.

She was in hopes that Walter would swear off drinking and try to reverse his condition, but that was not happening. He seemed to be drinking more, rather than less. She tried talking some sense into him but he felt that the war would be over by the time he was healthy, so what was the point in trying to quit?

And then, two weeks later, it was time for the most difficult departure. The day arrived for them to say goodbye to Jimmy at Union Station. The Marine Corps was sending him to boot camp at Parris Island in South Carolina.

"Don't worry about your granny," Walter said. "I will see that she is well cared for."

"I know you will. Please watch out for Carol too." Walter shook his hand, and Lizabeth embraced him.

"I will write you a letter every week," Lizabeth promised.

"I will send you guys my address as soon as I can."

"Keep your guard up," Walter said, as he faked a punch. "You will probably run into some of those crackers we met riding the rails."

"I'll do it, and I will miss having you to back me up."

Carol gave him a tearful kiss goodbye. He pulled away, gave them a wave, and hurried down the stairs to his train. It was difficult for Walter to say goodbye to his childhood friend; especially because they had planned on leaving together.

The next day, Walter joined the Civil Defense Corps. Over the next several weeks, he took classes in first aid, fire suppression, enemy aircraft identification, and anti-saboteur training. It wasn't what he wanted, but at least he was contributing something. However, it wasn't doing his health any good. When his squad finished their nightly rounds, they retired to Tom's Town Tavern and told tall tales of what they would do to an enemy who never materialized and drank until the early hours of the morning.

With the obligations the war effort had put on her company, Lizabeth knew she could not lose focus on her core business of women's fashions, because it was her most profitable division. Jennie was in charge of that division and had continued the expansion across North America and into Canada. With the war, the goal of expanding into Europe was put on hold. Sales were now in the millions of dollars, and there were sales reps all over the country and in Canada. The outlook for her company couldn't be better.

And then what she feared the most happened. The government sent out an edict that rationed clothing. Women would be given so many coupons a year for their purchases, and to further crimp sales, the government put out an advertising campaign promoting that it would be more patriotic to mend clothing than to buy. This was a dire situation, because she had promised not to make profits on her work for the military and now sales would be hampered in her designer clothing division.

Her women's workwear would have to carry the load. A number of those items were not on the restricted list. She was worried because she had promised not to lay anyone off for the duration of the war. She stewed over the problem for a few days and then called Walter and asked if she could come by his apartment. She wanted to run the problem by him. In his years with Tom Hannon, he had proven that he was a problem solver. He invited her to come over and have dinner with Terri and him.

She sat on the couch with Terri, while he fixed them a drink.

"How is Father doing?" Walter asked

"He's fine. You should stop by and see him some time. I think he is lonely with Cam gone."

"I would, but it invariably leads to a lecture on the evils of alcohol."

"Perhaps you could overlook that."

"There's not much point to a visit if I make all the concessions."

"You could humor him until Cam comes home."

"Act as a stand-in for the number one son?"

"Why not? With enough exposure, you might actually begin to like each other."

"Not likely. When he looks at me, I can tell he's wishing I was Cam."

"You could make the effort, despite that," Terri said in support of Lizabeth.

"Was teaming up on me the reason for your visit?"

"Of course not."

"Okay, Lizabeth, I will stop by and visit with him. Now what did you want to see me about?"

Lizabeth explained the problem with clothing rationing and how it was going to affect her business. "I promised not to lay anyone off and this rationing had to happen."

Walter pondered the problem for a moment. "The government will restrict the selling of textiles to you and also limit retail sales. Is that right?"

"Yes."

"Didn't you tell me you had warehouses full of material in the event something like this happened?"

"Yes. But I hadn't counted on restrictions at the retail level."

"And you have invoices to prove that you purchased your goods before the restrictions were put in place?"

"Of course."

"Have you forgotten what you did when the big department stores tried to put you out of business?"

"I ran them out of inventory."

"Exactly. And once again you have the inventory and your competitors are at the mercy of the marketplace. You might be the only dress manufacturer in America with enough material to outlast the war."

"But if retail sales are restricted, how does that help?"

"What do you think women will want to buy with their clothing coupons? The bland, cheap material restricted by the government going to wholesalers, or the quality, beautiful, colored fabrics you have stored in your warehouse? This might be the best thing that could have happened to you."

Lizabeth looked at him wide-eyed. "My goodness! Why didn't I think of that?"

"You were smart enough to put your money into inventory and that is what counts. In a couple of months, your competitors will be out of inventory and at the mercy of government restrictions. Retail buyers will be flocking to your door to get quality merchandise at the expense of your competitors."

"You just saved my business!" Lizabeth was ecstatic. "Would you like a job?"

Walter laughed. "You saved me on one occasion, Prince on another, and you funded my business. I'm just happy to pay you back."

"You have more than paid me back. You've inspired me, and I can hardly wait to start emptying those warehouses."

~

The next evening, Walter was at the tavern when he got a call from Luther.

"Hello, Luther."

"Can you meet me tomorrow night at Union Station?"

"Sure. What's up?"

"Prince is leaving for the Army."

"What! How is that possible?"

"I'm as dumbstruck as you. Kayla contacted me and said to contact you. I guess we will find out tomorrow night why he joined up."

"I thought he was all set to settle down with Kayla."

"Me too. I can't imagine what prompted him to join the service."

"What time should I be there?"

"Seven p.m. in the North Waiting Room."

"See you there."

When Walter arrived at the station, Luther, Ezra, Eddie, and Prince were there with Kayla. He shook hands all around.

"I was shocked when I heard you were leaving," Walter said to Prince. "What prompted you to join the Army?"

"I'm an American and we are at war. And I can use my knife and not get into trouble."

That got a laugh from everyone.

"You can tell the Army that you have already had bayonet training on the streets of Kansas City," Luther said.

"Where are you headed?" Walter asked

"Fort Benning, in Georgia."

"Facing Japs and Germans might be easier than facing Georgia rednecks," Ezra said.

"I know it. Charlene has helped me with that."

"Do you have everything you need?" Luther asked. "I have some extra cash."

"No. I'm good. You can check on Kayla for me while I'm gone."

"We will," Luther said.

"What about your profits from the club?" Eddie asked.

"Give them to Kayla. We are saving to buy a house."

"Well, son," Luther said, "you've come a long way from that shoeshine stand. You will make a fine soldier."

"Thanks, Luther."

"You stay safe," Walter said, as he shook his hand.

"I will."

Prince's train was called. He gave Kayla a long lingering kiss and then headed downstairs to the train. She was in tears as she watched him go.

"I still don't understand why he decided to join the military," Luther said.

"It's his way of paying you and Walter back for all you have done for him," Kayla said. "He knows that you would both join if you could, so he is going in your place. I tried to talk him out of it but you know how he is. He has his own code that he lives by."

"He doesn't owe us anything," Walter said, feeling humbled by the gesture.

"He thinks he does, and that's all that matters."

"That young man turned out to be something special," Luther said. "Let us know if you need anything, Kayla. We will pray that he stays safe."

Summer 1942

Cam had been sent to England by the Army to coordinate the Jeep shipments. He was now headquartered in London. Helen had moved back to Kansas City from Detroit and was living with her parents. In June, the nation had the first glimmer of hope that the tide of the war was changing in favor of the Allies. The Japanese had been defeated at the Battle of Midway in the Pacific, where four Japanese carriers had been sunk. And in August, the Navy and Marine Corps began the first offensive of the war, attacking the Japanese on the island of Guadalcanal.

Jimmy was with the 6th Marine Regiment at Guadalcanal, and Lizabeth was concerned for his welfare. His letters were upbeat, so she hoped for the best. Drum and Queasy were finishing their training and thought they would be shipped to a location in the British Isles.

Walter had been correct about Lizabeth being in an ideal position in the fashion business. Her competitors couldn't figure out how she could keep offering colorful fashions made of quality material. They were sure she had some special deal. They complained to the government but to no avail. Lizabeth had proof of purchases that were made before rationing, so there was nothing the government could do.

Retailers couldn't get enough of her designs and business was booming. She had an idea she had been contemplating for a few years and now that she was a leader in the industry, it seemed the perfect time to implement her plan.

She made an appointment with Mr. Harzfeld and was in his office early on Monday morning.

"Miss Braden. It is good to see you again."

"And it is good to see you."

"What can I do for you?"

"By any measure, our partnership has been a success. You were the first to have enough confidence in me to carry my designs, so you will be the first to benefit from my proposal."

"I'm listening."

"Your women's department is merchandised with all brands and designers mixed together. The quality of my merchandise is unique and should be featured where your customers can shop for skirts, dresses, and accessories without having to search through the entire department. I'm proposing that you build a Liz Braden shop within your women's department. I will help with the initial expense, because I want to create a template that I can show to other retailers across the country." She could see that he was interested but not completely sold on the idea.

"Picture the first advertisement," Lizabeth continued. "The Liz Braden Shop in Harzfeld's. And you will have an exclusive for ninety days to help offset the expense of setting up the shop."

"With the war effort and the rationing of textiles, all expansions have been put on hold, Miss Braden."

"That is the very reason that I want to strike now. I have the inventory and together we can show the public that everything in retail is not lackluster and made of sackcloth."

"Do you mind me asking how you managed to acquire your inventory?"

"It was the fire, Mr. Harzfeld. It taught me to never take anything for granted and to stockpile enough material to keep me in business for years. Most manufacturers put their profits in the bank. I put mine into materials, because they are my lifeline."

"Would I be correct in assuming the retailers who agree to your proposal will be getting the best of your inventory?"

"Yes. But because you helped me get started in business, you won't be held to that standard. You can turn me down, and it will not harm our business relationship."

"I'm not about to bet against you, Miss Braden. If you will give your drawings to my store development department, we will get started on our new venture by the end of the week."

"Thank you for your confidence in me, Mr. Harzfeld. I guarantee us both a significant sales increase."

Lizabeth left the department store ecstatic and with visions of Liz Braden shops in every department store in America. One of the keys to her success was to strike when her competitors least expected it. If everything went according to plan, she would be set up for a tremendous expansion when the war ended. She would start her own store development team to ensure that Liz Braden shops would be of the highest standard and uniformity across the country.

The holidays were subdued that year and people leaned more toward religion than gift giving, as everyone prayed for the safety of their loved ones and for an end to the war. After several encouraging victories in 1942, there was hope. The new year brought a newfound optimism that the world might survive the nightmare of Germany and Japan ruling the world.

After a long, cold winter, spring finally arrived. Lizabeth was on the sunporch reading a letter from Eileen. Her father was in his study. Eileen was donating most of her time to the war effort. She was doing USO tours across the country, entertaining troops and promoting war bonds. She was so busy making movies and touring that Lizabeth seldom saw her. Lizabeth worried about her, because she knew when the big push came for the Allies to invade Europe, Eileen might insist on going too.

She stopped reading and looked across the street at the neighbors working in their yard. This was the time her mother loved the most, when, in the warmth of the sun, she could get her hands in the dirt and create something magical to beautify the earth. And then she saw her mother's practitioner, Mrs. Allman, coming up the walk. She often stopped by to check on them and see how they were getting along. Lizabeth thought it was kind of her, but it brought back a lot of unpleasant memories of the religious practices that had failed to work. She greeted Mrs. Allman at the door and invited her inside.

"Would you like some tea or coffee?"

"No, thank you, Lizabeth. Is your father home?"

Lizabeth was instantly alarmed because the practitioner was extremely nervous.

"I'll get Father."

J.M. came out of the study holding a newspaper. "Hello, Mrs. Allman."

"Hello, J.M." Mrs. Allman started to cry, and Lizabeth's heart seemed to stop.

"Helen Rabun's father contacted the church and said to give you this telegram. I'm so sorry."

It was a bit hazy for Lizabeth after that. J.M. had collapsed on the couch after reading the telegram. She gently pried it from his hands and read that Cam had been killed in a London air raid. She vaguely remembered calling Walter and telling him to come home. She wanted to contact Helen, but she was trapped inside a body that wouldn't function.

Later, Aunt Julia and Aunt Erma arrived. She wondered how, because she hadn't notified them. The call to Eileen was the hardest she ever had to make. Uncle Ray tried to console J.M., but Cam's death seemed to take him somewhere beyond grief. When Walter arrived, he tried to comfort his father, but he knew by the look on his Father's face that Cam's death had crushed any chance of having a relationship with his father. The good son had been taken, and the bad son was here to remind him of that.

In the weeks that followed, Lizabeth tried to spend as much time as she could with Helen, because Helen was devastated by the loss of her husband and could barely function.

The memorial service was difficult, because the bomb had vaporized the building Cam had been working in and there was nothing physical to grieve over, only the memory of a loving husband, son, and brother. Lizabeth realized how naïve she had been about war. Before, it had been something that happened to other people in foreign lands. But now the war had come home to her.

After a month had passed and she had had time to grieve, she formed a scholarship fund in Cam's name for her employees, so they could continue their education. And she sped up production even more in her military division to make as many uniforms as possible to help the war effort and to honor Cam.

But the war and the business were no longer her main concern. Her father was not recovering from Cam's death. He sat in his study or took long walks and seemed to have no interest in living. He no longer showed up at work and Lizabeth had to hire another advertising man to take over his responsibilities.

After a while, she talked to her father and reminded him that he had three other children who needed his love and support. But it didn't seem to register, and he continued on a downward spiral. He had been given a gold star by the government to display in the window to show that the family had lost a loved one in the war. He ripped it up and disdainfully threw it in the trash, indignant that he should announce losing his son to war. Lizabeth urged him daily to come back to work because she needed him, but nothing seemed to penetrate the grief that consumed him.

Her other concern was Walter. She had lost one brother, and she was not about to lose another, so she was now on a mission to get him to stop drinking. He kept making promises to quit that he never fulfilled and continued drinking far into the night with his buddies. She teamed up with Terri to present a united front against his drinking, but so far, all efforts had proved fruitless. She was not going to give up, however, and she hounded him endlessly to quit for the sake of his health.

It was the first week in December. Walter was working at the tavern when he received a call from Jimmy's grandmother telling him she needed to see him right away. The urgency in her voice concerned him, and he expected the worst when he drove up to her house. She answered the door and invited him in. Jimmy's granny was a petite woman, not quite five feet tall. She was in her eighties and wore spectacles.

"Did you get a letter from Jimmy?" Walter asked.

She took an envelope off the table and handed it to him. He hesitated, afraid of what it might contain. He thought of Cam, then opened it carefully and read the words. Jimmy had been seriously wounded in the attack on Tarawa in the Pacific. The attack had taken place the week of Thanksgiving. Walter breathed a sigh of relief but was sorry to hear Jimmy had been hurt.

"Have you told Carol?"

"No. I wanted to contact you first."

"I will go by and see her right away."

"Do you think he will be all right, Walter? The government doesn't say much."

"I'm sure he will. I will make some inquiries and find out as much as I can."

"Thank you, Walter."

"You get some rest and take care of yourself."

"I will."

Walter drove to Carol's house. He would make this quick, so she wouldn't be too badly alarmed. He knocked on her door, and a moment later, she answered with a questioning look on her face.

"He's been wounded. The government sent a telegram to his grandmother."

She started to cry, so Walter put his arm around her and they went inside the house.

"How bad is it?"

"We don't know. Lizabeth knows some top brass in the military, so we will start our inquiries there. As soon as we hear something, I will call you."

"Thank you, Walter."

"I wish I could have been with him."

"I know you do. Let's pray that he is going to be okay."

"Will you be all right?"

"Yes. I will leave now and go see his grandmother."

Walter drove across town to Lizabeth's building and rode the elevator upstairs to her office. She had her head down, concentrating on some papers.

"Hey, there."

She looked up, surprised to see him. "Walter, is everything okay?"

"Some bad news, I'm afraid. Jimmy has been wounded at an

island called Tarawa. I was wondering if you could call your military contacts and get us some more information."

"Do you know how bad it is?" she asked with concern.

"No. Please find out what you can."

"I'll do it now. The Sixth Marine Regiment. Is that right?"

"Yes. Call me at the tavern if you learn anything."

"I will. I'm so sorry to hear this."

"I know. Thank God he wasn't killed."

It was a week later when she called. "Jimmy was hit by machine gun fire that shattered his arm," Lizabeth said.

"How bad is it, and where is he?"

"He spent a couple of weeks in a field hospital on Guadalcanal and was then airlifted to Australia. It was a serious wound, and he will have some long months of recuperation."

Walter wondered how it would affect Jimmy's boxing career.

"He's alive, Walter, and that we can be thankful for."

"You're right."

"I have his address, so we can start sending him letters."

"I'll pass it on to Carol and his friends at the tavern."

It was a few weeks later when Walter received his first letter from Jimmy. It wasn't Jimmy's handwriting and must have been written by a nurse or a friend at the hospital. Jimmy tried to sound positive, but Walter could tell by the tone of the letter that he was not the exuberant Jimmy of old. Jimmy thought he would be home in April. He wrote that unless his condition drastically improved, the war for him would be over. That was good news and bad news. Walter wouldn't have to worry about him being killed in the war, but the wound must be serious if he could not be rehabilitated into active service.

CHAPTER TWENTY-FIVE

Spring 1944

IN EARLY MARCH, PRESIDENT ROOSEVELT gave the war department permission to release a newsreel titled *With the Marines at Tarawa*. He wanted the American public to see the real cost of war and what American fighting men were up against.

Walter went to see the film. It showed the horror of the battle as Marines tried to storm the island, but were cut down by machine gun fire on the beaches and in the water. The images of those dead Marines floating in the surf off Tarawa shocked Walter and all those who saw the film. Walter felt that he should have been there with Jimmy. It depressed him even more and sent him on a downward spiral with his drinking.

He left the tavern early, because he was having dinner with Terri and Charlene at their home in Hyde Park. The two women were sitting in the parlor when Millie ushered him in.

"Hello, Charlene. How are you feeling?"

"I'm doing fine, Walter."

"Have you heard anything from Prince?"

"Not much. He's a man of few words and that has carried over in his letter writing. How about you?"

"The last I heard, he was still in Italy, with George Patton's Seventh Army. They are having a hard time taking any ground from the Germans."

"I hope he stays safe," Charlene said. "His life has been hard enough without the war."

"I'll check in with Kayla and let you know if she has heard anything."

"Any more news from Jimmy?" Terri asked.

"He should be home sometime next month. It will be a great day when he arrives." Walter needed a drink but it was obvious they were not going to offer one. Millie called them into the dining room for dinner.

"Have you heard any more from Drum or Queasy?" Terri asked, when they were seated.

"Queasy is still doing administrative work in London. Drum is now a navigator on a B-29. His squadron makes bombing runs over Germany. The missions are dangerous, and I worry about him."

"We have to hope for the best," Terri said.

"What is the latest with Helen?" Walter asked.

"She is not doing well. Lizabeth and I take turns going to see her. She is having a hard time adjusting without Cam. You should stop by and check on her."

"I keep telling myself that I will, but it never seems to happen. The least I could do for Cam is to comfort his widow. It's just that I wouldn't know what to say, and I'm sure my resemblance to Cam would make her uncomfortable."

"You have to stop feeling guilty about not being in the war," Terri said. "You can't isolate yourself from your family. You don't go to see your father and now Helen. You have a lot to offer both of them, if you would just realize it and make more of an effort."

"Your family has made the ultimate sacrifice," Charlene said. "It is a blessing that your father doesn't have to worry about losing another son to the war. It is a difficult time for everyone. The fates have not been kind to us with years of economic depression and now a world war."

"Maybe the end is in sight," Walter said. "They are sending more men and equipment into England every day. I'm guessing the Allied invasion of Europe will happen sometime this summer. If that's the case, the war should be over by next year."

After dinner, they had coffee in the parlor. Walter felt something was up because Terri and Charlene seemed tense and uncomfortable. After a few more minutes of idle conversation, Charlene excused herself and left the room.

"I can tell by your manner that something is up," Walter said. "What's going on?"

"This is not something out of the blue," Terri said. "You've ignored all my efforts to get you to stop drinking, and if anything, you are drinking more. This has been building for a few years, and I think we should put our relationship on hold for a while."

"What does 'on hold' mean?"

"We should stop seeing each other until things get better."

"In other words, you are asking me to choose between drinking and you."

"It's reached the point where I have no other options. I'm not going to stand by and watch you drink yourself to death."

"Have you considered that losing you might make me drink more?"

"I have. But the choice is yours to make."

"I don't do well with ultimatums."

"I know. I wouldn't be giving you one if I had another choice."

The phone rang. A moment later, Millie came into the room. "Telephone for you, Walter."

Walter thought something must have happened at the tavern. He had left Charlene's number with his manager, in case any problems arose.

"Hello."

"Walter. It's Uncle Ray."

Walter knew something serious must have happened for his uncle to track him down. "What is it, Uncle Ray?"

"I just got a call from the chief of police. An ambulance and the police have been called to the family home in Brookside."

"What has happened?"

"I don't know. I will meet you there."

He put down the phone. "That was my Uncle Ray. An ambulance has been sent to my father's house."

"Oh, no. Do you want me to go with you?"

"No. I'll call you when I know something."

Terri felt bad that this had to happen on top of the ultimatum she had just given him.

A slight mist was falling, as he turned the car onto his father's street and saw the flashing lights of the ambulance and two police cars. He feared an accident had occurred and hoped it was not serious. He parked the car and hurried inside the house. Erma and Julia sat in the living room on either side of Lizabeth trying to comfort her as she sobbed.

"What's going on?" he asked.

Uncle Ray put his arm around Walter's shoulder and moved him into the study. J.M. had his head down on his arm, as if he were sleeping. Walter put his hand gently on his father's face, and it felt cold.

"It was a heart attack, Walter. I'm sorry."

Walter was stunned. He tried to grasp that his father was gone. It was so unexpected and surreal. He tried to compose himself.

"I'm sorry for you, Uncle Ray. He was your only brother."

"Yes. I will miss him terribly."

Walter felt callous, because no tears would come.

"We didn't get along, but I admired him," Walter said. "I can't imagine what life will be like without him."

"It will be difficult for us all."

"I think losing Cam broke his heart. He didn't seem to have much interest in living after that."

"I'm sure it contributed to his failing health."

"Has anyone contacted Eileen?"

"Lizabeth wanted you to break it to her."

"Would you help me with the arrangements? I don't want to put any more on Lizabeth."

"Of course."

Walter went back into the living room to be with his sister. He tried to comfort her as best as he could, but losing her father was a devastating blow. Later that evening, he called Eileen and then Terri and gave them the bad news. It was a sad time for all of them to lose J.M. so soon after losing Cam. Walter stayed at the house with Lizabeth until Eileen arrived the next day.

It was a difficult week, but relying on one another and the support offered by friends, they managed somehow to get through J.M.'s funeral. Walter said goodbye to the last mourner who had come to pay their respects at the Braden home. He had lost his father and Terri, and they were both devastating blows. He headed to the tavern to have a drink and think about how to get on with his life.

~

After a week of being worn out with grief, it was time for Lizabeth to say goodbye to Eileen.

"Are you sure you will be okay?" Eileen asked. "I have to get back to work."

"Yes. Now go, and don't worry about me."

"I do worry about you."

"Mother would tell us to buck up and get on with life."

"If only she were here to support us."

"We have each other and Walter, and we should be thankful for that." She kissed Eileen on the cheek and sent her out the door. She waved as Eileen entered a cab and headed to the airport.

That night, Lizabeth tried to sleep but there were too many memories, and the silence in the house was unbearable. The rain beating on the rooftop and the sound of the streetcar that had once made her feel safe and secure now only heightened her loneliness and reminded her of how much she missed her family.

She couldn't live in the house alone with her memories, so the next day she rented a furnished suite on the top floor of a Plaza hotel. Walter didn't want to live in the house either. Selling the home was not an option, because she didn't want anyone else living there. It might be an exercise in futility, because she was trying to hold on to a time that no longer existed. But she could not let it go.

She called the lawn company and left specific instructions on the care of her mother's flowers and shrubs. With a heavy heart, she locked the house and walked away. It was now a part of her life suspended in time that she could return to whenever she wanted. The house was her own private time capsule, and it was comforting to know that she could go back to her girlhood home and be among the things that were once enjoyed by her family. However, she could not bear to be there alone at night with her memories.

~

In April, Walter, Lizabeth, and Carol were at Union Station waiting for Jimmy's train to arrive. Carol had received a letter letting her know the date and time. It seemed to Walter that it was a lifetime ago since they had said goodbye to Jimmy. He wondered what Jimmy would be like with the injury and with the trauma he had experienced with the Marines at Tarawa.

"It is so wonderful to finally experience a happy day," Lizabeth said.

"I tried not to think about his return," Carol said. "I was afraid it might bring me bad luck."

"You can let go now and celebrate," Lizabeth said.

"I'm sorry he was wounded, but not sorry the wound will mean a medical discharge from the service."

"We are all thankful he survived," Walter said. And then he saw Jimmy walk up the steps into the North Waiting Room. He was dressed in his Marine uniform. His arm was in a sling, and he looked like he had lost weight. A big smile crossed his face when he saw Carol running toward him. He put his good arm around her and held her tight for a few moments. Walter and Lizabeth walked over to him. He shook hands with Walter and hugged Lizabeth.

"Thank God, you are home," Walter said.

"I can't tell you how glad I am to be here."

"How's the arm?"

"I won't be doing any boxing. The goal is to rehabilitate my arm enough to get some use out of it."

"I'm sorry about that. Let us know if we can help."

"How's my granny?"

"She's doing great and can't wait for you to get home." Walter thought Jimmy was definitely not the exuberant Jimmy of old. He was more subdued, and his eyes looked tired and lifeless. Walter guessed it was from the stress of everything he had endured.

"I received your letters, and I was so sorry to hear about Cam and your father. They were my family too, and I'm going to miss them."

"Thank you," Lizabeth said. "You will always be part of our family."

"We know you are tired and want to get home," Walter said. "When you feel up to it, stop by the tavern."

"He promised me he wouldn't do anything for at least two weeks," Carol said.

"That's a good plan. Come by and have a drink with your friends after you get rested," Walter said.

"We do have one request to make of both of you," Jimmy said. "I asked Carol to marry me and she agreed. It will be a June wedding, and we want you and Lizabeth to stand up with us."

"How wonderful," Lizabeth said. "Congratulations."

"It would be an honor for us," Walter said.

"Please allow me to make your wedding dress," Lizabeth said. "We need some happy time at Liz Braden's Original Designs."

"Thank you so much for offering," Carol said.

"I was so excited to see you guys that I forgot to ask about Terri," Jimmy said.

"That's a long story," Walter replied. "Now get home to your granny, and I will fill you in later."

There wasn't much to tell about Terri. Walter had thought about giving up booze but invariably his friends showed up at the tavern and one drink led to another and before he knew it hours had passed and then days and his good intentions were lost in an alcoholic fog. When Cam was killed and his father passed away, it had changed him. Even though he was at odds with his brother and father, there was something in the family dynamic that had made him feel anchored. The alcohol helped with the grief and with his low self-esteem for being rejected for military service.

He knew he would lose Terri, but he didn't like her ultimatum. He did have to admit the drinking was affecting his health, because his stomach was swollen and he was having mental lapses where he would lose track of time and he had a hard time following conversations. He felt that if he cut back, that would be enough, and the symptoms would end. It was always going to be the next day when he would drink less, but the next day came and went, and he kept putting off his commitment.

It was a bittersweet time for Lizabeth. Jimmy had returned home, but Cory had finished his studies, received his teaching degree, and had joined the Navy as an enlisted man. Margie was upset, but Cory was determined to go, so all Lizbeth could do was to offer Margie her support. She encouraged her to be optimistic because the invasion of Europe had begun in June, and everyone felt the end of the war was in sight.

She was thankful and proud that her company had survived the Depression and, so far, the war years. When the war ended, Lizabeth would be poised for even greater success. She wanted to be the first American dress manufacturer to help in European recovery, and that investment should lead to further expansion. She would keep a close eye on her business, but first and foremost she would concentrate on Walter and how to get him sober. She had lost Cam and her father, and she was on a mission not to lose Walter. It was time to use all her determination on her brother. She was prepared to do whatever it took to cure his alcoholism.

She was aware that Terri had given him an ultimatum, and it had shocked her that he had chosen drinking over a relationship with Terri. It was time to enlist doctors, psychologists, and Walter's friends, to help him beat his addiction. And she would ask every member of the family to join her in the crusade to save Walter from himself. If there was a solution, she would work tirelessly to find it. Her first step was to confront him about his drinking, so she called him and he agreed to meet her at the tavern.

He pulled out a chair that fronted his desk, and she sat down. He eyed her curiously, as he went behind the desk and took a seat. "What is so important that you would leave your business in the middle of the day?"

"You and your health. That's what is so important."

"You aren't going to start preaching again, are you?"

"Yes, because I want you to stop drinking."

"Look around you. Drinking is what I do."

"Tom Hannon owned a saloon, and he didn't drink."

"I concede your point, but I'm not Tom Hannon."

"You are starting to have some serious health issues, and you have broken your relationship with Terri. What is it going to take to get you to change your lifestyle?"

"My lifestyle is doing just fine, and Terri broke up with me."

"Yes. As a direct result of your dependence on alcohol. You are in denial."

"You need to quit worrying so much. Just because something bad happened to Cam and Father doesn't mean it will happen to me."

"Would you be willing to talk to a doctor and a psychologist about your drinking?"

"I don't see that I have a problem."

"The military thought so."

"They were of the opinion that I wouldn't hold up under the stress of combat. There is no stress here at Tom's Town Tavern."

"The first step in recovery is for you to acknowledge that you have a problem."

"The only problem I have is that you keep hounding me. I've been drinking since I was fifteen; it's part of who I am."

"Nonsense. It is an addiction that you could beat if you would make a commitment to change your mindset."

"We don't all have your strength of character, Lizabeth."

"I'm not buying that for a minute. As a ward boss, you proved yourself time and again in some critical situations. You could beat alcohol if you started seeing it as an enemy, rather than a friend."

"You've done your homework."

"I'm learning all I can about dependence on alcohol. If I have to enlist every professional in the country in this battle, I'm prepared mentally and financially to take it on."

"I appreciate your concern, and I will take everything you have said under consideration."

"Now you are patronizing me."

"I assure you, I'm not."

"Okay, then. Will you join Alcoholics Anonymous?"

"No way. I don't want to spill my guts to a bunch of strangers. I can quit drinking whenever I want."

"We've always been a good team, Walter. We can beat this, if you will let me help you."

"You've always come out on top, Lizabeth. But there are some battles you might not be able to win."

"There might be. But this isn't going to be one of them."

"Duly noted. Now I have to get back to work." He escorted her to the door. "You have enough to worry about, so quit worrying about me."

"You've put me off in the past, but that is not going to work any longer. I'll be gathering my considerable resources for our next meeting."

"Jimmy and Carol's wedding is next week, so let's call a truce until we get them married."

"Okay. But don't think for a minute you are getting rid of me."

After she was gone, he headed to the bar. He needed a drink after dealing with the force of will that was Lizabeth.

⌇

The wedding was held at the Catholic church that Jimmy's grandmother attended. There were about 200 guests, many of them friends Jimmy and Walter had made over the years. Eileen had flown in for the wedding, and she sat with Helen and Terri. Walter's split with Terri did not affect her relationship with his sisters, who maintained hope for a reconciliation.

Because of material shortages, most wedding gowns during the war were made of rayon, but Lizabeth had acquired enough silk and lace in her inventory to make a beautiful dress. She wanted it to be special for Carol and for Jimmy. It was simple, but an elegantly designed sleeveless gown with a square neck, an A-line skirt, and a chapel train.

Walter stood at the altar with Jimmy and Lizabeth, as they waited for the bride to come down the aisle. Carol looked stunning when she appeared at the back of the church. Her father was at her side, as they proceeded down the center aisle to the altar. Jimmy beamed with pride as he took her hand, and they turned toward the priest.

Walter thought these Catholic ceremonies took too long. He was happy to see his best friend married, but he could hardly wait to get back to the tavern so he could have a drink. When the priest finally pronounced Jimmy and Carol, man and wife, he breathed a sigh of relief and shook Jimmy's hand and kissed Carol on the cheek.

Walter had enlisted Aunt Erma and Aunt Julia to decorate Tom's Town Tavern for the reception. Banners were hung with congratulatory messages. The largest one read "Mr. and Mrs. Jimmy Dolan." Centerpieces on the tables contained vases of Carol's favorite flowers that were a mixture of yellow and lavender daisies, pink roses, and carnations. Mini, white lanterns with tealight candles were positioned beside each plate. The wedding cake was three-tiered, sitting on a silver tray, with a porcelain bride and groom on the top tier. The tavern was so beautiful that Jimmy and Carol were stunned with delight when they walked into the room.

"Thank you, Walter!" Carol exclaimed. "Everything is so lovely!"

"The entire family was involved," Walter said. "We wanted everything to be perfect for you and Jimmy."

"You've outdone yourself," Jimmy said. "We are so grateful."

The Braden family and guests offered hearty congratulations and best wishes to the couple, and then it was time for everyone to sit and for Walter to say a few words.

"Thank you all for coming to this special occasion. Jimmy has been like a brother to me most of my life, and it gives me great joy to see him married to a wonderful woman like Carol. We wish them many years of health and happiness. And we want to thank Jimmy for his sacrifice in the service of our country. And also, we thank Carol for supporting him through the time of separation and loneliness."

He turned to Jimmy and Carol. "We know that because of the war conditions that you hadn't planned on a honeymoon. However, your friends have pitched in and booked you a honeymoon suite for a week at an Ozark resort. And finally, raise your glasses for a toast to Mr. and Mrs. Jimmy Dolan. May love and joy follow them all the days of their lives."

It was Sunday morning, the day after the wedding. Lizabeth was sleeping soundly from the late-night festivities when the telephone rang. She willed herself awake and picked up the receiver.

"Hello," she said sleepily.

"Lizabeth. It's Uncle Ray."

She was instantly alert with concern. "What is it, Uncle Ray?"

"It's Walter. He collapsed after a heavy night of drinking, and we rushed him to the hospital."

She could feel her heart pounding. "Was he drunk and then passed out?"

"I'm afraid it is much more serious. The doctors say it is complications from his liver condition."

"Are you at Research Hospital?"

"Yes."

"Okay, we will be right there." She hung up the phone and went to wake Eileen.

"What is it?" Eileen asked irritably, when Lizabeth shook her shoulder.

"It's Walter. Uncle Ray has taken him to the hospital, and he said it's serious."

The two sisters dressed quickly and rushed to the hospital, where they met with the doctor treating Walter.

"Why did this happen, doctor?" Lizabeth asked.

"It is a direct result of binge drinking. His disease has progressed from alcohol-related chronic liver disease to an advanced stage of cirrhosis of the liver."

"But he's a young man," Eileen said.

"He's also been a heavy drinker for twenty years," the doctor replied.

"What can we do?" Lizabeth asked.

"It is critical that he stop drinking. A few more of these episodes will kill him."

"Can you give us some advice on breaking the addiction? He won't join Alcoholics Anonymous, and I can't get him away from the tavern he owns."

"You have to convince him to quit. He knows he has a problem, but he is in denial."

"Why won't he acknowledge something that might kill him?" Eileen asked.

"That makes perfect sense to you and me, but the addict has a different mindset. A drink becomes the most important thing in life."

"Alcoholism runs in the family," Lizabeth said. "My mother thought it might be an inherited condition."

"That is a possibility, because some people seem predisposed to the condition."

"I wonder if hounding him endlessly does more harm than good."

"It's important that you don't let him alienate you. Express your concerns and support him as best you can, but realize beating this addiction is up to him. You can't make him do anything."

"What is your prognosis?" Lizabeth asked, afraid of what he might say.

"If he quits drinking, and we can limit the damage, he has a chance at a decent life. On the other hand, I don't see him surviving many more episodes of binge drinking."

"That is alarming to hear, but thank you for being frank with us," Lizabeth said. "Now we know what we are up against." She was more determined than ever to take on Walter and his alcoholism.

Walter stayed in the hospital for a week to dry out. Lizabeth waited until he felt better and was ready to be discharged before tackling his drinking problem.

"Are you ready to admit that you have a problem?" she asked.

"I can no longer deny the obvious," he replied.

"What is your plan?"

"I don't think quitting cold turkey will work. I'll cut back to two drinks a day for two weeks, and then one drink. At the end of one month, I will have quit completely."

"What does the doctor say?"

"He wants me to go cold turkey, but he will accept the plan if I'm serious about quitting."

"Are you?"

"I can only promise to do my best."

"The alternative is scary, Walter."

"I know. You are my main concern, Lizabeth. If I fail, it is not your fault."

"You shouldn't be worrying about me. And there will be no talk of failing. If we work together, we can beat this thing."

"I'm glad I have you to support me."

"Terri tells me she has been by to see you. Are you going to work things out?"

"That is a work in progress. She is waiting to see if I'm serious about quitting."

"We need her on our side. And getting back together will be motivation to help you quit."

"I agree."

374

"Do you need me to stay with you at your apartment?"

"No. If this is going to work, I need to be on my own with no supervision. I can't use you for a crutch."

"Okay. Jimmy will be back any day now, and we will enlist him to help us."

CHAPTER TWENTY-SIX

LIZABETH WAS MORE HOPEFUL THAN ever that the war would soon be over. The Allies liberated Paris in late August and were advancing on Germany. In the Pacific, the United States was winning victory after victory and using each island as a steppingstone toward the final defeat of the Japanese.

She made it a point to stop by Kayla and Margie's workstations periodically to see how they were holding up.

"What have you heard from Prince?" she asked Kayla.

"The last I heard, he had left Italy and was with Patton's Army somewhere in France. He doesn't write often, and when he does it takes over two weeks to get here. He could be anywhere by the time I get his letter."

"I'm sure not knowing is the hardest part. You have to hope for the best and have faith that he will be okay."

"I try. It gives me comfort to know that he can take care of himself. If anyone can survive the war, it will be him."

"He beat the odds against those Italian gangsters here in Kansas City, and they were just as tough as the Germans."

"I'll remember that, and thank you for taking the time to ask about him."

Lizabeth moved on to Margie's station. Margie looked up from her work.

"Any word from Cory?"

"I received a letter on Friday. He's on a destroyer with the Seventh Fleet somewhere near the Philippines. He can't say the exact location, but I can read between the lines and I follow the news. I'm guessing the Seventh Fleet is supporting General MacArthur's return to the Philippines."

"How are you holding up?'

"I'm plenty worried when I don't hear from him. I'm not sure he would tell me if he was injured."

"He would probably alert me to spare your feelings, and I haven't heard anything."

"I hope you are continuing to write to him. He needs all the support he can get."

"I send him all the news about you, the city, and the Braden family."

"Good. I know he is homesick and appreciates any news from home. I miss him something awful."

"I know. If you can hold on for a while longer, I'm sure the war will soon be over."

"I pray every day that it will be and that he comes home safely."

"I'm sure that he will. Keep the faith and try not to dwell too much on anything negative you read in the newspapers."

"Thanks for the pep talk, Lizabeth. I appreciate your support."

Jimmy had received a letter officially giving him a medical discharge from the Marines, so he went back to work at Tom's Town Tavern. Walter welcomed him back, and it was just like old times.

"What have you heard from Queasy and Drum?" Jimmy asked.

"Drum finished his required amount of air missions over Germany and he is now an instructor somewhere in England. He was lucky. I understand those missions over Germany are the most hazardous of the war. Queasy is still doing administrative work near London."

"I'm glad they are both safe. It will be wonderful when we get them back."

"Will it ever. I miss those two."

"Lizabeth called me," Jimmy said. "I understand that you have taken the pledge."

"She didn't waste any time in contacting you."

"I'm to let her know if you backslide on your commitment."

"And will you?"

"Of course not. We have too much history for me to spy on you."

"Hopefully, there will be nothing to report, and you will have a clear conscience."

"I'm pulling for you, Walter. I know it won't be easy."

"Thanks, Jimmy."

⁓

Walter made it through the holidays and even New Year's Eve without a drink. On a cold day in February, one of his old friends from the political wars came running through the tavern door.

"What's up, Barney?" Walter asked. "Is the city on fire?" He poured Barney a whiskey and waited for him to catch his breath and drink it down.

Barney wiped his mouth with his sleeve and looked Walter in the eye. "Tom Hannon is dead."

"What! You have got to be kidding."

"No, sir. City Hall is buzzing with the news."

Walter was stunned. Tom Hannon was bigger than life. He was even bigger than death, or so Walter had thought. He couldn't imagine Kansas City without Boss Hannon.

"How did it happen?"

"Heart attack."

⁓

Walter helped with the arrangements for Boss Tom. His widow and daughter wanted a private service with family and a few close friends. They did not want a spectacle that would dredge up old grudges from his political enemies and bring back unpleasant memories. Boss Tom had been in the spotlight for most of his life and deserved a quiet, dignified ending.

However, after the funeral, it was another story. Walter hosted a party at a downtown auditorium that held thousands, and it seemed that most of the city turned out to say goodbye to the man who for decades had ruled the city with an iron fist. It surprised Walter that even a large percentage of reformers had set aside their animosity and showed up at the wake.

Speeches were made and gallons of beer and whiskey were consumed throughout the evening and well into the night. It was such a special occasion that Walter felt it would be rude not to have a few drinks with his friends to honor Boss Hannon. He had had more than a few when Jimmy took him aside.

"You promised Lizabeth you would not start drinking again."

"I'm just having a couple to be sociable. The chance to celebrate the life of Boss Tom with my friends is a momentous event that won't come again."

"You've had more than a couple."

"I'm feeling fine, Jimmy. Quit worrying. After tonight, I will get back on the program and no harm will be done."

"Do you want to explain that to Lizabeth?"

"This will be our little secret. Lizabeth doesn't have to know everything."

"You are putting me in a bad position. If something happens to you, then it's on me for remaining silent."

"Just stick with me tonight, and I promise that when tomorrow comes all will be well."

"You are risking another stay at the hospital."

"That won't happen."

"You're letting all the hard work you put in go to waste," Jimmy continued to argue.

"Then again, I deserve a reward for all that hard work. I haven't felt this relaxed in a long time."

"Are you trying to convince me or yourself that it is okay?"

"Don't be such a fuddy-dud. Have a beer with me in remembrance of our years together with Boss Tom."

Jimmy knew it was useless to argue. All he could do was hope that Walter didn't get sick again.

The next day, Walter didn't feel so good, but the nausea was not debilitating and he was able to go to work. He convinced himself that if he took it easy on the booze and did not do any more binge drinking that everything would be okay. He kept a bottle in his desk drawer that he could nip on, and when Jimmy wasn't looking, he would have a quick beer with a customer. When the nausea returned, he knew he had crossed the line. When that happened, he cut back on his drinking. He felt that he had a workable plan that would allow him to have a few drinks to enjoy life, but not enough to put him in the hospital.

It was early in May. Lizabeth was having a company-wide meeting on the work floor when one of her military security guards ran into the room. "Miss Braden, you better come and see this!" She followed him in alarm, wondering what was going on. When they made it outside, people were pouring out of the buildings up and down the street. They were yelling at the top of their lungs and dancing in the street. And then, church bells started ringing all over the city.

She looked questioningly at the security guard.

"Could it be true?" she asked in disbelief.

"It's true all right, Miss Braden. The war in Europe is over."

She was so overcome with joy that she threw her arms around his neck and started sobbing. She wept for Cam, her father, Helen, and for all those who had been devastated by the war.

"You had better tell your employees, Miss Braden."

"Yes, I should. Thank you," she said, pulling away and wiping her eyes. She hurried back to the work floor, where her employees were looking at her questioningly.

"The day we have been waiting for has finally arrived. The war in Europe is over! Please leave the building and join in the celebration! We will be closed the rest of today and tomorrow! God bless you all!" There were shrieks of joy from her employees. They grabbed their belongings and ran for the door. The women who had joined the support group to help one another through the war years were quietly hugging.

"We can't believe that it's over," one of the women said. "It's hard to let go of the worry we've lived with for so long."

"It will take some time," Lizabeth said. "You won't be free from worry until your loved ones get home."

Kayla walked up to her. "We made it, Miss Braden."

Lizabeth put her arms around her. "I'm so happy for you. I hope you and Prince have a great life together."

"We will. As the spokesperson for my group, we want to thank you for all you have done for us and for the war effort."

"We did it together," Lizabeth said. "Now, all of you, please leave and go celebrate." She walked back to where Margie was quietly knitting one of her creations.

"Aren't you going to join in the celebration?"

"I'm happy the war in Europe is over, but the war with Japan goes on. I won't celebrate until it is over and Cory comes home."

"I'm sure it won't be long."

"I'm reading between the lines that his ship has left the Philippines and is somewhere near Okinawa, where kamikaze pilots are killing and injuring hundreds of sailors."

Lizabeth searched for something comforting to say, but she was also reading the devastating news from Okinawa. The Japanese were fanatical fighters, and it was estimated that any invasion of Japan would result in hundreds of thousands of casualties. She took Margie's hand. "Come with me and stand by the door and watch the celebration. It will give us hope for our own celebration when Cory comes home."

Walter opened the doors of the tavern, so people could move freely back and forth to the street. He announced free drinks for as long as the beer and whiskey lasted. He was so happy that Queasy, Drum, and Prince had made it through the war and would be coming home. It lifted some of the terrible burden he carried about not being able to fight for his country.

He knew that Lizabeth would be showing up soon, so he downed a couple of quick shots of whiskey and chased them down with beer. It was just enough to give him a buzz for the celebration but not enough for her to notice. Carol burst through the open door and, being careful of Jimmy's injured arm, embraced him and then hugged Walter.

"It looks like all of the old gang is going to make it home," she said.

"All except Cam," Jimmy reminded her.

"I'm so sorry, Walter."

"I know you are. Now go out in the street and celebrate."

Lizabeth and Terri showed up and then Uncle Ray and Aunt Erma. Aunt Julia and Uncle Ralph were not far behind. It was a wild affair out in the streets, with people letting go of all the frustrations and fears the war years brought into their lives.

Lizabeth and Terri were swept away by the joyous occasion and failed to notice Walter slipping away now and then to nip at his flask. Walter felt that he should be able to have a few drinks with his friends to celebrate the end of the war in Europe. The festivities had given him a perfect cover to drink, as long as he kept it within reason so Lizabeth would not find out. Lizabeth left around midnight, so Walter could then drink without constraint. He drank with his friends until the early hours and then went home.

The next morning, he was so sick that he couldn't get out of bed. He called Jimmy and told him he wouldn't be at work because he had caught a cold. He was sick for two days and vowed that he would never drink again.

That lasted until early August when Jimmy came running into Walter's office holding a newspaper. The headline read, "ATOMIC BOMB DROPPED ON HIROSHIMA."

"What is an atomic bomb?" Walter asked.

"A bomb that can wipe out an entire city."

"Then the war is over."

"Not yet. The Japanese have not surrendered."

"If we have a bomb that powerful, it should stop this war and all future wars."

"I would think so."

However, it took another bomb dropped on Nagasaki to end the war and begin another celebration. Walter had been careful about his drinking for three months, so when the Japanese officially surrendered, he felt that he could join in the party. He had become a master of deception where his drinking was concerned. Everyone's minds and hearts were focused on the end of the war and provided him with the cover he needed to feed his addiction.

However, it was getting difficult to hide the ravages that drinking was taking on his body. He told Lizabeth that he was having symptoms of withdrawal from giving up drinking. That allowed him to take the days off he needed to recover. She was naïve, because she didn't realize the addiction was more powerful than honesty. She trusted Walter to do the right thing.

Lizabeth went to Margie's workstation as soon as she heard that Japan had surrendered. They embraced each other with pure joy.

A week later Lizabeth checked back to see if Margie had heard from her husband.

"I received a letter from Cory, and he should be home in a couple of months," Margie said. "It will take the Navy that long to process all the sailors back into civilian life."

"It will be difficult to wait, but knowing he is safe is the main thing."

"I was so worried that he wouldn't come back."

"I know. It has been a difficult time for you."

"I want to thank you for your support. It was amazing that you never showed any resentment, given your history with Cory."

"Oh, at first there was resentment. Then I realized it was my own actions that sent him away. The bitterness ended when it became obvious you were a better match for him than I could ever be."

"He will always be fond of you," Margie said.

Lizabeth smiled. "Fond means that I came in second."

"I'm sorry. That didn't come out the way it was supposed to."

"That's okay. Your heart is always in the right place, Margie. I have some news that will help the time pass quickly while you are waiting for Cory to come home. The Liz Braden shops around the country are doing a fantastic business, so we are going to move to a much larger building at Eighth and Broadway. You will have an entire floor of employees for your division, so you had better start planning for the expansion."

"Oh, my! How exciting! I suspected you would be ready to pounce when the war ended. You have a knack for staying ahead of the competition."

"The end of the war will be the end of our military responsibilities, so we are going back to promoting fashion in a big way. It is what we do best, and my guess is that fashion will explode in the post-war years."

"You haven't guessed wrong yet. It was amazing that you kept us running smoothly through the war years."

"We can't rest on our laurels. Once Europe gets back in business, the competition from Paris and other European cities will be fierce. We are in the enviable position of setting trends, not following them. Our competitors will have a hard time matching our store-within-a-store concept. They will be fighting one another for the remaining floor space in department stores."

"How many employees will you have to hire?"

"Another hundred, to go with the four hundred we now have."

Margie shook her head in wonder. "I remember when your workforce was Erma, Jennie, and a couple of other girls."

"The Designers' Club has come a long way from that humble beginning."

"But it still feels like family."

"That is nice to hear. I hope it can always remain that way."

"When will you make the announcement about the expansion?"

"I will wait until all of our loved ones have returned from the war. Then the ladies of the Designers' Club will be focused and ready to begin a new era in fashion merchandising."

As she walked back to her office, Lizabeth felt a great sense of relief and freedom. She would not have to meet any more military quotas or worry about restrictions. Walter seemed to be doing well, and she no longer had to worry about losing anyone else to the war. The future looked bright and promising and she could hardly wait to get started.

It was early October, when Cory came home to Margie. She took a week off to be with him and then brought him by to see Lizabeth.

"I'm so happy that everything worked out for both of you," Lizabeth said.

"It is so great to be home," Cory said. "Thank you for the letters. They helped me get through some difficult times."

"Did you see action?"

"I saw some things that I don't ever want to see again," Cory said somberly. "How are you, Lizabeth? And how is Walter?"

"We are both doing fine. Walter is in good spirits, because Queasy and Drum will be home in a few days. Queasy managed to doctor their discharge papers so they will be traveling home together."

"I'm not sure the city will survive when the four musketeers are back in action."

Lizabeth laughed. "It will be good to see them together again."

"I saw Jimmy a few days ago. It is too bad about his arm."

"Yes, but as we learned with Cam, it could have been much worse." Cory nodded. "I had some shipmates who didn't get to come home."

"I'm sorry."

"Margie told me about your expansion plans," Cory said, brightening. "You are putting the war behind you quickly. Don't you want some time to catch your breath?"

"While I'm catching my breath, someone is sure to pass me by."

"That's our girl, Margie. Lizabeth is still running miles ahead of the competition."

"Never underestimate her, because she will prove you wrong," Margie replied.

"How is the job search coming?" Lizabeth asked Cory.

"I've been offered several teaching positions. Now I have to decide."

"Good for you."

"Thank you for insisting that I get my teaching degree."

"I'm glad it worked out."

"We will let you get back to work," Margie said. "Thanks again for everything you have done for us."

Lizabeth watched them go, with a pinch of envy for their relationship, but truly feeling grateful and hopeful they would have a long and happy life together.

Lizabeth, Walter, and the gang from the tavern were waiting on the tarmac at the downtown airport for the military transport aircraft that would be arriving from the East Coast with Queasy and Drum aboard. Walter wondered if the war had changed them in any way. A lot of the veterans he knew were quieter and more introspective because of their experiences in the war. He needn't have worried, because when the plane landed and came to a halt about 50 yards away, Queasy was first off, followed by Drum. A big cheer went up from the gathering, and they both hurried over and plunged into the crowd.

"It's great to be home!" Queasy said.

"I see you made sergeant," Walter said.

"Check out Drum. He's a first lieutenant."

"I'm checking out his medals," Walter said. "Did you win the war all by yourself, Drum?"

"No, that would be Queasy. Just ask him."

"We missed you," Queasy said, vigorously shaking Walter's hand.

"I'm glad you two are back," Walter replied. "You were right when you said this burg wouldn't be the same without you."

Lizabeth, Terri, and Carol gave them each a hug and a kiss on the cheek.

"Did you see combat?" a man asked Queasy.

"Heavens, no. I was much too valuable an asset to be exposed to the enemy. Drum saw enough combat for both of us."

"What's it going to take for a man to get a drink in this town?" Drum asked. With that, they were given the places of honor in front of the caravan of honking vehicles that swept them over the bridge to Tom's Town Tavern, where they found their reserved seats at the head table.

"I know you are modest, but tell us how you won all of those awards," Walter said. "And how did you become an officer?"

"The same answer to both questions. I managed to stay alive. When enough lieutenants were killed, they filled those slots from the lower ranks."

"He's not being flip about it," Queasy said. "I was in the group that figured the stats for the Eighth Air Force. We lost two thousand bombers and twenty-seven thousand crew members. It was the most dangerous duty of the war."

"How did you survive?" Carol asked.

"It was just a matter of luck. It's behind me now, so I would like to let it go."

"Fair enough," Walter said. "Welcome home, and from now on we will focus on the future."

Drum thought Walter looked unwell. He had a protruding stomach and a grayish tint to his skin.

"Are you okay, Walter?"

"Never better. Just a bit shaky from taking the pledge."

"You have quit drinking?" Queasy asked in surprise.

"Yes."

"Miracles do happen."

"This one was in the form of Lizabeth."

"Good for her. How is he doing, Lizabeth?"

"It's been a challenge, but we remain vigilant."

"She has you figured out, Walter."

"Tell me about it."

"How is business here at the tavern?" Drum asked.

"We are doing fine, but we need Queasy behind the bar and your gambling skills to kick off the post-war years. With you two back on the job, the future looks bright indeed."

"How is the arm, Jimmy?" Drum asked. "Walter let us know you were wounded."

"It's coming around, but I've had to hang up the boxing gloves."

"Sorry to hear it. Tarawa was a nightmare for the Marine Corps."

"Yea, but like you said, it's over."

"We'll drink to that," Queasy said.

When the ladies left, Walter fixed himself a whiskey.

"You are not backsliding, are you?" Drum asked.

"Nothing is going to stop me from drinking a toast to my childhood buddies for their courageous efforts in fighting the war." Walter held up his drink. "To Queasy and Drum. We are so grateful that you have returned home safely."

Being together was just like old times. Walter forgot about his pledge and drank with his friends far into the night. He felt that he deserved to celebrate their return. After all, he could quit drinking anytime he wanted.

He was off work for a few days after the bout of binge drinking, but he felt the nausea and being bedridden was a small price to pay to celebrate his friend's homecoming. He stayed sober for the next week, and then Prince came home and they were all invited to Eddie's club on the east side to celebrate. Luther was there with Eddie and Ezra. Prince greeted his four friends from Tom's Town Tavern, and there were handshakes all around.

"You made second lieutenant," Queasy said, checking out Prince's uniform.

"A battlefield commission," Prince said.

"Congratulations," Walter said. "That's a big deal."

"It is if you are black," Luther said. "There are not many Negroes in the officer corps."

"Second lieutenants did not last long in the infantry," Prince said. "I was one of the lucky few."

"I can sympathize," Drum said.

"You must have seen a lot of combat," Queasy said. "You didn't get that salad on your chest from wilting under fire."

"I found out there are no heroes when the shooting starts. My first night under fire was a nightmare. I would have given anything to be in the backroom of Luther's barbershop."

"We are proud of you for sticking it out," Luther said. "A lot of men would have cut and run."

"Plenty of men did. They could only take so much. Watching your friends die messes with your mind. You get the feeling you are going to be next."

"We are so grateful you made it home," Walter said. He found it amazing that this confident young officer had once been the terror of Woodland Avenue.

"Thank you. Let's move on to happier things. Kayla and I are getting married in two weeks and you are all invited."

"Good for you!" Walter said. "She is a lovely girl."

The bartender put their drinks down in front of them.

"I thought you had quit drinking," Luther said to Walter.

"It would be rude not to toast Prince on his return from the war. Tomorrow I will resume my march to sobriety."

"That's what you said last week," Jimmy cautioned.

"Prince is the last of our friends to return from the war. Don't deprive me of my last chance to celebrate."

Jimmy was worried, but he didn't argue because Walter had always bounced back from his drinking binges.

It was approaching two o'clock in the morning and all eight of them had bought a round of drinks. They were reminiscing about the 18th Street brawl and their battle with the Klan. Walter was feeling light-headed. He stood up to go to the restroom and tried to steady himself, but everything went dark and he pitched forward onto the table.

"He's passed out," Luther said.

"I'm afraid it's more than that," Jimmy said frantically, as he and the other men grabbed Walter and lay him gently on the floor. Jimmy checked his breathing and his pulse. "Call an ambulance," he said.

Lizabeth had arrived at the hospital quickly after getting the call from Jimmy. Walter was in a coma, and they moved him to intensive care.

She questioned the doctor. "Why did this happen? I thought once he quit drinking these episodes would stop."

"They would have, Miss Braden."

"What do you mean?"

"It appears that he has never stopped drinking."

She turned and looked at Jimmy for confirmation.

"I'm sorry, Lizabeth. It's my fault. I wish now that I had been more loyal to you than to him." There was a look of anguish on his face.

"It's not your fault, Jimmy. You could never be anything but loyal to him. It's my fault for not seeing what was going on. He fooled me completely."

"Don't blame yourself, Miss Braden," the doctor said. "Alcoholics are very clever at hiding their addiction. This was Walter's fight to win or lose, and I'm afraid he has lost."

"It couldn't be that serious," she said. "Give me more time, and I'm sure I can get him to stop drinking."

"I'm afraid Walter has run out of time."

"What do you mean?" she asked fearfully.

"Scar tissue has built up over the years and hardened, making it impossible for his liver to filter blood. In Walter's case, blood has ended up in the spleen and the spleen is being destroyed."

"Are you telling me there is nothing we can do to help him?" she asked tearfully.

"I'm sorry, Miss Braden. All we can do is make him as comfortable as we can."

"It isn't fair," Jimmy said. "He was going to give up drinking after last night's celebration. Prince was the last of his friends to come home from the war."

Lizabeth was crushed and could hardly think straight. Surely the doctor was wrong.

"I'm going to need another doctor's opinion," she said.

"I always recommend that, Miss Braden."

This was something she could not come to terms with. She had never failed at anything and now she was losing the most important fight of her life. It was totally unacceptable, and she was not about to give up.

"Will you stay with him, Jimmy, while I make some phone calls?"

"I'm not going anywhere."

Her first call was to Eileen at her Beverly Hills home.

"Hello."

Eileen's voice made Lizabeth tear up so that she could hardly speak. "It's me."

"What's the matter?"

"Walter is in bad shape. You need to come home."

"How soon?"

"Now. We'll talk when you get here."

Lizabeth hung up the phone and, after drying her eyes, called Terri. "Walter is very ill. We need you at the hospital."

"I'll be right there," Terri said.

She called Aunt Erma and asked her to inform the rest of the family that Walter was in critical condition. Erma told her not to worry, that she'd take care of things.

Terri came to the hospital and held Walter's hand for hours on end, and Jimmy checked on him throughout the day.

Lizabeth stayed at his bedside and wouldn't leave. She had food brought in and slept fitfully in a chair beside his bed. Eileen had made it home, and she tried to get Lizabeth to take a break, but she would have none of it. On the second night of her vigil, she was rewarded when Walter came out of his coma for a moment.

"Hey there, baby girl. How are you doing?" he whispered

"Not so well." She squeezed his hand in hers, trying not to cry.

"It's going to be okay."

"Only if you get better. I can't go on without you."

"Yes, you can," his voice was labored, and she leaned over so she could hear him.

"Mother knew that you were stronger than the rest of us."

"If I had paid more attention to what was going on with you, this would not have happened."

"Don't blame yourself," he whispered. "You did everything you could for me." His breathing slowed, as he fell back into a coma.

At dawn on the third day of Walter's hospitalization, Lizabeth was holding his hand and watching the sun come up through the window when she felt the life go out of him. She did not shed any tears as the nurse helped her from the room. She marched resolutely past friends and family without saying a word. While sitting by Walter's bed for three days, she had fallen into a depression so deep that nothing around her registered. All she could think of was that she no longer wanted to live.

Somehow, she managed to drive to her girlhood home in Brookside, retreating into the past because the present was too difficult to bear. In her old bedroom, she undressed, put on her nightie, and curled up in bed. In her world, she was living in the past. Eileen was sleeping beside her. Her mother and father were safe in their room and Cam was sleeping in his. Walter would be coming home soon, making noise in the kitchen, and she would go downstairs and ask him to be quiet. The depression was all-consuming and became strangely peaceful. It was like floating in a bubble that nothing could penetrate. She would not acknowledge anyone who tried to enter her make-believe world.

That was the condition Eileen found her in, and she immediately called the doctor. The diagnosis was a state of catatonic shock, and he said that she should come out of it in a day or two. But the doctor had never treated anyone with the force of will that was Lizabeth. The resoluteness that had propelled her to become one of the most successful designers in the world took hold and now worked against her. She was holding on to her fantasy world with a dogged determination that could destroy her. She would not eat, talk, or sleep.

Over the ensuing days, Eileen consulted with every medical expert she could find to help bring Lizabeth out of her trance, but nothing worked. Aunt Erma and Aunt Julia did their best to comfort Lizabeth and give her encouragement to go on, but they were unsuccessful.

The family waited for as long as they could before holding Walter's funeral. They had no idea when or if Lizabeth would come out of her stupor. Uncle Ray made the arrangements and the service was held at Grace and Holy Trinity Cathedral. Walter was much loved in the city and instead of hundreds showing up, thousands did. They spilled out of the cathedral into the streets. Terri, Jimmy, Queasy, and Drum led the solemn, sad, procession of cars to the cemetery, where he was laid to rest beside his parents.

After the funeral, Eileen stayed with Lizabeth night and day, coaxing her to climb out of the depression by reminding her of all she had to live for and the hundreds of people who depended on her. Lizabeth either didn't hear her or didn't want to. Eileen was afraid that her sister would die from a broken heart. Finally, she resorted to the last thing she could think of to get her back. She gently put her arms around her and whispered in her ear.

"I was outside the door listening, when Mother was on her death-bed and gave you instructions on taking care of the family. She would be disappointed in you, because you are not taking very good care of me."

The thought that Lizabeth was letting down her mother was the key to unlocking the door that she had been hiding behind. She blinked a couple of times, held tightly onto Eileen, and started sobbing, letting out all the pent-up grief she had held for Walter.

EPILOGUE

Christmas Eve 1971

AS THE YEARS PASSED, SO did some of the guilt Lizabeth felt for Walter's death. She realized there was nothing more she or anyone could have done to save him. It was almost as if it had been preordained. However, that did not ease the pain of living her life without him. After his death, she dedicated herself to her work, and the months and years had flown by. She witnessed a lot of changes over the ensuing years, but was gratified that much had remained the same.

Margie was still a major contributor to Liz Braden's Original Designs. She and Cory were devoted to each other and had adopted several children. Kayla was a valued employee and was in charge of production. She married Prince, and they raised three children. Prince sold his share of the supper club to Eddie, and after Luther died of a heart attack, had taken his place on the city council. Ezra had returned to the South to work in the civil rights movement.

Terri and Helen became good friends. They had the shared grief of losing someone they loved. Helen remarried and lived in Kansas City. Terri made several more local documentaries, but eventually moved to California, where she married a movie producer. She never knew that Walter was the one who made her first movie possible.

Jimmy and Carol separated but were still friends. Jimmy had some bitterness about his war injury and the lingering feeling that he was partly responsible for Walter's death. The stress became too much for their marriage to overcome. Lizabeth hired him to be head of her national security team. He had been an integral part of Walter's life and now he was the closest thing she had to a brother.

Queasy and Drum ran Tom's Town Tavern for a few years, but it wasn't the same without Walter. He was the heart and soul of the business, and it withered without him. Queasy became Lizabeth's accountant and Drum took care of her investments. She had sought them out because she trusted them, and through them, she could hold on to Walter. Queasy remained a bachelor, but Drum had fallen in love with Jennie and they were happily married.

Lizabeth was sitting in her office on the top floor of the world headquarters of Liz Braden's Original Designs reminiscing about the past. A knock on her door ended the reverie.

"Come in."

Little Mary Kelly, whom she had hired off the picket line all those years ago, came into her office. Mary was now a supervisor.

"It's noon, Miss Braden, and we are shutting down. I wanted to wish you a merry Christmas."

"Thank you, Mary. Merry Christmas to you too." After she left, Lizabeth watched out her window as a gentle snow began to fall.

She looked at her watch and then smiled. Eileen's TWA flight from New York was right on time. She followed its path as it came out of the south, flew past her window, made a tricky approach over the Missouri River, and landed on the tarmac of the Kansas City Municipal Airport. Eileen had retired from the movies and was producing and directing plays on Broadway.

Lizabeth's office was only a couple of minutes from the airport. She walked downstairs through the deserted production area and out to her car. It was a ritual she had performed every year since losing Walter. Eileen would arrive about noon on Christmas Eve. Lizabeth would be there to greet her, and they would drive out to the house in Brookside.

The Christmas tree was set up and ready to decorate. Lizabeth poured Eileen a cup of tea from their mother's sterling silver tea service, and they caught up on the news each had to offer. Afterwards, they retrieved the decorations from the attic, began to fill the tree with the adornments, and remembered Christmases past.

"The only time our brothers could be civil to each other was at Christmas, when they cut down a tree and brought it home for us to decorate," Eileen said, as she wrapped a string of lights around the tree.

"I think they must have called a truce, because it was a religious holiday and out of respect for Mother," Lizabeth answered, as she carefully placed the garland on the tree.

"I miss those Thanksgiving and Christmas dinners," Eileen said.

"I'm surprised Mother got anything done, the way everyone crowded into the kitchen."

"And we always had interesting conversations around the table."

"The way Father went after Walter there were more fireworks than anything. It was sad that they could never bridge their differences."

"Father wanted Walter to be like Cam, and that was never going to happen."

"There was a lot left to be resolved in Mother's relationship with Father and their relationship with Walter. Sometimes life doesn't give us time to put things right."

They reminisced about the history of each bauble, as they placed it on the tree. For the finishing touches, Lizabeth placed Walter's miniature golf bag on a branch. Eileen climbed the stepladder and placed Cam's star at the top of the tree. They turned off the lights, stepped back, and admired their handiwork. The tree's lights shone brightly out into the room.

"It's a beautiful sight," Eileen said.

"Yes, but it can never be as beautiful as it once was."

"That's because we were young and wrapped in a loving family."

"I miss Nana and Pop."

"Me too."

"We should be thankful that we still have Aunt Erma and Aunt Julia." Julia had retired after years of successfully running her home furnishing business. Erma still worked part-time at Liz Braden's Original Designs. Uncle Ray and Uncle Ralph had passed away.

"And thankful that we have each other," Lizabeth said.

"I've been thinking a lot about that. I've decided to retire and come back to Kansas City. We can get this place out of mothballs and start a new life."

"Why here in this house? We can afford to live anywhere we choose."

"But then we would have to listen to Mother, whispering in our ears about extravagance."

"That's true. She would want us to spend our money wisely, so I've been thinking about starting a Braden family foundation to go along with the scholarship funds."

"That is a wonderful idea. We can spend our senior years giving money away."

"I would love to have you home, if you are sure about retirement."

"I'm sure, and I'm hoping the Red Barn Players will take me back."

"The most accomplished actress of the century. Why would they not?"

"Have you given any thought to retirement?"

"No. I don't think I could ever leave my business."

"You could cut back your workload and be a director."

"It's something to think about."

⁓

That night they continued the tradition of sleeping together in their upstairs bed. When they awakened on Christmas Day, there was no smell of coffee drifting up the stairs or whispered conversation in the house, just the sound of the wind in the eaves, and their remembrances of Christmases past.

"I'll go make the coffee," Lizabeth said, putting on her robe.

When the coffee had finished perking, Eileen came downstairs. Lizabeth poured them both a cup.

"Thank you," Eileen said, as she sat down at the kitchen table.

"I've often wondered about something but never asked," Lizabeth said.

"Go ahead."

"Why have you never married? I'm sure you've had plenty of offers."

"I thought that would be obvious. I've followed your lead in not wanting anything to interfere with my career."

"I would hate to think that I am responsible for you not having a family of your own."

"Heavens, no. We all have to decide what path to choose. I chose acting."

"No regrets?"

"Oh, sure. I miss not having children and grandchildren. How about you?"

"No. I'm satisfied with the choices I made."

"Good for you. You became America's most successful designer, not to mention your success in other countries. Not many people can say that."

"Perhaps not. My only regret is not spending more time with those I loved."

"We all have regrets of one sort or another. All we can do is to keep going and do the best we can."

The next day at the airport, Lizabeth embraced Eileen. "You take care, sister."

"I'll see you in the springtime, when Mother's flowers are in bloom," Eileen said.

"I'll be counting on it," Lizabeth replied. She clung to Eileen for a moment, already missing her sister.

"I love you," she said.

"I love you too."

As she watched Eileen walk to her plane, the years unfolded as if they were yesterday, and she wondered if it had been worth the struggle. The hard times of the Depression, choosing a career over a relationship, and the long years of war weighed on her mind. Most painful was the loss of Cam, her parents, and especially Walter, because she had loved him so much.

She remembered Terri asking if her ambition was worth the sacrifice. She had replied that she wouldn't know until the end. The end was near, and her goals were accomplished, but she would trade them all if she could spend one more minute with her parents, Cam, and Walter.

Lizabeth watched Eileen's plane take off through the swirling snow and rise above the city, headed for New York. And then she did what she had always done to survive. She set the heartbreak aside and went back to work.